Molech
Rising

TODD MARTIN

Chapter 1

A long, terrified scream split the night. Candy Beaumont shrieked until her breath ran out. As soon as she inhaled, she screamed again. Her parents burst into the room when her second yell turned ragged. The door smacked hard against the wall. Her father shouted at an unknown and unseen assailant. Her mother cried out in confusion.

Stephen Beaumont looked around the room. Candy's skinny, eight-year-old limbs tangled in her sheets, and her dark hair was tousled. Her eyes were wide like she had been startled from sleep. Terrified tears ran down her cheeks. He couldn't see anything else amiss. The window was closed, and the curtain was drawn. Clearly, no one else hid in the room.

A Magic 8 ball lay on the floor in the middle of the room, and a flashlight rested by the head of the bed. He briefly wondered where they came from. Candy must have been playing with the toy with the lights out. When she had finished, she'd laid them by the head of the bed, and the ball had rolled to the middle of the room.

Rachel continued toward Candy, her dark eyes worried. She was a tiny, pretty woman at just over five feet tall.

Rachel gathered Candy into her arms and stroked her hair while she whispered, "Everything is alright. Mommy and Daddy are right here."

Candy clung to her mother fiercely, sobbing into her mother's breast. She was inconsolable for a few minutes. When she finally spoke, she stammered, "Monster... Monster came out of the closet!"

Rachel pushed her back far enough to peer into Candy's face. "Sweetie, there is nobody here but us. You were having a bad dream."

Candy peered around the room and then pointed to the closet. "It came out of there," she said doggedly.

Rachel eyed the closet door. It was slightly ajar, though she distinctly remembered closing it when she'd bid goodnight to Candy earlier. She turned and gave Stephen a 'Help me out here' expression.

Stephen saw his cue and walked over to the closet. Reaching out, he took the closet doorknob in his hand. The spider on the bottom of the doorknob was all but invisible. It wasn't venomous, but it was alive. His fingers closed on the doorknob like a great wall around the spider.

Startled, it started climbing the giant wall. Stephen felt the spider on his hand. Shouting, he jumped back, waving his hand around to shake it off. Dancing a little jig, he saw it go flying across the room.

His recognition of it came at the same time his bare foot came down on the Magic 8 Ball. The ball shot across the room and under the bed. Stephen did a violent half-somersault and landed on his back.

His breath chuffed out of him painfully with a muttered, "Damn!"

All of this had the unfortunate effect of scaring Candy all over again. She screamed, gripped her mother that much tighter, and started crying frantically. Rachel wasn't prepared for his reaction, either. She screeched and held onto Candy a little tighter. Her breathing turned into a shallow gulping. That alarmed the already frightened Candy. For a moment, the two of them were frantic.

Stephen lay on the floor for a full thirty seconds catching his breath. He paused, letting the initial jolt of pain subside. His selfish side came to the fore, and he shouted, "Shut up! Shut up!" He rolled over and got to his feet. "I'm okay. Everything is alright. Where the hell did that thing come from? I almost broke my neck!" He wasn't a big man at five foot ten, but in his anger, he was rather imposing to his family. He glared over at the closet door which had swung open the rest of the way after he'd let go of it.

Candy was shocked into coherence by her father's reaction.

She stared up at her father and admitted, "It's a Magic 8 Ball. Grammy gave it to me today when I was staying with her."

Stephen gazed at her for a moment and asked, "She gave you that? Why in the world would she go out and get you something like that?"

The guilt was evident on Candy's face. She wiped the tear tracks from her cheeks and replied, "Well, she didn't really give it to me. I found it in a box in her garage. It was all mixed in with stuff she was giving to charity. I asked her if I could have it."

"What were you doing in her garage? Were you snooping around?" Stephen questioned.

"No, I wasn't." Candy muttered. She hated it when her father was like this, grilling her for details. "She sent me to the garage to see if she left her wallet in her car. I almost tripped on the box when I went out there. When I looked in the box, I found the ball."

Stephen saw he was wearing at Candy's patience, but that was part of being a father. He wasn't going to be one of those clueless dads that had no idea what his daughter was up to.

"I don't need any attitude from you in the middle of the night, young lady. I only asked you a question."

Rachel stepped in at that point. "I don't think she meant you any disrespect, honey. We've all been through a bit of a shock, and it's bound to have an effect." She turned to Candy and coaxed, "Sweetie, what was it you thought you saw?"

Candy's face became taut. "I didn't think I saw something. An ugly little thing came out of the closet." She pointed at the now open closet. She continued, "He said 'Thank you for helping me.' Then he started dancing around the room. He was scary, and his voice was all…. scratchy?"

Stephen looked at her quizzically. "He? How do you know it was a he?"

"Daddy… he was naked. I know it wasn't a girl." Her face reddened.

"UUhhh… Okay," stammered Stephen. This was rapidly moving into territory that he wasn't comfortable with. He gave Rachel a pleading glance.

Rachel made a show of peering around the room. "Sweetie, there is nothing and nobody in here but us. It had to be a bad dream."

Candy shivered and declared, "Momma, I saw... something." Tears started welling up in her eyes. They could tell she was being sincere.

Rachel had never seen this much fear from Candy. "Sweetie, will it make you feel better if I stay in here with you tonight?" Knowing it would cause trouble, she didn't offer to let Candy sleep in their bed. Stephen would never go for it. She would hear his objection just from this little bit.

Relief flooded Candy's face. "Yes, Mama," she whispered. She leaned forward and hugged her mother fiercely.

That seemed to solve the situation for Stephen. He stood up.

"Well, I have to get up early to go to work so I think I will go to bed. Good night again to both of you." He leaned down and kissed them both goodnight, turned, and left the room.

Rachel thought, *Really? You aren't the only one who has to get up in the morning to go to a job.* She didn't say anything. The fight wouldn't be worth the satisfaction of the words. The important thing was her daughter's state of mind. She pushed away selfish thoughts and focused on her little girl.

She gave Candy a little hug "Let's see if we can get some sleep, Sweetie."

She had Candy get out of the bed. They straightened the covers together. "Okay, where is that ball your father almost broke his neck on?"

She didn't want to risk tripping over it in the middle of the night. Candy found the ball under the head of the bed. She also found a quarter and one of her dolls that she thought was lost.

Candy got into bed first. Rachel spread the cover out over her. She had Candy lay closest to the wall, as far away from the closet as possible to keep her from being nervous. She crawled into bed and laid her arm over her daughter.

"Good night, sweetie. I love you," Rachel intoned.

"Night, Mama," came Candy's the less than sleepy reply.

Rachel lay there quietly. She thought of how this night had played out. Stephen wasn't usually so selfish. *It must be the hour and the situation.* An excuse for him came to mind. *Never thought I'd hear the monster in the closet routine for real,* she thought.

Candy's breathing slowed down. She could feel her daughter's tension diminish beside her. Rachel relaxed and snuggled closer to her little girl. This moment was one she would treasure, years down the road. She closed her eyes and willed herself to sleep.

Neither saw the red eyes that glared out at them from the closet. They couldn't hear the curses that came from inside. Luckily for them, they couldn't feel the raw hatred that poured off the being that stood in the closet.

The demon stared at his new prey.

Chapter 2

Argass stood in the closet. He gazed out at his new host and her parents with an evil, hungry grin. The girl's fear and the mother's apprehension were intoxicating. A shiver of anticipation ran down his spine. This child's corruption would have to be handled slowly. She had not yet reached the age of accountability. He expected that Heavenly warriors surrounded her as they were with all small children.

The smell of Christianity was not in this house, but a careful survey of the place was in order. Maybe there were others of his kind here. He peered around quietly to see if he faced Heavenly opposition. Some of his own brethren could be equally as dangerous to him.

He thought of his last master as he unconsciously rubbed the depression in his abdomen. His last master had cut a chunk out of him and ate it. He supposed the hole in his grey skin would never heal completely. The present intruded on his thoughts. Caution was needed here. The Christian smell hadn't been in the grandmother's house, either. He had been stranded there for years, however.

Argass thought of the old Wiccan witch he attached to years ago. She had been an air-headed confection, easy to manipulate. It was simple to enter her dreams and impress upon her that her magic word was "Argass." She ignorantly called his name often without realizing that she had been invoking a demon. Those had been some very rewarding years until the time when the witch had passed on the willow wand.

He had bound himself to the wand for the passage ceremony. The new high priestess would see the wand as a symbol of her power. It was extremely likely that she would carry it with her everywhere for a long time. An opportunity to attach himself to the new bearer of the wand would present itself. Lead her into new avenues of sin. Stay with her at all times. That was the key to moving from the wand to the new host. The entire coven had been sure who she would pass it to. She was such a dedicated practitioner. He didn't consider she wouldn't do as expected.

8

The room was dim. Candles decorated every point of the pentagram on the floor. The members of the coven kneeled facing the altar. The stupid crone held the wand over her head as she intoned Argass' name. The coven's traditions dictated that she must choose the next bearer of the wand. Usually, the wand was passed to the next high priestess.

Ownership of wand was hers, however. Tradition was not law. Her decision could not be contested. She could give it to whomever she chose. At the end of her chant, she stepped around the altar and walked straight to the newest member of the coven.

The young woman named Liz looked up at her with a quizzical expression. Her expression turned to wonder when the old woman held out the wand and spoke.

"Sister, I choose you to be the bearer of the willow wand."

The women of the coven gasped. This was an outrage. Their outrage was a mere shadow of the fury of Argass.

He had howled out his "NNOOO!"

He cursed in the demon tongue. He railed at this stupid bitch. Before he could disentangle himself and leap from the wand, the young woman reached out and took it. Ownership had passed, and he was still tied to the wand.

Argass fidgeted at the memory. He ran a three clawed hand across his angular jaw and licked cracked lips with a slimy, grey tongue. His tongue caressed a cracked and broken fang. The break had come from a former master. He shuffled to the right to get a better view. His shoulder passed into the door frame. The breathing of the females was regular. They were going to sleep.

He was tired from his earlier display. Manifesting into the material world was extremely draining. The father had gone to bed and left the two females alone. The man would bear investigation later. Contention existed between the man and the woman. That could be a key to undermining any harmony enjoyed by the family.

Experience told him lies were the simplest way to destabilize a family. Get the little girl to lie and her parents wouldn't trust her. Get the wife to lie and break the husbands trust. An outright lie was never the place to start.

The best place to start with a grown human was slight exaggeration. A slight exaggeration almost always led to bigger indulgences. From there it was but a short step to the outright lie. Argass giggled in anticipation. This family would be performing for him in just a short time.

He shrank as he strode from the closet. At a mere three inches in height, he took to the air and glided onto the bed. The mother and daughter were completely unaware of him. He walked up and down their bodies. Argass studied their features.

Rachel's hand was under her chin. He stared at her hand and then peered down at his own. He spread his three-fingered clawed hand as he looked at it. An impish smile came to his lips. He reached out and dragged his claw through the woman's face. His hand passed through her as though nothing was there. She stirred in her sleep and rubbed where he'd scratched her.

"So you are sensitive to me. That is good to know," he rasped.

Stepping over to Candy, he sank his claws into the base of her skull and curled up behind her. She whimpered as a nightmare began in her dreams. Argass' eyes were half closed. He enjoyed the emotional pain of his new host.

The nightmare poured through his mind like a movie. He experienced her dream rather than seeing it. Shrill screams echoed in the darkness. The sound of dripping water seemed to come from everywhere. The image of a dancing form accompanied maniacal laughter.

Argass smiled and chuckled. The image was supposed to be him. It was good to know that he had caused such dread in this child. Candy whimpered in her sleep. Her pain was nectar that he hadn't tasted in years.

He had been in that damn box for such a long time. He and twelve of his brethren had attached themselves to items in it. He cursed this child's grandmother. She wasn't even aware of what was in her home. If she had, she wouldn't have slept in the same house with the box.

The box was so confining. They couldn't escape the box without aid because of their attachment to the trinkets. They had screamed and railed constantly. They had called to the woman to come and see what was in the box. If they could get her to pick up one of the items, they could get out. It was the only thing they all had agreed on. Argass cursed the memory of that time.

His escape from the box had almost been a triple escape. The girl had passed by the box. They had screamed at her in unison as she walked. It was so hard to get his fellows to act in concert. How many times had they bickered about working together to get out?

The discussions had always ended in violence. Each of the demons wanted to be in charge. He didn't understand his own kind. In every situation, his thoughts sprang to *What is in this for me?* Or *What can I get out of this?* Finally, Chella, Drex, and he had agreed that they would work in concert to get the girl's attention.

Chella was a singer. He crooned to the little girl to peek into the box, just to see what was inside. He kept up his song the entire time the little girl stayed in sight. His voice moved in range. At first, it was wheedling. Then it turned to almost a begging whine. Finally, it became a deep and forceful commanding tone. The sound was always balanced. It was never too much one way or the other.

Drex was a persuader. He spoke to the little girl, prodding at her curiosity. He talked about how shiny the ball was. His voice was smooth with an edge of desire. He willed the desire he was expressing to influence the girl to be curious enough to pick up the ball.

Her eyes had roamed over everything in the box. There was a cacophony of screaming. The demons in the box were excited. Each one begged, pled, commanded, and even threatened the girl to gain her attention.

Argass was a mover. He could manifest movements or illusions in the physical world. There was a bit of space between the ball and the hair dryer. That was all of the room he needed. He urged lightly to Chella and Drex to keep up their workings while he called the girls attention to the ball.

Argass sunk his claws into the ball. He seemed to almost mold his spindly body to the ball. He concentrated and began a low rhythmic chant. The ball began to shiver then to shake. It rattled and actually jumped up a bit and lightly clicked into the hair dryer.

The movement and slight noise caught the girl's attention. Her head snapped to their direction. Her focus was fully on the ball. Argass was fatigued from his work, but he couldn't feel it. He drew up his boney shoulders and crowed in delight.

He left his claws in the ball and waited. Drex stopped persuading and screamed at Chella to work harder. Chella reacted to the command with anger and told Drex to do his own work. Drex screamed for Chella to continue.

Chella made an obscene gesture. Drex leapt forward landing on Chella in a tangle of arms and claws. Chella responded by standing up while holding Drex over him. He threw Drex as hard as he could. Drex still had a good hold on Chella and wasn't about to let go.

They were both so off balance that they fell from the ball and landed in the bottom of the box. This was the very instant that the little girl picked up the ball. Argass was elated that he had succeeded. He felt nothing but contempt for his brethren who had failed to achieve their aim.

Argass had since found out that the little girl's name was Candy. *Candy*, he thought. *Rather fitting since you are a treat for me.* A thin line of green saliva trickled from the corner of his mouth. He closed his eyes and lost himself in the silky horror of the girl's nightmare.

He could feel her neck tensing and the change in her breathing. He gave her a particularly good show. He had been locked inside that little prison for a long time. This was a night for celebration. A maniacal little gurgle issued from his throat as he thought of horrors to feed her dreams.

Chapter 3

Liz woke with a start. She didn't see the flicker of glory's light when the angel passed through the wall. A light sheen of sweat dotted her brow. That always happened when the dreams came. Tonight's dream wasn't the one she always had. This one had been about Candy.

In her dream, Candy cried out in pain while some creature pulled pieces off of her and ate them. She tried to go to her but couldn't. Candy's screams had been like a hacksaw across broken glass in her mind.

The creature's eyes were so malevolent. It enjoyed what it did to her granddaughter. She fought her way forward to this evil thing. Her struggles woke her before she reached them.

"Where in the world did that come from?" she asked in the darkness.

She got out of bed and padded to the bathroom. She felt shuddered apprehensively as she crossed the room in the dark. Night time and dark were something that Liz dreaded. That was a fear that was born from her childhood. Her father used to punish her by locking her in a closet.

Liz flipped the bathroom light on. She stared in the mirror and saw the face of a woman who appeared older than her fifty-one years. The gray streaks in her brown hair were much in evidence. She didn't believe in dying her hair. She thought to change her appearance in that way was vain and pretentious. The crow's feet at the corners of her eyes were her care lines for her family.

She turned on the sink and waited for the water to get warm. The dream came to mind as she scrubbed the sleep from her face. She wondered if the monster in her dream represented her father. If that was true, Candy obviously represented her. The act of eating had to represent her father's abuse of her. The scar on the back of her hand stood out in stark relief against her skin under the running water. Memories flashed back to the last time she saw her father.

William Douglas screamed at her.

"Slut!" had blasted from his mouth.

Her back was against the wall. She sat on the floor where he had knocked her. Blood poured from her split lip.

She had feared him for a long time. Now she was terrified. He had made her uncomfortable with sexual innuendo. At first, they were little things, words or a look. Then it became more. He brushed her breast with his arm. As time went on, instead of his arm, he used his hand.

Tonight, she had had enough. She had slapped his hand away with a yell.

"Don't you touch me like that! I'll tell Mamma!"

He had cursed her, calling her a teasing little slut. He was so angry that she thought he was going to seriously hurt her. When she got to her feet, she ran.

Her father made a grab for her, but she shook him off. She ran through the old screen door without stopping to open it. His screams and curses fell behind. Liz had run to her friend Karen's house. Karen knew what her home life was like.

There were bloody scratches on her neck and arms from the screen door. Karen had answered the door after a minute of knocking, and her friend gave Liz a sorrowful look.

"C'mon, let's get you cleaned up."

Liz stepped through the door. She hadn't known she left her old life behind.

Liz's head snapped up and she peered in the mirror again. Cursing softly, she reached for a towel to dry her face. Candy's face came to mind. She didn't see the angel that whispered in her ear and then passed through the wall out of her house.

"This has to mean something," she mused as she laid the towel on the sink. She went to the nightstand, opened the bottom drawer, and pulled out a black box. She sat on the bed while setting the box on the bed beside her while she opened it.

Liz pulled out an abalone shell, a lighter, and a small bundle of sage tied together with twine in the shape of a cigar. She lit the sage with the lighter and blew the flame out when it got started well. She laid the lighter aside, picked up the abalone shell, and walked around the room.

The smoke from the sage wafted around the room as she waved it. She walked from room to room until smoke was in every corner of every room. When she was done, she put out the sage in the sink. She left the mostly unburned bundle on the counter to dry then headed back to her bedroom.

On the way to the bedroom, the thought occurred to her that some warm milk would help her sleep. She turned around and went back into the kitchen.

She saw the garage door still hanging open and didn't remember closing it. She shook her head ruefully and intoned, "This is a sure sign that I'm getting old." She had the doorknob in her hand and saw the box.

It was full of the items she was giving to charity. She thought, *I'm going to trip on that in the morning if I don't move it.* She walked down the three steps to the garage floor and picked up the box. She couldn't hear the cursing and screaming that was coming out of the box.

She felt a little thrill of fear balancing the box on her knee while she opened the car door and placed it inside. The little voices were screaming at her in a chorus. They wanted her to pick up an item from the box. She couldn't see or hear the slimy mass of tiny beings that writhed in the box. They reached for her, cried out to her.

One particularly lively little imp climbed to the end of the willow wand. He made a leap for Liz's hand to the catcalls of his unwilling companions. He missed and fell back into the box. The screaming in the box increased. The persistent imp didn't give up.

He climbed to the end of the willow wand one more time. Liz jostled the box while trying to open the car door. He made the leap again. He caught a precarious grip on Liz's thumbnail as she was letting go of the box. He held on long enough to be drawn from the box as his grip slipped. He fell to the garage floor.

The screaming in the box doubled in volume. The demon landed on the garage floor and howled in triumph. Liz shivered in fear. An impulse made her hurry to the door. She closed the garage door as the imp ran gleefully from garage into house with her.

Liz hated feeling afraid. That thrill of fear reminded her of the fear she felt around her ex-husband. Jeff would get angry and become physical. She had left him after a couple of good beatings.

She preferred not to think of the painful times. It had scared her to think of Rachel being around Jeff when he was angry. She never wanted to go through a moment like that again.

Liz cleared her mind and began to converse with the cosmos. She wouldn't call it prayer because she was just talking out her problems to what in her mind was the great consciousness of the universe. Whenever she did a cleansing ceremony, she thought it appropriate to commune with the Great Spirit. She expressed gratitude for blessings and protection.

Liz lay back down in her bed. She kept her mind on her meditation. This was a very good way for her to get to sleep. Closing her eyes, she concentrated on the good things in her life. Sleep came quickly.

The room was quiet except for Liz's breathing. The imp leapt up onto the bed even with the woman's head. He reached out and touched her forehead. "You are falling down a very dark tunnel. There are screams all around you. You are sooooo cold..." He giggled to himself and settled down to enjoy a night of tormenting a human in her sleep.

Liz stirred in her sleep. It took a few minutes, but the imp's suggestions started to produce results. She found herself standing on the edge of a huge cliff. The bottom couldn't be seen. She heard the voices of her mother and father behind her.

"What is the point of it all?"

"Why are you here?"

"Wouldn't it be easier to end it all?"

"No more pain."

"No more suffering."

She felt the suggestive pull of the voices. She wanted to jump. There would be no more problems afterwards. The voices were sweet. They were concerned. She brought her foot up to take that last step. She wondered where the bottom was. Liz shifted her weight forward and began to plummet.

This was wrong. Her father's voice..?! Her father didn't care about her. She felt the sensation of falling, and fear gripped her. Where was she? How did she get here? What was going on?

Liz woke with a scream. She was drenched in sweat. The covers tangled around her feet. She had been kicking to get free of them. She had knocked the clock off the nightstand. When she picked it up, she saw that only twenty minutes had passed. She felt like a wrung-out dishrag. This was going to be a long night.

Chapter 4

Candy sat on the couch changing channels on the television. She wasn't watching anything yet. The headache she had was aggravating. It wasn't too painful, but it was constant. Her resistance to it was wearing down. She hadn't become testy yet, but it was only a matter of time.

Argass sat on her shoulder with the claws of his right hand dug into her skull. He slashed through her bones with the other hand. His movements were insistent. He tried to make her headache worse. It appeared to be working.

He felt it well before the doorbell rang. That feeling came over him like a sickness. He wanted to throw up. He wanted to run. He wanted to flee. He felt the warmth at first. Then it began to sear him.

He was being pushed away. He got one last good look in the general direction before he was thrown through the front door. He wasn't thrown far. This was odd. Whatever it was had come from the direction of kitchen.

Rachel had just poured the morning's first cup of coffee when the doorbell rang. She reluctantly put the coffee pot back and went to the back door. The window revealed Angela Simmons from next door.

Mrs. Simmons was a nice lady but just a little too churchy for Rachel. *I wonder what she wants this early in the morning.* It wasn't usual for her to come by at this time of day. She opened the door, and Mrs. Simmons broke into a smile. She stood there holding a covered dish.

Angela Gail Simmons was a rather plump woman in her late fifties. She had been widowed a few years back when her husband Ben died of a heart attack. She was renowned in the neighborhood for her baking. She was a kindly woman with a heart of gold.

There were whispers in the neighborhood that she was prone to gossip. Rachel had heard her catch herself in the act. Mrs. Simmons had stopped herself with, "I shouldn't be saying anything about this. I'm going to pray about it." Then she would promptly change the subject. That had impressed Rachel. She was one of 'Christians' that Rachel had met that she thought was for real.

"Is everything alright, Angela?" Rachel asked. She had to continually remind herself to say "Angela" instead of "Mrs. Simmons." This lady's open and honest bearing practically screamed for a measure of respect.

"Oh, yes dear. I was up early baking for the church bake sale. Well, I realized I had baked more than was needed. I know your little angel enjoys my apple pie so I thought I would bring one over while it was still warm. I hope I'm not intruding." She intoned the last part with a slight bit of apprehension.

Rachel saw that she seemed to be a bit uncomfortable. "Oh no, it's no intrusion. You are welcome here. I hope you know that. Are you alright? You seem a bit on edge?"

"No, no dear. Everything is fine." Angela really didn't want to explain to a nonbeliever that she felt led by the Lord to make this visit. She had known this insistent gnawing in her mind before. It was something like an urge but more deeply felt. It could almost be called a need. When she had become sensitive to the Spirit's leading some years back, she learned to give in early. She lost less sleep this way.

She had followed the leading many times. More than a few had shown her something miraculous. She never knew what to expect, but she was long past second-guessing the Holy Spirit. She had resolved herself to make this little trip and see what the Lord brought from it.

"Well, thank you for the pie. We really appreciate it. Won't you come in?" This was a genuine, warm welcome from Rachel. The concern she saw in the other woman's eyes had broken down her usual business-like defenses.

"I was fixing breakfast for Candy. I had just poured myself a cup of coffee. Can I interest you in a cup?" Mrs. Simmons stepped through the door and, for a moment, silently marveled at how God paved the way for you when he sent you on a mission. This was not the usual hospitality she received from Rachel. She followed Rachel into the kitchen.

Argass stood there looking at the front door in confusion. He reached out and touched it. It was as solid as a rock. It shouldn't have been. He should have been able to reach through it as easily as moving through air.

He struck the door with his fist, swearing. His anger grew. He had followed the rules of this game. The child was his. He started howling and beating at the door with his fists and alternately kicking it. Then he realized what had happened.

He calmed himself. He let his mind reach into the house. He could feel the … LOVE… *gag… wretch*…. emanating from this disgusting monkey creature that just walked into the house. It was the enemy… oh, how it burned… The spirit of the enemy infused the being of this… this woman! He could feel the searing light pouring out of her. She was a fountain of his spirit! Argass jerked away from the connection and writhed on the front porch.

Candy's headache went away the moment Mrs. Simmons walked into the room. Argass looked at his body and his surroundings. He had grown back to his normal size. That woman was the cause. He hadn't felt the presence of God that strongly in years.

She had barred him from his prey with the protection she enjoyed. He realized this was only a temporary thing. The door and his size were the giveaway. He knew that when he reestablished his connection to Candy, his size would accommodate her.

He still had the link to the child. There was nowhere in the cosmos she could hide from him. As long as he still had his bond, he could come back later. He would try the door again after the hag was gone.

This woman was dangerous. She was actively communing with the Father all the time. He or his kind couldn't stand in her presence unless she started operating in the flesh and not depending on the guidance of the Holy Spirit. His thoughts drifted back to a time when he had seen this light in its strongest form.

How things had been better before that. He and his friends had taken over that whimpering fool in the tombs of the Gadarenes. They had this fool completely in their grasp. All in the region feared him.

He lived alone in the tombs. Oh, how he and his friends laughed at this Jewish wretch. They were forcing him to live in an unclean state. Every moment of pain and torment for him was a fine, delicate wine for them.

Then the Nazarene showed up. He was just standing there gazing at this monkey with such—*gag*—love and compassion. The twelve standing behind him, far behind him, appeared appropriately fearful. And well they should be. They were Legion, and all in the area feared them.

It wasn't fair! They had earned his pain! He had allowed them in, even invited some of them! There he stood with—*ugh*—love and light streaming from him. There was power there, too! Unbelievable, unimaginable power!

Argass sat on the porch brooding. They feared for their very existence. His command was inexorable. They couldn't resist him. There were the mighty conquerors reduced to begging for a crust of bread from him! Powerless, they could do nothing except beg to be allowed to enter into a herd of swine nearby. The utter shame of it all! *We were so angry that when he allowed us—and that is what it was— to enter the swine, we killed them. We sent them over a cliff straight to their doom.* He spit in frustration at the memory then plunged on in his silent discourse.

Yes, they floated for a time. Some of them for years as disembodied spirits. They had shown their power to the Nazarene! They killed a bunch of pigs! He waved his arms around in emphasis.

"It was nine years of floating before I found a suitable 'home' again," he muttered to himself. He knew he wasn't as lucky as some demons. Argass thought wistfully of how some of his kind attached to a family line and had a home for generations. Their bond was broken only when a person was saved or when a saved person actively rebuked the spirit in the name of Jesus, the Christ. "Someday, I will have a vessel like that." He encouraged himself.

There are ways back in, though, thought Argass. Some of these idiots threw around the name of the Christ like a magic word. *Most of these herd animals don't get it at all.* Argass grinned at that thought.

He liked that kind of 'Christian.' All he had to do was be quiet around them, and he could corrupt them from within. He capered about and almost shouted, "They didn't know what was going on until it was too late. A good percentage of the 'saved' aren't 'saved' at all."

Saliva dribbled down his chin, and he giggled to himself in a disconcerting way. He crowed, "Some of these fools believe that if you just believe in God you are saved." He lost control of himself in a fit of laughter at his own remark. He lay on the porch guffawing at his own words.

Argass had seen quite a few of the self-righteous intellectuals in their moment of death. He had watched from a distance of course. The humans were quite surprised to see the angels of God with sad faces. They didn't understand the sadness until the angels escorted them to Sheol—the holding place for the unrighteous dead.

Argass shivered at the thought of the Lake of fire. Sheol, he knew was bad. He had visited there once. Some of his 'friends' were bound there. He knew, though, that hell itself would be much, much worse.

Hell, he thought, *is the final place of judgment.* It was designed and created for Lucifer and his angelic followers. It wasn't originally intended to contain humans or his kindred, either. It was only when mankind chose to go their own way were the gates of Hell opened wide for them.

Argass didn't like to think of the place of final judgment. He hadn't asked to be born as the offspring of a human woman and an angelic father. He knew that he and his kind weren't supposed to exist. Argass was bitter about that. *What was I supposed to do?* he thought emphatically.

Like most people when these thoughts intruded into his mind, he pushed them away and thought of something else. He was, after all, beyond redemption. He knew this. For a short time after the fall of man, Argass wondered why humans merited redemption. The fallen angels hadn't been offered any kind of reprieve. Then he overheard Truvo, his master at the time, talking to the demon lord Gornog.

Gornog: "Did any of the fallen angels ever entreat the almighty to return to Him?"

Truvo: "Do not say that too loudly, my friend. Lucifer may hear you. You don't want to suffer his retribution as well, do you? In answer to your question, our overlord knew one of the minor fallen that tried to approach the throne for admittance. He was turned away by Michael with his blazing sword and the words 'You knew full well what you were doing when you rebelled. Your knowledge made your rebellion complete. Nothing of you can be saved from ruin.'"

Gornog: "If the fallen angels can't find redemption, then there is no hope for our kind."

Truvo: "That is why we fight to win. This is war with no quarter. We have no hope outside of victory."

Argass almost sobbed at this memory. He wondered how long the 'Christian' would be here. He really wanted to get back to torturing the child. She was like a cool drink of water after working hard on a hot summer day. He hoped that He wasn't going to intervene on behalf of the child.

She had opened the way for him. Argass was within his rights. She was young and ignorant, however, and that was often reason enough for a hedge of protection around an individual. He dwelled upon this for a moment before resolving himself to enjoy as much of her corruption as he could. Live for the present, after all.

He let out a bitter laugh at his thought then recalled again the angels of God. It had been a long time since he had seen one. It had been a long time since he had seen a fallen angel, too. He snorted. The high and mighty fallen angels didn't have much to do with a lowly demon, except maybe to bark orders. When they did manifest to a demon, it was almost always a demon lord of great power.

They manifested sometimes in the lives of nonbelievers. This happened only if it was within the plan of God to bring one of His "Children" to salvation. Angels never showed themselves as angels, either. They were afraid they would become objects of worship if people saw them as they were.

The last thing in the cosmos a holy or elect angel wanted was the worship of a human. Angels were created for the purpose of serving God. The holy angels existed and thrived in absolute bliss doing only this.

Argass remembered thousands of years ago before he died. He played his pipes for his lord's court. He had been born a satyr. He had his father's gifts of music and seduction. He had enjoyed seducing young women with his pipes. His lord had praised his talent many times. He'd claimed it was on the level of angelic song.

Argass checked the door again. The barrier was still there. He settled back down on the porch and lost himself in his brooding memories. He and his kind had made it their existence to thwart the plan of God for this creation. What else could they do?

Some twenty years ago, he had attached to a homeless alcoholic fool. He had motivated the man to brutally rape a sweet, young girl. The man had severely beaten the girl and left her for dead when he was finished with her. They had expected the girl to become a horrible woman, bitter and cold.

One night when she was crying out to God from her pain, He touched her. He showed her His love for her. He made her whole again. As time went by, little by little, He led her in His way until she learned to forgive the homeless fool who had so cruelly used her.

She became a rape crisis counselor in the slums of the inner city. She had planted the seeds of salvation in every patient who came through her door. She showed them she cared, and they listened to her. Many had been saved by her testimony.

Watching her over the years taught Argass a valuable lesson: Talk is cheap. Telling someone you know God and showing someone you know God are two entirely different things. He realized what most "Christians" never really wrapped their minds around. A life lived in the love of God was the best testimony a man or woman could give on behalf on their creator.

Inside the house, Mrs. Simmons followed Rachel into the kitchen. She could see Candy through the entryway to the living room. Candy was just sitting there watching television. Nothing seemed amiss. Still, for a brief instant, she'd had an uneasy feeling. Mrs. Simmons could have sworn she felt something very wicked close to her. She didn't know why she felt compelled to come over this morning. She was here on faith.

She set the pie on the counter while peering around the room. She prayed under her breath. The kitchen appeared bright and airy. Through the entryway, Candy appeared to her to be a darling little girl. She didn't know what she expected, but this wasn't it. That uneasy feeling had simply disappeared. She didn't know why she was supposed to be here.

She peered at Rachel and asked, "I take it you were preparing breakfast for yourself and your lovely daughter?"

Rachel positively beamed at that statement. She absolutely loved it when someone complimented Candy. She smiled and replied, "Yes, I was going to fix her one of her favorites, scrambled eggs and waffles."

Mrs. Simmons made a small face at that. "I'm so sorry. I didn't mean to interrupt your breakfast routine. I had thought to bring you the pie before it got cold. I will leave you to your breakfast with an invitation. My church is having a revival this weekend. You would be more than welcome." She started for the door before Rachel could respond.

Rachel was taken aback by the abruptness of Mrs. Simmons withdrawal. She almost stuttered, "Well—if you are sure—we will think about the revival."

Mrs. Simmons waved cheerfully as she closed the door behind her. Argass felt the barrier fall. He flew straight to Candy and perched on the back of her neck like an unseen parasite. Despicable little creature that he was, he was positively jubilant that the Nazarene didn't rescue her. It took a few minutes for him to get acclimated to her again. She had the stench of the Holy Spirit—*gag, uuhhgg*—on her. It was even in her hair!

He had to take her mind away from the thoughts of the nice lady. Curiosity of the saved was very dangerous when a demon was first trying to get established in a new host. He knew many demons that had lost a new host because of simple curiosity blooming into a saving faith. If he got her thoughts away from her curiosity, the smell would fade faster.

He spent the rest of the day trying to torment her into a bad headache again. He wasn't having very much luck at all. After some thought, he realized her word would be undependable to an adult since she was young. He would reveal himself to her again. He planned to show her his true appearance this time. He knew this would scare her desperately.

It scared any human to look upon him. He'd been around long enough to know that her parents wouldn't believe what she saw. After all, what adult in their right mind would believe that a child saw a demon? His true form was that of a satyr. Demon was just the word to describe a disembodied non-human spirit. Demons were things of myth and story in the modern age.

The Nazarene had told His disciples to accept the truth like small children. Argass found it strange that humans almost always leaned in the opposite direction of righteous instruction. He didn't mind this at all. It made his job easier.

He could see it now. Late in the night, he would rouse her from sleep again. He would caper about making sure she saw his goat legs and hooves. He would howl at her. She would scream like a maniac. It would be glorious. It would tire him severely, but desperate times and all that.

He found it very effective to wake a human by screaming into their ear. They couldn't consciously hear his wailing, but it caused them a great deal of spiritual discomfort. He expected her to wake up fearful. They usually did from a demonic voice. It was a reflex action.

The reflex dulled with age and intellect. After a time of frustration with her parents because of their unbelief, she would rebel. Willful rebellion made a host more open to control. Her parents would be dulled to her complaints after she pulled the "Monster in the closet" routine again. He relished the idea of corrupting her.

He thought of Candy as his prize. If things went the way he wanted them to, she would be a drunken, useless dope addict by the time she was seventeen and dead of suicide before her twentieth year. Argass settled on her shoulder and began to relax. He needed to rest if he were going to manifest himself to someone that he didn't completely own yet.

He would not have been so comfortable had he known that he was being watched.

Chapter 5

Dayanel had heard the call and responded instantly. It was out of the ordinary to receive an assignment so soon after completing one. Ordinary or not, he would do whatever was asked of him without question or reservation.

He thought for a moment of when he winked into existence at the will of God. Dayanel was aware from that moment on. The name he had been given reflected his power and being, meaning "Wind of God."

He was swifter than most of his brethren. Ordinarily, his job was to act as a gust of providential wind. He blew off a man's hat at the right moment. The man bent over to pick up the hat and found a discarded bible lying there beside it.

He remembered one time that his function was to blow some papers out of the hands of a young woman. When she walked out of her office building, he simply snatched them from her hands and let his breeze take them.

A young man rushed to help her. It was funny to see him chase some of those papers half a block. Finally, he came back to her with the rest of her papers in his hand. She had been impressed that a stranger had gone to such trouble for her.

Dayanel had not known that this young woman was an activist for the pro-choice movement in her city. He also didn't know that this young man was a student at the local bible college. He did know now, however, that after a three-year courtship they had gotten married.

The young man had become the pastor of a church, and his wife had given her life to the Lord six months after they met. Dayanel always marveled at how the Lord would work circumstances out for His glory and the benefit of His children.

Dayanel was an absolutely stunning creature to look upon. When he assumed human form, he was over seven feet tall, muscular, and had handsome sculpted features. When in angelic form, he was radiant. His radiance, however, wasn't his own. He was merely reflecting the glory of God all around him.

Dayanel had finished a short assignment. He'd blown dust into the eyes of a businessman on a bicycle path. He took no pleasure in causing any sort of pain. This, however, was a necessary thing. He stepped in front of the man and pulled dust up from the ground and swirled it in a whirlwind around the gentleman on his bicycle.

The blinded man rode the bicycled into a pothole. He was thrown neatly over the handlebars. He landed not ten feet from a park bench where an attractive young woman sat on the bench. She was startled at the accident and rushed to help the man. She laid aside the devotional study she was reading and went to his aid.

Dayanel was turning to go when a wave caught his eye. He turned and saw Shadrel, a dark-skinned warrior angel smiling and waving at him. It would seem that this little assignment had taken two angels guiding unsuspecting humans to their destiny.

He smiled and waved back. He looked and saw the man and woman talking to each other. Dayanel was amazed how many people found the beginnings of their salvation in a small act of kindness.

The knowledge that Shadrel would be in charge of watching over these two flowed into his mind. He couldn't explain how he knew; he just did. The Lord had placed information in his mind time and again. It never seemed invasive or intrusive. It was more like it drifted into his mind in an act of sharing.

He abruptly realized that this mission would take him into direct contact with the enemy. The thought of them always brought a wave of sorrow and confusion. He understood that they existed beyond redemption. He couldn't comprehend how his brethren had fallen. He was especially confused by his brethren's actions creating the Nephilim.

Dayanel's mind drifted back. He remembered the last time he saw a swarm of demons. The children of Israel were trapped in the wilderness. The Red Sea was behind them. Mountains stood on both sides. Pharaoh's forces bore down on them.

The children of Israel were afraid. If they could have seen what was really bearing down on them, they would have been in a total panic with terror. Demons of every sort, large and small, were in the midst of Pharaoh's forces. They slithered, walked, crawled, hopped, and flew around and through Pharaoh's army.

One of the largest demons of Lucifer's inner circle had his claws buried in Pharaoh's skull. The enemy had complete control of the Egyptian army. Dayanel wasn't worried, but he was curious. He wanted to see the Father's solution to this problem.

He didn't dream he would be part of the solution. He was so honored when he received his call and his instructions. The angel of the Lord himself stood between the Egyptian army and the Israelites.

The demonic forces stayed back, hissing and spitting curses and screams at this most powerful of angels. They were formidable, but they weren't stupid. They were waiting for an opening. Dayanel watched for the moment that the Lord had instructed him.

Then it came. Moses stretched forth his staff, and Dayanel went into action. He'd brought his wind to bear on the Red Sea. The extreme winds parted the waters. A path opened for the children of Israel.

Thousands of angels dove into the path. They upheld and guarded the children of Israel. Weak wagon wheels suddenly had angelic help. Old men had more vigor for this journey. Children were lighter for the mothers who carried them.

Dayanel saw one of his brethren whispering a praise song into the ear of Miriam, the sister of Moses. Dayanel chuckled while he blew the sea back. He knew that Miriam would think she had thought of the praise song. The song was still fresh in his mind when he came out of his reverie. He had a job to do.

Dayanel stepped from eternity directly into the Beaumont's unfinished and unlit attic. The beams of glory stopped pouring off of him as he stepped into fallen reality. He didn't want to give away his presence to the enemy.

He could feel the evil in the home and altered his perceptions in the general direction of it. He could see Candy and Rachel lying in the small bed. He also saw the imp with its claws dug into the skull of the child.

Something did not make sense. Dayanel peered around but didn't see what he was looking for. The house had a stench of evil. It wasn't this little imp. Something large was here recently.

He could sense the cause of the stench. Whatever it was, it was larger and more powerful than this little imp. The smell clung to everything. He paused to consider. Was this scent the enemy he was going to come into contact with? It hung thick in the air even after the thing had gone.

His orders were to observe the demon. He was not to act until the Father gave him further instructions. Dayanel hated this part of his job. He was an angel of the Most High God. As an angel, he didn't like allowing a disgusting little demon to amuse himself with a helpless child.

If he had his choice, he would have drawn his sword and cut this tiny demon to ribbons. The choice, however, was not his to make. He would follow his instructions with perfect obedience. Working this out was the Lord's problem, not his.

Dayanel concentrated, and his body blended in with his surroundings. He wasn't invisible, just difficult to spot. He spent some time observing Argass. He saw the gray, warty skin and the gaunt body. The wispy, balding pate over the red eyes was a stark look, reminiscent of an unholy hunger.

This being was starving. No, that wasn't it. The imp was empty. It was desperately trying to satisfy its need by tormenting the child. Its movements were insistent and hurried, to the point of being jerky.

The night passed slowly while Dayanel kept a discreet eye on Argass. The cretin was single-minded in his attempts to feed on

Candy. He didn't even bother to check his surroundings. Candy slept restlessly. Her mother tried to comfort her. The whimpers and small cries upset her mother. His heart went out to the child.

Children were usually protected because of innocence. The mother and father in this family were free of parasitic demons. Dayanel wondered at that. It was evident that they weren't Christians. They also had very little leanings in that direction.

The parents had been protected. The reason or reasons why they had been protected were unclear. Apparently, that protection was coming to an end. Once a demon was attached to a person in a home, it was only a matter of time before more came.

The enemy would use the little girl as their way in. The imp would use her temper tantrums to wear down the parents. They would give in to impatience or temper. Sooner or later, they would do or say something that the enemy could use. This city was rife with demons. They watched for openings. This family was in for a time of trial.

Chapter 6

Candy came out of the bathroom and turned toward the living room. Rachel watched the news on television. She'd told Candy to take her bath and get ready for bed.

As Candy walked down the hall, a huge hand slapped through the wall, passed through her, and snatched Argass off her shoulder. She felt a horrible chill for a moment. The chill went away taking the nagging headache, also.

Argass felt a horrible snatching jerk and realized he was in the grip of a gigantic demon prince. The huge, calloused hand was at least ten times larger than he was. Thick black hair looked like spines growing from the back of the hand. The knuckles were covered in calluses.

Argass was terrified as he passed through the wall in the grip of that hand. He felt the slap of the wall go past and found himself face to face with the largest demon prince he had ever seen. This monstrous being had to stand on the order of seventeen feet tall.

He had the form of a well-muscled man, but his feet were the cloven hooves of a huge bison. The demon prince brought Argass up through the ceiling to within six inches of his face. He studied Argass for a few moments then opened his gaping muzzle and screamed, "FOOL!"

His voice sounded like rusty cans being dragged across a hard surface and the sound of breaking glass. Some spittle flew from his mouth and hit Argass in the face. Argass realized that it must be venom, because it burned terribly. The little imp tried to make himself smaller, but he couldn't.

He was completely paralyzed in the grip of this terrifying creature. The demon prince spoke again. Rage distorted his speech. Argass could barely make out the words. The demon prince screamed so forcefully that the tops of his monstrous black wings trembled.

"Little imp! Where did you come from?! Who sent you here to ruin my plans for this town? Was it Graylar? He has always been jealous of the trust that lord Lucifer accords me! That sickening slug! I will rend the flesh from his pitiful frame with my bare claws! I will send your body back to him in tiny pieces. He will realize that I'm not to be trifled with. He will learn fear and trembling at my hand!"

Argass started choking and whimpering. "Please, my lord, no one sent me here. I escaped from a human talisman of power. I know not this Graylar of whom you speak. I don't even know the name of this town, Great Prince."

Tears of fear streamed down Argass' face. He realized he was pleading for his existence on Earth. He did not want to be cast into Sheol. He'd heard the wails of the damned coming from there.

Every new tempter was shown the torture that his brethren and the lost human souls endured in that horrible place. He did NOT want to go there. He knew that eventually his fate would be the lake of fire. That was something to be avoided at all cost.

His last master Kilbor raged at his underlings, too. Kilbor was a demon prince, but nowhere near the stature of this behemoth that held him now. Kilbor would have been a demon prince of a small town or village. This monster probably commanded an entire principality. He'd hinted at ties to Lucifer himself.

The demon prince squeezed Argass momentarily. He lowered the imp and narrowed his eyes. Slowly, the words came out of his gaping muzzle. "You have no knowledge of where you are, and you've never heard of Graylar? Is that your contention, little imp?" The voice sounded rather amused as the last words rolled out.

Argass tried to regain his breath and whimpered, "Yes, my lord. I swear on my existence that I have spoken truthfully."

The demon prince pulled back from Argass, and his muzzle broke into a hideous smile. "Indeed, little one, your existence on this plane does depend on whether or not you have spoken truthfully. I will investigate the truth of your words. Very thoroughly, I will investigate your claims."

The demon prince tittered at this last pronouncement. Argass was relieved that he'd received a chance to prove himself. Something in the demon prince's demeanor had changed, however. He was no longer thundering accusations. This seeming amusement was more terrifying.

The monstrous demon placed Argass on the floor and eyed him hungrily. "If you move, you will pay the price for disobedience, whelp." Those words welded Argass's hooves to the floor. Even if an angel of God had appeared before him, he would not have moved a muscle.

He stood there with his eyes lowered. He dared not meet the gaze of this prince. He did not know much of the workings of the inner court of Lucifer, only enough to show abject respect to those in power over him.

The prince looked down at Argass and grated out, "I am Molech, little one." At this pronouncement, Argass reached a state of pure, unadulterated terror. This demon, if indeed he was Molech, was one of Lucifer's favorites.

"I shall now test the truth of your claims. Woe to you if you have lied to me." At this, Molech leaned forward and put his fists on the floor in front of Argass. He lowered his head until it was on a level with the little demon.

Suddenly, Argass felt the cruelest invasion of his being he had ever experienced. This demon lord occupied his mind. He combed through Argass's thoughts maliciously. Nothing Argass could have done would prevent it.

The demon prince's face was a picture of savage delight. He had this little demon in his power. He violated the most personal parts of him at his whim. He enjoyed the humiliation that he inflicted on this little one. The worst part was Argass could see how much Molech enjoyed this.

Quite by accident, he found that the intrusion went both ways. Images exploded across his mind. He saw human children being sacrificed to Molech. He saw the hunger and enjoyment of the demon as the lifeblood was drained from the children sacrificed to him. He saw Molech prompt his High Priest to sodomize and beat a small boy he sacrificed to him on the altar.

He saw the pain and fear in the eyes of the child. He saw the confusion that comes from a child who is being abused by those they have been taught to trust. He felt the feeling of hopelessness that radiated from the boy after the beating. For a moment, he was the child, and he felt the violation of innocence that permanently scarred those it touched.

Then he was himself again. He had been violated by this superior power. He was stripped of pride. Finally, after what seemed like an eternity, Molech withdrew his mind from Argass. His face was a picture of perverted enjoyment and satisfaction.

Argass had hated his own kind. Moments like that reminded him that his not fully human birth had made the choice of his eternity. In all of the stories he'd heard, the Almighty Father had never subjected any of his servants to any unwilling invasion.

The lore of the watchers said angels enjoyed an open sharing of love and thought with their creator. They had nothing to hide from each other. Theirs was a bond of love and complete trust. Argass on the other hand had much to hide from those he served.

He was petrified that Molech had found his musings and was going to punish him for them. "Well now," hissed Molech when Argass had regained his sense of self. "I see that you don't view our dark father as the all-powerful being that he is."

Molech's voice took on the texture of velvet and molasses. He growled, "You have never stood in the presence of Lucifer, have you?"

Argass trembled and answered truthfully. "No I haven't, my lord." Argass realized that his worst fears had come to pass. This foul being had found and played with his most secret thoughts. He felt anger and hatred at that moment.

It was a useless feeling without release. He knew that he would never have an opportunity to revenge himself upon Molech. He simply hoped that he would never have to endure this type of invasion again.

"Unbelief on the part of a lackey is to be expected," hissed Molech with a casual flip of his hand that sent Argass flying. Argass was surprised at this. He had expected a railing rebuke at the very least. He hadn't understood what was going on. Confusion reigned in his mind.

Molech took on a commanding tone. "Where is this box of talismans I saw in your thoughts? I saw many willing servants to be gained. I would have them freed from their prison."

Argass lip trembled as he replied, "It is in a box in the grandmother's house, my lord, but she is planning to give the items in the box to charity."

"That is easily remedied." growled Molech. He let out a low hiss, and a spindly demon appeared at his knee.

"Yes, my lord," dripped the syrupy words of the newcomer, a low-level demon. He was still quite a bit higher than Argass.

Molech let out a satisfied growl and purred, "Jenoch, your quick response does you credit."

Argass heard the name and remembered. The name Jenoch meant 'whisperer.' In the time before the flood, this one would have been a sprite of power. He had been a guardian of safety for his brethren. He would have had a very powerful, suggestive voice. This pointed to an affinity with small children. His specialty now would be leading children astray. He could whisper effectively to the mind of a child.

Jenoch moved his five-foot six-inch boney frame in a very servile manner. He rubbed the orange skin of his shoulder against the calf of Molech like a cat. There was a layer of fur around his waist that grew so thick that it resembled a loincloth. His fixed his large, flat eyes on Molech and spoke in the voice of a small innocent child. "What would you have of me, Master?" The voice that came out of that face was so disquieting Argass shuddered.

Jenoch ground his small fangs on his lower jaw against the strangely horse-like teeth in the top. He glared at Argass and raised a normal appearing hand. When the hand flexed, retractable claws came shooting out. He wiggled his claws at Argass with a very wicked smirk on his face. Argass thought this freaky little demon would be trouble for him in a fight.

Molech leaned forward and touched the forehead of the subservient demon. "Retrieve these minions. You have my leave to banish the first one to question you to Sheol. If any question you after that, banish them as well. Once you are unquestioningly in charge, take them here and ensure that they guard the archangel pay system." Jenoch shuddered under this touch.

Argass noted that Molech passed information directly into the mind of Jenoch. He knew that high-level demons could do this. He'd never seen it done, though. Molech was indeed a powerful demon lord.

Jenoch's form took on a more serpentine appearance. His face became more feline, and his spindly body smoothed. His movements became more graceful and less shaky.

Argass suddenly realized that Jenoch was being imbued with power from his master. Jenoch's form swelled and became more robust. He still had the serpentine aura, but he was more muscular, more powerful. Jenoch trilled under the feeling of power he received, and his voice became deeper and more vibrant. It also became much more sinister.

When it was over, Jenoch's height had more than doubled. He stood easily twelve feet tall. His eyes had a powerful, red glow, and what appeared to be tears of blood trickled from them. His lower fangs protruded from under his lips, and the ridge of his brow had thickened. Small horns had sprouted from either side of his head, and the set of his jaw had become much more pronounced.

"Your will be done, my lord," pronounced Jenoch. Then, in a swirl of smoke, he disappeared. This caught Argass by surprise. He had never seen a demon disappear in this manner. Molech snorted in amusement at him. He reached forward and touched Argass on the forehead.

Argass's mind flew in all directions. Images exploded across his brain. Pain flashed behind his skull. He found himself curled into a ball, begging for mercy. As suddenly as the pain struck, it disappeared.

He opened his eyes. Argass suddenly realized that Jenoch hadn't disappeared. He had simply changed his point of reference in this reality. He still existed in this universe. The demon was traveling between the planes of existence. He could see Jenoch shuffling away in a weird half-light.

Argass realized he was surrounded by demons. This strange half-light was the point of existence for huge demon hordes in this place. He stood there in awe of it. All these years he had thought that there were no demons of consequence around him. Here he stood surrounded by a multitude of his brethren. He hadn't even known they were there.

Molech had correctly read his expression. He reached forward and touched Argass on the forehead again. Argass felt a slight thrill, but beyond that, nothing changed. Then Molech pointed off to Argass' right and hissed, "See what you have brought with you, little one?"

Argass was stunned to silence. Then a sense of terror came over him. He saw Dayanel hiding in the attic behind a large old chest of drawers. He could tell that the angel wasn't looking around. He gathered that the angel was following him. He realized that Molech knew that Argass had led the angel straight to them.

No wonder the demon lord had been so angry at first. A big part of him didn't understand why he was still being allowed to live on this plane. He had unwittingly done the worst thing that a demon can do. He had led an agent of Heaven straight to a demonic stronghold.

Molech correctly read his expression. He purred, "If all mistakes were punished with Sheol, then this plane of existence would be empty of demons, little one." He continued, "We must work with what we have. An unknowing mistake is better forgiven than punished. It creates allegiance and more attention to detail. Casting someone into Sheol only throws away a potential servant."

This reasoning made sense to Argass, but he didn't think of any demon lord as being forgiving. That seemed more the forte of the enemy than his brethren. He thought of the old saying '*If you can't beat 'em, join 'em.*' This could be a case of using proven wisdom to further one's own cause without concern of where it came from.

Argass snapped from his reverie. He realized he'd been spared punishment. That gave him a sense of allegiance toward Molech. Molech had made him aware of his mistake. Then he had forgiven him for it. Whatever else he was, Molech knew how to lead.

"What shall we do about this agent of Heaven, my lord?" breathed Argass, thankful that he was on this side of Sheol.

"We shall do nothing, little one. We will allow this agent of Heaven to believe we are unaware of him. That will give us the element of surprise when the time comes to capture and dispatch him. It is especially satisfying to watch an angel dissolve into nothingness when hacked in half by a demonic sword."

Argass wondered at this statement. He'd seen demons dispatched. He'd even watched a fellow demon in Sheol killed. All demons knew there were no angels in Sheol.

Where would an angel go when cut in half by a demonic sword? Wouldn't they only return to Heaven at the throne of God himself? Wouldn't they be honored for the sacrifice that they had made on behalf of Heaven?

That didn't seem fair to Argass. He thought bitterly that the fate of his kind was hardly fair. He hadn't asked to be born of human and angelic lineage. What was his kind supposed to do?

When that thought occurred to him, he felt Molech's wing slap the back of his head. "Thoughts like that do not win wars, little one," growled Molech. "You would be far better occupied pondering the downfall of this child that you have attached yourself to. She is a representation of all that is good. To corrupt her beyond redemption would be a personal triumph on your part. To fail in this corruption would be a personal failure."

Argass flinched inwardly. Evidently, his mind was an open book to Molech now. He wondered about proximity. He made a mental note to control his thoughts in the presence of his new lord. He considered for a moment how satisfying it would be to be the one who cut Dayanel down. This would surely please Molech.

A small imp appeared at Molech's knee and wheedled, "Master, you wished to be called when your pet human is crying out."

Molech smiled a horrible smile and replied, "Excellent! Now let's see how many of these pathetic humans we can lead astray. Take a squad of imps with you and torment the human. I need to go and receive my tribute before I tend to the little praying preacher. Keep him off balance and confused as best you can. I will take over when I get there."

Chapter 7

Dayanel had altered his perception earlier. He saw what Argass had not. The little demon had stumbled into a demonic stronghold. Surely this little demon would be destroyed for his folly. He was surprised to see one of the old demon lords in this little town. Of all of the demon lords he expected to run across, Molech was not one of them.

He was in vogue during the time of the Ammonites. He had been worshipped as a god, requiring human sacrifice. Human sacrifice was scarce in the world of today. Apparently, Molech had changed to mimic the times. Molech had always groveled to Lucifer. The thought of Lucifer angered Dayanel.

He remembered the before time. Lucifer had been the Heavenly choir director. Dayanel remembered that he even joined in the song led by Lucifer praising the Father. This was before time began, when Lucifer was an angel in the service of the triune God.

Dayanel didn't understand the motivation of Lucifer. He had occupied the highest position of any of the created beings. None were above him save the Lord himself. It made no sense at all to Dayanel. Why would anyone give up what Lucifer had to become what he is now?

When Lucifer offered himself up to the congregation as an object of worship, many angels readily took up his praises. He and his compatriots didn't sing for long. Father Yahweh was a jealous God. When He heard this praise being lifted up and offered to one of His creations, He made His displeasure known.

It was a rather strange moment in eternity. The throne became dark with anger. Lightning flashed in eternity. Throughout the Heavens, the words echoed,

"YOU SHALL HAVE NO OTHER GODS BEFORE ME."

The creator sent Michael forward to banish the rebels. The Lord's face was sad but knowing when he issued His command to Michael.

Michael rushed to do the bidding of his creator. With two-thirds of the host of Heaven behind him, Michael engaged Lucifer and his followers. The battle was brief. The energies that clashed were indescribable.

On a human scale, Lucifer was powerful beyond description. Dayanel had learned that sin corrupted the sinner. Lucifer had chosen sin. Everything about him became perverted. His power was degraded to a point well below that of his fellow archangel Michael.

Lucifer fought savagely but couldn't stand against Michael. Lights, lightning, and explosions coruscated in eternity. The amount of power unleashed was staggering. Dayanel remembered looking over at the throne just before the rebels were cast from Heaven.

There He sat on His throne, perfect in grace, power, beauty, and knowledge. His essence permeated everything in eternity. He was not in the least concerned about the outcome of this battle. This pitiful little rebellion had no effect at all in removing Him from His throne.

Some of the rebels seemed to realize that the Father had foreseen the rebellion and its outcome. He knew all, so surprise was not something that could happen to the creator. Regret was the last thing they felt before being cast down.

At the fall, the power and appearance of the fallen had diminished. They were less than a shell of what they were before. The fallen, at Lucifer's prompting, had engineered the creation of the Nephilim. Semyaza and his underlings had paid a terrible price for their folly. They were still paying that price. They had loosed terrible evil on the earth.

Argass and his kind made it their existence to thwart the plan of God for this creation. There were times when they thought they had won a great victory. Later, they would find their victory had brought about a great loss.

Dayanel snapped back from this line of thought. Molech reached into the mind of Argass. He could tell that Molech was aware of him. He made sure to appear completely oblivious of the demon horde.

He saw Molech empower a lower demon. The little one grew quite a bit in strength and power. The task given to this little one must be important. The now not-so-little one slouched away. He saw Molech point out his presence to Argass. The little demon now knew he was being followed.

He was shocked that Molech had let Argass live after such a blunder. Obviously, Molech was attempting to build some allegiance. Dayanel had heard demons boast of using the 'tool' of grace. Argass would now be a willing servant. He settled back to watch.

Molech realized that time was short. Pride overtook him when he was about to leave. What good was a wonderful secret if it was never shared with anyone? Molech turned to Argass and growled, "I must leave, but I need a witness to my activities this night. Since you are convenient, you will accompany me. This is an honor that you are receiving, and you will treat it as such."

Argass bowed before Molech and simpered. "Thank you, my lord." Fear quaked through Argass. He had thought this interview to be finished. To his disappointment and terror, his company was required. He didn't know what for. *Maybe he wants someone available for punishment,* Argass thought.

Argass had been present at several hundred sacrificial ceremonies. He had been punished many times for their errors. He'd lost a leg once when the sacrifice of a goat didn't go correctly. He'd lost an arm another time. That happened when a high priest had burned the incense at the wrong moment.

It had taken two months for Argass' arm to grow back. He hid for more than a year in blind terror. His demon lord at the time had been Dulock. Dulock was a junior demon lord of a small city. He never took responsibility for his own failures.

He wasn't a demon lord for long, only a few centuries. That, however, was plenty of time to destroy morale and ruin discipline. It had taken time to restore order. Some of the worst cases were simply banished.

Most of the demons that had served Dulock doubted Lucifer's power. Lord Satan didn't seem all powerful to them. Argass reflected on this for a moment. He prepared himself to accompany Molech to his destination. Molech studied Argass in a cool, somber manner.

"So, you served under lord Dulock? I am surprised that you are tractable at all. He was a bumbling fool. I questioned how he attained lord status. I had opposed him in open court before Lucifer himself. I wasn't aware that he had been given lord status until it was too late to say more. He set our cause back at least several centuries.

"He was the cause of the religious reasoning of the British colonies. The main cause was supposed to be money or, at the least, power. His mishandling of it caused the colonists to turn to our enemy. I've heard that Lucifer himself punished Dulock and consigned him to the Sheol. That doesn't do much good for those who served under him, though. I assure you, little one, I am a much better master than Dulock."

Argass didn't know what to think. He had received promises from demon lords before. It was true that Dulock was a complete fool as a leader. He was afraid to say anything about Dulock to anyone of worth. If he joined in the condemnation of his former lord, he could be prosecuted for his words. Argass had learned long ago that he didn't answer without being required to.

"Let us be about our business," Molech barked. With that, he reached out and took Argass by the arm. They rose into the air and shot through the ceiling. The speed they moved at amazed Argass. He saw they were heading toward a large body of sprawling lights.

Must be a large city, Argass thought. As soon as they flew over the outermost lights, Molech started to slow down. They were heading directly toward some tall smokestacks. Molech took them to a point above the smokestacks. Argass couldn't puzzle out why they were here.

Molech boasted, "No doubt you know of my past as the god of the Ammonite peoples. While I was their lord, they offered child sacrifices to me. That is precisely why we are here. This is the largest abortion clinic in the state. Each night, a worker disposes of the aborted babies in the incinerator as my tribute. Lucifer allows me this indulgence. It is a reward for my control over government officials. Those officials looked the other way when abortion litigation sneaked through the system.

"This is my work as it was thousands of years ago. Then they were knowingly offering innocent children to me. Now they are doing it out of greed and stupidity. Lucifer loves the irony. He has given me control of Aurora Financial Unlimited. That financial group funds all of the research into more humane abortion procedures."

With that last part, Molech started laughing and took a while to stop. "I have expanded what Aurora handles. We are moving into daycare centers. If I can't have them killed before they are born, then I will take them while they are young and corrupt them beyond redemption."

Molech's voice became excited. His breathing turned rapid when smoke poured from the smokestack. Molech moved forward into it. He appeared to be bathing in the smoke. He cupped handfuls of the smoke and moved it across his body as a human would soap during a bath. He had a rapturous look on his face as he writhed obscenely in the smoke.

Molech cried out in a hoarse voice, "This is the destruction of the innocent!" He moved his cupped hands to himself, stroking his body with the smoke and moaned. Darkness seemed to gather around him as his excitement built. Molech grunted as he stroked himself in an obscene manner.

Molech could see Argass' fear. A huge buildup of dark energy grew from the smoke. He knew that one of the most powerful sources of energy was the death of an innocent. This wasn't the death of an innocent. This was the intentional slaughter of many innocents. This was a large offering. The remains of ten babies fueled the smoke he bathed in.

It had taken more than a year to move two of his worshippers into positions in the abortion clinic. The doctor that he had moved in was performing abortions in Molech's name. The real power came from the offering, though. The disposal technician that destroyed the remains was in secret a priest in the worship of Molech.

He had requested that he be allowed to do this part of his job alone. He claimed he would treat the remains with dignity. No one saw him place the remains on the altar of offering and light the candles. No one saw him load the container of unborn remains in the incinerator. He was alone when he knelt with arms raised in prayer to Molech. The rapturous expression on his face was unseen when he pushed the button that began the incineration process.

At least no human saw any of this. A dozen imps always lingered in the room, cheering him on. Above the rooftop, Molech basked in the smoke. Argass had resolved to be very quiet. His face showed his fear and the hope that he would go unnoticed.

The smoke thinned and stopped. Molech turned his face to the sky. He didn't glance at Argass, simply floating a few feet from his position. There was a loud crack akin to distant thunder, and Molech was gone.

Chapter 8

Argass was relieved that Molech disappeared. He was also shocked. One second, he was there, and then he wasn't. What Argass didn't see was the method of movement that Molech used. Not all demons could do it. Only mighty demons could move across the Earth using the dimension of eternity as a gateway. A demon or an angel, if they were strong enough, could use eternity as a stepping stone. They could stride from one place to another hundreds or even thousands of miles away.

After Argass got over his shock, he knew that Molech expected results from him. Since he hadn't been given different orders, his task was to corrupt Candy as he had originally planned. Any change would be dictated by Molech. The last thing he wanted was to get on the bad side of the largest demon lord he had ever seen.

Argass flew back to Candy as fast as he could. He was familiar with her so finding her again was no problem. He wasn't very powerful, so this trip would take him a little time. He did not waste that time. He thought he should have a plan for this attempt at corruption. Sifting through his past, he came to something he thought might be useful.

From his estimation, the imp that was assigned to her didn't try hard enough. He should have filled her mind with a buzzing. He should have screamed into her ear day and night. He should not have given her spirit a moment's rest. Instead, at the first sign of the Holy Spirit, he had retreated. He had run like a cowardly little fool.

Argass resolved that he would allow Candy no peace of mind anytime he could detect that she was spiritually curious. He would not make that kind of mistake. He would show Molech that he was useful and cunning. Whatever it took, he would avoid being cast into Sheol. He came upon the Beaumont home and started a fast, almost vertical descent.

Passing through the ceiling, he plummeted into their home like a missile. Candy watched TV with her mother. Argass perched on the back of her neck like an unseen parasite and spent the rest of the evening trying to torment her into a headache again. He alternately screamed and whispered into her ear. Though working hard gained him very little result. There was only one thing for it.

Shocking her away from thoughts of security was his only option. His true appearance terrified humans. He planned to reveal himself to her tonight. That would do the trick.

He stopped his assault on her. He needed to conserve his energy for tonight's antics. Manifestation was a very demanding act. She would be so scared she wouldn't doubt that she'd seen something. Her parent's assurances would not affect her belief. That would be the start of a good rift.

Molech had seen Argass's surprise when he looked back at him through the doorway of eternity. He knew the little imp couldn't see him. He had laughed at the confusion he had caused in this new underling. He thought that Argass could make a fair tempter if he were trained correctly. His last master had been a complete idiot. Allegiance wasn't gained through fear. All that was gained from fear was avoidance and the appearance of respect.

Molech had thought of his own ascent through the demon ranks. He had been born a giant. His father was one of the original two hundred with Semyaza when they were watchers. His stature of more than sixty feet had guaranteed him a powerful position among his brethren. He ruled over a kingdom that covered hundreds of square miles. His word was law, his displeasure death. Life had been a sweet thing in his reckoning, until the time of the flood.

He had been sitting on the throne of his huge ziggurat when he heard the first explosion. The boom came from a great distance, but it was ear splitting in its volume. It pushed a wall of wind and debris in front of it. The sound of the initial explosion went on for more than a minute before it started to die down. He had climbed to the top of his ziggurat and surveyed the scene.

What he saw was unbelievable. They had all heard the stories of the coming flood and the fool Noah. No one he knew—Nephilim or human—had believed the story. The watchers had all been imprisoned. Their punishment was horrid. They believed the story to be a warning. This was what would happen if there was another incursion among the human women by the angels. None of the fallen angels had dared. There was the judgment, though.

A wall of water two hundred feet high came directly at him. The sky was black. The wind howled around him. He heard the cries of his people and could do nothing to help them. Rocks and trees and scores of bodies swept in the wake of the torrential wave. The rain fell like a rushing water fall. Then the wave struck.

He opened his eyes and could see. He could hear. He couldn't feel anything, though. This was very strange. He could see his body along with some of his servants being swept away with the wave. His body, as massive as it was, was just a broken and battered thing. He saw the bow of a tree protruding from his throat. The water around his body was a red froth. He was thankful that he couldn't feel that.

He suddenly realized THAT was his body. He didn't have a body?! Confusion cascaded through his mind. He had been told his fate by his father. He wasn't human, so he couldn't go to Heaven. From what he'd heard of it, he surely didn't want to be consigned the lake of fire. He and his kind realized there was only the gamble that the forces of Lucifer could win. He had thrown himself entirely into that struggle.

Now he was without a body. What could he do? It took time and many attempts, but he found that he could affect the mortals. He could scream and whisper to them. Some, he could influence more easily than others. Over the thousands of years since his death he had been able to possess a number of them. Those were the ones that he had enjoyed the most.

While in possession of one of these monkeys, he could feel again. He luxuriated in the bodies that he had taken over. He could eat and taste food again. He had actually caused one of his hosts to eat until his stomach burst. When his host died, he felt an odd jarring sensation as he was separated from the body. He would see the soul leave the corpse and feel nothing.

He preferred to take the body of a man. When there was no one else suitable for possession, he would take the body of a woman. He didn't like the variances in sensation, though. The female body felt different than the male. The rush of sensations caused a disjoint in his thoughts. He didn't understand the cause of the tumble of his thoughts. That scared him more than he would admit to anyone.

Molech was nearing his destination. His mind snapped back to the task at hand. More than two years of work had gone into his machinations. It was his hope to start a teaching system among the humans. False doctrine and false gospel were very useful tools. This area was going to be his test bed to bring information to Lucifer himself, if he could gain audience to present it. He was, after all, only a demon lord, not a fallen angel.

Chapter 9

This moment had been a long time in coming. Molech thought back to Job and the test that his master had put Job in. He and all of the dark forces of Lucifer were astounded that this simple human had stood in the face of all that could be dealt out against him and still retain his faith.

Molech himself had been in charge of the group of Chaldeans that had stolen all of Job's camels and killed all the servants save one. He had thought that this blow to Job's riches would have caused him to doubt. It hadn't.

Most humans of faith tended to shy away from the Almighty once it started costing them something. Molech knew that Job was the exception, not the rule. Job wasn't the only human that the Lord allowed Satan's minions to test. They were constantly receiving permission to touch the life of Christian after Christian. This puzzled Molech, but who was he to understand the methods of a creator that he'd only heard about in stories?

Molech saw his destination and smiled. A small amount of venom dribbled over his bottom lip and slid down his chin. He was too lost in thought to notice. He stared at a rundown little shack. Inside the shack was the product of two years' work for Molech. He believed that tonight was the perfect time to set his plan in motion.

The little human inside had been sufficiently humbled and stripped of all pride. Molech would make a willing servant of him by giving this human exactly what he thought he needed. Molech considered the time and effort he had poured into this work.

Molech's thoughts shift to when he first encountered this little human. Molech followed a seminary student home to a small but neatly kept apartment. The couple inside celebrated the birth of their first-born. A beautiful baby girl with sparse blonde hair slept soundly in her crib. Her father, Edward Cain, stood at the foot of her crib with a rapt expression on his face.

He was a man of average height, slightly thin. His bright eyes held an impish gleam. He pushed his dark hair back off his forehead and leaned on the crib. He looked down at the baby in the crib and was positively terrified. He had not been prepared for staggering jolt the realization of fatherhood had dealt him. He also wasn't prepared for the intense feeling of love that he felt for this tiny person.

Eddie was a deeply religious young man who had been brought up in a somewhat practicing Christian home. Throughout his childhood, he felt the presence of God. That was the only way he could describe it. God had always been with him. He had always believed himself to be different. He never seemed to quite fit in with the people around him. He found that this was true no matter who he surrounded himself with.

In his early teens, he had discovered the Bible while doing a report for school. He had decided to do a report on one of the Gospels. He didn't really know which one to do a report on, so he started at the book of Matthew and read straight through all of them. Halfway through the book of John, he had decided that this Jesus described in the Bible was the one he would follow for the rest of his life.

Every word he read rang true to him. By the time he finished the Gospels, he had rejoiced at the resurrection of Lazarus and nearly cried at the depiction of the crucifixion. Every time he felt emotion welling up, he stopped reading long enough to collect himself. He was, after all, a young man, and only women cried when they read books.

He didn't understand the grade he had gotten on the report. He had worked tirelessly on the project. He was disappointed when he got it back.

The teacher had given him a C+. He hadn't known the teacher was an atheist with antagonistic leanings toward Christians. It would have interested him to know that the teacher had made a copy of his report to review at a later date.

During his teen years, he studied the Bible and went to school. He led a rather boring life by the current social standard. His mother and father were a little bothered by his passion for the Lord. They believed "All things in moderation." When he had graduated high school, it was no surprise to his parents when he told he was going to attend seminary.

He had led a quiet Christian life up to this point. He didn't realize that someday his faith would be tested. He had excellent grades in high school. That afforded him a scholarship to the New Life Christian Academy. Though far enough away to feel like he was on his own, it was also close enough that he could go home on the weekends.

Two of the young girls in the neighboring town had tested his commitment to his faith. He had stayed true to his beliefs. He met Jan Thompson two months before graduation. Jan was breathtaking as far as he was concerned. She was of average height with flowing auburn hair. He could lose himself in her big brown eyes. She disarmed him with her disposition and laugh.

Her easygoing nature put others at their ease. Her friends told her they could trust her with anything. She would have made an ideal councilor, if she had gone into the field. After she started going out with Eddie, that path didn't seem important to her.

She was soon captivated by this young man. He wasn't like any other boy she had ever met. He was respectful and attentive to her. They spent hours talking, and he had never once brought up the subject of sex.

She grew to know him to be a deeply religious young man. She admired his commitment to his beliefs. It was their third date before he even kissed her. They had a traditional courtship for a little over a year. He had met her parents, and they had heartily approved of him. When she met his parents, the same was true for her.

Jan gave her life to the Lord six months after they started dating. She had told Eddie that she waited so long because she wanted to be sure it was for the right reasons and not because she was with him. He admired her truthfulness on this subject. The day he saw her baptized became the third happiest day in his life. The second was the day they said 'I do' in the little church they attended. The first was the day that Faith was born.

They had the normal adjustment time while they were newlyweds. They were getting used to living with each other and discovering each other's warts. There were a few arguments but nothing supremely difficult. They did have one large argument over time spent apart and how the household money was to be spent. All in all, they had a strong Christian start in their marriage.

A year and eight months after the wedding, their daughter was born. Eddie had gotten an internship at one of the larger churches in the city. He was the youth leader at Grace and Mercy Christian Church. About this time, Molech took an interest in this puny human.

He saw in this young praying preacher the makings of a grave threat. This young one was truly dedicated to his faith and could be a real problem for the dark forces later on if something wasn't done to negate him. He didn't know how far the Almighty would allow this one's faith to be tested. Molech planned to explore that limit.

He started with a new young assistant at the church. She was a pretty little thing named Amber Gray. She was on friendly terms with Eddie. He put one of his lackey demons to following her about. The little demon's job was to constantly whisper to her about Eddie.

"I wonder what Eddie is doing right now."

"I wonder if Eddie noticed the dress I wore today."

"Eddie is such a dedicated man of God."

"He is so handsome when he smiles at me."

"Did I just catch him staring at me?"

"I wonder if he thinks I look better with my hair up or down?"

He constantly prompted her to dwell on Eddie until her feelings began to follow those promptings.

Humans could be talked into feeling a certain way. Molech found that amusing. That was why the Christ had taught people to guard their thought life. If one thought a certain way long enough, he would start to act that way.

After a few weeks, Amber had wicked thoughts of Eddie. There was only minimal prompting from the demon. He had done his job expertly, and she was well in hand. In her mind, she had fallen in love with Eddie. Now the little imp was prompting her to reveal her feelings to Eddie.

"You could have such a fulfilling life with Eddie."

"He is the kind of man you want to spend the rest of your life with."

"God wouldn't let you have these feelings if they were wrong."

"He looks at me and I melt. I wonder how he feels about me."

"You will never know if you don't say something to him."

The work had been long and arduous for the imp, but it paid off. Amber asked Eddie if she could talk to him after work. Eddie had no idea what was coming. He was oblivious to Amber's romantic feelings for him. He had agreed to catch up to her after work.

The day for him had been like any other day. He had to confirm reservations that he had made for a youth outing just to be sure. He had reviewed the calendar for the next month. He made a note to submit a request for funds. All the while, another little imp screamed at him about Amber.

The little imp had a problem getting close enough to Eddie to be heard on a subconscious level. Tolerating the light of the savior that constantly emanated from Eddie challenged him. He couldn't stand to get closer than ten feet. The light seared him so badly.

He screamed for all he was worth about how Amber was so attractive. Did Eddie notice that she was wearing a rather low cut top today? It was useless for the little demon. Every thought, notion, or idea that he aimed at Eddie was turned away almost instantly.

Eddie had his thoughts on his savior. He didn't want to dishonor the Lord. Toward the end of the workday, the little demon gave up and limped gingerly away. He found himself in the presence of a greatly disappointed Molech. The demon lord vented his anger by cuffing the little imp across the campus with a single blow.

Eddie had met Amber at her desk and noticed that she was wearing perfume. This was something he hadn't noticed before. She appeared nervous but glad to see him. They walked outside to the parking lot. She had asked how his day went, and he had told her it was a normal day. He looked at her and asked, "What did you want to talk to me about?"

Amber took a deep breath and replied, "I was wondering what you think of me."

Eddie was puzzled at this and responded, "Uh, I think you are a nice lady."

Amber's expression was unreadable. She breathed, "I think you are a great youth leader and a great guy. I find myself thinking of you a lot. I guess I was wondering if you were in any way interested in me."

That genuinely scared Eddie. There was only one answer he could give her. "Amber, you know I'm a married man. I don't want to hurt you in any way, and I'm sorry if I ever gave you the impression that I'm interested in you. I honestly didn't mean to. I think you are an intelligent, beautiful young woman. Any man in his right mind would love to have you on his arm. I am married, though, and I'm very much in love with my wife."

Amber's tears had come, and she stood there with tears streaming down her face. She looked the picture of a broken woman, and Eddie had felt responsible for her pain. His first instinct was to reach out to her. That thought quickly fell away. It would be inappropriate to comfort her without another person present. She croaked in a broken, sobbing whisper, "I understand."

She turned from him and got into her car without another word. She left him standing in the parking lot wondering if there had been any other way to handle that. Eddie got into his car, drove straight home, and told Jan everything that had happened. Jan's reaction was predictable. She was angry at Amber but pleased with the way Eddie had handled the situation.

She had met Amber only once. She had thought Amber a nice enough girl. She could tell that they would never be great friends, though. The thing that bothered her most was that they both worked in a church. Amber knew that Eddie was married. They both agreed that they wouldn't bring it up again since it was already handled. There was no need for Jan to confront Amber.

Chapter 10

Molech had been livid. He had hoped to at least create doubt in the mind of the wife. He had hoped to nurture a wandering eye in Eddie. He had even dared to hope that something might blossom between Eddie and Amber. That would have made his job so much easier.

But no, this little pathetic Christian had stood against the temptations. He was a victorious Christian. Well, *not* for *long!* Molech called his lieutenants. He was careful not to punish them for his anger. Lucifer had advised him to start using the 'tool' of grace to win the loyalty of his minions. He had to admit that it seemed to be working.

His lieutenants appeared at his side. A few of them didn't even flinch when he turned to them. "This young preacher has become a bother to me. I want him and his praying faith neutralized."

One of his larger demons stepped forward, "May I speak my lord?"

Molech gazed at his brawny minion for a moment. "Speak."

"If I may be so bold, my lord, his shield of faith protects this man of prayer, but not those around him. We must focus our attack on those he loves. That will distract him from his daily prayer walk. He will become vulnerable to us. We can then pick away at him. In time, he will fall into our hands like overripe fruit falling from the vine.

The thought brought a smile to Molech's face. He stared full into the face of the master demon that had given this advice. He must retain this one, he thought. *This is a wily demon. I would do well to keep this one close at hand. Besides if his council fails I can always punish and blame him without blaming the entire horde placed under my care.*

Molech was silent for a moment then peered at the master demon and snarled, "Tell me of your plans."

The master demon smiled. He knew he had won a place in council. He planned on guarding this new position jealously. "Master, if you will but give me a small contingent of lowly tempters, I can start to pick away at his wife. Depending on how much protection she enjoys, we could harass her. I'm sure her misery will make her husband miserable." He continued, "Two small squads would be enough, my lord. One to keep the child awake at night, sapping their physical strength, and one to make the thoughts of the wife discordant and worrisome."

The master demon went on, "If she proves an ample candidate, we will be able to attack her mind and her resolve soon after the child becomes too much for her to handle alone."

Molech's smile grew even larger. This master demon was a find. He was pleased to have this one working for him. "You are now the captain of my forces. You are second only to me in this command. Know you this. Success is greatly rewarded while failure is greatly punished."

The master demon drew himself up to his full height, "I, Barak, pledge to you my loyalty and my absolute desire to see these monkeys burn in the lake of fire, my lord."

The assembled demons behind him hooted in excitement. There was no turning back now. An offer of allegiance had been made. It must now be answered or dismissed by Molech. This master demon Barak had gambled much, but there was much to be gained in the risk.

Molech was silent for a moment. Then he quite deliberately reached forward and placed a clawed hand on Barak's forearm. The sizzle of flesh and the smell of burned meat filled the air, but Barak didn't flinch or pull away. He was publicly throwing in his lot with Molech. This was a surprise, but a welcome one.

Barak was going to be an able captain. He was easily eleven feet tall. His long tongue snaked out and licked the pus from his segmented eyes. He shook his head, and the mop of silver hair bristled. He grinned, and his lack of a nose made his appearance even more alien. Barak's mouth was so large that he could easily have placed an entire human baby in that gaping maw.

He scratched his chin with permanently extended claws. The tips were slick with ooze that acted as a spiritual poison. One good swipe of his claws would be enough to produce bitter anger or howling fear. He adored flying through the crowed cities in heavy traffic. He would induce road rage in otherwise passive people.

"Kneel," ordered Molech.

Barak's face took on an expression of exultation. He half-closed his eyes in ecstasy and slowly bowed knee to the demon lord. Molech placed one hand on Barak's head and the other on his shoulder. "Let all those who serve me know that this demon, Barak, is now the captain of my forces. Any command given by him is to be obeyed as though it were from me. No disobedience will be tolerated. My wrath will be great for those who try my patience." Molech bowed his head and became still as stone.

Barak started to shiver then shake. A low cry escaped his mouth, and slowly, his form began to swell. He gained another three feet in height. His claws lengthened, and poison began to drip from them. The segments of his eyes split and multiplied, giving him more far-reaching vision. His limbs and torso became more sinewy. Large horns sprouted on the sides of his head, and small bat-like wings grew from his back. His fangs lengthened to the point that he couldn't fully close his mouth. Putrid saliva dripped down his chin. A look of pure pleasure settled on his face when Molech removed his hands.

"You are captain and guard. Do not fail me," rumbled Molech in a low husky voice.

"I will not fail you, my prince and lord," purred Barak.

"How will you set this grand plan of yours into motion?" growled Molech.

"My lord, I have heard that you sent an underling to fetch new forces. Might I use these forces to harry the young preacher?" questioned Barak.

"Word and gossip travel fast in the ranks, do they not?" rasped Molech. "Take what you deem necessary. I want this accomplished.

Take some of the more experienced tempters. I need to check on the progress of a little project. Serve me well and you will soon be part of that project as well."

Barak flushed with pleasure. He intended to serve Molech staunchly. "If I may take my leave, my lord, I will set plans in motion," Barak simpered.

Molech smiled. He enjoyed receiving the adulation of a demon that clearly understood his place. This Barak was a treasure indeed. Not only could he be a willing and able servant, he could also be an erotic pleasure for Molech. "Take your leave." ordered Molech huskily. "I will check on your progress soon, captain."

Barak slithered away with a sinewy grace. He called a lower imp over. "As soon as Jenoch returns, bring him and his imps to me. Tell him what has occurred here, so he doesn't make the mistake of disrespect. I would hate to have to punish one who so recently was empowered." The imp disappeared in a swirl of smoke. Barak reveled in his newly acquired power and position.

A short time later, Jenoch appeared at Barak's shoulder, "You sent for me, my lord?" uttered Jenoch.

Very good, Barak thought. *This one already knows his place.* "I have a special assignment for you. Serve well and you will be rewarded." Jenoch stood stoically before his superior. "Go to the little preacher's house tonight. Kill the child if the throne of Heaven allows it."

Jenoch shivered with excitement. Seldom was a lower level demon given the pleasure of taking human life. It was even rarer for that life to be an innocent child. He was being greatly honored with this task.

There was, however, great risk. He would have to stride past the angels of God. He knew the great possibility was that the All-Father would not allow this murder. He very well could be cleaved in half by a dozen angelic swords. The chance to try was intoxicating.

Then a thought struck him. I *need not take a direct route. We are all creatures of another dimension. I can approach from wherever I choose.* He gave a curt nod of respect to Barak before disappearing in a swirl of smoke. He passed through the dimensionality and emerged in eternity. Covering a short space, he then emerged half a mile from Eddie's house.

Chapter 11

Jenoch wiled away the hours until midnight. He made a circuit of every room in the house. He shouted at Eddie and Jan as he passed them. They didn't know why, but their nerves were on edge tonight. They didn't realize they were the target of a spiritual attack.

Eddie was preoccupied with his previous spiritual victory concerning Amber. He felt pretty good about himself. Jenoch realized that his defenses were relaxed. He wasn't glowing with the power of the spirit as this one usually did. He had Jan on her third cup of coffee. She was getting rather suggestive to him.

"You don't deserve a man as good as him," Jenoch screamed at Jan. "You aren't a good father," Jenoch yelled at Eddie. His plan was to antagonize Eddie all night. Then, if he was successful, the feelings of remorse from Eddie would be all the more palpable.

Jenoch wondered at the absence of Heavenly warriors. He realized that a mature Christian was more powerful in the will of Christ than any angel. He found, though, that Christians were guarded by angels most of the time. This was a promising sign. He was not being hindered, but then again, he hadn't made a move toward the child, yet.

He expected to see a ring of Heavenly warriors around the crib. He considered the gamble he was about to take. If he won this, he would gain so much. It was likely, he would meet his end this night.

You only gain much if you risk much, he thought. He was prepared. If this was to be his end, what an end he would make of it.

Eddie became jittery. Jan was outright annoyed. They were starting to get on each other's nerves. Jan decided to check on Faith before she lost her temper. She sat in the baby's room for a few minutes, watching her daughter sleep. She marveled at her love for this child. She thought of how lucky she was to be a mother. Jenoch continued screaming at her.

Shortly, she and Eddie got into bed. They made no move toward each other. This was not going to be a night of affection. Neither was in any frame of mind to show love to the other. After a quick peck on the lips, they both passed reluctantly into sleep that night.

Thirty minutes past midnight, Jenoch floated through the floor and down into the ground below the home. He judged the distance to the baby's room flawlessly. He slid through the earth and up through the floor. In the half-light of the room, this horror came up through the floor.

There was no brave warrior in the room, only an innocent and defenseless child. The nightlight shone beside the baby's crib. He thought that soon he would see the flash of an angelic sword arcing toward his head. This was strange. All was silent. Then he saw three angelic warriors. They had sorrowful and stern faces. They rose as one and passed through the ceiling. They were withdrawing from the protection of the home.

Jenoch could not believe his luck. He was in the room of a perfectly innocent child, and the Heavenly protection had been withdrawn. Exultantly, he stretched forth his hand, and a large, red tinged axe appeared. The night deepened in the room. In the moment at hand, darkness ruled.

He approached the crib with drool dripping down his chin. This disgusting creature was excited to the point of ecstasy. He wanted to savor the moment. It was not often that a demon was allowed to take the life of an innocent. The axe rose and fell. There was no sound. The child in the crib simply stopped breathing.

Jenoch started to lean forward. Perhaps he could make the child suffer before she was escorted to her maker. In an instant, a huge and mighty angel appeared by her crib. He was large and muscular, easily the most beautiful man anyone on earth had ever seen. Incandescent beams of glory poured into the room.

"The Lord rebukes you!" cried the angelic warrior. His voice was thunder. "You shall not make sport of this child of the Almighty." He reached out with his brawny hands and gently cradled the soul of Faith Ann Cain. He drew her close to him and spoke comfortingly to her.

Jenoch threw himself away in terror. Literally blinded by fear, he was powerless in the presence of such a one. He dove straight through the floor, desperately hoping to get away. All thoughts of bravery were gone. In their place was cold, craven fear. He couldn't stand before the light of Heaven.

The Heavenly warrior turned slowly. He cooed to the child. When he turned, a pinpoint of soft white light appeared. The pinpoint grew. It gained in brightness but not in glare. It continued to grow until unimaginable beams of pure white light filled the room. No longer a pinpoint, it was a doorway to the throne room of Heaven.

Close by yet far away rested a throne. Sitting on the throne was the creator of the universe. He waited. He had been waiting since before time began to welcome this child into His presence. Love so thick it could be felt washed over the baby. Faith remained perfectly secure in the arms of the angel as they approach the master of all creation.

Jesus stood and met the angel halfway. He was expectant, like a father seeing his child for the first time. "Thank you, Andarel. You did well." The warrior bowed his face to the ground in an act of unadulterated worship. Excited to see Faith, Jesus took her into His arms and walked back to the throne. He sat on the throne with her in His arms and told her how much He loved her. She knew it's true.

She was secure in the arms of her savior. She would never fear and never want again. For an instant, she thought of her mother and father. The Lord assured her that all was as it should be. She rested in the fact that, forevermore, she would be in the presence of the Most High God of the Universe.

She knew she was privileged beyond reason but so were all of them. Her perception shifted. She can see that Jesus was individually holding and comforting thousands of souls. It was a number beyond count. They were all receiving individual attention from him, yet it happened at the same time.

She was in a unique state. She was untainted by sin when she was brought into the presence of the Lord. She grasped and understood concepts beyond normal human perception. She accepted without question, because this was all she knew.

At four AM, Jan started awake. She had an uneasy feeling. She shook Eddie awake. "Eddie, something is wrong!" she wailed.

He stirred sleepily beside her. The tone of her voice roused him. Her manner made him uneasy. "What's wrong, honey?" he asked.

She hedged. "I don't know. I just have a really uneasy feeling. Will you check on the baby for me?"

Eddie thought she was being overly dramatic. He didn't say anything about it. He would humor her for the moment. "Sure, honey, you should relax." Eddie slid his feet to the floor. *Kinda chilly. Maybe I should start sleeping in my socks.* Eddie slowly trudged down the hall to Faith's room.

He felt something wrong when his hand touched the door. His stomach turned over when he saw the crib. There wasn't a mark on her. She was lying there normally. It was only a feeling, one that grew with every step he took toward the crib.

Invisible to Eddie, a dozen little imps cavorted around the room. They danced in glee over the death of the child. They screamed at Eddie and Jan about the death of their daughter. Jenoch himself yelled into Eddie's ear.

"She's dead!"

 "It's your fault!"

"You weren't a good father!"

"God doesn't think you deserve a child!"

"What did Jan do to the baby?!"

"What do you do now, man of God?" "Now you'll have the freedom that you've been missing!"

"How can you think that?"

"You didn't love her!"

"God has deserted you!"

Jenoch screamed this litany at Eddie over and over. Eddie's head swam as he touched Faith and realized that she was gone. He felt her chest, but there was no heartbeat. He tried to see the rise and fall of her breathing. Her little body didn't move. Panic gripped Eddied like a vise. Jenoch had both claws on Eddie's head. He kept screaming at Eddie, knowing that he was getting through.

Eddie's throat constricted. He let out a hoarse cry and ran from the room. He had to get to the telephone. He tripped over the end table in the living room in his panic and knocked the phone to the floor. Scrambling along the floor, he sobbed and cried, trying to reach the phone.

He finally reached the phone and tried to dial 9-1-1. For a moment, the phone had no dial tone. Eddie didn't see the little imp with his claws inside the telephone. Letting out a strangled cry, he moaned, "Please, God, help me." At this, the imp fell away cursing.

The phone sprang to life, and Eddie dialed 911. The operator answered, and Eddie almost screamed. Jan heard the commotion and got out of bed. Fear gripped her heart like a cruel vise. She had no less than eight small demons prancing around her. They were screaming at her.

"Your baby is dead!"

"You killed your baby!"

"You are a bad mother!"

"God doesn't love you anymore!"

"You should have died instead of your baby!"

"Did Eddie kill the baby?"

"Now you and Eddie can spend more time alone together."

"That was so selfish. How can you think that?"

"You shouldn't be allowed to have children!"

She heard Eddie in the living room. He was to the point of hysteria. Her heart was ice cold. She walked woodenly into the baby's room. Her feet wouldn't carry her to the crib. She knew what was going on, but her mind and her heart refused to accept it.

She didn't realize she had stopped breathing. Her emotions were so high her entire body clenched. A few steps inside Faith's room, Jan passed out and crumpled to the floor like a spent match.

The 9-1-1 operator heard Jan in the background. The operator tried to calm Eddie enough to get directions to the house. The throne of Heaven wept for their grief. Beyond that, however, was silence.

No one saw the angel step from eternity into the Cain home. The demons scattered as though they were on fire. No one saw the angel put his hands-on Eddie's shoulders and say, "A trial is a painful thing. The Lord doesn't like it any more than you do."

Eddie's breathing calmed. The angel released Eddie's shoulders and moved to Jan. He put his palm on her forehead and whispered, "Sometimes trials are necessary to strengthen your faith." Her sobbing eased but didn't stop. The angel stayed for an hour and then returned to eternity.

An hour and a half later, two sad and stern-faced EMT workers exited from the Cain home. They had taken notes on the appearance of the home and the state of mind of the parents. They wheeled the gurney carrying the body of Faith Cain slowly to the ambulance. No lights flashed as they drove away. Nothing could be done for the child.

Frank, the grizzled older EMT, had seen it many times. He already knew that this would be written up as a case of SIDS, or Sudden Infant Death Syndrome. His heart went out to the parents, such good people. He didn't understand why things worked the way they did in this world. He wasn't a Christian. He was a worldly man, but the finger of God was on his heart.

The angels that rode with him—and there were always at least two—knew that it was only a matter of time before this one gave his heart to the creator. Sometimes, he would say, "I don't understand why this had to happen," and they would smile. They saw the earmarks of salvation.

On this night, he spoke to a doctor. This doctor was a committed Christian. Frank's salvation had been set before the foundation of the world had been laid. He had the standard questions for one who had seen too much evil and not enough good. His doctor friend explained that the evil is the result of the free will of man to choose. Every time a person chooses against God, evil is given sway.

The conversation had lasted for more than an hour. Frank had walked away convicted but also wary. Two weeks later Frank Blanton invited Jesus Christ into his life to stay. He felt now he had a direction. The world still seemed cruel but the creator was much more real to him. In the end, most of his questions were answered. That had been enough.

Faith's body was delivered to the county coroner for an autopsy. He knew that the coroner would find that the child had simply died. She hadn't died of trauma, poison, suffocation, or drowning. SIDS was still something of a mystery to science. Some doctors postulated that a baby sensed a lack of love or welcome and just died.

Other doctors believed that there was a genetic defect that simply tells the baby to die at a pre-determined time. Some doctors believe that SIDS was God's way of ensuring that there will be plenty of innocents in Heaven.

Jan sat in the easy chair of their home. She had been given a sedative after she had been revived. Sitting with a glassy stare and tears running down her cheeks, she couldn't tell anyone why she was crying. She only knew something BAD had happened.

Eddie had been given two pills to give her if she became 'unruly'. The demons had returned one by one after the angel left. Nobody could see the little horde of imps that had surrounded Jan and continually screamed.

"You were a bad mother!"

"God took your baby because you didn't deserve her!"

"You and Eddie were bad parents!"

"Why did you let her sleep in a room alone?"

"She was alone when she died, and she was crying for you!"

"Eddie thinks it's your fault."

"Eddie thinks Amber would have been a better mother!"

"Amber would watch over her baby!"

"God is disappointed with you!"

"Your daughter died, and you slept through it!"

Eddie sat on the floor beside the chair that Jan was in. He felt more alone and more a failure than at any other time in his life. His daughter was dead. He didn't understand how God could have allowed this to happen. His wife was completely disoriented with grief. He couldn't do anything to help her. He felt more useless at that moment than he had in a long time.

He struggled with feelings of intense anger toward God.

How could God have allowed this to happen? Haven't I tried to be a good servant of the Lord? Is this how God repays those who love him? If this is how God rewards those who serve him? Do I want to serve him? Maybe the scientists are right and there is no God. Maybe I've been wasting my life on a God that doesn't exist. Oh, come on, Eddie. You've seen too much to believe that. You know there is a God. There is a purpose in this somewhere. What purpose is served in the death of a child? What purpose is served in the death of an innocent man? Jesus was innocent, and his death served to bring about your redemption.

Eddie slumped to the floor and sobbed. That was all he could do at this moment. He was beyond speaking. His pain was so great that the Holy Spirit had to make intercessory prayer for him. The Spirit stood before the throne and offered prayers on behalf of Eddie Cain. The throne of God heard those prayers and granted a merciful sleep to Eddie and Jan.

They both spent the rest of the night in dreamless sleep. Fifty of the Lord's angels appeared in the Cain home. The demon horde suddenly found it a distasteful place to be. Two of the angels placed their hands on the foreheads of Eddie and Jan.

Divine calm overtook them. They didn't know why or how. They only knew the sleep of the emotionally exhausted. Cares no longer troubled them. Worries no longer assailed them. They were given a brief respite from the troubles of this life.

Chapter 12

Two months passed. The funeral seemed so long ago. The usual time of grieving was over. All of the friends and well-wishers receded back into the woodwork. Half a bottle of Vodka hid in the closet in one of Jan's shoeboxes. Eddie didn't know that this was a usual hiding place for her. She had taken up the habit of drinking a couple of shots of vodka slowly each night before she went to bed. Not enough to make her tipsy, but enough to affect her mood and relax her. At first, it seemed a good idea. It relaxed her so much she didn't feel the pain of loss.

Then it became a nightly ritual. She couldn't have told you when it went from a desire to a need. She felt that this was something that she needed. It was no longer something to help her through the night. It was now something that she worried about.

Would she have enough to last her the rest of the week? Would Eddie find her secret little store? How much less would he think of her when he found it? Why did it have to be this way? Why couldn't she simply have some peace of mind? Why did her baby have to die?

When this last thought hit her, she would have to have a drink. She found that a little vodka in a glass of orange juice left no smell on her breath. Several glasses later, she didn't feel the pain any more. She was cautious with her behavior. She didn't want Eddie to know. She couldn't bear the shame of her actions.

She thought if she hid this part of her she could appear to be the dedicated little pastor's wife. She was so wrapped up in her own pain she didn't see Eddie was hurting for her as well. In her grief, she had become a creature of self. She hadn't done it consciously, and she hadn't meant to do it. It had simply happened.

She was human, and she hurt beyond what she could deal with on her own. She completely forgot to rely on the Lord. It never occurred to her. Eddie was unaware of her practices. She was leading Sunday school classes under the influence of a few shots of HELP.

It was a bright Friday morning. Jan sat at home after her third shot of nerve tonic. She planned on spending a lazy day cleaning up the house and catching up on chores. She was completely unprepared for the phone call from Eddie. He was at the Church. He usually spent his Fridays in his sermon development. He hated being bothered on Friday.

She thought that today was a day of freedom to do as she pleased. That was why she had allowed herself the 'nerve medicine'. She answered the phone uncertainly. "Hello?"

"Hey, honey, it's me" Eddie's voice came on the line. "I'm in the middle of my sermon notes, and I left my Greek language reference at home. I was going to come and get it, but the car won't start. Carl says he will take a look at the car, but I have no way to come home. Could you please bring it to me?"

Eddie didn't see the three little imps that stood on the hood of his car. One reached through the hood and made the engine non-responsive. Jan hesitated. She did *not* want to drive after drinking so much. She wrestled with herself.

A battle raged within her. *Tell him the truth! No, you can't tell him. What will he think of you if he sees what you've become?* A huge blanket of shame washed over her. The little imp hovered at her elbow. This battle had been won long before it ever occurred in reality. This was a weakness that was known to the enemy. She didn't have the heart to tell her husband of her dependence on alcohol.

They had planned for this long in advance. They had fed her a steady diet of shame for her affliction. They suspected she would continue to hide her dependence. Most humans did. They hoped they would be able to alert a slothful police officer to her driving.

"Okay, honey," she piped. "I'm in the middle of cleaning the oven, so I'll drop it off at the door so I can get back and finish this up before it dries."

"Thanks honey," crooned Eddie. "You're a treasure."

This only increased her guilt. The imp sat on her shoulder grinning broadly. Jan walked slowly with little coordination to the car once she had retrieved Eddie's book. She got in and steeled herself for what she was about to do. She took several deep breaths, thinking it would sober her. She hoped she could do this without incident.

She started the car and backed out of the driveway. Undetectable to human eyes, the car was covered by ten small demons. They all howled with glee. Three other demons had been sent ahead to see if they could find a police officer.

Jan backed out of the driveway, almost dropping into the ditch. She didn't realize how badly her coordination had been affected. She started toward the church, eleven miles from their house. She drove at a snail's pace.

Her speed was far too slow for a normal driver. She was coming close to the stretch of road where the road ran parallel to a large fishing creek when she realized that her speed was far below normal. She thought she was handling the car pretty well so she decided to pick up the pace.

Three of the demons had found the local police officer and prompted him to patrol past this road. He traveled in the opposite direction as Jan approached the creek. He was looking around. Generally, no one was out fooling around in this area. He was shocked to see the car coming at him on the wrong side of the road.

Jan hadn't expected to see the police car rounding the curve. She realized she was headed straight for him. She overcorrected, went straight off the road, and into the deep, cold creek. The impact, when the car hit the water, knocked Jan out cold. The car filled rapidly while Jan was unconscious.

Officer James Denton screeched to a halt and leapt from his car. He ran to the creek and fumbled with his gun belt. He didn't want the encumbrance of the belt, the gun and the extra rounds. He couldn't understand why the belt wouldn't loosen. Two imps holding his gun belt together went unseen.

When the car was almost covered, Officer Denton grew frantic. "Oh, Jesus, please help me!" At this, the two small imps screamed in pain and fell away from him. The belt slipped off with ease, and he jumped into the water.

He swam to the driver's side of the car and tried the door handle. It was locked. He tried banging on the window. The pressure of the water inside the car acted as a brace. He couldn't break it.

He swam quickly to the other side of the car. Frantically, he yanked at the door. It was not locked. He opened the car and grabbed Jan. She wouldn't budge. He reached and pushed the button on her seatbelt. The belt came free, and he pulled her out of the car. He was quickly running out of air.

They broke the surface, and he had her head cradled in the crook of his arm. He wasn't a strong swimmer, but he managed. He swam slowly to the shore. He finally made it to shore and pulled her out of the water. She looked bad. She was limp as a ragdoll, and her lips were blue. Her head lolled to the side as he tried to lay her gently on her back.

She wasn't breathing. He started to administer CPR. She had a nasty bruise on her forehead that he assumed she got from the steering wheel or the windshield. When he blew into her mouth, he came away with a slight taste of alcohol and vomit.

He was in a quandary. He couldn't leave her, but he had to call for help. He decided to administer CPR to charge her body oxygen. A few minutes later, he ran to his car radio. In short urgent sentences, he called for an ambulance at his position. He ran back to her.

Officer Denton kept telling himself to keep going. He was determined to do what he could until an ambulance got there. He continued CPR, alternating fifteen chest compressions then two breaths. She was ashen and completely unresponsive the entire time.

Demons around him screamed for him to give up. They stood or hovered at a distance. The demons didn't want to chance this one calling upon the savior again. Now and then, one would get brave and leap through him. Fifteen agonizing minutes later, the ambulance showed up.

The EMT's took over, but their faces were grim. They had little hope for Jan. One of the EMT's was Frank. He recognized Jan. Sorrow coursed through him with the recognition. His demeanor had change since the death of Faith Cain. He had struggled against the Lord in his life. Faith's death had stirred something in him.

Frank pulled out the defibrillator. His younger partner was administering CPR and using a breathing bag to help Jan breathe.

"Lord, please help this young woman." He connected the leads and set the defibrillator to charge then opened her shirt.

The defibrillator chirped to let him know that it was charged. He told his partner to stand clear. He leaned over Jan's body and applied the paddles to her chest and abdomen. Jan's body rocked with the jolt. There was no pulse. He applied a second shock with the same result.

He set the defibrillator to charge again. His partner continued working on Jan.

"Lord, I'd love to see this woman draw breath again, but your will not mine." With his first prayer, the demons had backed away. With this giving over of will, the demons fled the scene. Frank attempted shocking Jan three more times. She was completely non-responsive.

Frank put his hand on his partner's shoulder. "I think this one is gone, Billy. I'm going to call time of death at ten-fifteen AM."

Billy pulled the breathing bag away from Jan's face and stood up to get the gurney from the ambulance. Frank hated this part of his job.

He got on the radio and informed the hospital that they were on their way with a D.O.A. The hospital gave the standard response. He and Billy went down the bank and picked up Jan's body. Officer Denton stood there shivering.

He was soaking wet with a defeated look on his face. This was the first time he'd administered CPR. He was afraid he'd done something wrong. That was the story the imp sitting on his shoulder fed him.

"She died because of you!"

"You were too slow!"

"A better officer could have saved her."

Tears came unbidden to his eyes. Frank saw this and made a mental note to speak to Officer Denton later. An angel sat nearby on the bank and smiled. He could see the hand of God in this. The Lord would turn something horrible into something for his glory. The angel thought of the scripture in the book of Romans.

Romans 8:28 (NIV) And we know that in all things God works for the good of those who love him, who have been called according to his purpose.

The angel knew Frank had been called to witness to Officer Denton. He also knew that the finger of God was on the life of the questionable officer. God would take this man and mold him into something beautiful in the eyes of Christ, All for the glory of God.

Frank prayed silently for Officer Denton. The little imp on the officer's shoulder screamed and jumped away. The thought of God and the 'meaning of it all' came to Officer Denton. This was strange for him. He never thought of such things. He always busied himself with the next ticket or possibly the next bribe that came his way.

He felt a strange pang at his conscience. He didn't see the Holy Spirit whispering in his ear. God was not here to condemn him so much as He was here to love him.

Chapter 13

The phone rang, and Amber picked up. She was unprepared for the gruff officer's voice on the end of the line. "Hello. This is Officer Tatum with the city police. I need to speak to a Mister Eddie Cain." Thoughts buzzed in Amber's mind. She wondered if Eddie was in some sort of trouble.

She decided this couldn't be the situation. "Sir, he is out of his office for the moment. Could I take a message or ask him to call you back?"

Officer Tatum hesitated before his voice came back. "Please have him call me at 555-3918 as soon as you possibly can. It is important."

Amber's head swam as she jotted the number down. She didn't know what to think. She didn't know if it was Eddie's wife or a congregation member. The thought of his wife brought the terrible thought that Eddie was free now. That idea was pushed away violently along with the little demon who had planted the seed of it. He giggled as he fell away.

Feelings of terrible guilt washed over her. Tears came to her eyes. She decided she would find Eddie to tell him of the phone call. She got up, and her gait was a little shaky. She found Eddie a few minutes later. He was in the community kitchen fixing a sandwich. His eyes narrowed at the sight of her.

She could see his body tense up. She knew he was nervous to be in her presence alone. She decided to get this over with as quickly as possible. They were still rather formal around each other now. "Officer Tatum called with the city police. He needs you to call him back."

A look of surprise came over Eddie's face. This was completely unexpected. "Did he say what he wanted?" Eddie asked.

"No. He wants you to call back as soon as possible." She held out the scrap of paper with the number on it. Eddie took the paper, and Amber turned on her heel and went straight back to her desk.

Eddie didn't notice Amber's abrupt exit. He was too engrossed in thought of what this could be about while staring at the number on the paper. He put the note in his breast pocket, picked up his sandwich, and headed back to his office.

The room was more like a large walk-in closet, but it was his. His worn swivel chair creaked as he sat down. He set down the sandwich and pulled out the scrap of paper. A little nervous, he picked up the phone and started to dial the number. He messed up once and had to start all over.

He was getting so nervous and didn't know why. He didn't see the two imps standing in front of his desk screaming at him.

"Your wife is dead, man of God!"

"It's your fault! You should have seen this coming!"

"You weren't a good husband!"

"Your baby is dead! Your wife is dead! Why have faith?"

"God could have prevented this if he really loved you!"

"If there is a God, would he do this to his servant?"

"Do you want to love a God like that?"

"City Police." A voice came on the line.

"Uh…. Yes, this is Eddie Cain. I was asked to call an Officer Tatum." Eddie stated.

"Please hold," came the nasal response.

Eddie wiled away the seconds by drumming his fingers on the desk. He didn't know why, but he was growing increasingly anxious.

"Officer Tatum speaking."

Eddie spoke, "Yes, this is Eddie Cain. Our secretary said you wanted to speak to me."

There was a pause, a long pause. Officer Tatum's voice came back on the line. "Mr. Cain, I'm very sorry to have to say this to you. There was an accident on Old Mill Road, about five miles from your church. I need you to come to the city morgue to identify a body."

Eddie's face went completely numb. He heard the words as though they came from a place far away. He heard his own voice reply, "Who do you want me to identify?" Tears started to form in his eyes. He knew before the answer came.

"We believe it is your wife."

He dropped the phone.

For a few moments, Officer Tatum spoke saying, "Hello? Hello?" Then he realized that he wouldn't receive an answer. He hung up and dialed the main church number. Amber answered the phone, and Officer Tatum apprised her of the situation. Horrible grief and concern for Eddie washed over her. She was silent for a few heartbeats.

Officer Tatum spoke forcefully. "You need to get in there and make sure he is alright. Have someone bring him down here. Don't let him drive here alone." Amber was shaking as she assured the officer it would be taken care of. Amber got up and walked quickly to Eddie's office. She knocked lightly and opened the door.

Eddie sat at his desk. Tears streamed down his face. A look of hopelessness covered his countenance. Slowly, his eyes came into focus. When Amber registered on his consciousness, Eddie felt an additional and undeserved pang of guilt.

It was enough to break the dam. Eddie collapsed onto his desk. Sobs racked his body. A low scream came from him and slowly built into a devastating, mournful cry. Amber didn't know what to do. She felt guilty and afraid. She wanted to go to him, but knew that she would only make things worse.

She ran from the office and through the back doors. She found the elderly groundskeeper puttering with the rose bushes. She was babbling when she tried to tell him what was happening through her tears. After a confusing few minutes, William Blain understood.

He assured Amber that he would take care of Eddie. William reached a shaking hand into his pocket to make sure that he had his car keys on him. The shake was a nuisance, but Parkinson's did that.

Most people would be resentful, but William had walked with the Lord long enough to know that this was actually a blessing in disguise. He would someday soon be with the one he served. That wasn't too much to bear for such reward.

William started his shaky walk into the church. He had only gotten through the doors when he heard Eddie. He didn't remember ever hearing such a mournful cry coming from another human being.

The old groundskeeper did his best to support a Shaking Eddie to his car. They rode to the Coroner's office in silence. William prayed for this wounded young man for the entire drive. When he pulled up to the Coroner's office, Eddie bolted from the car.

William set the brake on the car and slowly followed Eddie into the building. It was a few minutes before her found the office he was looking for. He heard Eddie's sobs from down the hall. *This is terrible,* he thought. *First, he loses his daughter and now his wife. This might break that young man.*

The coroner had told Eddie of the level of alcohol in her blood. "She must have been drinking for a while to have built up such a tolerance," he explained to a sobbing Eddie. He walked away for a moment and returned with a sedative to settle the preacher's nerves.

What the coroner couldn't see was the prompting he received from the demonic realm. The whole time he administered the sedative, the demons screamed at Eddie. It was a strange otherworldly sight. The coroner was a completely carnal man. The demons could only scream at Eddie, but they had their claws deeply buried into the medical examiner. The worldly doctor was a man who wouldn't accept the gospel of Christ.

He believed that the Bible was a big history book. He was open to the demonic control being directed toward him. He was easily manipulated as to the amount of sedative to be administered to Eddie.

The doctor came over. "Here, take this. It will calm you down." He offered two tiny white pills in a cup and a little paper cup of water.

Eddie had mechanically taken the pills. He hadn't even asked what it was. The change in his mood was incredible. In twenty minutes, he went from total despair to being strangely detached from his grief. Eddie was shocked at how much difference he felt when the sedative took effect. The piercing despair had lost its grip on him.

He understood why his wife had turned to alcohol if this was the benefit she sought. He determined that he would try to understand why she had done what she had done. He went home an hour or so after he had identified her body. He had never felt emptier in his life when the sedative wore off.

He set about the task of searching for Jan's hiding place. He reasoned that it must be hidden if he had no knowledge of it. He found it when he searched their bedroom. It was in a shoebox at the foot of their bed. He couldn't believe she had hidden it in such an obvious place. Then again, he wasn't looking for it.

He wondered for a moment what it was that she saw in this clear liquid. Then he remembered the calm that the sedative had given him. This had become so important to her life that she was willing to drive under the influence. A desperate desire to understand seized him.

Eddie went to the kitchen and got a glass. He hesitated for a moment, but it was only an instant. He didn't see the demons all around him screaming at him.

"You know you want a drink!"

"You need to find out why she drank!"

"What kind of husband doesn't know his wife is in pain?"

"She died because you weren't there to help her!"

"If you had paid more attention to her, this wouldn't have happened!"

This litany played through Eddie's head every night for the next few months. While this continued, he drank more and more vodka. The effect was the same. He would drink a few drinks and feel strangely, happily detached. Despair and absolute depression would leave him.

In his drunken state, Eddie thought of the unfairness of God. While in a stupor, he thought that it was cruel of God to make life so uncertain. All the while, the imps were all around him. They were slowly able to stand closer then to even touch him.

They fed him a false gospel. Things that he would never have accepted before seemed to ring true in his state of mind.

"GOD IS THERE FOR THOSE WHO PRAY TO HIM!!"

"IF YOU ASK FOR SOMETHING IN MY NAME, YOU WILL RECEIVE IT."
"

GOD IS A FATHER WHO GIVES GOOD GIFTS TO HIS CHILDREN."

"IF YOU DON'T RECEIVE WHAT YOU'VE ASKED FOR, IT IS BECAUSE YOU HAVE TOO LITTLE FAITH."

Chapter 14

Eddie stood in the convenient store. He was spending the last of his money after being released from the church some months earlier. Unemployment insurance was due to run out soon. He didn't have any idea what the future held for him. The cashier rang up his order. "Twenty-three dollars and fifteen cents," she intoned.

It was a strange moment. Eddie realized that he had a dollar more than the order called for. He said, "Let me get one of those Lucky Lot Lottery tickets, too, please."

She asked, "Do you want any specific numbers?"

"No." Quietly, he thought, *Lord, I claim this winning lottery ticket in the name of your son, Jesus Christ.*

In that moment, the imp went to report to Molech what had happened. His master had left him with explicit instructions. Minutes later, the little imp was bowing before his master. Molech exulted at this. He nearly danced with joy. This was the moment he had waited for from the time that he had decided to corrupt this man of God.

Molech then disappeared in a swirl of smoke. He went to the Demon Lord that watched over gambling in this area and called in a lot of favors to gain this advantage. Molech thought the demon lord had done well. The demon lord had assured him that Eddie would be one of three winners. Everybody knew what religious people automatically did with the number three.

From that moment on, Molech had made himself a constant companion to Eddie. He was searching for the key to destroying this Christian's life and drag as many of these foul monkeys down with him. Watching this young preacher fall from grace to despair was wonderful. It had been like savoring a fine wine. He meant to enjoy all of it that he could.

Eddie went home that night to a dreary and rather messy apartment. Patches dotted the walls where the plaster had been badly repaired. Sometimes at night, the pipes rattled, and he could swear he heard voices coming from them. The tiny bedroom was taken up by the worn double bed. The bed sagged in the middle and had to be full of dust mites.

The apartment had the lingering odor of stale beer and kitty litter. He'd had to move from the house, because the church held the house for interns. The elders were as patient with him as they could be, but his days as a preaching intern were definitely over.

He turned on the television as an afterthought. He'd just started on his fourth mixed drink for the night. He remembered the lottery ticket in his pocket when he heard the drawing come on at ten-thirty. There was a hope but not much when they started giving out the winning lottery numbers.

Eddie was shocked to hear the first two numbers that he recognized as the numbers on his ticket. He was rather serious about it when he took the ticket from his pocket and started comparing it to the numbers on the screen. He realized he might make a mistake and dropped his ticket and then started jotting down the numbers from the television commercial. When he was sure he had them all, he picked up his ticket and started his comparison.

He was dazzled by the fact that all of the numbers matched. He couldn't believe it. It took a moment to register on his mind. Suddenly, he went from being poverty stricken to having a ticket worth more than five hundred thousand dollars! His mind reeled. He couldn't believe what had happened.

He had prayed over that ticket, and now he was being blessed. Eddie poured himself another glass of 'celebration' and was feeling the effects.

The lottery ticket stayed in his shirt pocket. He wasn't going to let it out of his sight until he cashed it in tomorrow. He was on top of the world. Thoughts of Jan and Faith were nowhere to be found. He had drifted so far from who he had been. He was unrecognizable as the same man.

It wasn't long before he collapsed onto his rather smelly bed and slept the sleep of a drunkard. Ten little imps danced around the room, celebrating. These imps were the lowest on the demonic food chain. Their gray skin appeared somewhat reptilian as they pranced back and forth in front of Eddie. Their eyes were as hard as agates. They enjoyed watching a human slowly self-destruct.

They chanted to Lucifer loudly as they each took positions around the bed, forming a five-pointed star around Eddie. Eddie lay there in his drunken sleep while Molech drifted slowly over him. The tempo of the chanting became more urgent.

Molech hovered face down directly over Eddie. For a moment, ecstasy spread over his face. "You are a Christian, little man of God, so I cannot possess you no matter how far you fall from grace." Saliva dribbled unchecked over his lower lip. "But I can empower you for my purposes," he hissed.

"You have wandered so far from your savior. Now I can use you to do my bidding." Moving deliberately, Molech came close to Eddie and breathed on him. "Charisma is a trait in humans, but it is also a spiritual gift. I am giving you the demonic equivalent of charisma. You will be a most effective speaker for my purposes."

Eddie didn't see the saliva that dripped from Molech's mouth into his own. Strangely, it didn't pass through. It lingered on his lip before evaporating.

Eddie stirred in his sleep. He was troubled by visions of a giant, flying spider weaving a web around him. He felt despair come over him. The loss of hope was devastating. His mind gravitated to the ticket and the security it offered to him. Eddie had become a carnal Christian. The love of God was no longer the most important thing in his life.

The next morning Eddie showered, shaved, and put on his cleanest clothes. Laundry day hadn't come for the week yet. He drove to the lottery office with the ticket in hand. The day seemed beautiful to him. The sun was shining. His head was much clearer than it had been in a while. He didn't stop to wonder why.

He was busy planning what he would do with the money. He offered a little thanks to God as an afterthought. *There really is power in the name of Jesus.* He drove on for a few miles, and the realization struck him. *I claimed that winning ticket in the name of Jesus Christ, and exactly as the Bible says, I got it.* Then the scripture came to mind:

John 14:14 - You may ask me for anything in my name, and I will do it.

It's true! You can ask for anything in his name, and he will do it. He made a promise, and he can't break his word. God can't tell a lie. Molech saw the expressions on Eddie's face and heard the muttering as he drove. He felt positively gleeful at Eddie's progress.

Molech was twisting Eddie into a powerful weapon to seduce people into a false gospel. This little man had the perfect background to draw thousands from the foot of the cross. Molech placed a scheming hand on Eddie's shoulder in an act of ownership. Eddie pulled up in front of the lottery office.

He fed Eddie a steady stream of lies about Jesus. "Yes, that's right. Jesus *has* to do what you ask. When you invoke the name of Jesus, God has to act because he has to give validation to the name of Jesus. You can have anything you want and put it all on Jesus' tab. After all, you are one of his children. He *wants you* to be happy."

Eddie practically bounced out of the car. He was abuzz with nervous energy when he walked up the steps. He saw winning the lottery as a validation of his status with the Lord. It was a reward for his years of faithful service. He considered that it may also have been a little of an apology for the taking of Faith and Jan.

His earlier teaching was fading from memory. He used to know that the only validation needed for a Christian was the fact that Jesus willingly went to the cross. The savior bore their punishment for them because he loved them. To ask for more validation than that was to show a lack of faith.

"Good morning, sir," chirped the woman behind the counter.

"Good morning!" replied Eddie in an exuberant tone. "Where do I go to cash in a winning lottery ticket please?"

She raised her right arm and pointed down the hall. "Go to the third door on the left. You will need to speak to Alice. Congratulations, sir, and have a nice day."

Eddie turned and walked up the hall. He got to the third door and knocked. A quiet voice invited him inside. He opened the door and walked in. The office was sparsely furnished. There was only one picture on the walls. It was a picture of the crucifixion of Christ. *A fellow Christian,* thought Eddie. This gave him a common ground before he even spoke.

"May I help you?" the lady behind the desk asked.

"Yes, ma'am, I'm happy to say that I have a winning lottery ticket from last night's drawing. I need to see about cashing it in."

"Well, let's see what we can do. You are the first one today, but our computers indicated that there were three winning tickets out there. You will have to share the winnings with the other two winners."

His thoughts gravitated to God wanting him to be willing to share, so he said, "That's fine with me. The Lord shared five loaves and two fish with five thousand people."

She was taken aback by this show of faith. In all of her years working in the lottery office, this was the first person that seemed willing to share. He even seemed to mean it. "He certainly did. By the way, my name is Alice Cunningham. I'm very pleased to meet you, sir."

"I'm Eddie Cain, and I'm pleased to meet you as well."

Eddie reached into his pocket and pulled out the ticket. He offered the ticket to Alice and asked, "Do I give this to you?"

"Yes, you do, along with your driver's license and your social security card."

Eddie took out his wallet and gave his license, social security card, and the winning ticket to Alice.

Molech prompted Eddie to say something churchy. Neither could see the demons in the room. Her little office was almost full. There were imps and even a few lords, but commanding the room was Molech, who was a little surprised. He hadn't expected this degree of precision.

The demon lord had done his job well. It turned out that Alice was a wayward Christian. She hadn't been to church in more than a year. Her religious husband had left her for another religious woman. They had been a church going family for more than fifteen years. She'd had no idea what was going on behind the scenes in her perfect little marriage.

She was the classic believing Christian who had been burned and her faith suffered for it. She was ripe for what Eddie was about to say. "Ma'am, you aren't going to believe this, but this is the first lottery ticket I've ever bought. I felt the pull of the Holy Spirit telling me to buy the ticket. I prayed over it when I bought it. I claimed it in the name of Jesus, and here I am claiming the winnings."

Inwardly, Alice was stunned, but didn't want to show it. "That's interesting sir. May I ask what you do for a living?"

"I was the youth leader at Grace and Mercy Christian Church until my wife died recently," Eddie replied.

Pity careened through Alice's mind. She could easily relate to Eddie's loss. She immediately moved into caretaker mode. "I'm so sorry. I know the loss of a loved one. You have my sympathy."

Eddie received her remark with seeming grace and replied, "The Lord helps those who help themselves."

"He certainly does," replied Alice.

She had input the winning lottery ticket into the system. The system prompted her for his information. Three small imps stood on her desk, yelling.

"This man of God has the keys to eternal life."

"This man is the real deal, not a fake prophet."

"Here is someone who has the real answers."

"He is so humble, and God has favored him."

The imps danced with glee when her posture relaxed. They knew how to judge a person's reactions by their body language. *I've got to tell Edith about this young man,* Alice thought. Meanwhile, the computer in front of her was blinking while waiting for an answer. She came out of her reverie and realized that she needed to give final authorization to the ticket and its owner.

She typed her name and her employee number into the system and received a green light. "Is there a particular account you would like this deposited into?" Alice asked.

"To tell the truth, I don't have a bank account anymore," confessed Eddie.

"That is not a problem." replied Alice. "I can have a bank draft drawn up for you in a moment."

"That would be great," exulted Eddie.

"So where do you attend church?" asked Alice.

"I've been on sabbatical for the last few months," Eddie replied. "Where do you attend services?"

"I go to Faith and Hope Baptist church," Alice replied, with a tinge of conscience. She knew it had been a long time since she had attended. She pushed away the condemning thought.

The little imp behind Alice jumped onto her shoulder and simpered.

"This is a true man of God! You could learn a lot from him."

"Your friend Edith would love to hear what this man has to say."

Alice's mind readily received these thoughts. She made a mental note to call Edith tonight. She reminded herself to be conversational with Edith. She didn't want her best friend to think of her as a religious fanatic. She didn't see the demons in the room prompting her. She was unaware of the conflict she was embroiled in. There was a plan in place, and she was part of it now.

They would put Eddie in the spotlight as an evangelist. The demons intended to use Eddie to draw believers away from the Cross. If the plan succeeded, the forces of darkness would claim a great victory. If it failed, Eddie's testimony would be the basis of a host of souls rejecting Christ. Either way, they couldn't lose.

The computer prompted Alice for the correct form for the printer. The flash from the screen caught her eye.

"Oh, I need to load the printer with the specific form."

She reached into her purse and pulled out the key to her desk drawer. Unlocking it, she pulled out the blank bank draft.

She was only allowed to have two blanks at any given time. This was a security measure in the event that the lottery office was somehow robbed. She loaded the special paper into the printer and hit the enter key. The bank draft printed in a moment, and Alice pulled it from the printer and handed it—along with the tax statement, his license, and social security card—to Eddie.

"Here is your draft, and you will need this tax statement for filing your taxes at the end of the year." Eddie looked down at the draft. It was printed for one hundred and fifty-one thousand dollars. That was a far cry from the over two-hundred thousand Eddie knew was his share. *Taxes*, thought Eddie. Uncle Sam seemed to get a good bite of the apple before it fell from the tree.

"That draft is as good as currency at any bank. So you can choose which bank you would like to open an account with. If you want a recommendation of a bank to use, I recommend New World Bank. They recently opened a branch here in town, and most of their services are free."

"New World Bank, huh?" Eddie asked. "I think I will give them a try." The idea of saving money was attractive to him. He still didn't have a job.

A thought occurred to him. "When are the services at Faith and Hope Baptist church?" asked Eddie. He'd thought this idea came from the Holy Spirit leading him to a new church home. He didn't see Molech standing beside him with a wide grin showing yellowed fangs dripping spittle. This little wayward Christian was shaping up to be a nice piece of clay in the hands of the demon lord.

Alice was caught off guard at that question. Thoughts careened through her mind. *I haven't been to church in ages. He will know that I've been lying to him. He wants to come to my church.*

The imp on her shoulder put her mind at ease with comforting words.

"Everyone is welcome in the house of the Lord." It hissed into her ear.

She hesitated for only a second and said "Sunday services are at nine AM and eleven-thirty AM."

"Where exactly is the church?" Eddie asked.

"It's about three miles outside of town on route 21. I usually go to the nine o'clock service."

"I will see you there." Eddie smiled his goodbye, turned and walked out of the office.

Chapter 15

Alice picked up the phone as soon as Eddie walked out. She called Edith Barnes. Edith was a tall thin woman in advanced middle years. Her husband had passed away eight years ago. Her children all lived out of state so she seldom saw them. She had become incredibly lonely so she'd thrown herself into her work.

Edith was the regional director of the Happy Care Daycare chain. She had almost tripped into the job when she started volunteering at the local daycare. She had taken on more and more tasks while volunteering. She was completely familiar with the workings of the business side of the daycare.

She was approached by a representative of HCDC. The corporate office offered her a position as the regional director. The offer came with a nice hefty salary. Edith was surprised but pleased by the offer. Once she found out what it entailed she accepted. She had basically given herself a free business education by investing only her time.

Edith picked up the phone on the second ring. "Edith Barnes. May I help you?" she intoned mechanically.

"Edith, it's me Alice. You aren't going to believe what happened."

Edith was pleasantly surprised by Alice's call but was puzzled by the breathless introduction she got from her. "Alice? Is something wrong?" She was a bit worried.

Alice heard the worry in Edith's voice and apologized, "Edith, I'm sorry. I didn't mean to scare you. Everything is fine. How have you been?"

Edith was slightly mollified by the response and responded, "Oh, you know how it goes. Never a dull moment but I love it. One of our daycares two counties over is having a staffing problem. I have to go over there. I need to find out why their turn over is so high. They lose one employee about ever three months. Something like this is usually a poor management issue. I think I'm going to have to replace the manager or the whole management staff."

Edith's voice had been thick with pride. She liked being the regional manager. It made her feel important that her opinion carried weight. That was why pride had crept into her heart. An imp skipped on her desk. He didn't own her, but he could influence her.

Alice considered Edith's response and replied, "Well, I'm happy for you, but I'm glad my job is easier than yours."

They both laughed at this, and then Edith recovered, "So tell me, what had you so breathless when you called?"

Alice warmed up to the subject again. "You aren't going to believe this. I just had a young man come in here. He had one of three winning tickets from last night's drawing. When I told him he'd have to share the winnings, it didn't bother him at all. He said that Jesus expects us to share. Then he started talking about how this was the first lottery ticket he'd ever bought and how he'd prayed over it in the name of Jesus.

"He told me he felt prompted by the Lord to buy this ticket. He's the youth leader of the big church on the edge of town. Edith, I swear I think the Lord is with this young man. He spoke so confidently about the Lord, and he won a lottery after buying one ticket in his life. Do you know what the odds of that are?"

Edith had to admit that Alice made a good argument. Edith wasn't one to accept snap judgments, though. She thought for a moment. "I'd like to meet this young man, Alice."

Alice divulged, "He's coming to church on Sunday at the nine o'clock service. Do you still attend there?"

Edith slowly responded, "Well, yes, kind of. But I haven't been in months."

This reply somehow made Alice feel better. Misery loved company. Alice replied, "Don't feel bad. I think you know how long I've been out."

Edith replied, "Yes, but you at least had a reason. I didn't. I stopped going because I was lazy one Sunday morning and thought I would sleep in and lie around. I should know better than that."

Alice was quiet for a moment. "We have two choices. We can sit around chastising ourselves, or we can agree to meet for church. Want to meet this Sunday morning at nine so you can meet this young man?"

Edith perked up and said, "Alice, you've got a deal. Maybe this is a turning point that we can both start going back to church. I know I've missed it."

Alice asserted, "Okay then. I'll see you Sunday. I need to get back to work."

Edith answered, "Yes, so do I. Talk to you later."

They both hung up. Alice perused the copy of the young man's driver's license. "I wonder what God has in store for you, Mr. Eddie Cain?" She put the copy down and straightened the mess on her desk. This was turning into a most interesting day.

Argass had been studying this neighborhood. He used the trick that he'd seen Jenoch use. After he'd altered his perception, he could see that this area was abuzz with demonic activity. He didn't inspect his surroundings long. He wouldn't risk being away from Candy for very long. He made himself aware of only the earthly plane. He started toward the Beaumont home.

Candy had taken her nightly bath. She was lying quietly in bed. Argass floated through the wall and hovered over the bed. Candy had a slight cold chill when Argass settled onto the pillow beside her head. She was almost asleep, but his arrival woke her up. She became restless and fearful. Argass countered this by cooing nice words of comfort into her ear.

"You are in a land of candy where you can eat all the sweets you want. ... Your mother and father gave you a new puppy as a present... You found a cute kitten and your mother said you could keep it.... Grandma Liz is taking you for a pony ride."

When she calmed down, Argass reached down and sunk his claws back into her skull. There was a momentary thrill for Argass. This was always an instant of triumph. Argass felt a brief surge of relief. He had worried that Candy would have resisted him. She was young, and rules for the young were unclear. This time, however, they seemed to be in his favor.

Argass wondered how far the rules had been stretched in this instance. He'd had several hosts that he had completely overlain. After that, his personality was completely in charge. The host was just a small voice in the background and very easy to ignore. He'd had more control over those hosts than any others. At the point of complete possession, his spirit overlaid the soul of the host. It was almost like having his body back.

He looked around carefully. There didn't seem to be any of the hosts of Heaven about. The girl's parents couldn't offer any protection for her. They never prayed as a family. They didn't even understand prayer. A better opportunity probably would not present itself.

Argass pulled his claws from Candy's skull. He stood and moved to a better position in the bed. When he was at the midway point of Candy's body, he lay down on top of her. He concentrated and slowly started to grow. He stopped growing when he was exactly the same size as Candy.

He rolled over onto his back. He took care to arrange his limbs in the same fashion as Candy. In an almost inaudible voice, he called to Candy. "Candy, let me in." He kept repeating it. It became a chant. Candy's body started to relax.

Argass' body became blurry. His diffused form started to sink into Candy. Argass was ecstatic. He was starting to overlay Candy completely. *Soon, she will be mine.* Slowly, bit by bit, he sunk into Candy. For a long moment, it seemed success was at hand.

Argass felt a terrible shocking burning sensation. The word "NO!" rang out through the night. Argass was thrown from Candy in a violent jolt. He flew up through the ceiling for a moment. Gravity took over and he made a small arc. He landed beside Candy's bed dazedly. He felt as though electrical fire ants were eating his flesh.

The sensations lasted for a while. Argass was terrified. He looked for a legion of angels to appear and drag him off to Sheol. Nothing happened. No angels made an appearance. He didn't dare to move. An hour passed and still nothing happened.

Argass finally relaxed. If something was going to happen, it would have happened by now. He stretched out his hands and walked to the bed. There was no barrier blocking his way. No voices sounded. No lights flashed. He leapt back onto the bed beside Candy. Still nothing happened.

Argass pondered this situation. It seemed that he received certain freedoms. He couldn't completely possess or overlay Candy yet. He didn't want to push his luck by trying again. If he disregarded the warning, something sterner would happen next time.

There was never any guarantee of ownership. The Father loved these stinking monkeys so much that he protected them at all cost. Argass remembered a child he was trying to corrupt in ancient Egypt. The child was taken from him at the Father's will because blood hadn't been painted onto to the doorpost.

Argass had been so incensed. He had worked for years to corrupt this firstborn son of a prominent merchant. The child was of the perfect age. At twelve years he was old enough to question his father's beliefs and methods but not old enough to understand the wisdom behind those decisions.

Argass reflected on these memories before returning to the task at hand. He settled back and drank in the emotional distress that radiated from Candy. This was always a good time for a demon. He was sure he would be allowed to corrupt this child without interference. That is as long as he didn't go too far too soon.

Chapter 16

Sunday morning dawned bright and clear. Alice's alarm clock went off. She was excited because this was going to be her first time back to church in almost a year. She was also secretly hoping to see that handsome young man again. She would never admit it to herself though. He was after all young enough to be her son. That would be completely improper.

She got up and bustled around the house getting ready. She made sure to use favorite perfume. She seldom wore perfume, but this was a special occasion. It was her first day at church in a long time. At least that is what she told herself. She didn't see the little imp caper about her bedroom, as she got ready. He screamed things like.

"Wasn't he such a handsome young man?"

"Did you see the way he kept looking at you?"

"Such a spirit filled man of God, full of compassion!"

She soaked these things up like a sponge. She went to the phone and dialed Edith's number. Edith answered on the first ring. "Hello?"

"Edith, this is Alice. We're still on for church aren't we?"

Edith responded, "Yes. I'm nearly ready."

Alice queried, "Do you want to meet at the church or do you want me to pick you up somewhere on the way?"

Edith considered this for a moment, "Let's meet at the church. That way if one of us has to leave for some reason it won't inconvenience the other."

Alice thought this was a sensible idea, "Okay then, I'll see you there at 10 till 9." Edith gave an affirmative and they both hung up.

Alice practically skipped out to the car. She didn't know why she was so excited or at least she wouldn't admit to herself why. She got in the car, checked her mirrors and started the short drive to the church.

Eddie rolled out of bed as soon as his alarm clock went off. His shabby little apartment was sporting some new furniture now and he had purchased some new clothes for church today. He got up and jumped into the shower. He'd gotten into the habit of shaving in the shower a few years back. He considered it easier. All he had to do was keep his razor and shaving cream in there and it was much easier to clean up than cleaning razor stubble from the sink and vanity top.

He got out of the shower and toweled himself off. He did all of his little grooming rituals and then went into his bedroom and started putting on his new suit. He had bought three. One was navy blue. One was dark brown, and one was black. He put on the black one. He put on a white shirt with a black tie that had 'John 3:16' in red metallic letters on it. He'd gotten a haircut yesterday, so he thought he didn't cut that bad of an image.

This was going to be his first time back to church since.... well in a long time. He didn't see Molech standing behind him. Molech was rather pleased at how his pet human was shaping up. He would be introduced to another of his unwitting agents today.

Molech watched Eddie puttering around getting ready. He was doing things like putting on a tie clip, putting on his watch, filling his pockets with little odds and ends. Molech was always puzzled at the human attachment to things. They surround themselves with things. Oh well, he guessed he would never understand it. He would be satisfied as long as he could control this pathetic little bag of watery mush.

Eddie went to the refrigerator, which was fully stocked now and poured a glass of orange juice. Eddie wasn't big on breakfast. He could eat it if it was there but most of the time preferred not to. He downed the orange juice, checked his watch, and headed out to his car.

Alice pulled into the church parking lot and was surprised to see Edith already standing there. "Well, she does live closer than I do." She muttered.

She couldn't explain the little pang of something like jealousy that she felt right now. She realized she had invited Edith here to meet Eddie, but now she wanted to have Eddie all to herself. Then it hit her. She was being foolish. Eddie was a much younger man and nothing but friendship would ever happen between them.

She chuckled at herself. She was glad she got a grip on these feelings. Now she felt better. She parked the car, got out and walked over to where Edith stood.

"How in the world did you get here so fast?" Alice asked.

"I put my makeup on in the car. I've gotten into the habit of doing that. I know it's not exactly safe, but it saves a lot of time." Edith replied.

People milled around them, some went into the building to find a good seat and others stood around to socialize. Alice wondered for a moment where Eddied was. She checked her watch and relaxed. The time was only 8:45 so there was still time.

Alice checked around and saw Pastor Johnson standing outside the front door. He was shaking hands of the people that were entering the building. "*I hope he isn't still doing that when we walk in. He'll say something like 'We haven't seen you around in some time' and then I'll be caught.*"

Pastor Johnson was a portly man of average height. He nervously ran a hand over his balding head while talking with another man. Only a few members knew that his crooked nose was due to a rather wild lifestyle. That was before he joined the ministry.

Edith stood there looking around and she wondered, "*Why is Alice so keyed up? She's wound up tighter than a spring. I wonder if it has anything to do with this young man. I certainly hope not. Neither of us is a spring chicken. I guess it could be because it's been so long since she's been here. I feel a little out of place myself.*"

Edith noticed Alice's head turn and her face took on an expression of expectance. She stared in the same direction as her friend. There was a young man approaching. He was about 20 yards away. He was a handsome young man in a black suit. He appeared broad shouldered but not muscular. When he got closer she noticed he had a cleft chin. When he got closer still, a smile broke out on his face. He had obviously recognized Alice. Edith glanced back at Alice. She was smiling as well. That settled it. This was the young man that Alice was talking about.

Eddie stepped up to Alice with his hand extended. "Ms. Cunningham, it is so nice to see you again. I trust you are doing well?"

"Yes, I'm doing just fine, but call me Alice. Ms. Cunningham sounds so stodgy." Alice practically purred.

There was a momentary silence and then Alice announced, "Mr. Cain, I have a friend here I'd like you to meet. This is Edith Barnes. We've been friends since writing on stone tablets was fashionable."

Alice and Eddie both laughed but Edith stood there with an expression of consternation on her face. "I don't see how that was so funny." She groused. That set Alice and Eddie into a fresh set of laughter.

When the laughter was over Eddie insisted, "If I'm to call you Alice then you have to call me Eddie." He turned to Edith and extended his hand. He spoke warmly, "Ms. Barnes, it is a pleasure to meet you."

He had such a warm inviting smile and his words sounded so sincere that Edith's defenses automatically went down, and she rejoined in a titter, "Oh please call me Edith. It's nice to meet you too Mr. Cain."

"Eddie" he corrected her.

"Alright then, Eddie" She surrendered.

Eddie looked from one to the other and asked, "Shall we go in ladies?" They stared at him dumbfounded. For an instant, they didn't seem to know what he was talking about. Their faces cleared and they both seemed to start,

"Oh! Yes." Alice prompted.

He gestured that Alice should lead the way. When Alice turned to the entrance she was relieved to see that pastor Johnson had gone inside. At least she wouldn't have to face that embarrassing moment.

Nobody saw Molech walking behind Eddie. His towering form was hulking behind and above Eddie. His gait was strange because he matched Eddie's speed. His height was so much greater. He took a step, waited, took a step and so it went. He stayed close to Eddie. This was enemy territory. He planned to keep his pet within arm's reach at all times.

He saw one of his lieutenants. It was Jenoch. He commanded, "Go and make sure my bidding is carried out." With that Jenoch took off, his claws were scrabbling on the concrete of the sidewalk. Eddie reached out and opened the door and held it for Alice and Edith. They both thanked him as they passed through the door.

Alice led the way down the middle aisle to about the middle of the church and found an empty pew. She slid in first. She hoped Eddie would take his seat next. Eddie however was determined to be a gentleman. He gestured for Edith to be seated next, which she did, smiling. Alice's face momentarily took on a sour look. She realized how foolish it was and rearranged her features. They quietly waited for the service to start.

It was a strange site inside of the church. There were angels walking with their charges, demons walking with their charges and a smattering of angels and demons alone roaming among the aisles. Occasionally an angel glared, or a demon hissed. The impression of truce or neutral ground was in force here.

Pastor Johnson walked along the front row of pews. He shook hands with everyone there. Jenoch walked behind him. He whispered in the pastor's ear as Molech had commanded outside. The pastor didn't seem bothered. He didn't seem particularly tense or upset. As a man of God, he should have been more sensitive to such things.

A bell rang out. The pastor walked to the middle aisle in front of the altar. He stood there for a moment. Then a young boy and a young girl walked forward. He was holding what appeared to be a set of stacked trays while she was holding a set of stacked plates.

They each presented their items to him in turn. He took the plates from the girl first and turned and walked up the steps to the altar. He

104

placed the plates on the altar. He walked back down the steps and took the trays from the boy. He walked up the steps and placed them on the altar. As soon as the trays touched the altar the boy and girl turned and walked down the aisle.

The entire time Jenoch followed and whispered in the pastor's ear. Pastor Johnson cleared his throat. He gazed out at the congregation. He glanced around until his eyes rested on Eddie. Jenoch whispered furiously into his ear. He stared at Eddie for a full 10 seconds and then shifted his eyes down. He walked to the lectern. He put his hands on both sides of it.

"Good morning to you." He intoned in a deep carrying voice.

The congregation responded with "Good morning Pastor."

It wasn't in unison. It sounded rather ragged. Jenoch still stood behind the pastor. He still whispered to him. The pastor's face became a bit haggard and then he seemed as though he'd made a decision.

Molech's face split in a wide grin. The pastor reached down and pick up a sheaf of papers.

"I uh.. I worked on this sermon all week. I worked on it and tried to polish it. I tried to make it applicable for life today. I was hoping that it would be a message of hope for someone going through a struggle here today. I did all that and I'm not going to preach it. As a matter of fact I'm not going to preach today."

The congregation was confused. They didn't know what he was going to do. His face took on a resolute quality.

"No, I'm not going to preach today because from the moment he walked in I've been getting the impression that this young man has our message for the day. At first, I was trying to ignore it but the more I tried to ignore it the more insistent it became. So to the young man in the black suit" He turned to Eddie "Why don't you come up here and share the Lord's message with us today?"

Molech leaned down until his muzzle was an inch from Eddie's ear and growled, "Go. Feed my people"

Without hesitation Eddie stood up and walked straight down the aisle. He walked up the steps to the lectern. Without a word the pastor surrendered the lectern and went to sit at his customary place in the front row. This was where he sat when individuals made announcements immediately after the service.

Chapter 17

A slight buzz ran through the congregation. People whispered to each other. There was a great deal of confusion throughout the room. The demons in the room grinned while the angels looked stern or sad. Eddie cleared his throat. He began in a soft voice.

"My name is Eddie Cain. Up until some months ago I was the youth leader at Grace and Mercy Christian Church." There was a buzz of recognition at the name running through the crowd.

"My wife and I lost our baby girl to SIDS or at least that's what the doctors told us. I personally don't believe that. I think we are approaching the end times when Satan will have full control of the world.

"I believe that the Holy Spirit is gradually being withdrawn from this world. I believe it is getting harder and harder to be a Christian. It is already a social faux pas to talk of Christian things.

"I believe that the day is soon coming when it will be a social faux pas to be a Christian. That will be followed not long after by the laws being passed that it will be illegal to be a Christian. Those laws will be punishable by death.

"We live in a nation that was brought into existence based on Christian values. Now we hear how talking of Christianity is against the constitution. The worldly people say 'separation of church and state'.

"That is not what the constitution says. What the constitution says is that the U.S. can't favor one religion over another. It doesn't say you talk of Christian things in public.

"The world is trying to trap us with this. If you can't talk of Christian things in public, then you can't preach in public. If you can't preach in public, then you can't call the lost souls to the Lord.

"Jesus gave us the parable of the sower. In the parable of the sower the devil and his workers came along behind the Lord and stole the seed that was sown. Think of how much easier it would be for the devil if he didn't have to do that. If the seed isn't sown one of his problems is completely removed."

A buzz of agreement swept through the church at Eddie's words. One elderly lady piped up, "You know he's right. I'd never given that a thought."

The pastor sat in the front pew with a wan smile on his face. He was convinced that he had done the right thing by listening to the prompting that had nagged him.

Why did he feel guilty then? Why did he feel like he'd betrayed his flock? He knew he hadn't worked that hard on his sermon. He knew it was a repeat from a couple of years back. He had shuffled it around a little and hoped that nobody would remember.

He knew he should put more work into his messages. He knew his prayer life was lacking. For a little more than a year, he'd felt like a hamster on a wheel. He couldn't seem to shake the feeling that nothing mattered. Nothing he did made difference in these people's lives. He should pray about this tonight and seek the Lord's guidance. Yes, he should but he probably wouldn't.

The church quieted again, and all attention turned back to Eddie. Eddie began to speak again.

"Ladies and gentlemen, I say to you that we as Christian people have to step forward and start preaching again. We need to sow the seeds not only in the church but out in the world.

"We as a Christian people need to reach people that are out there. Coming in here to receive the word and teaching of our pastor is a good thing but we need to reach out of our comfort zone and say, 'Here I am Lord, send me.'

The church became animated. Eddie had reached into their hearts with his words. They responded to his every word. Eddie saw the pastor smiling at him. He didn't know he was making the pastor absolutely miserable.

The pastor was sitting there thinking *When was the last time I stirred this congregation with words from the Lord?*

Molech was gleeful. He crouched behind Eddie and fed him the words. His little pet performed perfectly. He had this church in the palm of his hand. Molech motioned for Jenoch to approach. Molech whispered something to him and he walked back to sit invisibly in the pew beside Alice.

He leaned over and started whispering in Alice's ear. The angels in the room started to worry. Each of them heard the throne of Heaven say "Peace" into the quiet of their minds. Then the voice was gone. With that they calmed. The will of the Father prevails in all things. Freedom of choice for man must be preserved in this world.

The congregation focused on Eddie. He coughed for a moment and the pastor mouthed 'under the lectern'. Eddie caught that and looked. There was a cold unopened bottle of water. Eddie took it and opened it. Before he took a drink, he mouthed a thank you to the pastor and took a sip. He swallowed coughed again and cleared his throat. He began to speak again.

"Ladies and gentlemen, I believe that the Lord is calling this church to become the sower for him in these end times. I believe that the Lord is saying that he wants someone or a group of someone's from this church to step out in faith.

"Place your personal safety in his hands to preach the word of God to the lost in the streets of this city and possibly this state. This church needs to consider a tent ministry like the one that the apostle Paul demonstrated.

"He preached out in public and he was a tent maker. As a church you need to remember, it is up to the people of the church to sow the seed. It is up to the Lord to make the seed sprout and grow.

"So many people give other's the word of God and then are disappointed that they don't get a convert to say the prayer of conversion." Eddie leaned forward at this and bit off every word as he uttered them. "It isn't up to you to save souls. That is the Lords job. He only wants us to sow seed."

Eddie straightened again and spoke in normal tones again. "Think about it. How can the Lord prepare a harvest if the workers, that's you and me, don't sow the seed in the first place?"

Molech didn't whisper in Eddie's ear at this point. He straightened and took a step back. He believed he had created a masterpiece. His grin was hideous to behold. He had gotten exactly what he came for. Now he was going to watch it come to pass.

Jenoch, still in the pew, whispered alternately between Alice and Edith. Eddie's face was calm when he looked out over the congregation. He didn't feel prompted to say more. He thought the best thing to do was share this with the congregation and step down. "Ladies and gentlemen, I know this is making for a very short sermon, but I don't feel prompted to say more. I hope this message has helped the church and I hope I haven't said anything wrong or out of line."

An excited buzz ran through the church. Who was this thin young man who had set the church aflame with his words? He had certainly captured their hearts here today. As Eddie spoke the last of his words he turned to step down. The pastor stepped up beside him and gripped his arm. He deliberately spoke close enough to the microphone that the whole church heard him.

He jibed, "Oh come on now, you don't think you are going to get away that easily do you?" The congregation laughed and waited for the pastor to speak. "Ladies and gentlemen, I think we need to give our thanks to this young man for such stirring words today." The church erupted into applause.

When the clapping died down an elderly gentleman with a gleam in his eye raised his hand to be recognized saying,

"Pastor? Pastor?"

The pastor recognized the man and responded, "Yes Mr. Edwards, you have something to say?"

Mr. Edwards cleared his throat and spoke, "Yes sir I do." He looked around at the whole congregation and declared, "This young man has given us a stirring sermon. Now, we all know that every word of it was God's own truth." There was a murmur of assent that ran through the crowd.

Mr. Edwards continued. "This young man says we need to start a tent ministry like the one that Apostle Paul had. Well I say he's right. Furthermore, I say we use that large pavilion tent that we purchased two years ago and have only used once. I think the Lord had us buy that tent just for this purpose. I move that as a church we begin a tent ministry as the given word of the Lord has commanded us here today."

Again, a murmur of assent ran through the room. The pastor considered this and noted, "Deacon Edwards, I understand your words. While I agree with them, my duties with the church are such that I couldn't find the time to dedicate to such an added ministry"

Alice raised her hand and didn't bother to be recognized before standing up. The pastor was taken by surprise. He hadn't seen Alice in quite some time.

Nonetheless he said, "You wish to speak Ms. Cunningham?"

Alice was shocked that she found the steel in herself to do this. She piped, "Yes I would. I move that the young man who preached here today would be the perfect candidate for the preaching portion of the tent ministry."

A rumble of approval went through the room. Eddie's face became stricken. He spoke up, "Now wait a minute, I'm not worthy of such a post."

The pastor regarded him and snorted, "Young man, if the Lord waited around for someone worthy to help him nothing would ever get done. Now be quiet, you've been nominated. The church has to vote."

Eddie choked out, "Hold on. I'm not even a member of this church."

The pastor glared at him sternly, "Young man, I realize this is your first time here. I also realize that this is probably because of the tragedy in your life that this is probably the first time you've been to church in a while. You are here because the Lord led you here. You are here because the Lord wants you to heal and in your healing this church will heal right along with you. Do you dispute that?"

Eddie was quiet for a moment. In a small voice stated, "No."

The pastor smiled and almost boomed, "Let's get on with it then. All of those in favor of the tent ministry raise your hands." Every person in the pews raised their hand. Some of them raised both hands. Pastor Johnson laughed and chortled, "That is the first time in years that we've had a unanimous vote." Then he requested, "All those in favor of this young gentleman… Eddie Cain I believe, to head up the preaching portion of the tent ministry raise your hand." Once again, every person in the church raised a hand. The pastor declared "Excellent"

He took Eddie's right hand in his and shook it vigorously. "Welcome to the church and the ministry young man." The pastor glanced out at the congregation and announced, "Ladies and gentlemen, now comes the most unpleasant part. How do we fund this ministry? The church is running on a shoestring budget as it is. I'm not complaining mind you and I'm not trying to extort more money out of you."

Edith Barnes stood up and requested, "Pastor, may I speak?"

The pastor peered at her and affirmed "Certainly Ms. Barnes."

Again, Pastor Barnes was taken by surprise. Here was another member that he knew hadn't attended in a while. Edith looked around the church first and then she stared directly at Eddie Cain.

Edith announced crisply, "I know that most of you know I'm the regional director for the Happy Care Daycare chain. As the regional director, not only am I in charge of monitoring the operations of all of the Daycares in my region I'm also in charge of certain public relations responsibilities. The Happy Care Daycare chain has a charitable donations budget. I am within my authority at this moment to pledge in the name of the Happy Care Daycare chain One

Thousand dollars per month for as long as the Daycare functions or for as long as this ministry is in service."

Pastor Johnson was stunned. A little jealous part of him thought she had never pledged anything like that to support her home church. The church rumbled its approval and Edith sat down. As soon as Edith was down Mr. Edwards was standing again.

"Pastor?" He asked.

Pastor Johnson replied, "Yes, James?"

Mr. Edwards spoke, "Pastor, I pledge to match that pledge under the same conditions."

The church applauded now. Pastor Johnson thought, "*This church has never gotten behind me like this. I've poured my soul out for these people. Pretty boy here shows up and gives one sermon and he has received the two highest pledges ever given at this church.*" Pride was a bitter dish to dine on.

Eddie was stunned. He got up this morning to go to church. Now he was the preacher of a traveling church. He was nervous, but he felt privileged.

The pastor seemed to glare at him for just a moment. He didn't understand why the pastor stared at him like that. Had he done something wrong?

Jenoch was puzzled. Molech's pet had delivered a sermon that was completely true. There was no false doctrine or lies in it. From where Jenoch stood that didn't make sense. He would *not* ask Molech about it. He didn't want to be punished for impertinence.

Chapter 18

The phone rang for the third time, and Roger picked it up. "Rest Easy Investigations. Roger speaking. May I help you?"

"It's me honey. I'm sorry to bother you at work, but could you pick up Brennan's prescription on your way home?"

"Sure, honey no problem."

"Thanks. You are such a dear." She followed with an almost syrupy "I love you."

Roger leaned back in his chair and crooned, "I love you, too."

Amelia replied, "I'd love to chat, sweetie, but I can't right now. See you tonight?" The last held an apologetic note.

"Okay." He heard the line go dead.

Roger Carter flexed his muscular frame. Thirty-six wasn't old, but sometimes he felt stiff from sitting for too long. The chair creaked when he leaned forward and hung up the phone. He had the disciplined personality needed to run a security company in modern day America. He loved the challenge of maintaining the company while also being a field operative. He was his own top investigator.

Roger looked back his computer screen and took a slow deep breath. He had been poring over some data from an investigation for a high paying client. The client was a large restaurant chain and wanted to know if one of its competitors had stolen ideas from their ad campaign.

He had analyzed the data and the footage exhaustively. He thought that any connection between the ad campaigns was purely coincidental. He didn't like this, but it was the truth. He wouldn't compromise the truth for profit. That was one principle that he ran his business on.

A lot of his competitors would have fudged the data to make a connection. This was not his style. He was a committed Christian and truth was important to him. He thought of his client's reaction and cringed, but only slightly. He thought, *They pay me for the truth, not for a lie. If they want a yes-man, they can hire somebody else next time.*

He shut down the system and started his daily office closing ritual. His mind drifted to Brennan. Brennan was his son by his first wife. He wondered what he was doing for the night. With luck, he'd be able to call his ex and get him for the night. She constantly went out and left him with a sitter.

She was the typical 30-something divorced party girl. He hated the idea that Brennan didn't receive the attention he needed from his mother. He liked how much time he spent with his son. He hated that most of the child support he paid went supported her lifestyle. He wanted a more active role in Brennan's life as his father.

He had vowed inwardly when the divorce happened that, no matter what, he would be a father to his son. He refused to be a weekend-only dad. Before he opened his security company he had spent a couple of years as a bounty hunter. The huge amounts of back child support owed by deadbeat dads amazed him. No wonder there was such a stigma on deadbeat dads.

He saw the tide turning though. More and more mothers were leaving family and children for other men or for jobs. Sometimes it boggled his mind to think of it. He used to think that there was nothing stronger than the bond between a mother and her child. He now knew that was an illusion. It was whatever was acceptable to society at the time.

The boundary of social acceptance was constantly being pushed. The push was always beyond what was shameful or sinful in the past. He mulled it over and thought, *This society has forgotten how to blush...Oh, listen to me. I sound like some Biblical sage. People could do a lot better than listen to me.*

Roger thought of what and who waited for him at home. Amelia was a petite woman with an open and friendly way about her. She was shorter than he was. That was one of the thing he found appealing. He like the way she kept her brown hair short giving her an almost pixie-like appearance. He loved her, but she was also a friend and confidant.

They had met about a year and a half after his divorce. Roger had become bitter and hadn't expected to find companionship. He'd met his first wife at a bar. That should have been a warning sign.

Her name was Susan Hamilton. She was a beautiful vivacious girl and a bit of a flirt. That should have been his second warning sign. She loved attention, another clue missed.

They had fallen for each other rather quickly after meeting. It was a whirlwind romance followed by a quick marriage. Brennan came along not long after the first year of their marriage. The divorce papers had shown up not long after the third year of their marriage. Now that marriage was dust.

He had become bitter and not in a good place to get over the hurt. He sat in his favorite coffee shop when Amelia walked in. She ordered a double mocha latte with cream and sat down at the bar beside him. It wasn't a move on him, it happened to be the only seat available. It was more out of necessity than anything that she started a conversation with him.

"What a day, huh?" Those were her only words, but her eyes were so innocent and inviting that he couldn't help but answer.

"I know what you mean. I think it would be better if we could do a rewind for a few hours at a time." They had sat and talked for two hours before they realized how much time had passed.

She was struck by his aloof nature. She could tell that he was guarded because of pain. She wondered at the source of the pain. He came across as an open and moral man. *Open and moral,* she thought. *Very funny! How many times have I had that exact thought to find that the guy was a complete jerk?*

She decided Roger was interesting. Beyond that he would have to earn her trust, no matter how funny he was. This thought drifted through her mind as she was getting up to leave. It was an awkward moment for them both. Each wondered if the other would ask for a phone number. Both were afraid to take the necessary step.

It seemed the opportunity passed with nothing of consequence happening. Then, Roger stammered, "Uh... I know this is different, but could I get your phone number?" Inwardly Amelia cheered but didn't let it show.

She tried to nonchalantly write her name and number on a napkin. It was evident that she was trembling. Her "0" was crooked and she forgot to write her last name. She passed the napkin to Roger who was also rather shaky. His mind raced when he took the napkin from her.

What are you doing?!

The last thing you need right now is a relationship!

Remember what the last pretty lady did to you?

What are you thinking?

You already know how this is going to turn out!

He'd put the napkin in his pocket with thoughts of misgiving. Neither of them saw the angelic escorts with them. Neither had heard the promptings of the angels. This had been an ordained moment. The father had decided that these two needed to get together.

Roger's mind shifted back to the present. He wanted to spend as much time with his son as he could. He'd offered his services to Susan as a free sitter. Saving money was the bonus in it for her. His bonus was time spent with his son as a real dad. He planned to impart his beliefs and morals to his son like a father should.

He reached into his pocket to confirm that the car keys were there. It was an absent-minded gesture, but one that he had adopted as part of his routine. The phone rang as he was about to walk out. He debated as to whether or not to answer it and caution won out.

He picked up the phone and intoned, "Rest Easy Investigations, Roger speaking. May I help you?"

A familiar voice came on the line. "Roger, it's m-me, Susan."

He heard her sniff. She was crying. His blood ran cold. All he could think of was that something was wrong with Brennan. "Susan, what is it? Is Brennan Okay?" His voice was thick with worry.

"No, Brennan is fine." She sniffed again. He waited for her to compose herself. She piped in a small voice, "Dean and I have been having a hard time lately. We really had a big fight."

Roger tried to be compassionate, but it wasn't easy. "I'm sorry to hear that," he replied as softly as he could.

If the truth were told, there was a little part of him that was dancing a jig inside. Resentment still clung to him toward her. He recognized that and was ashamed of himself. He heard her sniff again.

She mused, "I was wondering if Brennan could stay with you guys for a while. We need time to work this out. I don't like him seeing us fight all the time."

Roger jumped at this chance, "Sure, drop him off at the house and we'll be glad to keep him."

There was a long pause on the line. The silence was always awkward between them. She mumbled, "Thanks Roger. This is a big help."

"No problem" was his reply. He heard her hang up.

When dial tone came on the line, he dialed home, and Amelia answered. "Hey, honey. It's me. You aren't going to believe this. Susan called crying all over herself and asked if we could keep Brennan for a while. She and Dean are having some trouble. She doesn't want Brennan to see them fighting all the time. I hope you don't mind but I told her to drop Brennan off with us."

Amelia took a moment to process all of this. She knew this was a dream come true for Roger. Brennan coming over was no problem for her. She would have liked to have been in on the decision making, though.

She wrestled with herself over this. Guilt fought with pride for a moment. She didn't like what she was thinking. A few seconds had passed, and Roger's voice came back on the line.

"Honey, I realize I should have spoken to you first before I said yes, and I'm sorry. It's just that he's my son." His voice was so contrite.

Amelia felt terrible for feeling the way she felt. She backpedaled, "No, honey, I'm sorry. He is your son and I'm supposed to stand behind you one hundred percent. I know the situation, and I shouldn't let my pride get in the way. When do you think she will be dropping Brennan off?"

He supplied, "It's after four o'clock, so he's home from school. She will probably be doing it within an hour or so." She thought for a moment and replied, "You do realize this presents a babysitting problem?"

He asked, "How so?"

She replied, "Well, you work until four o'clock, so you can't pick him up from school. He can ride the bus home, but he isn't old enough to stay at home by himself. I work at home, but you know I have a lot of client meetings. I never know when I'm going to be at home. We can't dependably say we can be home when he gets off the bus."

Roger thought about that for a minute. He really hadn't thought about that part of it when he made the leap to say yes. He remembered one of his clients was in a child custody battle. She'd raved about a new Daycare in town called the 'Happy Care Daycare'. She was very pleased with it.

He offered, "Well I heard about this new Daycare in town called the 'Happy Care Daycare'. We could call them."

Amelia thought about it for a second and responded, "Roger I don't want to hurt your feelings but I think I should call them. You are a guy. You would ask about when we are supposed to pick him up and how much it costs and then you wouldn't have any more questions. Brennan is a child, not a pet. We need to know that he will be cared for responsibly."

He thought about that for a second and she was right. He didn't have the foggiest idea what kind of questions to ask them. "Fair enough" he settled.

She said, "Okay, I'm going to call them and see first if they have any openings, then we will go from there. I'm going to get off of here to go ahead and take care of that. Love you, honey."

"Love you, too."

They both hung up.

Roger got up from his desk with a feeling of satisfaction. He opened the door to leave. He flicked the light off as he passed over the threshold. He thought of home and his family as he closed and locked the door.

Roger silently prayed. "Thank you, Lord. You've given me so much. I know I don't deserve all the blessings, but I try to live up to your word."

Chapter 19

Amelia walked into her little home office. She sat down to her computer. She had thought *If this daycare is new they won't be in the phone book. I'll check online and see if they have a web page.* Sure enough, they did have a web page. She read through some of it. It was the standard stuff you would expect for a daycare.

"We provide a safe nurturing environment."

"Children are our first priority."

"Children are the resource of the future."

"Feedback letters every month report the progress of your child."

"Each district has a child psychologist on retainer to aid in behavioral issues between parents and staff."

Amelia clicked on the 'Find Locations' button and looked at the list that came up. "Well this is convenient." She thought. "They are only about 3 miles away. I wonder why I don't remember ever seeing this new place."

She wrote down the phone number. She picked up the phone and dialed the number. The phone rang, and a soft feminine voice answered, "Happy Care Daycare, Judy speaking. May I help you?"

Amelia replied, "Yes ma'am, I was wondering do you have any openings?"

"Why yes we do ma'am, we still have several openings", was the reply.

Amelia offered, "I read through your web page and a friend of my husband highly recommends you. My husband's son will be staying with us for an extended period on rather short notice. We both work so we will either need a sitter or Daycare. I was wondering if I could bring my stepson in tonight and tour your facility?"

The soft voice came back on the line, "Why yes ma'am that would be fine. We certainly wouldn't expect you to employ our services based on a phone call."

Something about this lady's attitude bothered Amelia. It was close to cloyingly sweet. Amelia confirmed, "Alright then, as soon as my step-son gets here we will come down there."

Judy replied with, "We look forward to seeing you." They both gave their goodbyes and hung up.

About 15 minutes later Susan dropped off Brennan. She was a mess. Her eyes were puffy, and her cheeks were red. It was evident that she had been crying. Amelia greeted Susan coolly. They didn't like each other.

Brennan walked into the house with a big smile on his face. He was carrying a large suitcase. Brennan was a boy of eleven years. He had his father's facial features but his mother's sky-blue eyes. Amelia thought, *"When this young man grows up, he's going to be a lady-killer."*

He was slightly shorter than average height for his age, but his form belied that he would be naturally muscular like his father. His expression most of the time was of adamant curiosity with a hint of rebellious pride. He was quick to laugh and had a good sense of humor. He was also quick to anger and easily placed blame.

Susan gave Amelia a grateful glance, "I appreciate you all doing this", she asserted.

Amelia felt a pang of sympathy for her and stated, "It's no problem."

Susan turned to Brennan and instructed, "Brennan, you be good for your father and Amelia. I love you."

Brennan appeared a little sheepish, "I love you too mom."

Susan turned back to Amelia, "Thanks again." Then she turned to go without waiting for a response.

Amelia thought, *That is one emotionally torn up woman. I'm going to have to pray for her and Dean.*

Amelia turned to Brennan, "Hey buddy, why don't you leave your suitcase down here for now. We need to run to a Daycare center to see if it is suitable for you. You can't get off the bus here because I don't know when I'll be here because of my clients."

He groused, "Awww man!! A Daycare!!? I'm not a little kid." She came back with, "I know you aren't Brennan. Legally you can't be left at home alone until you are 12 and you aren't there yet. Now come on. Let's get in the car and go up there."

He turned around grumbling a little but marched resolutely back out to the driveway to get into the car. She unlocked his door for him then walked around the car and unlocked her own. She got in the car.

It was like getting into a sauna. She rolled down the window and started the air conditioning as soon as she got it started. She backed out of the driveway and headed toward town.

Brennan complained, "How long am I going to have to stay at this Daycare every day?"

She thought about it for a minute, "Well your dad gets home every day around 4:30. I don't have client meetings every day. On most school days you shouldn't have to stay there for all that long. My best guess would be anywhere from a half hour to an hour. Your spring break is coming up though. Those days you will probably be there for at least 8 hours." She heard him groan and she didn't blame him. He was at an independent age. Daycare sounded like something for a little kid.

They drove in silence to the Daycare. Sure enough it was on the right about three miles from home. She saw the nice new building with the new backlit sign. She didn't know why she hadn't seen it before. She pulled into the parking lot and they both got out.

The placed seemed standard for what you think a Daycare should be like. The front had a large picture window. The front area was for the toddler's. There were four of them playing with one of the worker's. They were rolling a ball back and forth. The kids were obviously enjoying themselves. Amelia thought, *Like that isn't a contrived image. I have to hand it to them. They know what they are doing.*

She and Brennan walked through the front door. A young lady walked toward them. She appeared to be in her mid to late twenties.

She had blonde hair and a nice figure. Amelia could see by her eyes that she was intelligent. She wore a manufactured smile on her face.

She greeted, "Hello and welcome to the Happy Care Daycare, my name is Judy, may I help you?"

Amelia answered, "Yes, my name is Amelia Carter. We spoke on the phone a little while ago. This is my step-son Brennan."

Judy smiled, "Oh yes, would you like me to take you on the grand tour?" She laughed a little at that.

Amelia replied, "Yes please." Judy responded, "Alright, if you'll follow me please."

She took them around the facility. She showed them the play area, the learning area, the rest area and the timeout area. The timeout area had a number of small cubicles in it. Each cubicle had a desk in it and that was it.

The learning area had a bookcase full of children's books and several computers with Children software logo's running on the monitors. The rest area had mats on the floor. The play area had lots of children's toys.

Amelia liked the fact that it was nice and clean. "As you can see this is a pretty standard Daycare setup. We at HCDC take our work with children very seriously." Amelia couldn't say she liked Judy. She couldn't complain about the facility or how it appeared they did things though.

"Do you mind if I ask your rates?" Amelia asked.

Judy stated, "$50 a week per child. That rate applies whether your child attends or not. You are paying for the slot your child occupies, not just the service provided."

Amelia was familiar with this. It was the pretty standard rate and how it worked. She had some friends who had to do the same thing.

Judy queried, "So Mrs. Carter, are you interested in utilizing our service?"

Amelia answered, "Yes ma'am, I believe we are."

Judy prompted, "If you will come with me, we have some paperwork to fill out. Brennan will be tentatively registered with us. Every child we take on goes through a 30-day probationary period. We can't guarantee that a child will be a good fit."

They followed Judy to her office and filled out a mountain of paperwork. The forms were for health insurance, basic information, emergency contact, and selective liability waivers and so on. Judy made special mention of the child psychologist the daycare had access to.

Amelia finished the last page and complained, "I think I'm going to need a splint for my hand."

Judy laughed and contritely opined, "I know what you mean. I'm sorry for that but we do have to cover the business end of things."

Amelia offered, "I understand. Is there anything else?"

Judy answered, "Yes, there is a starting charge of the first two weeks in advance."

Amelia replied, "Alright."

She reached into her purse and pulled out her checkbook. She wrote out the check and handed it to Judy. Judy accepted the check with a thank you. Amelia stood with an expectant glance at Brennan.

"Ready to go buddy?" She asked. He stood looking sheepish.

Judy escorted them back to the front and instructed, "Brennan, you will need to ride bus 21 here tomorrow. She pulled a slip of paper off her clipboard and gave it to Brennan. "Here is a note for the bus driver so he will let you ride here. Just give it to him and get off the bus here. You understand?"

Brennan gave a nod of understanding. Judy gave him a pat on the shoulder. "Mrs. Carter, don't worry about a thing. We will take good care of Brennan when he is with us. I hope you both have a great rest of the day."

They left and headed back to the house. After all that paperwork Amelia felt drained. She decided that they were going to have takeout for dinner. She checked her watch. She guessed that Roger was at home already.

She called him on her cell. He answered the phone and she told him they were on their way home. She asked him what he thought of takeout tonight. He told her he'd already ordered pizza. She was so thankful. She asked if he ordered breadsticks and he answered yes. She told him thanks and they would be home in five.

Chapter 20

The next day was a normal day. Amelia didn't have a client meeting. She decided that she would let Brennan get off the bus at the Daycare to start his new routine. She gave him a half hour there then went and picked him up. He was exultant to see her when she got there. That was a nice surprise.

Day three of Brennan's stay she hadn't had a meeting. She picked up Brennan from daycare early to get a start on dinner. She decided that she would try to fix home-made biscuits tonight. They got out of the car and went into the house. Amelia was done with her work for the day so she walked straight into the kitchen. She got out all of the ingredients that the cookbook showed in the recipe for biscuits.

Twenty minutes later Amelia swore under her breath. She glanced around to make sure that Brennan wasn't within earshot. Sometimes watching her language wasn't easy. Her mother could fix biscuits and make it look easy. Her mother's biscuits were delicious. Amelia was not her mother. She worked wonders on a keyboard. On a stove she was an amateur.

She worried that Roger wanted her to be this "Be-All End-All" homemaker. She took a moment to apologize to the Lord. She shouldn't have sworn. She knew that the Lord still loved her, but she didn't want to offend him callously. She dumped the misshapen dough into the garbage disposal. She would have another go at the biscuits before she gave up.

Amelia measured out the flour again. She heard footsteps coming into the room.

"Hey Amelia, what are you doing?" came Brennan's soft voice. She peered up at his curious expression.

"I'm fixing biscuits for dinner tonight." Amelia answered.

His face lit up in a small grin. "You mean you are trying again?" There was a light chuckle behind his words. She realized he was playing.

"Yes, I am buster and if you don't watch it, I'll make you eat two of them." He laughed and ran from the room.

"You will have to catch me first." came the shouted reply.

That was her cue. She dropped the measuring cup and chased him through the house. The play fight lasted for ten minutes. He was fast for his age or was she slow for hers? She finally cornered him behind the couch. She used her weight and the training from Roger to pin him. She mercilessly tickled him until he, however falsely, admitted he'd be happy to eat two of her delicious biscuits.

She was thankful that she got along with him so well. It was due to the fact that they both loved his father so much.

She got up and let him catch his breath and offered, "Sorry kiddo, but it's back to the kitchen for me or we won't have any dinner tonight."

He replied with "I don't really have to eat two biscuits, do I?" She chuckled, "You don't have to eat any if you don't want."

She was slightly out of breath. Brennan was a handful when they were wrestling. She was of slight build and he was still growing. She realized in a couple of years he would be too strong for her. She trudged back into the kitchen while Brennan settled himself on the couch.

She heard the TV come on and she knew he was surfing channels. She wasn't bothered about leaving him alone with the television. They had long ago blocked all of the channels with offensive programming. They were the only family she knew with more channels blocked than they allowed to be viewed. Roger had stated, television started out as a good tool but like all other good tools, give the devil time and he will twist it into something terrible.

She got to the counter and picked up the dropped measuring cup. She started measuring out the flour again and wondered what she had done wrong the last time. This was starting to become a chore she didn't like. She really wanted to be able to make homemade biscuits, but she didn't want to deal with the learning curve.

"Why can't we just use those frozen biscuits?" she thought. She reminded herself that she had taken on this little mission after she heard Roger remarking to a friend that he loved his mother's homemade biscuits. *"OK girl, you wanted to do this now follow the recipe and do it."*

It was quiet in the house, so Amelia zeroed in on the sound as soon as she heard it. Brennan had fallen asleep on the couch and was snoring. She thought that was a little funny. Then she thought of the last few nights.

He'd awakened with bad dreams. He'd been fearful after waking up. He acted like something was chasing him. When he finally came to his senses he couldn't remember his nightmare.

She had spoken to Roger more than once about it. She wondered what could be causing such bad night terrors. Roger believed it was because he was starting puberty. She didn't agree. The nightmares were starting to really cut in on Brennan's rest. This was becoming something of a concern.

She dumped the flour into the mixing bowl and reached for the butter. She measured out the amount and started toward the microwave to soften it. She was paying special attention to every step. She wanted to get this right. She made a mental note to speak to Roger about Brennan's loss of sleep.

Brennan lay on the couch. His face was relaxed and his jaw slack. His position had caused his mouth to open. That was the reason for his snoring. Something settled on his chest but he didn't feel it. The being that sat on his chest caused his nightmares.

The imp on Brennan's chest flexed his slimy claws. He giggled maniacally and shook himself like a dog. The demon blinked his single eye and glared at Brennan. He had been a Cyclops in life. The lobes on his sharply pointed ears wobbled with the movement of his head. Spittle dripped from his chin and evaporated.

He had battled the angels for thousands of years since his death. Fear drove him to watch and try his best to corrupt this young son of

Christians. His name was Grablek and it meant slimy spike. He remembered the last time he had had a charge this young. It was a young boy whose family was in hiding from the Nazis.

He had tempted the young boy into rebellion easily enough. The close quarters and lack of food made it a simple task. The shelter was small, so they didn't move around much. He'd tormented the boy into thinking that conditions would be better in a prison camp. He'd clung to the child's back when he'd sneaked out in the night. He had willingly led the German soldiers back to the hiding place. The boy had watched with tears in his eyes, while they had butchered his family.

His father had died first trying to protect the family. He heard his mother's cries when they beat her with their rifles. His sister had gone quietly with a disdainful glare at her attackers. She did however spare a look of disappointment in his direction. He hadn't expected the bullet that ended his life. They were finished with his family. He was after all a Jew and the Third Reich had no use for any Jew.

Grablek's thoughts shifted to the time before the flood. He remembered the great battles between the Nephilim. He had been killed in one of those battles. He was a guard for his lord. It had been his job to keep watch for the enemy.

He had never seen the enemy. He had never seen the cut from the axe that took his head off. He was, and then suddenly he wasn't. That was what death was for him.

His earthly lord had been one of Semjaza's inner circle. They had all assumed their fortress was impregnable. They had viewed the younger Nephilim as weaker. They had ruled for so long unchallenged. The attack had been unexpected.

They thought the young ones were just posturing. When the attack came in full force they knew they had been mistaken. It was too late. He and all of his brethren had been killed. He'd had a difficult time adjusting to not having a body. None of them had known what to expect. He'd spent the next 30 or so years watching the larger newly dead Nephilim demons battle for position.

Brennan stirred in his sleep. He couldn't hear the soft song of his step- mother in the background. She was singing a slow praise song. It made Grablek uncomfortable. He didn't like being in the home of committed Christians. He especially hated being in the home of Christians who actively praised God when no one else was around.

This was a sign of authenticity that dashed the hope of any demon that came near. First, the praise would start and then the spirit would invade the room. Everything would go so disgustingly white, pure and painful that it was all an imp could do to leave the room screaming.

It was painful to witness the worship of God. It hurt so much to be in the presence of the Holy Spirit while it accepted and prompted the worship of the Father. Amelia was far enough away that Grablek stood the noise. It was rather sickening but he tuned out the words and pretended that he didn't hear references to Jesus. Oh how he hated that name. The name had destroyed any hope of victory or even amnesty.

With the coming of the Christ all demon-kind had been condemned for their actions. Grablek brought his attention back to the task at hand. His master Molech had instructed him to wear down and corrupt this child of Christians. This was no easy task and he worried constantly.

True praise or true prayer called to the Holy Spirit. Either of these drove him from the room. The father and the mother were of one accord spiritually. The enemy had placed a hedge of protection around the family. His window of opportunity was small. His punishment for failure would be horrible. He'd had to make the most of every opportunity.

This was the reason he sat on the boys shoulder practically twenty-four hours a day. He'd endured as much pain as he could stand in the presence of worship. He screamed at the boy constantly.

"Your father doesn't love you!"

"Your step mother hates you!"

"You are a burden to your father!"

"Your mother doesn't love you!"

"You are so dumb!"

"You are an ugly little toad!"

He'd thought of it as a challenge. Then he realized that it was much more than a challenge. He found that he gambled with his existence. Molech would banish him to the pit if he showed no progress. This thought terrified him. When he was about to give up hope, the boy started to respond.

Chapter 21

He saw the seed of rebellion start to germinate. Late at night Brennan had lain awake and listened to the thoughts that Grablek fed him. Brennan thought he was starting to think for himself. He was only mimicking the thoughts that Grablek fed him. Last week was the first time that Brennan had acted on one of those thoughts.

They had been at the breakfast table. Roger had asked Amelia what her plans for the day were.

"You never ask me what I'm going to do!" Brennan burst out. Roger was disturbed by the disrespect behind the statement. His face grew stern and he stood from the table.

"We need to talk man to man in the living room." said Roger.

Brennan's face blanched at this. He knew he had crossed the line. He didn't like the look of disappointment on his father's face. He got up from the table slowly and followed his father into the living room in conspicuous silence. He noticed that Amelia had been silent through the entire exchange.

An hour later Roger and Amelia sat on the couch together. They talked about the exchange that had happened with Brennan at breakfast. Roger wanted to keep Amelia informed as to what was going on. He was however at a loss for the cause of it. There wasn't a change in the way that they had treated Brennan. Neither of them realized divine guidance was at hand.

Getrel reached out an unseen hand and touched Roger on the forehead. A thought flashed through Roger's mind.

Roger prompted, "Do you think it could be anything from this new Daycare that he's going to?" This caught Amelia completely off guard. She hadn't even made the connection.

"I don't understand why you would even say that. How could they have anything to do with Brennan acting out?" She returned.

Roger replied, "We really don't know what goes on there. What they are teaching the kids when we aren't around? We need to ask Brennan what his day is like when he is there."

Amelia answered back with, "Do you remember the interview we did with them? They invited us to pop in at any time and check on Brennan."

Roger balked at this and he hesitated for a moment. "Yes, but when you go in to check on your child they have complete control of the situation. You remember how they led us around by the nose through the place every time we showed up?"

Amelia answered back with "Well… yes but you can't say that every time you want to check on your child something shady is going on."

"I'm not saying that." Roger shot back, "All I'm saying is that it bears more investigation." Amelia didn't see the imp on the table screaming at her.

"This is so unreasonable."

"Who would do any of this??!!!

The imps name was Redix. He was a rather bizarre little creature. His name means "Slimy One." He was about four and a half feet long when he wasn't attached to a host. He waved his scarlet tentacles about nervously. He was not humanoid. He was octopoid. His breath came in uneven chugs of crimson gas as he screamed at the two mortals. It looked for the world like his breath was blood.

In life he'd been an aquatic Nephilim. He'd served the lord of the Ocean. Some of the humans called him Neptune. His lord had many names. All of which he was afraid to use. He'd been killed by a bolt from above. The Nephilim that called himself Zeus had struck down a group of twenty.

He'd been in the middle of that group. In his spirit form Redix floated through the air like a squid swimming in the ocean. His grandfather had called himself Kraken. His black razor-sharp beak could sink painlessly into humans. He preferred to sink it into their skulls.

He was the type of demon that was difficult to exorcise. He used his beak and all of his arms in concert. Only devout prayer could remove him. The only time he'd been ordered out was when Jesus had walked the world.

Redix snapped back into the moment and started screaming again. "You can't say that without taking into account the other side", what that meant Redix didn't know but it seemed to work every time. Sometimes the lower ranks had to act simply because they knew the reaction that would be drawn. Understanding wasn't necessary.

The orders from Lucifer's cabinet came slowly. What do you expect when failure means banishment to the lowest plane? His thoughts drifted to Jaxon, the closest thing he ever had to a friend. He and Jaxon had been servants in the citadel of Neptune. They were both clarions. They announced the presence of visitors or even enemies at Neptune's court.

When the false Zeus had attacked, Jaxon had led the defense group he was in. Years after his death, the demon Jaxon had been ordered to corrupt a young monk. The young monk would later be known as Martin Luther.

Jaxon had adopted a tactic of harassment instead of seduction. The young monk would sit for hours arguing with voices that no one else could hear. Martin Luther was rather eccentric, but his sincerity was without question.

Waning attention from Amelia brought Redix back to the moment at hand. He'd had little enough influence in the conversation. He continued his ranting. There was nothing else he could do.

Roger realized that the conversation was going nowhere. He didn't understand Amelia's emotional involvement. Experience had taught him not to belittle her feelings.

He prayed under his breath. "Lord, please help me be the husband you want me to be." He gathered his thoughts, "We need to find out more information before we make any real decisions. Let's agree to investigate further and talk about this later."

Amelia didn't know why she was so invested in this conversation. A cloud lifted from her mind when Roger offered his prayer. They didn't see the angel that appeared. Nor did they see the way that Redix had shot away like scared rabbit when Getrel made his entrance.

Redix' first thought was simply to get away from the angel. He remembered his position and anger flared up. He braced himself and turned. In a moment his tentacles had sharp hooks on the ends.

He screamed, "Fight or flee angel!" Getrel considered drawing his angelic sword. Then the word of the Lord drifted into his mind.

"The Lord rebukes you", was Getrel's reply.

The words hit the demon like a freight train. He slammed backwards through the wall leaving a smell of singed flesh behind. These were the same words that Michael had uttered to Lucifer when the devil had tried to take the body of Moses.

The room brightened. The pall over Amelia and Roger lifted. They sat on the couch and discussed how to investigate the practices of the Happy Care Daycare chain. The mood of the conversation was much lighter.

Outside the house Redix was furious but also rather pleased. He had learned the Achilles heel of this family. The chink in Amelia's armor was her desire to understand and be understood. This was a frustrating human desire because God doesn't give all the answers. He wants his children to live by faith.

Roger on the other hand was weary and worn when it came to emotional subjects. He was a man of actions. Emotions seemed to elude him. When Amelia reacted distressed emotionally, Roger started to shut down.

Emotional issues were problems he couldn't see. He was not equipped to handle her emotional pain. He wanted problems or issues that he could do something about. He could fix a broken washer. He could repair a leaky faucet. Emotional problems gave you nothing to put your hands on. In that sense Roger was very frustrated.

Redix realized he could capitalize on this. With any real luck he could drive a wedge in this family and cause some major strife. Redix hovered for a moment and thought of how best to use this information. He knew he couldn't attack Roger and Amelia alone. He thought, *I'm going to need some help.*

Chapter 22

Names of demons that he had worked with in the past rolled through his mind. He needed someone strong but also someone manageable enough, so he could stay in charge. Slag came to mind. Slag was what the doctor ordered, immensely strong but didn't care to be in charge. Redix concentrated on Slag to get a feel for his location.

He was in luck. Slag was only about fifty miles away in the next county. Redix put on the speed to find his associate and tell him of his plan. He found him roughly 25 minutes later. Slag had attached himself to a despondent drug addict. His host was so far gone that all of the other demons had abandoned this pathetic creature.

Redix yelled out, "Slag! I have work for you. It is something that I'm sure you will enjoy." Slag didn't respond. *He's sure is single minded but he's obedient to orders.* Redix changed his approach. He yelled "Slag! I have fresh meat for you. It's a family with no demons attached to them. They are fresh for the picking!"

Slag's eyes slid into focus at that.

"Redix, is that you?" Slag was slightly intoxicated on human emotion.

"Yes, it's me, you idiot. Did you hear what I said?! I have fresh meat for the both of us, but I can't pick it alone. I need your help."

Slag seemed to become more alert. Redix didn't know if it was the insults or the familiarity of another demon, but something was working.

Slag seemed to set his jaw at this. "I have sustenance here. The others have gone. What is it that you offer that is more than this?"

Redix ground his beak at this. This was the one thing about Slag's personality that drove him insane. Slag was always looking for the comfortable. He was never really willing to take the risks for the big prize. This was the one thing that would always relegate Slag to the lower realms of power.

Redix wanted more. He wanted to hold sway over a vast area. He wanted to be in Molech's inner circle. He had never done more than receive orders from his dark master. He had resolved, if the opportunity arose he would impress the ancient god of the Ammonites.

"What is it that I offer?!" questioned Redix indignantly. "I offer you fresh emotion, something that you haven't tasted in years. You may continue to satisfy yourself with this stale creature or you can come with me." Redix gathered himself and stood before his compatriot haughtily.

Slag's grip on his host loosened. "Are you sure this is fresh meat?" Slag asked.

Redix scoffed at this. "Have I ever led you to a host that was unfulfilling?"

Slag drifted in thought for a moment. Of all of the hosts that Redix had brought him, he couldn't complain that any of them weren't ripe for the picking. Slag's grip on his host slackened.

He knew if he left the hordes of the enemy could come crashing down around his creation. He leaned back and looked at his host.

"You aren't much of a banquet anymore are you?" This thought drifted through his brain while he slowly came to the decision that he would join Redix in his work.

He released his grip on his host. He had to unwind the two living pythons that served as his arms. His hands were literally two mindless fanged snake's heads. The power of his grip came from the fact that he would sink the snake fangs into his host. The grip served as an anchor point.

He was another demon that could only be driven out by prayer. In life he had been a keeper of animals for his master. The animals he kept were used in experiments with the humans. He had bred the beautiful stallion that had been used to father the race of the centaurs.

He had died from poison. His niece had brought him a drink on a hot day. The drink had been poisoned by several different types of venom. His death had been agonizing. He had writhed in agony for more than a week before dying.

Before his death he had tolerated the humans. He knew that, because of his nonhuman heritage, he was beyond redemption. His existence was a bitter thing now. He'd made it his business to punish the humans for how his birth had come about. In his mind man's fall had brought about his existence and eventual punishment. He would take his vengeance where he could.

Slag rose into the air and faced Redix. "All I can say is that this better be worth it."

Redix grinned and hissed, "Just follow me and you won't regret it." Redix took off with Slag close behind. They didn't see the angel slowly descending on the now abandoned host. The host was lying on the ground in a fetal position.

He was a young man in his early twenties. He seemed young to measure his time as an addict in years. He came down from one of his worst binges. He'd been at a friend's place partying. He had mixed his drugs of choice. That had caused a bad reaction in him. He'd become belligerent at first. When his belligerence had gone without consequence, the demon had driven him to violence.

He'd attacked his friend's girlfriend. He didn't realize it was her until he had punched her in the jaw. He hadn't seen his friend coming at him until it was too late. It had been a bad beating. The drugs had numbed him a good deal but not completely. He'd lost a tooth to a kick from the girlfriend once he was down. Two of his ribs were badly cracked.

He'd crawled away from their home. He spat blood and the pain in his side prevented a deep breath. He had tried to stand a couple of times. The shooting pain in his side didn't allow that. He hoped he could make it to the community park. He planned to sleep in the bushes near the duck pond. He'd almost made it there when he'd passed out.

It was twilight when he woke up. Drug withdrawals rocked his body. It had been a while since his last fix. The headache had already started. He was nauseous. He dreaded the stomach cramps and vomiting. It had never been this bad before. He was hurt and bad from the feel of it. He had no money and no prospects for a fix.

He was scared. He lay there for what seemed like an eternity. Phantom spiders and roaches crawled on his flesh. The flashes of fear and pain came quicker now. Paranoia took a terrible toll. All he wanted was relief. If that meant death, he had no argument.

Somewhere in the midst of his agony he felt a hand touch his shoulder. He couldn't have seen the lone angel whispering into the ear of the old man. The old man was a bitter former preacher. He had given up his post of preaching the gospel when he felt that no one was listening any more. This small angel had breathed on the ember of faith the old man had left.

A rush of compassion such as he had never known swept through him. Before he knew it, he stepped forward and placed a hand on this vagabond's shoulder.

The old preacher leaned down, "Son, you look pretty beat up. I know you are in pain. I'll help you if I can but that stuff you've been using isn't helping you at all. I'll help you get off of it if you let me. If you would rather not, say so and I'll leave you alone."

Time passed slowly. The old man was about to turn and walk away. A gaunt hand reached out and a rasping voice, "Please help me."

The old man felt some apprehension at the responsibility that he now felt. He thought, *"Lord, is this what you want from me?"* This was the first time an offer of help had been accepted. He was committed. He would not let this man go without trying his utmost to help.

Hesitantly at first, He reached out and took the hand. Truthfully, the gentleman was afraid,

The elder gentleman said, "Ok young man, get up now. I have a place not far from here. It isn't much, but you are welcome there." Those were the first words of kindness that the host, Terry, had heard in years. It struck a chord in him. He felt a bond immediately forming between himself and this old man.

They struggled together to draw the younger man to his feet. Terry cried out once in pain because of his ribs. Once he was on his feet, Terry saw a look in the old man's eyes. He could only describe it as hopeful.

With a voice scratchy from non-use he rasped, "My name is Terry."

The older man drew in a ragged breath and said, "I'm Carl. Lean on me a bit if you need to. My home is this way."

Carl stepped off slowly to lead the way home. Terry winced in pain and took a tentative step with him.

He watched as the two men began their journey. They were so different. One was lost and the other was saved. This was the way the Father worked. The lone angel offered up a song of praise. There was hope now where before there had been none. *This is how God works*, Thought the angel. *He waits until the humans are empty and then he acts. There is no doubt that the blessing is from him.*

Terry and the preacher, leaning on each other start their trek into the night as the angel ascends back into the Heavens with a song of praise and thanksgiving.

Chapter 23

Redix and Slag arrived at the Carter home as dinner was coming to a close. It had been a quiet evening. Redix drifted through the ceiling with his companion. The home was bright but there is no presence of Heavenly warriors.

"This is going to be easier than I had hoped", thought Redix. They hovered over the family while the dinner conversation was winding down.

Redix turned to Slag and ordered, "You start working on the woman. I'll work on her husband. When you get a chance see if you can soften up the child. Every offering is accepted by Lucifer's court."

Slag had been eyeing this clean family with a gluttonous lust. This was fresh meat. He was glad he had decided to follow Redix here. He only hoped that they would be allowed to truly tempt this family.

They had all the earmarks of Christianity. They had spiritual pictures on the walls, all of which contained the savior. They were sitting at a family dinner. This was something that by and large American families didn't do unless they were Christians. God made family an extremely important thing in his word so in this day and age Lucifer had undermined it.

Slag allowed himself to float down to within three feet of Amelia. He noticed that she was pretty, by human standards. She wouldn't be so pretty when he was finished with her. His specialty was drug addiction. If he could find a chink in her armor and get her to respond to his leadings, within a year he would have her as a strung-out drug addict.

Redix, on the other hand, eyed Roger. He thought, "You are like every other puny man on this planet. God made your kind as the highest creation of this universe and you don't even know your station. I will tempt you in the same way that I have tempted and brought down so many other so-called 'Christian' men.

"Lust is the besetting sin of many men. You are no different little monkey. I will use your natural urges against you. You will fall away from this woman you profess to love, and she will see you for the unfaithful creature that you are. I will expose you and on your day of shame I will laugh at you while you are abandoned by those who profess to love you most in this world."

Redix turned to Slag and growled, "For the next few days, we do nothing but observe their conduct. It is there that we will learn their weaknesses. Don't let the woman out of your sight. Her weaknesses will become apparent if you are patient.

"Remember, they are unaware of us. Christians know of our existence, but they prefer not to think of us. They exist in this strange three-dimensional plane. We exist in a dimension above that. This task was assigned by Molech. Don't fail me."

Slag was shocked at this remark. Who was Redix that Molech assigned him work? He made note of this. For the next week Slag followed Amelia while Redix followed Roger. Slag found that Amelia was a perfectionist. She couldn't leave something she had done alone if she thought there was something wrong with it.

Slag started to work against Amelia at her chores. A stain would stubbornly stay on a plate she washed. The dust bunnies would blow away before she got them into the dustpan. She proved to be easily frustrated. That spoke to Slag of a driving need for security. She wanted things to go the way they were supposed to.

Amelia's perfectionism gave Slag a way to tempt her. It was very effective to frustrate her chores while screaming at her. Slag screamed disparaging remarks about Roger while thwarting her work.

"Roger doesn't help with the household chores much anymore!"

"I spend more time with his son than he does!"

"Do all men just give up on the relationship when they feel like they've won the woman?"

Slag attacked Amelia every chance he got. She worked at home most of the time. That meant she was constantly in his presence. A few days after his arrival his hard work bore some fruit. Her frustration was evident by the thin line her mouth formed. Her patience lacked most when it came to family.

Slag fed her venom about all men. Redix had contacted some of his fellows and retrieved some information on Amelia. Her main failing in relationships was her lack of trust. Her need for security undermined her ability to trust.

Slag suggested that Roger was noticing other women. Amelia was susceptible to this. Her trust in Roger was eroded due to his inaction. She had lost respect for Roger. Slag knew that this alone would cause a human woman to act in a selfish way. He decided to merely point out Roger's inaction and watch them drift apart.

Redix found he had predicted correctly. Roger's besetting sin was lust. He fought against it like most Christians do. The internet had made it too easy to indulge in that failing. Roger cursed himself for this more than once. Eventually though he was drawn back to his secret sin. He was careful to keep it hidden. He thought as long as nobody knew about it then the damage was minimal.

Redix found that after lunch Roger's stomach was full. His appetite was satisfied, and Roger's defenses were at their lowest. Then he could scream instructions with the most effectiveness.

"I wonder what women look like in Hawaii!"

"Do they really do that sort of thing in Korea?"

"Do African women really want a man who values them?"

"I wonder if Amelia thinks of these things."

"You sick man, you know Amelia doesn't think these disgusting thoughts! How dare you think such things about a Godly woman!"

This last one increased Roger's guilt. Redix loved to push punishment on top of corruption. It was a two for one deal that he couldn't resist. Lucifer's strategy was to get the humans coming and going. Tempt them while telling them they deserve to stray. Once they have strayed become the loudest voice condemning them. If a tempter played his cards right he could completely drown out the Holy Spirit in the ear of a believer.

Slag noticed that Amelia spent some of her quiet time writing down her thoughts. He could tell she was wavering when she wrote words like "Jealousy" and "Undependable." He knew he'd made real progress when those words appeared on the same page as "Roger." She associated his name with these failings. Redix was happy to hear that.

She didn't see him as the leader of the home any more. She saw him as an authoritarian or a weak man. Slag congratulated himself on his hard work. Redix was had a rather bountiful harvest himself. Roger became a regular for internet porn. He no longer saw Amelia as his object of desire. He started believing in the unbelievable female image. No woman could live up to this.

Redix enjoyed entering the home without feeling searing pain. A by-product of their tempting was the family prayer life suffered. They used to pray together every night. Now those prayer times came fewer and further between. The light of the creator no longer permeated this home.

Redix called Slag over during the family meal. "It seems we have succeeded in our task here. What have you learned of the woman that you can share with me?" Slag perked up at the question. He like that Redix was asking his opinion. It showed him that Redix thought him capable.

Slag scratched at his chin with a clawed finger. "The woman has lost respect for the man's leadership. She also has responded to leadings of resentment toward the boy. Given a little time, we could fan that resentment into animosity between them."

Redix was surprised at Slag's advice. Slag wasn't the total muscle-bound idiot Redix had taken him for. His analysis showed some real thought and planning.

Redix didn't want Slag to know of his lack of trust and merely chuffed, "I see. I will begin to work on the son's respect for authority.

Continue to harry at the woman. If we do our work skillfully, the boy and woman will be adversaries soon."

Slag nodded his agreement. They spoke no more for the duration of the meal. At the end of the meal the boy went off to his room. Redix followed him. While the woman cleaned the kitchen, she threw a disparaging glance at the man. Instead of helping her, he got up and turned on the television. Neither of them spoke.

Chapter 24

Roger was increasingly uneasy. He wasn't at peace any more. It took a few days for him to notice it. He realized that the family had drifted away from God. He wondered how long it had been since he and Amelia had offered up earnest prayers together in the name of Jesus.

He sat there at his desk and felt like such a failure. He had let his guard down and the family had fallen prey to the world. He didn't know that demons had taken up residence in his home. If he had he would have been far more vehement in his resolve. He decided that he would talk to Amelia when he got home tonight.

Roger didn't like living in a home where he didn't feel comfortable. This house wasn't comfortable any more. He thought of the times when they prayed together in the living room. A feeling of peace came over the home when they finished. He knew this woman was his godly wife. He felt convicted that he didn't treat her that way. He wanted those days back again. He asked himself what he was going to do about it.

He knew that they loved each other. Somehow, they had lost sight of that. He examined that thought and didn't like what he saw. He was tempted to soften his role in this. Roger didn't want to face that he was failing in his duty as a husband. He forcefully faced the fact that his failure was due to selfishness and laziness. He didn't want to add cowardice to that list.

He knew that somehow, he had lost sight of how much his wife meant to him. For all he knew his behavior had driven her into her shell.

He thought, *"If I'm going to face this, then I'm going to face it. No flinching and no excuses."* He didn't see Redix hovering beside him. He didn't hear the imp's words telling him the fault was with Amelia. Roger pushed the negative thoughts away with conviction.

He must share with her what bothered him. Roger knew she would have been bothered as well. He realized that he hadn't been the perfect husband. She probably had a list of his shortcomings. That thought scared him a bit, unworthy as it was. The longer he sat there the more certain he was of the path he must take.

Roger didn't see the Angelic warrior holding his sword high. The radiance emanating from the sword bathed the room in an incandescent light. It was the light of God. Roger didn't realize it but the light of Christ was convicting him of hidden sin. To his credit, like King David before him he didn't hide from his sin.

In the presence of God, he bowed and admitted his sin and repented of it. In his heart he made a covenant with the Lord. He would go home and set things right with his wife. He would put his home in order. The throne of Heaven smiled. This man was not so inconsequential.

The Heavenly warrior sheathed his sword and flew back to the throne. He was there in the blink of an eye, offering praises to the Father. Roger was steadfast in his resolve. He set about doing the little things that he did every day to close the office. He made sure the answering machine was on, and that the alarm system was set.

For the first time in weeks Roger felt the prompting of the Holy Spirit. Before he left the office, he knelt by his desk.

"Father, you are God and I'm not. I ask your help in setting my house right. You appointed me the spiritual leader of my home. I know I can't handle what I'm facing. Please give me as much help as your will allows."

Roger thought of this and thought a lot of help would be welcome.

He didn't see Redix jump up and down on his desk. The imp screamed at him for all he was worth. Redix manner was urgent. The smoke that came from his body may have had something to do with it. He was in a room with a Christian in communion with God.

Roger gathered his thoughts and pushed away the negative that seemed to be including itself and prayed,

"Lord, you know best. Please lead me in this and I will do the best I can to follow in your will. Whatever you decide or do, I thank you for your decision and your part in my life."

Roger rose from his kneeling position. Redix had dove through the wall to escape the room. Sparks had been jumping off him just before he screamed and made his exit.

Rumbles came from the throne of Heaven. The name "Ascendel" split the Heavens in a thunderous peal. "Go and assist" was the command. Roger didn't see the room brighten with the glory of more than a hundred angels. He didn't see the cherub Ascendel settle into the room and place his hand on Roger's shoulder.

"Favored are you among men, Righteous Warrior." The angel intoned. Roger visibly relaxed. He suddenly felt like he was doing exactly what he should be doing. Roger felt a thrill as he put his hand on the office door. He knew he was going to have to face some conviction at home. He was going to have to face not being the father or husband God wanted him to be.

His sins had been removed from him as far as the east is from the west. If that was good enough for God, then it was good enough for him. Roger got into the car and drove home. He thought the entire way of how he would approach Amelia. How was he going to say this to her? He hated the idea of facing his sin in front of her but there was no way around it. If she was going to be his helpmate, and his wife he had no choice but to reveal the deepest and most base part of himself.

Part of the problem was fear. He was afraid to admit his darkest failings to her. The thought of it filled him with shame. He thought if he shared this part of himself, she wouldn't love him anymore. The thought of losing her was unbearable. No man can be good enough. That doesn't stop men from wanting to be the man of their wives dreams.

Roger held on to the hope that Amelia was in the same state he was in. The drive home seemed like the longest drive of his life. Roger was both scared of what might happen but anxious to see this through. He pulled into the driveway and prayed. *Lord, I'm going to do what I promised. I ask you to touch Amelia's heart and help us through this time of testing."* He killed the engine and got out of the car.

He walked to the front door like a condemned man to the gallows. Roger couldn't explain the fear that coursed through him. He also couldn't see the imps standing on the sidewalk by his front door. They screamed.

"Your wife will leave you, if you tell her the truth!"

"You don't deserve the love of a good woman!"

"You can't tell her what you've been doing. It will crush her!"

"How can you call yourself a Christian?"

The imps couldn't get closer to Roger than a few yards. Ascendel stood beside Roger with his sword drawn. The light of Heaven poured from him. The imps blistered and burned but they didn't dare leave. They knew they would face terrible wrath from their master if they failed. They fought as hard as they could.

The spirit of God spoke through Ascendel.

"LEAVE THIS PLACE AND NEVER RETURN. THESE ARE MY CHILDREN WHOM I LOVE!!!"

The words hit the demons like a bomb. They screamed in pain and scattered like roaches when a light is turned on. Their skin blistered and burned. They recoiled from the words of God.

This family was now under the protection of the Father himself. No demon would be able to enter the home without suffering agonizing pain. Before the protection could be breached Roger or Amelia would have to stumble again. Causing a human to stumble in most cases isn't all that hard for a demon. It is a different matter when the human is a practicing Christian. They were forbidden fruit.

Roger opened the front door and walked into the living room. He heard Amelia and Brennan in the family room. From the sound of it, they were wrestling. Brennan was getting the best of his step-mom. He heard Amelia grudgingly admit defeat. Brennan let her go with a light airy laugh. He was about to mess up a happy moment. This little scene made Roger feel even guiltier than he had before.

He put his briefcase down and called to Amelia. "Hey honey." He heard the commotion settle down as Amelia and Brennan walked into the living room. Amelia came through the doorway before Brennan. She had a questioning expression on her face. She could tell by the tone of his greeting that something was up.

He gave Brennan a hug and prompted "Hey, sport, would you mind watching TV while mom and I have a little talk?"

Amelia's face grew grave at this announcement. She had no idea what he was going to say to her. That scared her a little.

Brennan returned the hug and answered, "Sure, Dad." He turned and marched lightly into the living room.

Without a word, Roger took his wife's hand and led her into the kitchen. They sat at the kitchen table, and tears formed in his eyes. He gazed deeply into the eyes of this woman that he loved so much.

Tears slid down his cheeks. "Honey, I need to tell you I'm sorry. I realize that I haven't been a good husband or father lately, and it's because I've been selfish. I didn't mean to hurt you or Brennan, and if I could, I would take it all back. I've been caught up in my own desires.

"To tell you the truth, I've been caught in the web of pornography for the past couple of weeks. I've been convicted of this, and I'm doing my best to repent. I'm so sorry if I've made you feel like you aren't enough for me. I know that you are hurt, and I promise I will sit here and listen to any complaints that you have about me. I want to fix our marriage because you are my wife, and I love you so much.

I've always seen you as a woman that I don't deserve to have, and now I've proven that point." By the time he finished, Amelia's face was wet with tears. This tore through him like a knife. It destroyed him to think that he had hurt her so deeply. He sat up about to speak again. She stopped him with a finger over his lips.

"I've been praying so hard for you. I knew something was wrong, but I didn't know what it was. I didn't know why you were so distant, and I was worried that you didn't love me anymore. I even asked Brennan to pray for you. I called my mother day before yesterday and asked her to pray for you.

"She thought it was because you were on a dangerous assignment. I didn't tell her any different. I don't want my family to judge you because they think you've hurt me. I know you love me, and I know you didn't mean to hurt me. I really wish you could have come to me sooner. It really hurts to see you drifting away. It's hard not being able to talk to you because you are in a foul mood.

"I won't pretend that the pornography issue doesn't bother me, but I have to think you are really serious about repenting of it if you've brought it to me. I know it takes a lot for a man to admit this to any woman, especially his wife. I was so scared that you were going to leave me.

"I had actually invested in a mutual fund in my own name. For the past few weeks, I've been placing two hundred dollars each week into the fund. I was so fearful that I thought I had to plan for my future. I'm so sorry to say that I've been stealing from the family. I know I'm giving you a reason for my actions, but a reason is not an excuse.

"I want you to know that I'm sorry for this, but that I was also flying blind. Under normal circumstances I would never take anything without your knowledge. The fact is that I didn't know where you stood. You weren't talking to me anymore. I've felt so guilty about doing this. All I had to draw on was what happened in my first marriage. It scared me so badly that I felt I had to do something to protect myself.

"I'm so glad that we have talked about this because I've felt like I've been stealing from our family. It really hurts to think that this is the person I've become. I know your conduct doesn't excuse me from what I've done. I'm asking you to forgive me for this, the same as you are asking my forgiveness for what you've done."

Roger was taken aback by her confession. He had not expected this at all. His view of her was momentarily jaded. Then he realized that he had admitted spiritual unfaithfulness to her. How could he expect her to be any better of a person than he could be himself? He felt a certain amount of self-loathing for being so judgmental.

He took a moment to take stock his situation. He had come home expecting to be ostracized for his conduct. He had fully expected to be persecuted and belittled by his wife. Instead he had received relief, love and a confession of guilt that had been prompted by his actions. The ugly head of self-righteousness that had reared up at her admission now cowered in the corner of his mind.

He was humbled by the understanding on Amelia's part not to persecute him for his behavior. This was grace if he had ever seen it. He couldn't begin to describe the feelings he felt for her now. How could he have ever thought that a picture of a woman was exciting when this vibrant caring woman was his wife?

His ex-wife's specialty was guilt and laying it on thick. He had come to expect that from all women. There were times when he was blown away by her simple love and lack of an agenda. To his discredit these moments gave him pause waiting for the other shoe to drop. He was glad that they were admitting their faults to each other. They were trying to live as married Christians in a fallen world.

Roger leaned forward and kissed Amelia. It was a quick, deliberate *"Do you still love me?"* kiss. He cleared his throat and whispered, "So does this mutual fund deliver a good return on investment?"

They both laughed, and Amelia replied, "Well, yes, it does. It is one of the best in the market right now. It has history of returning between twelve and fourteen percent per year."

Roger thought about this for a moment and asked, "Do you think that we should keep the mutual fund account?…under both our names." he quickly added.

Amelia was relaxing now. She was glad things were turning out as they were. She had thought she was losing her husband.

Instead, after a few tears and growing pains they were starting an investment portfolio. She was grateful to God that things were working out.

"Yes, I do." She replied. "We need to consider what our future will be once we reach retirement age."

Roger reached over and placed his hand on hers. She took his hand and they both looked at each other for a moment. This marriage survived. Ascendel sheathed his sword. The light of Heaven was no longer needed from it. The Holy Spirit was shining brightly in the two believers in the room.

Ascendel bowed knee and gave thanks to the Lord for his part in this. He broke into angelic song. The entire home visibly relaxed. When his song was finished, Ascendel stood and drew his sword. He manifested himself in full glory. The light cascading off him was brighter than the sun.

He stepped into eternity and shouted, "Another victory for the lamb!"

Chapter 25

Molech could not remember a time when he had been so angry. These two tiny Christians had eluded his forces. They were still strong in their marriage while precious time had been spent in sowing discord between them. He had listened to glowing reports from Redix. "The family was beginning to break down" and "The light of Heaven fading from the home."

He stood on a hill not far from the home. The house blazed with the light of Heaven. His forces had lost the battle for this family. He ground his teeth at the thought. So much time and work had been wasted.

The marriage hadn't been sundered. In a strange way they were closer. The lamb of God had stepped in and salvaged the marriage with *LOVE!!!* His forces had been at work for months. Something about this nagged at him.

It was always after the work was undone that Molech was reminded of the scripture in Romans 8:28.

"And we know that in all things God works for the good of those who love him, who have been called according to his purpose."

The verse cut through his mind like a knife. None of his work was safe from the Lord. His anger was vicious and unforgiving. He sat there on his makeshift private throne while Redix and Slag lay on their bellies before him.

His voice was like dried reeds as he rasped, "I remember you telling me that the family was falling into our hands like over-ripe fruit. It would seem that the fruit was not so ripe for the picking." These words stung Redix. He was terrified. He knew that his existence on this plane was in jeopardy.

He replied, "Master, many apologies. The enemy sent an emissary that we did not expect. There was no way for us to plan for this outcome."

"No way?!" screamed Molech, "No way!" his anger was threatened to take his control from him. "What do you mean there was no way?!"

Redix and Slag tried to make themselves appear even more insignificant. Redix looked up. He realized that someone was going to be punished today and that the only thing he could do was try to make sure it wasn't him. He thought for a moment that Slag had been a good friend.

They had been friends for thousands of years. He had known Slag since the time of the Exodus. They had always dealt with each other on amicable terms. This was the one relationship he had not betrayed. For a moment what he was about to do pained him, then his fallen nature took over and it was no trouble at all.

"Master, we had the family under control until Slag lost control of the woman." Redix screeched.

"What is this?" screamed Slag as he turned to Redix. "I only came at your request! Now you turn on me to save your own skin?"

"BE SILENT!" bellowed Molech.

Slag went quiet immediately in the face of such anger. His mind worked furiously to turn this situation around.

"You will note, my lord, that it was the woman who failed to offer persecution when the husband repented. She was still full of forgiveness when her husband came to her with his failings." hissed Redix.

"Why did the husband repent if you were doing your job?" screamed Slag.

Molech cuffed Slag aside and replied curtly, "You shouldn't blame others for your failure." Molech paused and seem to consider Slag for a moment. "You realize that I'm going to punish you for your failings?"

Slag whimpered, but Molech was unforgiving. "Master, I've only tried to do your bidding. I've only tried my best to make sure your will is carried out." simpered Slag. Molech took a moment to revel in Slag's abject apology.

"Simply trying is never good enough among our kind, you must succeed to gain the prize", sneered Molech. He reached up extended his claws and tore a hole in the fabric of reality. Horrible screaming and wailing came from the hole. Slag began to beg but Molech was inexorable. Molech took Slag by the neck and tossed him unceremoniously into Sheol.

Redix suffered a momentary pang of guilt. He realized that the loss of the Carter family was not Slag's fault. If anyone was to blame it was himself. Redix was the one who had made the decisions concerning the family. He didn't volunteer this information to Molech. He was perfectly content to allow Slag to be punished in his place.

Redix reflected on his moment of betrayal. He did not relish the sight of Slag being thrown into Sheol. For a moment, he had a sense of remorse. Then all remorse died within him. He was a being without remorse or repentance. He was beyond redemption. That is the fate of all demons.

After tossing Slag into the hole Molech wiped the hole with the palm of his hand. This closed the dimensional rift. Redix was afraid. He had never seen any of the demon lords do this. Opening and closing a dimensional rift to the hereafter is extremely difficult. He had served one demon lord who claimed he could do it but had never done it in front of his lackey's.

Molech turned to Redix and spoke. There was no mention of what he had done. It was something he wouldn't brag about. He had done it so many times that it was commonplace.

"So little one, you contend that you had nothing to do with the failure of corrupting the Carter family?" snarled Molech in a playfully malicious tone.

"Well... I... Uhhhh... Master, I only wanted..." began Redix in pathetically unconvincing tones.

"Relax, little one. You've done what our kind has done since we were brought into being. You've laid the blame for your failure elsewhere other than your own doorstep. What do you think Adam and Eve tried to do before they faced their own sin in the garden?" Molech provided.

Redix relaxed a little at this but stored the realization that he was dispensable in the back of his brain.

Molech's head snapped up. He was absolutely still for a few moments and then purred. "My little pet is praying. I think I will go provide him with some slight direction in his prayers." Molech took two steps forward, and in a puff of brimstone, he was gone.

Redix stared at the spot where Molech had disappeared. He waved his hand back and forth to get rid of the stench of sulfur. Now that he was alone, he considered the events leading up to Slag's banishment. He considered making plans to cover any future failure.

He made a mental note to guard his thoughts from Molech. He knew that the demon lord could read his thoughts and invade his mind at will. He knew that all demon lords do this. He was sure that Molech could.

Redix went over the plans that he knew of the Carter family and those concerning Eddie Cain. He worked out ways that he could enter those plans. He planned to make himself more valuable to his master. Redix knew how many demons were working with Eddie Cain. He wondered how many saw him as a leader. He knew that he had the allegiance of at least two of them.

They were minor imps, but any support was better than none. He knew that the plan forming in his mind was an all or nothing gamble. That was better than the surety of being thrown into Sheol when the next thing went wrong. He contacted one of the imps without the knowledge of Molech. *All seeing, yeah right!*

The little one showed up quickly. "You called me, Master Redix?"

"Yes I did Griktar. You did well to respond so quickly." Redix cooed to the underling. He wanted to build some allegiance between himself and this one. The best way to do that was through flattery. *"They are extremely wary of angels and humans but for some reason they lower their defenses around their own kind. That is when they should be watching out for themselves the most.*

No Angel has ever lied to a demon. It is not in the nature of an elect angel to lie, even to a demon. They speak only the truth. Legions of demons have lied to each other to spare themselves wrath or to keep themselves from facing the truth that they have failed in the task that has been set for them."

Griktar was a slithering little demon that specialized in gossip. His size deceived many. Nations and churches fell to gossip. This little one, though his size was diminutive, wielded great power. His name in the demon tongue meant gossip. Like his namesake, he had a disturbing appearance. Gossip is to twist the truth.

Griktar was a being that offered camouflage in nature. He could utter the most preposterous things into the ear of a human and they would be believed. If you could cut through the image that his innate power generated, you would have seen a small demon that was slight of build. He was mostly humanoid in form. He used his retractable claws to hold onto his host. His claws gave him purchase on a human who was particularly resistant.

Griktar found that he seldom needed to employ his claws. It was laughable. Most humans were willing to believe the worst of their neighbor. It didn't matter how farfetched that worst was. He greatly enjoyed planting falsehoods into the minds of those around him. Before his death he was a messenger for the court of Nimrod

Griktar turned to Redix and simpered, "Forgive me master, but I was under the impression that you weren't working on the project concerning the little preaching man named Cain." The words were half accusation and half wonder. He wielded great power among the humans. Among his own kind he knew his place.

Redix chose his words carefully. "It is true that I am not directly involved in the Cain project. Don't we all seek to make ourselves

160

more valuable to the master? Just as I am sure you will be a valuable servant if my plans work out successfully. Of course, if they don't you will not be mentioned or implicated in the least. This is my gamble and mine alone. I would appreciate your help in this. I assure you that the reward will be great. If I am elevated, you would be one of my most trusted advisors."

Griktar enjoyed the flattery. He would pass information to Redix as long as it didn't cost him anything. He had played this game for millennia. He practiced deception on a daily basis. He always saw the attempts of the less proficient coming a mile away. He would stop at the point that it would be traceable back to him.

Griktar intoned, "The little preacher has set about spreading the message of how he called upon the name of the Christ to gain a winning lottery ticket. He has found a few converts who serve as his core group of believers. If all goes according to the masters wishes he will be setting up a tent and preaching his false gospel to an open-air congregation by the end of next week."

This was welcome news. Molech would be much easier to work around if he was content with his pet project. All Redix had to do was find a way to enter the project and make himself valuable to his master. This was not going to be easy. But then, what thing worth having isn't worth working for?

Redix knew that he was of little use to Molech now. He probably wouldn't even be called upon in the next few days. He had time to observe what was going on. Redix concentrated and altered his perceptions. He traveled to the vicinity of where he knew the preacher was. He knew his master would be nearby. He was right.

He saw the preacher and less than an arm's length away was Molech. The demon lord bent low and whispered something into the preacher's ear. Redix allowed himself to fall straight down. He passed into the ground. He kept his head above ground and stayed within a hundred yards of his master. He concentrated on his hearing. It heightened enough to hear the whispers that Molech was speaking into the human's ear.

"You are such a righteous man. No, this isn't pride. It is truth. It would be prideful if you claimed it to other people. There isn't anything wrong with you realizing that you are so humble. How many other people could have prayed and have God answer their prayer.

"You are favored of God. God loves you more than he does a lot of these people. It is up to you to deliver his message of prosperity and love to them. You have been chosen above all others for this special task. The God of the universe is depending on you to get his message out. You are such a privileged man. What would God do without you?"

Eddie's face lit up as this stream of words slithered into his mind. Molech nearly had his pet human trained. He couldn't inhabit Eddie because he was a Christian who thought he was doing the Lord's will. He had drifted so far that he couldn't discern what was of the Lord anymore.

Redix took note of Molech's behavior. He didn't know a demon could speak into the ear of a Christian. It appeared if a demon didn't stare into the light of Christ, then they could stand to speak in its presence. This was a neat little trick that the higher echelon evidently didn't want to share with the lower ilk.

It was obviously one of the things they considered the trappings of power. They were always seeking mean little advantages over each other. Redix was present when Jesus had pronounced, "Any kingdom divided against itself will be ruined, and a house divided against itself will fall." These words had stung Redix.

He hated thinking of anything that reminded him of his eternal fate but there was nothing for it. He was doomed and damned, but he would make as good an end for himself as he could. He hoped that in the end he would stand rebelliously before the Lord screaming curses at him while he was being banished to the lake of fire.

One of the things that Redix hated was cowardice. He was guilty of it at times. Those were the times he wanted to expunge the most. In his opinion there was nothing worse than a coward. His definition of coward changed every time he infringed on what he perceived a coward to be.

He rationalized it with, "Humans do the same thing and they are God's favorites!" He reflected on the human's excuses.

"It was only a little white lie."

"I only said that to avoid a fight."

"I didn't tell them the truth because I didn't want to hurt their feelings."

"I didn't tell them about Jesus because I didn't want to make them uncomfortable. I'll let my life be my witness."

"I know adultery is wrong, but I love her so much, and God is a God of love. Surely God will forgive because of this."

"God wouldn't let me have these feelings if they weren't right."

"I know this is a sin but God will forgive for it later."

"I know I'm not perfect, but I'm better than my neighbor."

"I know God abhors homosexuality and abortion but who am I to judge these people?"

He counted these things off to himself like a child's bedtime prayer.

Redix snapped back to reality. Molech left his pet, stepped through eternity and disappeared. He had no idea where Molech went. He knew that if he stayed around the human, he would learn of the plan in detail. If an opening presented itself he would provide an answer, thereby redeeming himself to his master.

Chapter 26

"You're hired." stated the woman behind the desk. "When can you start work?" Liz was momentarily caught off guard. She hadn't expected an answer this soon. She had thought she would go home and it would be a few days before she heard from the law offices of Sidney and Brashton. They were in need of a fast typist who was well versed in the newest word processing software.

Liz was a little bit of a computer geek. She'd always been in the right place at the right time to receive a new copy of the latest word processing software. She was well versed in several of the latest systems. She didn't know the hand of God had always ensured that she received the newest program.

Well......, Uh, to tell the truth, I didn't think you would offer me the position on the spot." countered Liz.

"That is understandable." Ms Clermont mused. "We have need in the firm that is rather urgent. If you find that you can't take the position we will understand." Ms. Clermont was a good negotiator. She was keeping Liz on the defensive.

She didn't want Liz to know that she was the one in the position of power. The firm wanted her to come and work there. That gave her a bit of room to negotiate. Ms. Clermont didn't want Liz to realize that. The lower she kept Liz's starting salary the more of the pie the partners held.

"No, it isn't anything like that. I'd love to work here. I didn't expect the offer so soon. I will need to make arrangements for my granddaughter to attend a daycare. I am currently her daycare and I don't want to leave my daughter and my son-in-law with no-one to watch her."

Ms. Clermont smiled and proffered, "We, at this firm understand family needs. If you want the position, we can wait for a few days until you make other arrangements. We would however like to offer you a different position. Your qualifications make you a good candidate for a legal assistant. We have such a position open at the moment. It will require training, but the company is willing to invest in you.

"You will be required to attend our parent office's workshop. That will be your initial six weeks of training. The rest of your training will be on the job. You will assist and experienced legal assistant for one year. All of the training, initial and OJT would be in our Chicago office.

"The compensation for the legal assistant position is twice that of the secretarial position. All travel expenses are covered by the firm. The company will also assist you in making the move to Chicago. The standard health and vacation benefits apply."

Liz was shocked at the offer. It took a moment to respond. "When you say the standard health and vacation benefits apply, what do you mean?"

The response was almost mechanical. "New employees receive two weeks' vacation for the first 3 years. The Health package is the standard 80/20 plan with a $500 deductible per year."

Ms. Clermont smiled. She was pleased with the situation. She was in complete control. Liz was off balance and had no idea that Ms. Clermont employed courtroom tactics on her. Ms. Clermont raised a slender hand to brush back a strand of her brown hair. Liz was also disconcerted by the offer and her powerful presence.

Ms. Clermont projected a carefully crafted air of concern. The truth was that she couldn't have cared less about Liz or her granddaughter. Her only concern was winning the moment. In the courtroom winning the moment meant winning the case. In the office winning the moment meant increasing her value to the partners.

She wanted to become a partner. In every sense of the word, Beverly Clermont was a material girl.

"My goodness." breathed Liz, somewhat flustered. "That is a welcome offer, a few days is all I need to make arrangements."

"Today is Wednesday. Shall we say that you will be starting on this coming Monday? I will ensure that your plane ticket and room reservations are made ahead of time. If you need to change the arrangements or if something comes up please feel free to call me", Ms. Clermont proffering one of her business cards.

She enjoyed controlling the conversation. In the courtroom she had to be careful of what she said and how she phrased it. In conversations like this she could let herself go and take full control. The average layman didn't understand they were being controlled.

Liz was a little dazed. She hadn't expected all of this. She thought she was simply applying for a job. She didn't know that she would be offered the job and demanded an answer so quickly. Neither of the ladies saw the imps dancing around the office. They were capering about in absolute glee. Ms. Clermont was under their complete control. They would make a suggestion and she would find a way to implement it.

There was a strange hesitation when it came to Liz. Ms. Clermont on the other hand was a willing tool in their hands. She had been instrumental in getting several of the more serious criminals in the area declared incompetent. She knew well that these individuals were completely sane.

They enjoyed short stints in low security halfway houses. Meanwhile their crimes were brushed away by the justice system.

In this country, it is legal for a woman to walk into a clinic and say, "I would like an abortion." literally translated "I would like you to kill the baby growing inside me." But it is federal offense to break a bald eagle's egg. What is wrong with this picture?

Liz gathered her thoughts for a moment. She didn't want to appear dull to Ms. Clermont. She didn't realize that Beverly Clermont was only one of the lower echelons of Sidney and Brashton. "Thank you so much for your time, Ms. Clermont. I look forward to working with you."

Ms. Clermont smiled and replied mechanically "We at Sidney and Brashton anticipate many happy years with you as well." Liz stood and walked out of the office.

She didn't understand her feeling of being disoriented. She was a person who was always in control. Suddenly she had met this woman and her world was no longer her own. She didn't see was the literal hive of demons that surrounded Ms. Clermont.

Ms. Clermont was searching for the next step up in the world. She wasn't concerned with her eternal destiny. Liz on the other hand, at least tried to keep an open mind. That truth would explain the Heavenly warrior who was waiting outside the office door for her. Liz reached into her bag and pulled out her cell phone.

She hated these things, but they proved to be useful. She remembered a time when calling someone in public meant finding a pay phone. She called one of the numerous numbers that she had considered for daycare. The lady on the other end of the line seemed responsible. After a few minutes she set up an appointment under the name of Rachel Beaumont for the following day at 2:00 PM.

She thought of how easy it was to set up an appointment for someone else and thought, "Today's society is such a weaker version of what it should be." She keyed the number to her daughter.

Rachel answered on the second ring. "What's up, Mom?"

Liz began, "I know this is short notice, but I was offered a job today. The job pays well, I might add. I didn't want to bother you with my financial concerns, but I need to take it. I've done some research, and in our area, the most acceptable Daycare is the Happy Care Daycare chain. They seem to have the highest customer satisfaction. I've set up an appointment for you and Stephen. I know this is sudden, and I'm sorry, but I have to pay my bills."

There was a silence on the other end of the line for a moment. Then Rachel's voice came back. "Mom, I understand that you need to pay your bills. I'm sorry if we have been a burden to you. I never really thought about how you need to pay your bills, too. I'm really sorry, and I didn't mean to think of you in such empty terms. If you've set up an appointment for us, then that is fine. I trust your judgment."

Liz listened to this with a slight twinge of conscience. She had only spoken to the person at the other end of the line. She didn't know them from Adam. As far as she knew, they could possibly offer Candy up on their next full moon ceremony. This thought pained her so badly that she came back to reality. She shook off the little imp that was feeding ideas to her. The imp fell to the ground in astonishment. This had never happened to Rakal before. His mind swirled in confusion.

Chapter 27

Rakal was an imp from the lesser circles of the Nephilim. He was rather strange in appearance. He moved his bright green body in quick jerky movements. He had been trying to sink his beak into the soft place at the nape of Liz's neck. He couldn't seem to get a good purchase though. The presence of the angelic warrior was no help to his peace of mind either.

His masters had found that sometimes he could connect to a wayward Christian. He distorted their belief in the future. He laughed at the thought that so many Christians believed that the future is solid. They get so fixated on it that they completely forget free will.

Rakal rolled onto his back. "What is going on? This one has been mine for a long time! I know she isn't turning toward the cross! What will I do if Jenoch finds out about this?! Jenoch has no tolerance for imps that fail! This isn't going well at all. I was hoping for something easy and a place to relax. This is turning into some really hard work to satisfy the overlords."

Rakal hated trying to ensure a human's allegiance. It was a lot of work, and it was also never a sure thing. These damn monkeys were so fickle sometimes. Liz had been easy to influence for so long. He had taken his position in her life for granted. That wasn't the case anymore. She was staring to think for herself. This was turning into a house of cards that he wanted no part of.

He had seen this far too many times not to recognize the warning signs. This whole setup was going to fall apart sooner or later. He wanted to be gone when it did. Jenoch had been newly empowered. That should mean he didn't have the power to track his underlings yet. If he did that would mean that his empowering was a large one indeed. He bet that Jenoch's empowerment wasn't earth shattering.

He'd put a lot of work into Liz. He didn't just want to let that go. He had to think of his reputation. He called to one of the helpers. The helper imp's head popped out of the ground not ten feet from him. "What do you need?" it hissed.

Rakal yelled, "She's broken free. I need help getting her back under control!"

The imp's head sunk back underground. A few seconds later 7 imps came lunging up out of the ground. They headed toward Liz. The little horde fanned out forming a wide arc. They started bringing the arc directly back at Liz. The angelic warrior drew his blade. This was going to be a struggle.

The first imp caught a wasp in his claws. He shook it to make it angry. The whole time he headed toward Liz to release the angry insect. The imp made a swooping dive. He tried to get under the angels' guard to release the wasp. The angel took a knee and swung at the imp.

The imp rocked back and released the wasp as the blade cut him in half. Red and black smoke billowed in the air as the little demon dissipated.

The wasp, suddenly free and furious, was looking for a target of its rage. If it stung Liz, it could shock her enough to make her easier to control. The angel reached out and caught the wasp.

He held it to his mouth and murmured, "Peace." Then he released the now calm insect into the air.

Three of the imps had worked together to form a dust devil. The miniature tornado contained dust, twigs and the occasional rock. If they could engulf her it would put her attention solely on herself. She would be in more of a state of mind to influence. One of the demons had several sharp rocks he intended to hurl at Liz in the hope of cutting her.

The angel rose from his crouch. He placed himself between Liz and the oncoming dust devil. The three imps cackled and screamed at Liz and her angelic protector. When the dust devil was about fifteen feet from Liz two things happened at the same time. The imp with the rocks threw one hard. The angel rose into the air singing and manifested himself in full glory.

The rock struck Liz's handbag. She didn't even notice it. The dust devil collapsed so violently that it resembled and implosion. The imps went flying as if hit by a bomb. One tumbled backward and down sliding into the ground at an angle. One sailed up into the branches of a tree. The one in the lead however was blasted back so violently he lay on the ground in a smoking heap.

The last three imps had flown into a homeless man sitting on a bench nearby. His head snapped up and looked at Liz. He stood and started walking straight at her. Liz had just gotten to the edge of the parking lot, heading toward her car. The man's face was twisted in a grimace of anger.

The angel saw this. He glanced around and saw a police officer getting out of his patrol car. He flew over and stood behind the officer. He took the officer's head in both hands and ordered, "See!"

The officer's head snapped around, and he saw the man headed toward Liz. He yelled out, "Hey! You there! Stay there! I need to talk to you!"

The man turned and saw a large, muscular police officer with a stern face. He turned and ran away.

The angel flew back over to his post beside Liz. She paused beside her car, digging through her purse. She was blissfully unaware that she had ever been under attack. The angel reached into her purse and pushed a pack of gum out of the way. Her car keys were underneath it. Liz let out a relieved little sound and grabbed the keys.

This was not good. Rakal had seen the whole thing. One lone angel had routed all of his helpers. His charge had angelic protection. It also didn't look like he was going to be allowed to just take her back. If he couldn't take her back, his punishment would be dire. Liz wasn't even a Christian. He would have to face the punishment of losing a non-Christian. That was an amateurish mistake. He couldn't bear that.

A cowardly thought came to mind. He acted on it immediately. "Bellus?!!" he called out.

A smaller, humanoid grey imp appeared at his elbow.

"Yes, master, what can I do for you?" Bellus simpered in a servile manner.

Rakal had contempt for Bellus because he was such a weakling. He was only good to whisper at a human. Weak as he was, he was still more than any human could handle.

Rakal knew that Marduk was toiling in obscurity of late. He knew that was the safest duty a demon could have. To toil on a high-profile job was to invite oblivion at the slightest failure. He decided that he would seek out Marduk and offer his allegiance to the once-great demon lord. Rakal noticed Bellus's fidgeting out of the corner of his eye.

He turned to Bellus and replied, "Bellus, I need to report to the master on how our progress is going. I need you to tend the human cow while I'm gone. I don't trust the others with this, only you. Do you think you can keep her in submission until I get back?"

Bellus swelled at this request, "Master I will do my best to justify your faith in me."

Bellus immediately jumped to Liz's shoulder and began the arduous and rather painful task of trying to bring Liz back into the demonic fold. At this announcement Rakal took his leave. This left Bellus trying his best to gain Liz's attention. It was actually rather admirable of the little fellow's determination. He didn't cry out once while he perched on Liz's shoulder and attempted to whisper horrible thoughts to her.

These were thoughts that Liz had grown immune to and easily shook them off. Bellus tried to come up with something more. He tried frightening her. He tried planting desire in her. He tried to distract her from her current train of thought. All of this, he tried to no avail. He was a junior tempter, so his bag of tricks was nothing compared to those that he served.

He was trying as hard as he could. After several hours of screaming at her he changed tactics. He tried to work his claws into the skin at the nape of her neck. He couldn't seem to get purchase on her. That was worrisome. He fastened himself to the collar of her blouse. He leaned his muzzle close to her ear and began a calming chant.

Bellus chanted at her for a couple of hours. That didn't make her relax. He didn't seem to have any effect on her. He shifted position to whisper in her other ear. He found that he could hold on to her shoulder without digging in claws. He decided to change the subject of his chanting.

He added Rachel's and Candy's name in his chant. Nothing made a woman reckless like subject of her family. Liz stopped in the middle of her reading. Bellus could tell his chant had reached her. He increased the cadence of his chant including threats to her family.

Liz put down the magazine she was reading. She seemed to notice the Bible tract that sat on the coffee table. She picked it up, not seeing the angels hand on it when she picked it up. White hot power ran through her straight into Bellus. He leapt from her screaming. Smoke poured from his body.

He felt like he'd just walked through a forest fire. Bellus found out rather pointedly that he was not going to be able to affect Liz on his own. He didn't stop to wonder why Rakal hadn't given him any of Liz's established weaknesses. This would have made his job so much easier. His lack of experience had made him an easy mark for Rakal. He had no idea that Rakal wasn't coming back. Rakal had left to search the arid regions for Marduk.

Chapter 28

The phone rang, and a young crisp voice answered it. "Happy Care Daycare, Barbara speaking, May I help you?" came the voice on the other end of the line. Rachel thought the voice on the other end of the line was a little too happy for her taste but didn't say anything about it.

She quelled her attitude and offered, "Yes, my mother, Liz Douglas made an appointment for my husband and I. We would like to come in for an interview with the daycare staff. We need a sitter for our daughter and my mother recommended you after some research."

"Well, your mother made a well-informed recommendation Ma'am. Our interest is the well-being of the children that are brought into our care. It is our aim to aid parents toward a good upbringing" countered the happy voice. Rachel wondered for a moment if this was a practiced line. If it was, it was a good one. Someone had taken time to craft it.

She slipped into a more relaxed state. Barbara's tone, along with the words had a genuinely calming effect. She didn't see the two imps that appeared as soon as Barbara started speaking to her. They screamed words of comfort and encouragement at her. They capered about around her, as they screamed. If luck was with them, it was entirely possible that they could take a hand in the fate of her child.

The practiced liturgy in the demon world is "Get them while they are young. Bend them to the will of Satan and they will be ours."

The imps were screaming as hard as they could in her face.

"These are good people!"

"You can trust them!"

"If they couldn't be trusted they would have no customers!"

"Children are our greatest asset!"

"These people truly love children!"

"They have people clamoring for their business. They must be doing something right!"

The screaming had its desired effect. Rachel was at ease in her own home. She grew more relaxed, while the demons grew more excited. Enticement was one of their favorite tactics.

Molech taught his minions much of enticement. After a sin has been introduced, it quickly becomes routine. When something is new that is a different story. He taught them to consider the first taste of a dish that was really enjoyed. It is a succulent experience for the demon and the human both. He taught them that to get a human to do something that is out of Character is an adventure.

He explained that is the principle behind the law of diminishing returns. A human would be able to enjoy a few hands of cards when first introduced to the game. Before long it takes hours of play before satisfaction comes. It is the same way for a human lost in sin. When they first give themselves over to it, a small amount will bring satisfaction. After their initial exposure, more and more of the sin is needed to get the same charge out of it.

Barbara spoke into the phone, "Will 2 o'clock tomorrow afternoon work for you and your husband, Ms. Douglas?" Rachel was caught momentarily off guard. She hadn't been referred to as Ms. Douglas in years. "Tomorrow afternoon at 2 should be fine. My mother is Ms. Douglas. I am Mrs. Beaumont. My husband's name is Stephen. I will have to call you back if the time won't work. This is far too important not to do together."

Rachel was starting to wonder about the cost. She didn't make that much as a kindergarten teacher and while Stephen's job was more technical and demanding, he was still relatively new in his field. He was a few years from being able to demand a high salary. She had to admit that cost would be an issue if this place is that good and in such demand.

"I completely understand that this would be too important an issue for one parent to decide upon alone. I will note it in your file and should you decide otherwise you can call our hotline and let us know." The words came across as too smooth. Rachel's head swam, and she didn't know why. She couldn't see the demons.

Rachel set the phone down on its' cradle. She still didn't quite understand the conversation that had just taken place. She made a mental note to speak to Stephen about the appointment. In her mind, it was already set in stone. Her daughter would be attending the "Happy Care Daycare" daycare and that is all that there was to it.

She had only spoken to these people on the phone. Her defenses had been torn down quickly. She wasn't suspicious at all. She was willing to entrust her child to these people on their words alone. She didn't have a clue how much she was being manipulated.

The imps on the table in front of her were dancing in glee. She had proven to be a malleable subject. She had bent to every idea they had handed her. She had offered almost no resistance at all. They had offered her idea after idea. They fell into ecstasy when she accepted an idea without protest.

A few weeks later Amelia sorted through the mail while she was talking to Roger on the phone. She had called to ask him to pick up some things on his way home from work. They both seemed to be running on automatic at the moment. She gave him the usual list, "milk, bread, butter …"

The whole time she was going through the mail to see if there was anything interesting other than bills. She was saying her "I love you" goodbye to Roger as a letter from Brennan's daycare caught her eye. Her mind turned back to the letter from the daycare. This was nothing out of the ordinary. They were to receive reports twice a week for the first three weeks and then monthly after what they called the initial period.

The reports were to inform them of how Brennan was adjusting to life in a daycare environment. They told how he was interacting with the other kids, whether or not he is behaving himself. Roger and Amelia had thought it was a good service provided by the Daycare. They thought of it as a way to see any warning signs ahead of time. They hadn't stopped to think that Brennan had been acting out since he'd been in Daycare. None of the reports they had received had given them a clue as to what was causing his behavior.

Amelia opened the envelope and opened the pages that were neatly folded inside. She recognized the familiar wording.

"Is adjusting well to the new environment"

"Is becoming popular with the other children"

"Always seems to be a big help to the interns aiding the group."

"Is interacting very well with her peers"

Wait a minute, HER peers? That didn't make any sense. Something about the wording seemed so familiar but what was with the "her" stuff. A thought popped into Amelia's head. She didn't see the angel standing beside her, whispering into her ear.

She remembered saving the first few letters that they had gotten from the Daycare. She thought that it was a proud moment. She was pleased at the potential they recognized in Brennan. She went to the hall closet and reached up to the top shelf. She had placed the letters with the memorabilia. She had planned on making it into a scrapbook for Brennan when he was older.

She didn't know where the idea had come from. She usually reserved photos and special occasions to be placed in the scrapbook box. She didn't see the angel that had been carefully following her every time she opened one of the letters. The angel whispered words of encouragement into her ear.

He tried to instill a sense of pride in Amelia for these simple form letters. He knew, because of his instructions, how she would react. He whispered a few hints into her ear as she retrieved the box from the closet.

She was burning with curiosity by the time she got the box to the kitchen table and had the lid off. The letters were right there on top. She flipped through them until she came to the bottom letter. Then a light went on in her brain and she couldn't believe what she was seeing.

The letter in her right hand was exactly like the letter lying on the kitchen table. The only differences were the name and the personal pronouns addressing the sex of the child. *These are nothing more than well thought out form letters. They haven't been observing Brennan. They are sending these to us for appearance sake. If they aren't really observing the children in the way that they say then what the heck is going on at that place?*

She paced the kitchen while her thoughts boiled. *"Wait a minute. Brennan didn't start his behavior issues until he had been there for a little over a month. I wonder if this place has anything to do with it. I can't wait until Roger gets home so I can show him this."* Amelia was sufficiently curious and upset.

The angel realized his job was done. This assignment hadn't lasted long at all. The whole assignment started when he was directed to the "Happy Care Daycare" to confuse the eyes of one of their clerks who were stuffing letters into their respective envelopes. He had made sure to switch the envelopes for the Beaumont's and the Carter's. He didn't know where any of this was going but he followed his instructions to the letter.

Chapter 29

The angel had been gone for about five minutes when Roger pulled into the driveway. He did his usual, briefcase, keys and parking brake before he got out of the car. He didn't know why but he was in a curious mood. He didn't see the angel who had been riding in the car with him. He didn't hear the words of prompting to him. The effect of those words was evident however.

Roger suspected something was amiss. He walked through the door into the living room with a feeling that something wasn't quite right. That was about the time that Amelia came into the living room and announced,

"I'm glad you're home. I want you to see something." She spun on her heel and walked from the room. Roger raised an eyebrow at the imperious demand. He followed her into the kitchen without a word. She walked straight to the island, which had two pieces of paper on it.

She turned to him, "Take a look at these for me, will you?"

His mood was ambivalent as he responded, "Sure honey." Then he bent over the pages and read each one carefully.

His investigator's eye saw the similarities immediately. The differences were subtle and well thought out. He was however thinking in detached terms. He hadn't connected these letters to his family and to another real family. He always thought of work in a detached way. This kept his emotional stability safe. He straightened up to give Amelia his assessment. He saw the expression on her face.

Roger realized this wasn't a case for work. This was about his family and another real family. They were being deceived in a deliberate and deceitful way. The alarm bells were going off full tilt in his head as he bent down to study the pages. His investigator's mind registered what Amelia hadn't seen. The name and address of the letter's recipient was right there in full print.

Stephen and Rachel Beaumont
2412 Tunnel Hill Road
New Crest, KY 40001

A plan formed in his mind. He wanted a moment to think of how this should play out. He wanted to be stealthy, but he didn't want to be deceitful. He realized these people were being lied to as well. He didn't want this family to know what was going. He did, however, want access to any future letters they might receive.

This would allow him to compare letters they received to the ones that he and Amelia had already gotten. This would prove or disprove any intentional deceit by the Daycare. He hoped this was simply a coincidence. As he entertained the hope he considered that it wasn't.

His cynical nature took over and he thought, *"There is no way this is a coincidence. These people are milking the public while building a good moral public image for themselves. Aside from the financial gain, what could be the purpose in that? This is a national Daycare. They can't simply be trying to promote a sense of good will to the public."*

Roger's face was grave as he straightened up and contemplated Amelia. "How in the world did you notice this?"

Amelia's face was slightly grim when she replied, "I've been so proud of Brennan because of these reports, I've been storing them to put in a scrapbook for when he gets older. I noticed the similar wording. Then a red light went off when I read that "She" was interacting well with her peers."

Roger stared at his wife for a moment processing this. He offered, "I see that the recipients of this letter live close to here. We need to contact them to give them their letter." He paused and gave Amelia a pained look. "I know you won't like what I'm about to say. If we want to find out what is going on, we shouldn't tell them of our suspicions. If we do they might pull their child out and we would have no way of knowing if this is a one-time fluke. There is no way a judge is going to accept one form letter as evidence that a daycare isn't doing what it promises to do."

A red flag went up for Amelia. "Are you saying that we need to make friends with these people under false pretenses?" She was shocked at her own tone of voice. It was severe but that was how she felt. She didn't agree with the thought of making friends with someone out of material need.

Friendship should be based on mutual trust. If that trust isn't there, then there is no friendship. What Roger was suggesting went completely against what she thought of as a friend. She thought about it for a moment and couldn't come up with a good counter argument.

She knew that Roger knew his job and his business. She knew he wouldn't suggest something like this lightly. She considered what Roger had obviously already concluded. She was forced to agree that Roger's reasoning was sound. They would have to befriend the Beaumont's with an ulterior motive. She didn't like the idea, but she liked the idea of taking chances with the welfare of children even less.

Amelia conceded that they must contact the Beaumont's and offer an olive branch of friendship. The mistaken letter would be their pretense. This chain of thought made her castigate herself. This was not going to be easy and it wasn't going to be enjoyable. Amelia liked making friends, but she despised people who made friends for a reason. Using people was not something that was usual to her.

Roger could see the struggle behind her eyes. "Honey, this is not something we are doing to these people. It is something we are doing for them and their child." He stated.

Amelia digested his words and replied, "I realize that, and I agree with you but that doesn't make this any easier for me. I've always hated fake people and now circumstance demands that I become what I hate."

Roger contemplated her words for a moment and replied. "God always seems to strip our sense of pride from us at one point or another. This could be one of His moments of showing you that there is nothing in you that saves you. Only His grace and love that saves you. I know this sounds terrible, but we deserve no sense of pride before the Lord. If we boast in our salvation, all of the pride in that boast should go to the saving grace of Jesus Christ."

These words were something of a blow to Amelia. They revealed to her that she had a sense of pride at being a good Christian. For a moment she felt chastised. She did not like being corrected. It was a hard thing when a dose of humble pie got handed her. Amelia took a moment to gather he thoughts.

She prayed. *"I know you are showing me something unclean in me. Please help me grasp it and then to shun that nature in me. I don't want to be anything that you don't cherish."* Amelia felt a calm settle over her. In this moment she knew that she was in the Father's will.

She turned to Roger and admitted, "You are right honey, I'm sorry to be so stubborn. Tell me what it is that you think we should do."

Roger brightened. He clearly hadn't expected her docile response. "Well, what I think we need to do is contact this family and try to establish a rapport with them. We will say that we have their letter and we can use the daycare as a reason to continue the conversation so that we can get to know them.

"The most important thing is to form some sort of relationship. I know that sounds cold, but it is our only option. As we get to know them we can reveal the truth to them if it is safe. If they are unresponsive to our Christian views, then we will have to remain silent on this issue. We don't know if these people have any religious views. They may have no problem with the practices going on in the daycare."

This was logical to Amelia, but she still didn't like it.

Roger quickly added, "We don't need to lie to these people. The Lord never lied once to anyone. That shows that there is no real need to ever stray from the truth. We need to be careful what we reveal to these people and when."

This made it much easier for Amelia to accept. They weren't going to lie. They were going to try not to volunteer information at an imprudent time. Amelia was thankful for the way that Roger had stated things. He presented it in such a way that Amelia could accept them. She hated gray areas. As far as she was concerned God didn't deal in gray areas. He only described light and dark, truth and lies. Any deviation from this was from the enemy.

The enemy..... She thought of this. How much of her life was exposed or open to the enemy? This sort of hit her in the chest at the moment. She didn't like the thought that God wasn't protecting her.

Amelia turned to Roger and offered, "I know this is something that you believe needs to be done. I don't disagree with that, but I will not become a fake friend. If we start a relationship with these people, it will be a relationship that honors God. We will not use these people and we will give them every courtesy that we possibly can.

"We will not represent anything other than the love of Christ to these people. For all we know they are lost and God has sent them to us to help save them. We will honor the love that Christ has shown the church. We will be the light for this family as we should." The last sentence had a note of finality. As far as she was concerned this wouldn't be done any other way.

Roger silently prayed, *"Lord, you have brought us this far, I ask that you bring us to a place that helps those that this company is using."* Roger felt a calm come over him.

He reached out and took Amelia's hand. "Honey, I think the Lord is using us in this to save the souls of those that he loves. I can't explain it but I feel that the Lord has brought us to this." They stared at each other for a moment. Knowledge passed between them that they would do this in a way that honored God.

Amelia was a little nervous when she picked up the phone. She dialed the number and after three rings the phone was answered, and a feminine voice came onto the line. "Hello?" Amelia heard.

"Yes." She intoned, "My name is Amelia Carter, my husband and I have a son in the 'Happy Care Daycare'. We recently received a progress report, but the report was on a Candy Beaumont. I'm sorry to bother you but I think we have received the report that was supposed to go to your family."

Silence greeted for a few seconds. Then the feminine voice came back. "Oh alright, I know what you are talking about. I'm sorry for my confusion but I haven't even opened the mail yet. Hold on a second, I have the letter we received right here."

Amelia heard the shuffling of papers for a few seconds and then the voice came back again. "If you have ours, I wonder whose letter we have. The letter I'm holding is regarding a Brennan Carter."

Amelia was shocked for a moment. This was a classic case of switching. This was strange. If the letters got mixed up you would expect a random shift in who received whose. It wouldn't be a perfect swap of only two letters.

Neither Amelia nor Rachel saw the angel now exiting the Beaumont home. His job completed, he'd been called back to the throne room of Heaven. His instructions were to ensure that both of the letters got to the other home. It was a simple matter for him to place a hand over Barbara's eyes as she sorted the letters and suggest to her that she saw something that she didn't. Then it was a simple matter of standing guard over his handiwork until they were delivered.

This proved to be more than a little difficult. He couldn't be in two places at once. He was extremely speedy though. He was able to get from one place to another without losing the location of the letters. The forces of darkness had no idea what he was guarding or why. This left them at a loss to be effective in deterring him.

Amelia took a deep breath before she spoke. "That letter is for me and my husband. My step-son's name is Brennan Carter." Amelia was stunned by the way this was playing out. It seemed like it had been arranged. Then she realized that God knew the end from the beginning. Setting up something small like this might seem miraculous to us but to him it was child's play.

Here came the part that Amelia didn't like much. She started to feel like she was being dishonest. She considered how to proceed from here. "I'm so glad to hear that you have our letter. This makes things so much simpler. We have every letter they've sent us on Brennan and I was worried that we wouldn't find this one. I'm making a scrap book for him after he gets older." Amelia finished a little flatly.

"That is a really good idea", proclaimed Rachel. "I think I might do that too."

Amelia saw an inroad here. "I could show you the layout I'm using for Brennan's scrap book if you like."

Rachel responded to this enthusiastically. "Hey! Yeah! We could do that when we meet to exchange letters."

Amelia took a moment and asked, "Do you know the coffee shop 'Runners' on First Street in town?"

Rachel quickly responded, "Yes, I know it. I Love their mocha latte and the atmosphere there is always warm and inviting." Amelia processed this.

She thought to break more ground about the coffee shop. "Have you ever spoken to the manager? I've heard that he is such a nice man. He lost his wife some years back to cancer. It is such a sad story, but he is always so warm and happy. I overheard a conversation about him between the servers one time." informed Amelia. "Well, anyway, we can meet there and exchange letters, if you like."

Rachel mused, "Really, that sounds interesting. I'd love to hear the story from him some time. There is nothing like hearing the story of tragic love from the people who have experienced it." That struck a chord in Amelia. She was a hopeless romantic.

She saw an avenue of commonality between herself and Rachel. "I know what you mean. I'm a sucker for a good love story."

Amelia saw traits in Rachel that she appreciated. She felt guilty for having a motive. Then she thought, *This is the reason God brought our families together.* "Have you read Romeo and Juliet?" Amelia heard a little squeal on the other end of the line.

"Oh yes! I absolutely loved it when I read it. William Shakespeare was such an imaginative writer. He seemed to know the way women think, better than most men."

This statement struck a chord in Amelia, and all thoughts of plans left her. She agreed with Rachel's sentiment and couldn't help herself.

"I know what you mean. Sometimes I wonder if men understand women at all. At times, I think Roger agrees with me to get me to shut up. Then there are times when I see confusion written all over his face.

"Last week I told him we needed to buy a new shower curtain for the bathroom, because we had bought a new towel set for the bathroom and it would clash. He didn't understand."

Amelia and Rachel spent the next hour on the phone simply chatting and getting to know each other. They found that they had similar tastes in foods and recreation. They were both raised by strong women with the decided lack of a male authority figure in the home.

In Rachel's case, there was no man present. In Amelia's case, her father was a chronic workaholic. She remembered weeks at a time in her childhood without even seeing her father. There were months when they shared no more than a hello and goodbye.

Amelia didn't like to think of her child hood. There were parts of it that she had intentionally blocked out. She didn't block them out because they were terrible. She blocked them out because the memory of them hurt. In her mind there was enough unpleasantness in the world.

By the time Amelia hung the phone up she had decided that she liked Rachel. She had enjoyed the conversation. They had gotten off the phone due to the necessity of household chores and the duty of motherhood.

That was another thing that they had in common. They were both afraid of making a mistake raising their children. They had agreed that they would meet at "Runners" the day after tomorrow to trade letters. Amelia found that she was looking forward to the meeting. It would give her a chance to get to know Rachel better and, in the background, to get the letter for Roger. Roger had already made a copy of Candy's letter and had started a little portfolio of their planned investigation.

Rachel glanced up at the calendar. The phone had brought her mother to mind. She had been hoping it was her mom when she answered. She hoped that Amelia hadn't been put off by the slow start. She hadn't spoken to her mother in a few days and that bothered her. She and her mother were very close, and they seldom went more than a day without talking. There were times when she would brag that her mother was her best friend.

When Rachel was growing up without a father she remembered that her mother had told her it was the two of them together against the world. She had always felt proud of that. She felt that no matter what she would always be able to stick with her mother.

Chapter 30

Jenoch was furious. He couldn't believe that one of his tempters had deserted his post. Even worse, another had been completely defeated in his task. He hated trying to corrupt a Christian family. He knew the fault did not lay with his tempters. The fault lay with the faith of these Christians and the power of the cross.

He cuffed Bellus to the side for lack of anything better to do. Molech reproached him, saying, "Use the tool of grace." He hated the tool of grace. The thought of any type of forgiveness or tolerance was disgusting. His kindred were demons and they lived to thwart the will of God. For them to do less than that was unforgivable.

How was Lucifer able to use this tool of grace and still preach that all that the Father wanted was wrong? Many things that Lucifer said conflicted with other messages he gave. Jenoch couldn't put them together in his mind. He was sure he'd heard conflicting messages from on low.

He couldn't understand how they were supposed to win. He knew that the Father had created all things. He knew that the Father knew the end from the beginning. The Father's power was without equal. He didn't understand this belief that the will of Lucifer would prevail. Sometimes he thought it was blind hope rather than face the thought of failure.

Jenoch raged. He couldn't understand how this Christian family could have found this connection. They hadn't found the connection!! They had stumbled upon it!! It was nothing more than coincidence!! Circumstance had led them to the truth of what the demon horde had been up to. Circumstance!

He knew it wasn't circumstance that had led these people to the truth. He didn't want to bring up that the Father had seen this before time began. He decided that he wasn't going to tell Molech about this. He knew the price for hiding this would be great but the price for telling him would be as great.

Fear filled him. That price was something that he was willing to forestall for as long as possible. Jenoch thought for a moment. What could he place in the path of the Christians to delay them? He didn't want them to find more than the connection that they had found. He needed to tempt the husband and the wife or …. Wait a moment….

He could attack the child. If he sent his forces after the child, the mother and father would be too distracted to do anything more with the information gleaned on this day. Jenoch smiled to himself. He knew he had found the only answer open to him. He would do everything he could to bend the child to his will. He would send the bulk of his forces against Brennan Carter. He knew the child would have the least protection against temptation.

He called his minions to his side. Several large imps appeared. "The child of the Christian family, this little one, his name is Brennan, I want him tormented and brought away from the cross. Don't let his family have a moments rest on his concern. Use every means at your disposal.

"Bring me news that they are seeing doctors and psychologists. I want him disturbed to the height that is possible. Bring me news that the family is starting to fall apart. I don't want their Christian faith to save them from any trouble. Tempt them. Try them all. Bring me news that the child is rebellious. Bring me news that the husband has strayed from his wife. Bring me news that the wife now views another with the respect and love of a wife. I want this family destroyed. Is that understood?!!"

The imps around him all bowed in acquiescence. They stole glances at each other in apparent confusion. They wondered how they could achieve all of this. They knew better than to ask how. They disappeared in a puff of sulfur when Jenoch turned his attention on Eddie Cain. He knew that the forces surrounding Cain were immense. If he could get the Carter family in close contact with Eddie Cain, they would be surrounded by evil.

Amelia was anxious. She was going to meet Rachel at the coffee shop. She was nervous, but she was also looking forward to meeting

Rachel. Rachel came across as someone that could be a friend. She pulled into the parking lot and checked her reflection in the mirror. Her hair wasn't exactly the way she wanted it but then again it never was.

It was a familiar place, but she hadn't been inside in a long time. She got out of her car and straightened her clothes. She decided against taking the small voice recorder Roger had given her for this "interview." It seemed like a deceptive thing to do, and she really did want to be friends.

She walked in the door took a moment to cast about the room. The hostess approached her, "May I help you?"

Amelia answered, "I'm meeting someone here. Her name is Rachel Beaumont. There should be reservations for us today."

The hostess scanned her clipboard and her eyes brightened. "Ah yes….. We have you right here. Mrs. Beaumont arrived about five minutes ago. We've already seated her. She is in the second to the last booth on the right. If you'll follow me, I'll show you to her booth."

They were walking toward a booth with a young dark-haired woman. The woman looked up from her menu. Amelia realized this must be Rachel. Rachel stood as the hostess approached.

The hostess turned to Amelia, "Here is your party ma'am. If you need anything else, call on us." Amelia murmured a thank you as the hostess faded into the background. Rachel stood there stark for a moment.

Amelia stepped forward, "Rachel, it is a pleasure to finally meet you." Amelia's earnestness appeared to disarm Rachel.

Her face softened, and she replied, "I'm pleased to meet you as well. Would you like to sit down and see what's on the menu?"

Amelia paused a moment, "No, to tell you the truth I've been here a few times and their turkey club sandwich is excellent. That is what I've been planning to order since you suggested this place."

Rachel seemed to contemplate her menu for a moment and then

replied with, "Well if it so good that you would plan to order it a week in advance, I think I'll give it a try."

She folded the menu in front of her and for the first time peered full into the face of Amelia. They both sat there for a moment and Amelia remembered why she was here.

"Oh yes, before I forget." She reached into her purse and pulled out the letter that she had brought for Rachel.

"Oh yes, of course, slipped my mind for a moment." She reached into her own purse and pulled out a letter in the same green and white format as the one that Amelia was holding. Neither of them saw the tiny imp that clung to Rachel's letter. When they traded letters, the imp felt the presence of the Holy Spirit in the one receiving the letter. He dove off with a terrified wail.

The imp had envisioned being burned by the holiness of God. His warty gap-toothed appearance was normal for his kind. He wasn't particularly notable in any sense. After he hit the tabletop he scurried back over to Rachel's purse and jumped in. He screeched a few choice curses at Rachel before he ducked his head down inside the bag.

Rachel looked up after scanning her letter for a moment for a moment. "You know", she commented. "I thought about your idea of making a scrapbook. It seemed like such a good idea. I was wondering if you would mind showing me how to turn these letters into a scrap book as we get them."

The words cut through Amelia. She couldn't believe what she was hearing. She and Roger had wondered how they were going to get a peek at the subsequent letters. The opportunity had presented itself in such a way that it couldn't be coincidence.

Amelia took a breath and paused for a moment. She had to honor God in this moment. She knew He had planned this for her. She thought, *"Lord, this had to be planned. There is no way this is a coincidence. This is the thing we were so worried about. You just handed it to us.*" She had stopped believing in coincidence a long time ago.

After her initial shock she took a moment, "Well, yes I'd be happy to. Making scrap books has been a hobby of mine for the past few years."

Rachel started a little at this, "Are you serious? I've always thought that was so interesting but didn't have the 'umph' to get started." They talked for the next few minutes until the waitress brought their orders.

Rachel picked up her sandwich and took a bite. She seemed surprised for a moment while she chewed and swallowed. She spoke up, "I see what you mean about this sandwich. This is excellent."

Amelia swallowed the bite she had taken. "I get this sandwich every time I come in here. I don't know what spice it is that they put on the turkey, but it has such an original flavor. I've tried to duplicate it at home, but I haven't been able to."

They both attacked their sandwiches for the next ten minutes. They shared thoughts about what spices could be used to make them. Rachel knew she tasted a hint of onion while Amelia could swear that she could taste a bit of Thyme. They couldn't quite agree on the ingredients but enjoyed the sandwiches all the same.

Chapter 31

While they sat and ate an elderly gentleman started walked around the tables and talked to the guests. He was deliberate in the way that he approached each table. It was evident that he was a manager who wanted to make each guest feel welcome. His demeanor was warm and unimposing. When he spoke, it was with an air of genuine caring. Something about this man was rather comforting.

He approached their table with a little smile on his face. When he got within a few feet he prompted, "Ladies, I hope you're enjoying your meal." Rachel and Amelia both stopped and looked at him at the same time. They were both surprised by this gentleman's approach. Neither felt threatened.

A flash of insight struck Amelia and she spoke up. "Yes sir, we are enjoying these turkey club sandwiches immensely. I wonder if you could tell us what spice is used on them."

He gave a jovial laugh and complained, "Now if I did that, you wouldn't have to come here to enjoy the flavor now would you?" Amelia was a little disappointed for the lack of an answer.

The silence seemed to prod him into action. "Actually," he continued, "We use a hint of onion powder, a touch of thyme and a little paprika on the turkey after we shave it into the sandwich mix."

"Thank you so much, I'll have to try that at home. I love the flavor. I have this sandwich every time I come in here" offered Amelia.

"You see", he lamented, "Now you won't have a reason to come back in." He said this with a twinkle in his eye.

He didn't know why but he felt led to stay there and talk to these ladies. He could tell by their response that the one to his right was a Christian, but the other was evidently "in the world." He stood there for a brief moment. He made his decision. He thought the best way to proceed was an introduction.

"I'm only teasing you ladies. My name is Harold Ashton and I'm the owner of this establishment. I hope you find everything to your liking." The name hit Amelia like a wet cloth in the face. This was the man that she had heard about in rumors. She had heard of him mainly through the members of the church that frequented Runners.

She couldn't help herself, "I know who you are. I've heard about you through my church, you're the one who lost his wife to cancer last year." Amelia regretted saying it as soon as the words left her lips. She hadn't meant to be so blunt and crude.

She could see the tears form in Mr. Ashton's eyes. "Oh sir, I'm so sorry. I didn't mean for it to come out like that. Please forgive me." Amelia felt the tears coming to her own eyes. She raised a hand to her mouth and hesitated. Rachel watched this exchange with what appeared to be fear. When Mr. Ashton spoke, there was no malice in his voice at all.

He spoke softly, "So, you've heard of my Meriam? She was a wonderful woman. I didn't deserve her. We married young you see, and I was a little bit of a rebel. She was always going to church and praying for her friends. I thought that was all well and good for her, but I wanted to live my life on my terms.

"My only excuse you see is that I was young. As the years of our youth passed I witnessed my wife being a faithful servant of the Lord. She never missed church and if somebody in the congregation was sick then she would be right there to help out. As I said before, she was a wonderful woman and I didn't deserve her.

"We tried in our early years to have children, but it wasn't to be and I could tell that it really hurt her. She wanted to be a mother so badly. I was afraid to go to the Dr. because I was afraid I was the reason we couldn't have kids. I thought if she had found a better man she would have been a mother.

"Meriam forgave me for my stubbornness, something to this day I still say I didn't deserve. I would go out with the boys and she would sit home reading her Bible and praying for me. There was even a time when I came close to having an affair, but when I looked at the woman standing in front of me offering herself to me, I realized I had much better than this at home.

194

"It was her example that made me strong enough to turn away. It was her love that made me see that she had something that I didn't. I've never in my seventy-one years met anyone who was as patient and loving as the woman I was lucky enough to call my wife.

"It was a little over twenty years ago that my stubbornness broke and I gave my life over to the Lord. I know as sure as I'm sitting here that I wouldn't be in the kingdom if it weren't for that woman.

"I loved her so much and I owe her more than I can ever tell another person." His words started getting thick with emotion as he charged on.

"I came home from work one day a year and a half ago. I found Meriam on her knees praying. This was nothing unusual but as I entered the room her voice was thick when she asked me to join her.

"I knew something was wrong. I knew by the tone of her voice that something had happened. Without a word I knelt beside my wife. For the next half hour, I offered up the most fervent prayers I've ever offered. I didn't know what was wrong, but I knew that something had upset her deeply.

"I wanted comfort for her so badly that I stopped praying for her purpose. I prayed for her. I knelt there with her begging the Father to comfort this woman who had been such a comfort to me. As I say, it was about a half hour and I felt her relax beside me. I saw her start to straighten up. She had a look of serenity on her face.

"That was when I got scared. I didn't get scared for her. I got scared for me. Somehow, I knew, I knew what she was going to say. We stood and walked into the kitchen. She poured us both a cup of coffee. We sat there for a little while drinking our coffee and holding hands. Finally, she glanced up, 'I got news from the doctor today.'

"My blood froze in my veins when I heard those words. Then I realized she had been praying for me because of the news. She wasn't scared at all. She had been preparing herself for this all her life. This was the next step for her. The doctor had told her that she had cancer growing around and into her brain stem. It was aggressive and had grown rapidly.

"She had gone to the doctor a couple of weeks before complaining of trembling fits in her hands. There was no way at the rate of growth and the location of the cancer that anything effective could be done. They offered to make her last few hours as comfortable as possible, but she refused. She wanted to spend her last moments on this earth with me, comforting me as she departed.

"I remember the expression on her face in those last few hours." Tears flowed freely down his cheeks now. He wasn't trying to hold back his emotions, "She was happy that her Lord was calling her home, but she was worried for me. She knew that I was angry with God for taking her from me.

"She was the only person in the world that I'd ever felt whole around. Her last words to me before she passed were 'I love you Harold, but Jesus loves you more. Love him as he deserves.' It was then that I realized why she was being taken now. I think it was because the Lord knew that I loved Meriam more than I loved him.

"He knew that as long as Meriam was on this earth with me he would never have my full attention. For a while I felt responsible for her death. Then I realized that God is sovereign and does his perfect will. I wasn't responsible for her death. God was using her death to make something good from it.

"Her death, as much as I hated losing her, forced me to lean on the Lord harder than I ever had. I'm closer to the Lord now than I've ever been and every day it gets better. I'm looking forward to the day when I go home to be with the Lord. I will see Meriam there but more importantly, I will see my Lord."

He took out a handkerchief and mopped the tears away. Amelia was already wiping her eyes with a napkin. Rachel had tears in her eyes but appeared abashed by the situation.

Amelia spoke up at last, "Oh Mr. Ashton, thank you so much for sharing that with us. You have a beautiful testimony."

The imps in the restaurant had all retreated to the darker corners. They couldn't stand the light that was pouring from this witness of God. Several of the imps were regulars because their hosts liked to eat there. The regulars would dive out the window as soon as Harold walked in. They knew what was coming. This man was a faithful witness and would share the testimony of Jesus Christ with anyone who would care to listen and several who didn't care to listen.

"Well," he prompted. "I've taken enough of your time. I will leave you to finish your meal. Please feel free to come back any time." Amelia assured him that they would. He turned and walked back into the kitchen. He had the same feeling of fulfillment that he always got when he knew he had done what the Lord wanted of him.

Chapter 32

Amelia turned to Rachel, "Wasn't that a beautiful story?"

Rachel hesitated for a moment and answered truthfully, "I've never heard anything like that in my life. To tell you the truth I don't know what to think. He made a lot of references to 'the Lord' and 'God'. He is obviously a 'religious man." Rachel finished here a little flatly.

Amelia could tell that Rachel didn't understand a lot of what was said. It was to her credit that she admitted it.

Amelia offered, "Christianity isn't about religion. It is about relationship. God doesn't want us to have religion. He wants us to have a relationship with him. That is why God created us."

Rachel gave Amelia a searching look, "How can anybody know that?" The question escaped her lips before she had time to think. It was more of a musing than a question. She didn't really want an answer. The question was her shield from the subject.

If God really existed and wanted a relationship with people wouldn't he make it much easier to understand than this? How could anyone want a relationship with a god that let suffering happen on such a huge scale? People were starving to death in the world and where was god? Wars were killing innocent people, sickness run rampant, starvation was prevalent in the world and where in all of this was God?

Where was this loving God that these Christians keep talking about? Rachel felt armed after this thought and wasn't particularly worried that Amelia would provide an answer. She knew that no real answer was forthcoming.

Amelia felt a stir in her soul. She knew that a lot hinged on this conversation. Here was a wayward child of God asking her for direction without knowing that she was doing so. Amelia retreated into her thoughts for a moment and silently prayed, *Lord, I know you've brought me to this moment. I ask that you guide me through it in your will. Please guard my mouth and don't let me say anything that is untrue of you. I believe that you will work this out for the best and I thank you for that. You are my Lord and my God."*

Amelia carefully phrased her response. "If you were God and you wanted people to understand that you were real and you were speaking to them but you also wanted them to have faith in you, how would you do it?"

Rachel seemed bewildered at the question. "I have no idea."

Amelia considered this for a moment, "If I were God and I wanted people to believe that I existed I would send them a message. I would send them a message that would tell them not only that I existed but a record that would tell them the future in advance. That way they would have a way to measure the credibility of what the record told them. The record I'm talking about is the Bible.

"The Bible is a record of the history of mankind in advance. We are told exactly how history plays out before it happens. The Bible is the only book that is the basis of a major religion that contains prophecy. There is no prophecy in the Koran. There is no prophecy in the book of Mormon. There is no prophecy in the Hindu Vedas.

"Prophecy is God's way of saying this is my stamp of approval. I am here and I want you to search for me in the same way you hunt for treasure. I love you more than you can understand love."

Rachel appeared rather shocked at Amelia's declaration, "Wait a minute. I thought the bible was a group of old stories that people told their children, so they would be good."

Amelia gave a lighthearted laugh at this statement. "The Bible is a record of history starting from the beginning. The Bible is also a list of rules for mankind to live by.

"In modern times there has always been a question as to how accurate the Bible is. In 1947, a young shepherd boy in Kumran discovered the Dead Sea scrolls. They verified for Christendom that the scriptures had been translated accurately for thousands of years. When you examine the evidence of how accurate the Bible is you actually have to wonder why people even begin to believe that the Bible isn't true."

Rachel rallied at this. "Okay, what about all of the contradictions in the Bible?"

Amelia was prepared for this. "Name a few of them and I will answer them for you." Rachel seemed to balk at this. Amelia had been expecting this reaction. She knew that most atheists didn't really understand the bible in a way to try to be-bunk it.

She waited for a few seconds for Rachel to supply her with an argument she could explain.

Finally, Rachel stated, "Ok the bible says that Adam and Eve were created directly by God and that they were the only humans when they were created."

Amelia answered, "Yes, that's true."

Rachel got a small look of triumph on her face as she challenged, "Well if that's true then where did Cain get his wife?"

Amelia had her answer ready as soon as Rachel stopped speaking.

Amelia replied, "On this question you have to use deductive reasoning. If Adam and Eve were the first two humans and Cain was their son there is only one of two places for Cain to have gotten a wife. Cain's wife was either his sister or his niece. There is no other answer."

Rachel came back with "But the bible specifically forbids incestuous relationships."

Amelia replied, "Yes it does, but that decree wasn't given by the Lord until the time of Moses. It was then that the species was degraded to the point that intermarriage could cause some serious birth defects."

Amelia wasn't going to go much further than this. She knew that you couldn't argue anyone into the kingdom of God. What she really wanted was to get Rachel thinking. The decision to follow the Lord had to come from an earnest heart, not a heart defeated by human argument.

"I'll tell you what," Amelia prompted. "Let's put this debate to rest, if you have any questions feel free to ask, I don't want to make you feel like I'm beating you over the head with a Bible."

Rachel wasn't quite ready for this. She had expected this to turn into something ugly. She was grateful for the respect that she was being shown.

Neither of the ladies saw the angelic warrior standing between them with the table passing through his lower body. He was standing there with his sword aloft shining the light of Heaven. This was one time that the gospel was going to be shared without interference. None of the imps could be seen in the shop.

Amelia's voice carried her conviction, "The one thing that I want you to understand is this. Mankind is burdened with the spiritual disease of sin. God is the only one who has the cure. God loves Rachel Beaumont so much that he sent his only son to earth to live a perfect life, die an atoning death and rise from the grave three days later showing God's approval of his sacrifice. He did all that so that you could be with him when you die."

Rachel seemed to be a little confused at this statement. "Hold on, I thought that Christians believe that God is all-powerful."

"He is." said Amelia.

"Well, if God is all-powerful and he wants you to be with him when you die then all he has to do is say so and it will be that way." Amelia regarded Rachel. This was a rather insightful thought.

"It is true that whatever God wishes becomes reality, but you have to consider that God is a gentleman. He isn't going to force his company on you after you die, when you wouldn't have anything to do with him during your lifetime. God doesn't send people to hell. People send themselves to hell. They want to live their lives their way with no consequence to a higher authority. Since God is the ultimate authority he simply grants their wish to be away from him. That is what hell is, the absence of the presence of God."

Rachel seemed to think on this for a moment, and then replied. "Well if people live their lives outside of the presence of God then how can hell be so bad?"

Amelia wondered how this line of conversation was going, "People don't live their lives outside of the presence of God. They live their lives outside of the will of God. There is a big difference in the two.

"Imagine living your existence without any hope at all. You have no hope that things are going to get better. If you are in pain, you have no hope that it will ever stop. If you are poor you have no hope that you will ever be financially sound. If you are sick, you have no hope of getting well. The absence of God is the absence of all hope. That is part of the torture of hell.

"I've heard some commentaries say that there won't be any real flames in hell. I don't know how they can say that after the graphic description of hell in the Bible. All I truly know is that whatever and wherever hell is, I don't want to be there. That is actually part of a Christian's motivation for turning their life over to Christ."

Rachel looked rather surprised at this statement; "I thought Christians gave their lives to Christ because of this warm fuzzy feeling they got standing before the cross."

Amelia laughed a little at this statement. "Lord no, can you imagine basing your entire life on a feeling that you have once? I couldn't do that. If I did I'd be wondering about the experience for the rest of my life." Rachel didn't voice it but that was precisely what she thought.

She had always thought that Christians were uneducated people. They were people who based their entire existence on a moment of frenzied emotion. Those emotionally charged people were too afraid to turn from such a decision. It didn't matter how much information they were presented.

Rachel pondered these thoughts. The angel whispered in her ear.

"These words are true."

"Your God is calling you."

"Pay attention to the words of the Lord."

"God Almighty loves you."

Rachel thought that she was going to have to investigate this further. Maybe Christianity could bear further scrutiny from her.

Rachel was snapped out of her reverie by Amelia saying, "Let me cover the check this time."

Her first thoughts were *"This time? What does she mean this time?"* Rebellion flared in her but was disarmed by the warmth of Amelia's voice.

"Okay, well thank you for the lunch." Rachel responded.

Amelia hurriedly wrote something on a napkin. When she looked up, she proffered the napkin to Rachel.

"Here is my phone number. Call me when you want to talk about the scrapbook. I'd be more than happy to help you."

Rachel's mind went back to the scrapbook. She had forgotten about it in the wake of her religious confusion. There was a small part of her that was afraid but the larger part of her was curious for more. She wanted to know more of what Amelia had that she didn't.

"Thanks, I'll call you in the next couple of days."

They both got up and started for the door. As they walked toward the door Mr. Ashton walked out of the kitchen. He waved a friendly good-bye to them.

"You ladies have a nice day now."

"Thanks, you too." Amelia called back.

Chapter 33

When they cleared doorway, Amelia noticed a large crowd had gathered at the far end of the parking lot. She was curious as to what was going on. She had parked near where the crowd had gathered. There was a small wooden podium and a man was standing behind it. The man was wearing a dark suit. He wasn't imposing but he did have an air of authority about him. His voice carried well over the everyday sounds that you expect.

"I'm standing here in front of you today as proof that the Lord answers prayer for his faithful followers. I was a young seminary student and the Lord allowed a tragedy to come into my life." Tears ran down his cheeks and the crowd answered with silent support. A few of the ladies in the front of the crowd leaned forward with looks of pleading on their faces. They seemed to be offering their support for this young man unconditionally.

"My daughter died in the night of what the earthly doctors call S.I.D.S." he proclaimed. "I don't believe this." His words came as an angry snarl. "The devil took my daughter from me. The devil took my daughter from me because I had failed my family as a husband and a father.

"I loved my wife and my daughter. What I didn't know was that the devil was laying a trap for me. I thought I was such a good man that the devil couldn't do anything to me. I was wrong.

"After my daughter died, I immersed myself in my 'church ministry'. I didn't see that I had abandoned my wife to her grief. I didn't see that she was spiraling down with no hope of recovery. I was the good little preacher boy that was doing all the right things.

"I was visiting families and working on programs to help feed the poor. People would tell me how sorry they were to hear about my daughter and how I was doing such good work in the face of tragedy. Yes, I would think to myself, God sure is lucky have me. I can get things going.

"It wasn't until after my wife died in a freak accident that I found the vodka under her side of the bed. She had turned to alcohol to numb her pain. She hadn't come to me because I wasn't being the husband that God had made me to be.

"I can see now that she was also ashamed of turning to alcohol. She needed support from me and I didn't give it. She needed her husband to love her like Christ loved the church and I failed her. I had shut down emotionally because I couldn't deal with the death of our daughter.

"I didn't blame my wife for our daughter's death, but I should have told her that. She probably thought that I thought she was a bad mother. I have to live every day of my life knowing that I failed my wife. I have to live every day of my life knowing that I failed my baby daughter.

"I sincerely hope that you find better than I have had to endure. I sincerely hope that you find it at the foot of the cross before the hand of God withdraws from you and the devil is given sway in your life.

"I went through a spiritual pilgrimage after my wife died. I lost my job from the church I was working for. They believed I had lost my way. Lost my way....... What man wouldn't lose his way after his child and his wife are taken from him?

"There were nights when I would pray and pray, and no answer was forthcoming. I wondered where God was. I mean I really wondered where God was. I know you are looking at me as a preacher, but a preacher is only a man who is telling you what God wants from you in this life.... I didn't know what God wanted from me." Eddie had leaned forward and tapped the podium as he uttered each word).

"I thought God had abandoned me. I didn't know that God had a larger plan for me that I didn't see. Like Joseph as a prisoner in Egypt, God had a plan for me through my suffering. Like any of you, when I was going through my trial, all I knew was my pain.

"When you hurt that much it is really hard to focus on anything other than your own pain. If any of you have thought of yourself as unrighteous for not seeing God in your pain, then let me relieve you of that notion. When Jesus was in the garden of Gethsemane he was focused on the pain he was enduring.

"He offered prayers for others during that time, but his primary focus was on the pain, fear and shame of the cross. His ultimate aim was to give his will over to the Father, but he did ask that the cup be taken from him. If you bang your finger with a hammer, for a few minutes all you are going to think about is how much that hurts.

"Don't you think God understands that? He made you. Don't you think God understands the people that he created? God isn't looking for perfect people. If he was then there would only be one perfect person for him to choose from and that person was HIM.

"What I'm saying to you is that God understands when you get preoccupied with your pain. He understands that we are creatures of self. That is how he made us. He wants us to be creatures of self who are willing to share that self with Him.

"Now that doesn't give you license to wallow in self-pity and remorse for the rest of your life, but it does give you license to understand that you are human and to accept God's forgiveness when you ask for it humbly.

"Please understand me. God's grace doesn't give you a license to sin. It gives you a license to live unencumbered by guilt when you are trying to live within the will of God. If you are trying your best to live the way God wants you to then the grace of God is upon you.

"If you are using a formula to say, 'Well, God understands that this is too hard for me, so I'll do what comes naturally.' Then you are walking outside of the will of God and you are tempting his wrath.

"It doesn't matter that you are a better person than your neighbor. What matters is how good are you compared to Jesus Christ? None of us have earned the grace of the cross. It is a free gift from the Father through his son Jesus Christ.

"If you are outside of will of God today and you want his forgiveness all you have to do is pray for that forgiveness acknowledging that Jesus is the path of salvation. Jesus said I am the way the truth and the life. No one comes to the Father but by me. Jesus is the door. He is the gatekeeper. You can't get to Heaven any other way."

Somebody in the crowd spoke out. "How do you know God answers prayer? He doesn't seem to have answered yours." Eddie seemed to falter for a second. Then his face firmed with resolve, and he spoke up. "I was in the worst state I've ever been in. I was to the point of believing that God didn't exist.

"I am ashamed to share this with you, but my pride is nothing in the face of the Lord's plan." Some of the ladies in the crowd actually mopped their eyes at this last remark. "Since my wife had found solace in a bottle of vodka, I decided to try it. I can see why she did it.

"You have no idea how much relief you get after a few drinks. The pain you felt is nothing like it was before. It seems so far away. I am so ashamed to tell you that I fell into the habit of drinking. There was such peace in the bottle. I could take a few drinks and my troubles didn't matter anymore.

"It didn't matter that I had failed as a husband and a father. It only mattered that I didn't feel this horrible pain any more. I was ready to live the rest of my life away from God with a shot glass in my hand. I didn't care about happiness any more. All I cared about was numbness.

"When you get to the point that all you want is to not hurt anymore then you are pretty much at rock bottom. If I couldn't stop hurting, then dying was fine with me. I'm not standing here to tell you how to live your life because I'm so much better than you.

"I'm here as a witness to the Lord. I'm here to tell you that God loves you. I'm here to tell you that the only way to God is through his son Jesus Christ. Your eternity depends on what you do with the person of Jesus Christ.

"If you reject him, then he will reject you before the Father. If you acknowledge him he will acknowledge you before his Father. I know from where you are standing that this all seems rather pat. I can't prove anything to you.

"God calls you to step out in faith. I know you are sitting there thinking 'You want me to give the rest of my life to an idea that you can't prove?!' I can't explain this to you in any other way than to say that the Bible says, 'The fool has said in his heart that there is no God.'

"As I'm standing here preaching to you, we all know that there is a God. We know that this didn't happen by accident. Nobody in his or her right mind can look around and say that this whole world is a product of random chance.

"All of that aside though, how do I know that God answers prayer. Well let me tell you. A few weeks ago, I was in the little apartment that I had rented. I was out of money and out of prospects. I was literally to the point of giving up.

"I didn't care if the Lord sent one of his angels to claim my soul and take me home. To be honest with you I wasn't really sure that I believed any of this stuff anymore. I had bought a lottery ticket. It was a spur of the moment impulse purchase. I really didn't expect anything to come from it, but something told me when the cashier handed it to me to pray over it right there.

"I remember thinking that this person is going to think I'm some kind of nut, but I did it. I stopped right there in the store and prayed over the ticket that she had handed me.

"I prayed, 'Lord, I don't know what this means, and it might only be an exercise in obedience but I feel the need to pray over this ticket right now. I'm not going to be a hypocrite. I really haven't felt your presence in some time. I wish that I could feel you with me more than I have but if you want me to pray over this ticket then I will.

"Lord I ask you to bring as much of your kingdom forward through this ticket as is possible without violating free will. I know that this is the one thing that has encumbered you through the ages. I give over my will to yours and ask that you do with this as much as your will provides. I also say that if none of this benefits me then you are God and I am not. I accept your will for my life.'

"When I finished that prayer I remember thinking, 'You simple minded idiot, do you really think you are going to win anything with that?' You can imagine my surprise when that night the lottery drawing took place and I had a winning ticket.

"I remember the thrill that ran through me when I realized I had won a lottery for almost half a million dollars. I thought, 'I won't have to work for a few years.' When I got to the lottery office I found that there were two other winners, so I only had a one third share of the winnings but let's face it, one-hundred and fifty-one thousand dollars is nothing to sneeze at.

"I can't tell you how blessed I feel. The money is truly a blessing. I feel more blessed to know that God had never left me. Actually, one of the people who arranged this open-air preaching works for the lottery office and I believe God led me to her. She organized everything so fast you wouldn't believe it."

Somebody in the crowd spoke up, "You already know that God doesn't approve of gambling and you want us to believe that God gave you a winning lottery ticket?" Eddie didn't miss a step. He turned in the direction of the voice and spoke in clear and deliberate tones, "It isn't gambling when God is in it. God is the only sure thing in this world and I'm here to tell you that God wants the best for you."

An older gentleman in the crowd spoke up, "God doesn't want us to give even the appearance of sin." With that he turned and walked away from the crowd. Eddie didn't know where his reply came from. It seemed to leap from his throat. "I spend a whole dollar on a lottery ticket and that makes me unworthy as a preacher? Moses and David were both murderers. David was a man after God's own heart, but he was a murderer, an adulterer and a terrible father."

The crowd seemed to answer back with their support. The gentleman was getting into his car now, but the crowd had dismissed his comment completely. Amelia's attention was on the gentleman and his car.

Chapter 34

Amelia came out of her reverie while watching the gentleman get into his car. She felt as though she had been asleep. She realized that Rachel was gone. She didn't exactly know when Rachel had left. She knew she wasn't here now.

She couldn't believe how powerful the words of this young preacher had been. She had been completely enthralled by his words and his passion. She didn't see the angel standing behind her holding his sword aloft. There was a huge bright light emanating from the sword. This holy light had broken the spell that had been holding onto Amelia's consciousness.

Amelia made a mental note to tell Roger about this. Her head seemed filled with a sort of fog as she turned toward her car. She faltered forward a few steps and then glanced back. The preaching was over now, and the crowd had gathered around the young preacher.

Some of the older gentlemen were around him patting him on the back. The ladies were clearly admiring him from a distance. Two or three of them showed obvious interest in this young man.

Amelia reached her car without realizing it and mechanically opened the door and got inside. She had fastened her seatbelt and put the key into the ignition before she realized that her surroundings had changed.

Suddenly everything was back to normal. She was herself and everything made sense again. She didn't completely understand what had happened, but she did feel the need to talk to her husband about it. She reached up and started the car. She was going to talk to Roger about this.

Molech was standing behind Eddie with a satisfied expression on his face. He was happy with the reception his little preacher was getting. He thought that this little man of God was going to further his plans effectively.

"Give it some time and he would be able to coerce thousands to a false gospel. Even if his little preacher is found to be a false preacher by the Christians it will be too late. His message will have swayed many and the humans who publicize the truth won't realize that they are disillusioning many more. Exposed preachers are a powerful way for the forces of evil to point and say,"

"See, Christianity is as fake as anything else!"

"These are the same people that say, 'You are going to hell' and now see how they are really living!"

"Christian preachers only want your money"

"Isn't it funny how they say they are concerned for your soul but then pass the collection plate for a 'love' offering."

Molech was jarred from his reverie when one of his captains stepped forward and spoke. "May I ask a question my lord?" asked the captain warily.

Molech considered his officer for a moment and resisted the urge to punish him. He had to keep reminding himself of lord Lucifer's orders to show compassion and understanding to win loyalty. Molech's voice was a low growl when he answered, "Pose your question."

His captain seemed to know that Molech had little patience for this, so he phrased his question very carefully.

"My lord," he simpered, "You allowed the preacher to preach a message of the Gospel of our enemy. Some of us were wondering why there wasn't more false seed in the message. You allowed the shadow of gambling in, which was easily quelled because of the reference to the Living God. The message preached today had the full gospel message in it. It is possible that his words led some to the cross."

Molech smiled when his captain finished his question. "I see that you don't look to the future. A false message from the start is a ringing gong to the enemy." Molech felt mollified as he instructed,

"Gather your forces captain and I shall teach you something."

The captain became stark white at this remark but carried out his orders to the letter. The last thing he wanted was to be punished by Molech.

Molech settled himself onto the ground as the horde gathered round him. He reached out and picked up a tiny imp and put him on his knee. The imp was trembling but didn't dare protest. It was a terrible parody of Christ's Sermon on the Mount. He spoke in a ringing voice that carried to the gathered throng of demons.

"Blessed are the worldly because theirs is Lucifer's kingdom."

"Blessed are those who seek vengeance because it shall be theirs."

"Blessed are the arrogant, because they shall have their desires."

"Blessed are the angry because they shall know vengeance"

"Blessed are those who seek self-satisfaction because their search is eternal."

"Blessed are the wicked for they have no need of God."

"The kingdom of Hades is like a treasure that a man finds and desires with all his heart. This is our treasure and we are the gate keepers."

"We my children are part of Lucifer's grand plan to overthrow our creator. Since we have power of our own we have no need of God the Father who would impose his will on us whether we desire it or not.

"It is true that God created us, but he can't control us. We are free to choose, and we have chosen. We have chosen the forbidden fruit of total freedom. We have chosen to oppose an oppressive God for our own rights and desires. We have chosen to live and exist outside the will of our maker and we will prove that he is powerless to stop us. We will rally in the courts of Lucifer and we will be there on the day that Lucifer lays the Father low.

"We will be held in high favor when Lucifer is lord and we are all allowed to do as our will pleases for us to do. I have personally seen Lucifer when he is fully manifested. He is a glorious all-powerful angel. The father made a mistake in creating an angel who was more powerful than himself. Lucifer himself told me that he was going to create his own paradise.

"This one would be for us, not for the humans. The Father went too far when he favored the humans over us. We are his greatest creation. Lucifer went to the Father and demanded an explanation of him. He was thrown from the Heavens for his trouble. This came from the so called loving god."

Molech and the assembled demons didn't see the angel watching them. He had a bitter expression on his face.

He growled in a low voice, "And he gathered them around himself and began to teach them. The Lord sent me to be a witness against this today. I will stand in the presence of God Almighty on the Day of Judgment and I will be a witness against you.

"This blasphemous parody of the Lord teaching his followers will not go unpunished Molech. You may rally your troops now, but you have no chance against the Almighty." With that the angel rose into the air. He passed through the bough of a large oak tree. In clear sky, he manifested himself in full glory and stepped into the kingdom of Heaven. Molech and his followers were so engrossed in their revelry that they didn't notice the angel.

Roger had gone into the office for a few minutes to tie up some loose ends. Brennan was with his mother today and Amelia was meeting with the mother of the child who had received their form letter. He was interested to hear how that meeting turned out.

He had located the file that he had forgotten to bring home. It sat on top of his desk right where he had left it. Sometimes he wondered if his mind was slipping. There it was right where he had placed. He'd put it there for the specific purpose of not forgetting it, and he had forgotten it.

He picked up the file and walked out of the office. He locked the door automatically as he left. He got into his car and realized that he was low on gas. He decided to stop at the little gas station that was about a mile from the office. He pulled up to the gas pump and realized that he didn't have his debit card in his pocket. He decided that he would pay with cash.

A quick check of his wallet revealed that he had thirty-eight dollars, more than enough to get gas for the trip home. He got out of the car and hit the intercom button. "fill-up on pump seven please."

"Pump seven set for cash fill-up" came the mechanical reply. He pulled the nozzle from the pump and began to fill the car.

The wind was high today. It was strange to see the wind blowing so hard at this time of year. Roger didn't see Dayanel using his wind to keep imps at bay. He'd blown the weaker ones away. Roger noticed that the pumps were different from the way they were the last time he was here.

He walked in through the door and glanced around. He went to the back of the store to get a soda. He found the brand that he was partial to and grabbed one out of the cooler. He walked up to the pay counter and put his drink on the counter.

"Eighteen forty-one on pump seven", the woman behind the counter asked, "And how will you be paying sir?"

"cash ma'am" replied Roger.

"Oh alright", returned the woman behind the counter. "I thought you might use our new 'Archangel Pay System.'" She indicated with a flourish toward the new pay terminal to her right hand. Roger peered in the direction she indicated and saw a new terminal that was a small, digital connection.

"That is connected to the world-bank system by satellite. Transactions are done in real time. Within seconds after a transaction, the currency is taken from your account and deposited into the receiving parties account. You don't even have to swipe your card in a reader. You pass your account card over the scanner. The card has a smart chip in it that can be read by the scanner up to three feet away."

Roger thought about this for a moment, "If the scanner reads the chip and handles the transaction, then where is the data maintained about your account?"

The lady behind the counter beamed at his question. "The data for every transaction and every account is maintained in a database in a supercomputer somewhere in the Arizona desert. From what I understand, the computer system is maintained in a bunker a hundred feet below ground. They were serious about protecting the data when they designed this system."

Roger couldn't help but think about the cashless society of the end times. This could be the precursor to the financial system that will be used by the antichrist. The one used to control the financial system of the world. It would be a simple matter to transfer the smart chip from a card to an injectable media.

Injecting the small chip into human flesh could be used as an argument against loss. Account security would be easier to maintain. If there wasn't a card to steal, then you are safer from theft.

"This sure seems a lot like the pay system that the Bible talks about in the end times," stated Roger.

He glanced up at the woman behind the counter. He saw that her face had fallen. She no longer had the welcoming expression that she'd had a moment ago.

"Oh, great," she intoned. "Now I get to hear from another one of you Bible thumpers. You know I'm just doing my job here. I'm not the devil. I didn't design or build this thing. I'm not forcing anybody to use it. I guess you are going to tell me that I'm sending people straight to hell and that's where I'll be going if I don't get rid of this 'infernal contraption.'" She made quotes in the air with her fingers as she said it.

Roger was surprised by the sudden anger. He had only made an observation, and she had become openly hostile. Where was this coming from? He took a moment to frame his response when he saw something out of the corner of his eye. It was like a shadow moving from the wall to the cashier. It didn't have form or substance, and when he stared at it, it was gone, but he was sure he had seen something. *Must have been a trick of the light*, thought Roger.

"Ma'am, I haven't said anything like that to you. It isn't up to me to judge you or your actions. That is for God to do. I was only making an observation. If you've been berated by other Christians about this, let me take this opportunity to apologize for them. I'm sorry if you've been mistreated simply for doing your job."

He pulled a twenty-dollar bill from his wallet and handed it across the counter to her. "Just put the change in that charity-jar. You have a good day now." Roger indicated the donation jar beside the register. The cashier appeared rather stunned by his reply and didn't say anything as Roger turned and walked out of the store.

Chapter 35

Roger hadn't seen the imps dancing on the counter while he was in the store. There was one particularly large imp on the wall near the cashier. It was this imp that Roger had sensed and seen in the form of shadow.

The Holy Spirit had touched Roger at exactly the right moment. He had reacted with reserve and caring instead of anger. Anger was what the imps were trying to draw from him.

The largest imp spoke to his fellows as Roger walked out of the store. "You know there for a second, I thought he actually saw me. He turned and stared directly at me or at least in my direction. The last time that happened was with that evangelist in Georgia. Remember the pain we felt when he called upon the name of our enemy to banish us?

"It felt like a thousand hot knives being driven into me at once. There for a second, I thought he was going to start praying. If he had, I was going to dive through the wall." His fellows voiced their agreement with various nods, grunts, whoops, and whistles.

Then from the back corner came a hiss and the air seemed to grow cold.

"You openly admit that you would abandon the post I assign you?!" Jenoch's form passed through the back wall. The room grew deathly silent. None of the imps spoke. The fear in the room was palpable. Jenoch swept forward toward the imp who had spoken. "Answer me, little one!!" Jenoch's snarled in rage.

The imp fell to the floor on his face. "Forgive me, master. I spoke in fear of our enemy." He whimpered.

"The only one you need fear is me, little one. I hold your existence in my hand." With this statement, Jenoch flexed his claws and slammed his clawed hand down on the little imp's leg.

A scream of agony cut through the air. Jenoch's claw had pinned the imp's leg to the floor. Jenoch prepared to address the assembled demons. Suddenly, a bellow of rage echoed through the room. A form struck Jenoch from the side. For a moment, silence ruled supreme.

Jenoch had been bowled over and his grip on the imp was gone. He sailed a good fifteen feet through the air and came to an abrupt rest when he struck the floor. As if a switch had been flipped, noise resumed. The air was filled with the screams of the imps that wanted to be away from here.

Jenoch looked through stunned eyes at the largest imp he had ever seen. This barrel-chested behemoth stood easily nine and a half feet tall. His emerald green, reptilian form shook with rage as he faced Jenoch. He opened a wide muzzle and emitted a bellowing howl. His huge muscular arms were now cradling the imp that Jenoch had been punishing. He laid the imp tenderly behind himself and then turned to Jenoch.

His voice was a ragged screech as he bellowed, "You hurt Regmar! Bornock will make you pay!" Jenoch jumped to his feet. Fury was a living thing within him. His authority had been blatantly disregarded, and he had been personally attacked. He was going to make an example of these two.

When he was finished, none of this little brood would dare to show any disrespect to him again. Jenoch flexed his claws and stretched his muscles as he began to circle the one who called himself Bornock. He could clearly see that Bornock was an imp. What didn't make sense was his size and strength.

Jenoch had never been hit so hard. He couldn't believe that the blow had come from a lower level demon. Jenoch spared an instant to glance around the room. He was looking for the imp who seemed to be the tensest. That would be the one who knew the most about this Bornock.

He zeroed in on a little furry and fanged imp clutching at the tables edge. He made a mental note to speak to this one individually but for now there was work to do. Jenoch snapped his attention back to Bornock. He studied his opponent as he circled him. He was searching for weak spots.

Bornock's upper body was extremely developed. He would be a strong opponent in a wrestling match. Jenoch didn't want this to draw out for long. He wanted all here to see how he had completely outclassed his opponent. Jenoch thought now was a good time to test this new strength that Molech had given him. Surely, he was more than a match for this imp, giant though he was.

Jenoch decided to match Bornock strength for strength for a short time. This would allow him to test his strength and show the assembled demons there how strong he truly was. After the decision was made, Jenoch charged. Bornock hesitated for a second and then charged as well.

Bornock was bellowing, but Jenoch was silent. *Let the fool scream and rage. True strength has no need of bravado.* They slammed together in the middle of the room like two big trucks. Jenoch's superior bulk and strength won him the advantage he was hoping for. He caught both of Bornock's hands and gripped them in his.

It appeared as though they were playing a perverse version of the children's game 'Mercy.' Jenoch couldn't believe his own strength. He found that Bornock was easily manageable. He spun on the spot dragging Bornock over his shoulder and slammed the giant imp to the floor. It was a blindingly fast movement that left Bornock stunned.

That was all the time that Jenoch needed. He raised one clawed foot high and brought it down mercilessly on the knee of the imp. There was a loud cracking sound, and then another scream of agony pierced the air. Jenoch reached down and seized the scruff of Bornock's neck. He hoisted the imp off the ground while, with the other hand, he dragged his claws through thin air.

The air seemed to part and then suddenly the screams of thousands upon thousands of tortured souls reached the ears of those in the room.

Bornock was whimpering and screaming now. "Regmar! Regmar! Help Bornock! Regmar help Bornock please…." The last please came out as a whimper.

The larger imp seemed to realize his fate. He was being thrown into the abyss for his actions. There was nothing anyone was going to do about it. Jenoch noticed Regmar cringing in the far corner of the room. This situation caused the little imp some real emotional pain. Jenoch wondered whether he should throw the little imp into the abyss as well.

He could always decide on that later. For now, he wanted to deal with the more immediate problem. When the rift was large enough, he brought his arm holding Bornock around slowly. He wanted all here to witness the fate of this one.

Bornock whimpered. He cried like a human child over the betrayal of a friend. Jenoch could read that this Bornock was a simpleton. That didn't excuse his actions. The crowd of assembled demons seemed to strain while watching the action. Jenoch pushed Bornock through the rift, and all present listened as his screams grew more and more distant. Jenoch wiped his hand over the rift, and it was gone.

"Are there any more here who would question my authority?" Jenoch asked these words quietly. There was no doubt about the venom in them. The air in the room seemed to chill as none of the demons dared look directly at Jenoch. They feared that he would take it as a challenge.

"I wish to speak to the one called Regmar," snarled Jenoch. There were several gasps from the crowd, but no one spoke. Regmar stepped forward on trembling knees and threw himself face down before Jenoch. His wounded leg still bled from being impaled earlier.

Regmar whimpered as he begged, "Mercy please, Master."

Jenoch decided to toy with this one. "It would seem that I was attacked because of you, little one. Did you dare to set your imp on me?" The last question came out as a low growl, and it was enough to make Regmar sink into the floor.

Regmar's voice was a high-pitched squeal when he replied, "I didn't set him on you, master. I would never defy your authority. I said nothing to Bornock to make him attack you. He did that of his own choice."

Jenoch leaned forward and commanded, "Tell me how you engendered such loyalty from the simple-minded one."

Regmar took a moment to compose himself and replied, "Bornock was like a lost child. I was simply nice to him, and suddenly, he was following me around everywhere. I didn't complain. He was so big and strong that none of the others bothered me anymore. I would never have set him on a superior, though. I fear those above me."

Jenoch reflected on Regmar's reply, and intoned, "It appears that you understand the principle of loyalty. That is a leadership trait. Instead of punishing you, I will place you over this group of demons. Their success is your success. Their failure is your failure and, therefore, your punishment.

Jenoch turned to the assembled demons. "This is your group leader. Obey him as you would obey me. Any who disobey or show disrespect to him, disobey or show me disrespect. This will be severely punished as you have seen." Jenoch noticed that several of the larger imps were watching the floor with expressions of disgust on their faces.

To ensure his meaning had been clear, he asked the group at large, "Are there any here who do not understand what I've just commanded?"

None spoke. Jenoch thought he saw one imp raise his gaze hopefully but then look down again. Jenoch touched Regmar on the shoulder, and a small burn formed there.

Jenoch hissed, "This burn will never heal. It will be ulcerous and a cause of constant, annoying pain. If you ever need me, simply touch it and speak my name. I will know that you need me, and I will come. If any of these disobey you, I will banish them. If any of them show you disrespect, I will punish them. As long as you do what I ask of you, you will be a leader among your fellows. If you fail me, you will be punished in much the same way as your friend Bornock. Do you understand little one?"

Regmar shuddered under the gaze and nodded. He was exhilarated at the prospect of being in charge, but he was terrified at the prospect of failure. He would do his best and hope for empowerment later. Those who were empowered were rarely banished to the abyss.

"I will see you again in two days' time. I want to hear how you have enticed more people into accepting this pay device. Our master's plan needs this to be accepted by the general public, and you are only one of thousands of groups of demons pushing it onto the public."

Jenoch rose from the ground and floated forward until he passed through the wall. Regmar watched him go with a bit of trepidation. This would be Regmar's first test of leadership. All present had heard Jenoch but as the old saying goes 'When the cat's away, the mice will play'. One word from Regmar would be enough to get one of his fellows banished.

It appeared that Regmar had gone from the protection of a huge imp to that of a junior demon lord. Regmar realized he was more secure now than he'd ever been. Before now, his word meant punishment at the hands of Bornock. Now his word meant banishment to the abyss. He wielded much more power now.

That thought of filled him with an unholy joy. He truly had power now and he intended to use it. He found his voice and called the assembled demons into a circle around him.

"You heard the captain!" he ordered in a strong commanding voice. "I'm in charge here and we all know what our mission is. We need to work on getting greater acceptance for the pay device in this community."

Regmar motioned to two small imps to his left. "You two, you will attach yourselves to the clerk. Where she goes you go. You will constantly repeat things into her ear. Constantly mention the convenience of the pay system. You will convince her that it is a wonderful new advancement within a week. If not we will seek other methods."

Regmar turned to three larger imps and began to speak. "You three…" He saw the defiance and hesitation on their faces. "You look as though you don't want to take my orders. Perhaps I should call the master and have him explain it to you." At this the three imps went pale. All three immediately assumed submissive postures. Each one offered up his most fervent desire to serve Regmar.

"Fine then, you three will stay near the cash register. If a customer doesn't pay with that method, you will scream obscenities at them. If they are not Christians, pass through their bodies while threatening them. Promise them death and destruction. Promise them hurt and harm. Do your utmost to make paying at the register an unpleasant experience.

"Scream at them that they are holding back progress. Yell that they should use the pay system. We will try this for a week and see how it works. If we need to increase your number, we will." Regmar scanned the assembled demons and asked, "Who here specializes in greed and lust?" Four particularly feline demons raised their clawed hands.

Regmar crooned, "Excellent, you four will station your selves at the Archangel pay terminal. All who pay there will receive positive messages from you. How they themselves might find a way to profit from it. Promise them good things will come their way. Tell them they are good people, beautiful people, that they will be successful. I don't care what you promise them. I want them thinking they paid the right way." Regmar swept his arm around the room.

"The rest of you divide into teams of two. I don't care who you pair up with. I want you to take turns tormenting those who don't use the pay system. I want you to continue to offer praises to those who do. I want this place to be a hive of activity.

"You will have a perimeter of one mile around the shop. Once you reach your perimeter distance, come back here and await your next turn. Is there anyone here who doesn't understand the orders that I've given?" None of the assembled demons spoke.

"Very well, you have your orders. Carry them out. No lazing about! I want all here doing their best to further the master's plans." With that Regmar clapped his hands together. It sounded like a gunshot.

The assembled demons scattered to their posts. The shop was abuzz with activity. This plan had formed in Regmar's mind moments after being given authority. He seemed to wear the mantle of authority well. Time would tell.

Jenoch was about leave and report to Molech. He stopped when he heard an imp mention the new little foundling Argass. He didn't trust the little demon. He was found so 'innocently.' He would check on Argass before going to see Molech. He thought this would be a good way to make himself more valuable. A good captain always watches his master's back.

He recalled the conversation between two lower imps. They muttered that Argass had spoken out of turn about Lucifer himself. He planned to bring this to Molech's attention. Molech would undoubtedly probe Argass' mind and find the truth buried there. If it was true, then Molech would probably banish the imp and be thankful of his choice of captain.

Jenoch selected two imps that he trusted. He called them to himself and they came in an instant.

"Observe the family that Argass is tempting. Don't interfere. You will only watch." He spoke to them in clear menacing tones.

He pointed at the closer of the two, "You take the father and you take the mother." He commanded, indicating the other imp. Don't let yourself be seen and if you see or hear anything suspicious I want you to come and report it directly to me. Is that understood?" Both of the imps bowed low and indicated that it was perfectly clear. They both disappeared in a swirl of smoke.

Amelia couldn't go anywhere without the watchful imp tagging along. He wouldn't tempt her. He also wouldn't offer advice to any imp who did attempt to tempt her. He knew his place. Likewise, his companion knew his assignment. They knew the best way to stay as safe as possible in the demonic ranks. That way was to do exactly as you are ordered. When your master is ranting at you, be completely silent and servile.

Roger wasn't aware that he had an unseen spy. Everywhere he went the imp went with him. It was especially hard on the imp when Roger was driving to or from work. It was his habit to tune the radio to praise music. He joined in the singing. The imp found it hard to stay in the car during this.

Chapter 36

Eddie sat at the small table in his rundown apartment. He had struggled with his sermon all week. Deep down, he knew he'd been going in the wrong direction with it. But it seemed so real that it must be true. He could swear that he heard the loving voice of the Holy Spirit. The words came to him and he had been writing them down.

He worked for a few minutes. The words made him uncomfortable. He stopped, got up and walked around for a little while. He debated with himself as to the content of the sermon. He gradually allowed himself to accept a doctrine that he knew was wrong. He told himself that the road to false doctrine was slippery. Then he plodded a little further down it.

Eddie knew that God is not a genie. Eddie also knew that God is sovereign. He thought *"God can't be commanded by the will of men."* Eddie also knew that God is far more concerned with a person's spiritual welfare before their physical comfort.

Eddie didn't see the angel whispering the story of Elijah. Elijah obeyed the word of the Lord and called for a drought. The Lord provided for Elijah by ensuring that he was fed by ravens. After that he was fed bread and water from an old widow and her son. That was a miracle where an oil jug and a supply of flour were not used up until Elijah called for rain on the land.

Eddie considered this. The provision of the Lord was bread and water. It was not extravagant, but it did meet the needs of Elijah. There is nothing wrong with being rich. But the Lord wants you to be rich in the spirit.

Eddie had been taught all of this. It was when his mind started down this path that Molech became more active. He covered Eddie with his bulk and take on the persona of a loving father. He crooned to Eddie. Eddie mistook this crooning for the Holy Spirit.

There had been a few spirit-filled Christians who had recognized his voice as one of the enemy. Every time it happened it was immediate. That hadn't happened with Eddie. Eddie was ripe to hear something good about himself.

Molech spread his wings and wrapped Eddie in them. He covered Eddie no matter where he went. In these moments of crisis Molech kept his eyes closed. He listened intently to Eddie debating with himself.

He had been watching this little wayward preacher for a while now. He knew how to approach Eddie with new thoughts. He had to take it slow. Letting Eddie get used to an idea and then accepting it was time consuming. It had to be done this way. If he didn't ensure an idea was grounded in Eddie's mind, it would be shaken off.

He heard Eddie say, "God is not a genie."

As soon as he heard this he started to counter it. "Of course, God is not a genie, but God wants to answer your prayers if you are faithful. God doesn't bless his wayward children because they are under discipline. Doesn't every father want to give his children what they want? Doesn't the smile you see when you give a good gift make you feel good? God longs to give you the desires of your heart."

Eddie relaxed after this and walked back over to the table. He started working on his sermon again. As soon as he sat down Molech whispered his message anew. He whispered a lack of faith destroys the power of God to grant your request.

An imp shot through the ceiling and knelt before Molech. "Master, I know you said you didn't want to be bothered. I must beg your indulgence. I bring news most dire." The imp lay before Molech trembling. He fully expected to be beaten severely. He hoped not to be banished to Sheol.

It was with great effort that Molech mastered his anger before he spoke. He almost reached out and pulled the imp apart then he remembered the instructions of Lucifer. *Never destroy a messenger BEFORE you get the message. It could be important.* Molech gritted his teeth and breathed deeply for a moment.

"This better be important, little one. I am in the middle of fragile workings. This better be dire news indeed. If not, you have sacrificed your existence on this plane," Molech growled.

There was a long silence before the imp spoke in a shuddering whisper. "Master, the parents of the young charge of Argass have obtained sensitive information about the Daycare's corporate ownership, though they haven't realized it yet.

"The father, Stephen, received the magazine in the mail. He placed the magazine in his briefcase. It appears that he means to read it on his break at work. They have also formed a friendship with a Christian couple. The husband is an investigator. I was sent to warn you that it may only be a matter of time before our plans are exposed." This last part came out as a whimper.

Molech was silent for the space of a few moments. Then he reached out his hand and took the little imp by the scruff of the neck. In a low and menacing voice, he snarled, "Go back and tell Jenoch to do everything he possibly can to keep this from happening. I will need time to form a backup plan."

"Yes, my master," the little imp cried and streaked away in terror.

He knew that Jenoch would use him and his friend to regain the information. If they couldn't regain it, he would wish to destroy it. He would do almost anything to keep Stephen from reading it. The imp thought frantically. If they failed in this, there would be hell to pay.

As the imp disappeared, Molech turned back to the task of corrupting this young preacher. He crooned and gently stroked the Eddie's back. He wanted Eddie to feel cold chills down his back. The preacher would mistake it for the moving of the Holy Spirit. This trick had worked many times, and it seemed to work now.

Eddie went to his knees in an ecstatic state. He prayed aloud for a moment and got up. He walked straight back to the table and started writing every word that Molech whispered into his ear. Eddie had tears in his eyes and kept mumbling, "Father, I'm not worthy."

Molech laughed an evil laugh. They worked through most of the night. Eddie truly thought he was preparing a message from God for his children. He thought this must have been what it was like for Moses. The words flowed from pen to paper as the night passed into morning.

The tent had been set up in the parking lot of the shopping center. Eddie's volunteers had obtained permission from the shop owners. The day was hot, so they had the ends of the tent rolled up. A nice cross breeze was blowing through. It wasn't air conditioning, but it was the next best thing.

Eddie was about to step up to the podium to address the crowd. They were waiting expectantly for him to share from the Word of God. His core group of 30 followers had grown dramatically. There were at least 200 people out there sitting in the chairs. That wasn't even counting the people who were milling around on the sidelines.

They were always there. That group of people who were curious but scared of the culture. It was an unfamiliar setting for them. Usually you could reach a few but most of the time the largest majority walked away after a few minutes. They were the ones who were afraid to commit to anything.

Nobody saw Molech kneeling behind Eddie. He had his clawed hand on Eddie's shoulder. A manic evil grin was on his face. Saliva dripped from his drooling jaws. This was going to be the beginning of the payoff. He had given Eddie the false doctrine of "Name it and Claim it."

This was very effective on the east coast. If he were at all lucky he would leave this crowd today witnessing the corruption of at least 10 souls. Lucifer would be pleased with him. He wondered at the honor he would receive from his master. He played little scenes over in his mind.

Eddie made his way to the podium. He stepped up to the podium as Roger and Amelia drove up. Brennan was in the back of the car. They got out of the car to go into the store.

Amelia looked up and announced, "Hey honey, it's that young preacher I told you about. He was preaching the day that Rachel and I met. He is a powerful speaker. We should listen to what he has to say."

Molech noticed the Christians as Amelia ushered Brennan out of the car. He sought to see how many of his trusted lieutenants were near. Eddie stood at the podium and found that his mouth was dry. He took a tiny sip of water from the bottle inside the podium before he started to speak.

"Good morning to all of you in the name or our Lord. I hope this day finds you all in good health and good spirits. It is a lovely day for us to have an outside service like this. The Lord is surely smiling on us this day.

"We are all here for one reason so before we get started let's open with a word of prayer." Eddie paused for a moment to see if the crowd was going to respond. They all obediently bowed their heads at his words. Eddie bowed his head and began his prayer.

"Father in Heaven, we come before you this days asking for your blessing and your help in understanding your word and your works. We ask that you open the eyes of those present and the hearts of those that should be here listening to your word.

"We acknowledge that you are the all-knowing, all-powerful God and we thank you for this opportunity to share this time in your name, learning from your word and sharing in your grace. I ask that you give me the words to speak to your children and I ask that you touch hearts today and bring souls into conviction. All of this I ask in the name of your son, Amen."

The assemble crowd answered with their 'amen' and Eddie took a moment to look around at those gathered to hear him speak. For a moment he allowed pride to swell in him. These people were here to listen to him. Eddie felt good about himself.

"We are all here because we have an interest in the things of God. People who are of the world don't understand this. If you are here and you aren't a Christian, then the Lord is working on you today. I'm here to tell you man and woman, boy and girl that God loves you.

"The God who made the universe loves you. YOU are special to him. He doesn't care that you don't think so. You might not get picked first for the baseball team and you might not be the most popular in your class but God who spoke the entire universe into existence thinks you are special and He loves you.

"God isn't only the creator, he is your Heavenly father and you should think of him as a father. When Jesus prayed he called the Lord Abba. Abba is Hebrew for father. It is most closely translated into our language as daddy. Father generally seems strict and forbidding. Daddy on the other hand generates an image of a loving and caring adult male figure.

"We are talking about someone who truly cares about you and wants what is best for you. We aren't talking about someone who barks orders and hands out punishment when their desires aren't met. I want you to think about that for a moment.

"If God loves you so much and you are so special to him don't you think he wants to grant you your hearts' desire? I'm here to tell you that he does. Man is Gods' highest creation. He loves us more than anything else he's made. He loves us so much that he decided to take our punishment for us.

"I'm sure that those of you who have children understand that. When your child is facing punishment, don't you feel like you would rather take the punishment for them than to watch them go through it? That is exactly how God feels about you; only multiply the feeling by about a million.

"There is no way we can fathom how much God loves us. I am thoroughly convinced that we will never fully understand how much God loves us even after we've been in Heaven for 10,000 years and have seen example after example of God's perfect love.

"I don't think we will fully understand it even after that long in intimate fellowship with him because …… He is infinite…… There is no end to God so there is no end to the love of God.

"Think about that people. There is no end to the love of God. Another thing I want you to think about is this. There is nothing you can do to make God love you any more than he does right now. God loves you as much now as he did when you were an innocent child.

"There is nothing you can do to earn more love from God. God already loves you as much as he ever will. He sent his son to die for you. How much love is that? How many of you would allow your child to die for anybody?"

Eddie paused for dramatic effect here. He glanced around the crowd. They all stared at him intently.

A voice came into his mind. It wasn't a loud voice, but it was prideful. It only uttered one sentence but what a sentence it was.

"They are yours."

For a fleeting instant, fear bubbled up in Eddie. He considered momentarily running from the podium, but the voice was so soothing.

It was as though he heard a voice saying, "Speak the words I have given you child."

Eddie's will broke, and he perused his notes. He gathered his thoughts and began anew.

"Is it so hard to understand that someone who loves you so much would want to grant your request? The only thing that stops God from giving you your requests is your faith or the lack of it actually. If you have given yourself over to God and your desires are those of the God who made you then any request you make will be granted.

"I'm not telling you that God is a cosmic genie. God is sovereign over the universe that he created. What I am saying is that if your will is within the will of God then any request that you make of him will be granted.

"I know that there are those of you that will say that Jesus was a man of poverty so if we are to emulate him then we shouldn't ask for anything that would put us in a position of wealth. I'm here to tell you that there is nothing wrong with being rich.

"Job was the richest man in the world of his time. Being rich isn't bad but lacking in faith is a crippling thing. If you don't believe that God can do something, then you shouldn't even ask for it.

"A lack of belief is a block to the power of God. If you ask God for something and you don't really believe he can do it then your disbelief will stop the power of God in your life. If you believe though you can ask for anything in his name and it will be granted for you."

Roger turned to Amelia at this point and whispered, "Are you sure this guy was preaching the word the last time you heard him? He handed the crowd a false doctrine. He is handing out the 'Name it and Claim it' doctrine."

Amelia couldn't disagree, and she was slightly stunned. "Roger, the last time I heard him speak he gave a good gospel message. He didn't say any of this stuff last time. He did say something about winning a lottery, but it didn't last long, and he was straight back to the gospel."

Molech saw the little Christians in the back talking to each other. He could tell by their body language that they were uncomfortable with this sermon. He needed them to leave quickly. He didn't want them to challenge the doctrine that Eddie was dishing out. He saw the set of the man's jaw. He was preparing himself to say something.

Molech whispered to one of the imps behind him. The imp went flying toward the Christians. The demon got to them quickly and decided that the child would be the easiest to use in a diversion. He reached out and stuck his clawed hand into Brennan's belly. He started clenching and unclenching his fist violently.

The effect was instantaneous. Brennan's face went pale. His gorge rose up in his throat.

He turned to Roger and groaned, "Dad, I think I'm going to be sick." No sooner had the words left his mouth than he threw up. His head pitched forward, and luckily, it landed in front of his shoes.

He had just finished drinking a red crème soda. It looked for the world like he was throwing up blood. Amelia's eyes went wide with horror. Roger immediately shifted gears. The welfare of his son was the only thing that concerned him. All thoughts of the sermon left him.

This episode caused a stir in the crowd. People backed away from them. Nobody saw the imp remove his hand from Brennan and go streaking back to the podium. Nobody saw the grin on Molech's face. He was pleased. The imp had done his will perfectly. This would deserve a reward later.

Molech watched as Roger scooped Brennan up and carried him to the car.

Amelia was saying, "Honey, that was awfully red. Do you think we should take him to the emergency room?"

Roger answered without turning around. "That is exactly where we are going. Try to hold on, Buddy. We will get you some help as fast as we can."

Brennan's stomach had stopped roiling, and he was regaining his composure. Roger had put him in the car as easily if he had been a baby. Roger got in the car and started the engine. Amelia had gotten in while he was buckling in Brennan. Roger drove slowly from the parking lot, but his motions were tense.

When they gained the highway, Roger turned on his flashers. He pushed past the speed limit while driving to the hospital. They were several miles from Mercy General. They were a mile from the hospital when Brennan spoke up.

"Dad, I know you don't want to hear this, but I'm feeling better now. Do you think maybe I ate something bad?"

Roger peered at Brennan in the rear-view mirror. He was going to tell him to sit back and relax. When he saw Brennan, he could see that

Brennan appeared to be fine. Roger didn't want to take a chance with his son's health.

He turned to Amelia, "Will you check him over to make sure he isn't putting up a front for us?"

Amelia unbuckled her seat belt and turned around. She reached out and put her palm on Brennan's forehead. He felt normal. She put her finger under his left ear and felt the rhythm of his pulse. It was normal. His eyes were normal and not glazed. His breathing was normal. His skin wasn't cold or clammy to the touch. As far as she could tell, he was being truthful.

She gave Brennan a little smile, "You scared us, buddy."

He smiled sheepishly at her. "I'm sorry."

She stared at him, "Buddy, you don't need to apologize for getting sick. We know you were really sick. We want you to feel better."

These words were comforting. His mother would never have said this to him. She would have kept goading him for inconveniencing her. He felt a pang of guilt at this thought. Sometimes, he wondered why his mother didn't love him the way Amelia did. Amelia gave him a pat on the cheek and turned back around in her seat.

She buckled her seat belt, "He appears to be fine. His pulse is fine. His skin is normal to the touch. His pupils are reactive, and he seems completely coherent. I don't have a clue why he threw up like that unless he'd eaten something that didn't agree with him. If that is the case, then whatever it was is back there on that parking lot."

Roger considered this for a moment. He was torn between taking Brennan on to the emergency room anyway and wasting money for a hospital visit that wasn't necessary. He looked in the rear-view mirror again.

"Brennan, promise me that if you start feeling bad or funny again you will let me know right away?"

Brennan's face was earnest, "I promise, Dad. If I feel like that again, I'll let you know, but I feel fine now."

Roger thought about it for a moment. He decided that they would take Brennan home to rest. He didn't want to take any chances. His decision came in time for him to turn around in the hospital parking lot.

"I think we will take Brennan home for now. If you need to go to the store, we can do it later or maybe tomorrow if you don't mind." Amelia agreed. They rode most of the way home in silence.

Brennan sat in the back seat hoping for some noise, any at all. His parents rarely rode in silence. They only did that when they were arguing or really concerned. Brennan felt a little guilty for getting sick. Nobody saw the angel flying above the car. This family would not be antagonized again today. They had earned a break.

Back at the open-air sermon, Eddie had asked the crowd to join him in a moment of prayer for the poor young child that had to be carried away. The crowd had become silent and heads were bowed. Eddie orated a flowery prayer about the love of God for the innocence of children and how the hopes and prayers of this group were with the family.

He had known that he had to acknowledge the incident, but he didn't want it to become a major part of the sermon. He had to dispel the nervous energy in the tent. His use of the prayer was actually to his advantage. He appeared to earnestly care about the child's well-being. A little voice in his head offered, *Children are always good for building your image.* He didn't know the child and didn't care to. He couldn't muster much more than mild curiosity as to the boy's sickness.

It was an annoyance he had turned it to his advantage. He wanted to make sure that his message was getting the attention that it deserved. Molech stood behind Eddie with a satisfied smirk. He had chosen well with this little preacher. He could tell that this little man knew how to handle a public setting, an innate gift that Molech intended to use to the fullest.

Chapter 37

It was a couple of days after the scene at the open-air sermon. The phone rang, and Rachel put down the shirt she was folding and picked it up. "Hello."

The line crackled for a moment. Then she heard a clear voice, "Rachel, this is Amelia. I was calling to see how you are doing. We didn't get a chance to say a proper goodbye the other day. I wanted to make sure you were alright."

Rachel hesitated for a moment. She had been battling within herself over the last couple of days. She was torn between curiosity and fear of what Amelia had told her. She wanted to know more. She also felt an odd fear for the knowledge she was seeking. She didn't see the demon that constantly followed her screaming:

"What makes her think she has all the answers?!"

"You don't want anything to do with those fanatics!"

"What would your family say if you did this?!"

That last one always invoked a response. Rachel started to squirm. Not very many of her loved ones were Christian. If what Amelia was telling her was true, then the people she cared the most about were doomed. She couldn't bring herself to say anything.

Amelia could tell that Rachel was uncomfortable. She wasn't sure of the cause.

"Rachel are you there?" she asked, concern in her voice.

Rachel came back to the conversation abruptly, "Oh, yes… sorry. My mind was wandering there for a moment."

Amelia gave it a moment, "Rachel, are you alright? Is there anything I can help you with?"

Rachel was quiet for a moment. "No, everything is fine. I was doing the laundry today. What are you up to?"

"Well," offered Amelia, "aside from calling to see if you were alright, I was wondering if you and your family would like to come by our house for dinner this Wednesday night. I'll ask Roger if he will fire up the grill. After dinner we can get started on your scrapbook if you like."

This struck a chord in Rachel. She really wanted to start that scrapbook for Candy. It would be a nice gift when she was older. She thought about it for a moment.

"Let me see what Stephen is doing that night. If we can come, I'll call you back in a little while to let you know."

Amelia offered, "That sounds great, I hope you guys can come over. It would be a nice break in the middle of the week."

There was such warmth in her voice that Rachel was taken momentarily off guard. She stopped thinking about Christianity and the whole spiritual thing that she was hung up on. She felt she could genuinely be a friend with this woman. Amelia heard the hesitation and didn't exactly know why. She felt prompted to offer a prayer for Rachel. So, Amelia silently prayed.

"Father, I know you love this person I'm talking to. I know that she is one of your children as much as I am. I pray that you will protect her and extend the shield of my faith around her until she finds her own. Please bring her into your kingdom."

This was a short prayer, nothing really special in comparison to all of the prayers heard. Yet the throne of Heaven smiled. Amelia felt a sensation of peace come over her.

The spirit alighted on Rachel's shoulder. He spoke words of comfort and love into Rachel's ear. Rachel was so overcome with a feeling of peace and friendship that she immediately spoke into the phone.

"Amelia, I think we can accept your offer of dinner on Wednesday. I'll still call Stephen. If there are any problems, I'll call you and let you know. Is that alright with you?"

Amelia beamed into the phone, "That will be great. We will be glad to have you over. I'll let you go now unless there is anything I can do for you. Is there anything I can help you with?"

Rachel hesitated only for a moment, "Actually, I have some

thoughts about what we were talking about. How about I make a list of questions that we can talk about on Wednesday night? I'd like to be able to articulate the questions and your answers together."

"That will be great." affirmed Amelia. "We will see you on Wednesday night."

When the Holy Spirit entered the home, the demon fell over screaming in pain. He flew from the house in agony. The little imp knew that he would be punished but who could stand in the presence of the Holy One? This wasn't fair. He had worked and worked to gain the ear of this lost one.

Who were the Christians that they could call upon the power of the savior and steal the work of the imps? He hated these favored creatures. He was both disgusted and jealous of their physical bodies. He missed the sensations of eating and drinking. He'd died so long ago that it was a painful memory. He had possessed a few humans, but it wasn't the same. He could tell the body wasn't his. The sensations always felt off somehow.

The imp broke from his reverie and watched the house. It was ablaze with the light of Heaven. He didn't know what was going on inside. Whatever it was, he knew it wouldn't be good news for him. He thought for a moment of what was going to happen to him.

For a long moment, considered going into hiding. Maybe he could find another demon lord to serve. This idea didn't stay rooted for long. The first thing another lord would do is read his mind. That would reveal how unreliable a little piece of trash he was. So, he resolved to get as close to the house as he could and watch. The more information he could pass on the better it would be for him.

He knew that when he went before his master he would be burned and scarred. Better to be burned and scarred by the enemy while trying to do his assignment than to run like a coward and risk an early trip to the abyss. He crept closer to the house. His flesh started to smolder, so he backed off a bit.

He altered his perception so that he could see through the house. He would keep a vigil on the home until he could enter it again. He watched as Rachel put the phone down. He could see that she was experiencing such peace. He could see she was relaxed and content. He knew she was thinking of that Christianity thing.

He could always tell when the word of God was starting to take root in a human. They always seemed to see the world differently. They seemed for a short time to be free of the concerns of this life. He would have to hope that she would prove not to be the good soil in the parable of the Sower.

He would come into the picture as soon as he was able. Then he would do what he could to snatch the seed of the word from this one. He would try to fan her worries into life again. Worry could sometimes overshadow the little light that was starting to take root in her. Hopefully the time he'd spent with her had made her rocky soil. Hopefully the word wouldn't take root.

Rachel picked up the phone and dialed Stephen's number. The phone rang once… twice… then Stephen picked it up on the third ring.

"Marshall's Securities, Stephen speaking, may I help you?"

"Hey honey, it's me. I was talking to Amelia on the phone. She and her family have invited us to dinner on Wednesday night. I told her I had to call you to make sure our schedule was clear. I don't have anything going on. Can we go?" Rachel finished.

Stephen smiled. He liked that Rachel had enough respect for him that she asked and didn't simply tell him they were going. He couldn't remember any of his co-worker's wives showing them this type of respect. Her approach made him want to give her whatever she asked for.

He looked down at his desk calendar and saw that Wednesday night was clear.

"This sounds like something you really want to do." He noted with a playful note in his voice. "Sure honey, we can go. Get the directions and the time and we will be there with bells on."

"Oh, alright, Thanks honey. I'll call her back and get the information. We need to take the Daycare letters too because she is going to show me how to start a scrap book for Candy."

She pulled out the drawer to the kitchen cupboard. She knew she had put those letters in here somewhere. Her hand closed on them when she heard Stephen's voice.

"Ok sweetie, I'm in the middle of something so I'm going to have to let you go. We can talk later on tonight. Okay?"

She heard the question in his voice. "Okay hon. Love you. Oh wait, can you pick up Candy on your way home tonight?" Rachel asked.

Stephen's voice came back with a hint of impatience.

"Sure honey, I'll swing by the Daycare on my way home. I really do need to get back to work".

There was a pause then Rachel's voice came back on the line, "Ok honey. I'll talk to you tonight. Love you."

Stephen heard the little click as Rachel hung up. He wished it were always so easy to make his wife happy. He set the phone back down on its' cradle and started looking at the paperwork in front of him. His desk was covered with several paper trails he was mapping out for his superiors.

He had laid out the file for Aurora Finance Unlimited. They were a large customer. He wanted his work to be flawless. He didn't approve of where the investments were going. Their investments made sense financially. The investments themselves were sound. He was having trouble with the moral aspect of how they were making money.

The company was a cutting-edge technology investor. The bulk of their investments were going to abortion research. A large portion of their profits came from the work of abortion clinics. Oh, the wording of their portfolios was saying all the right things. The liberal public would eat it up. Stem cell research was sited often. They listed things like

"Research to help the aged and the infirm"

"Research into technologies to prevent birth defects

"Research that could possibly lead to a cure for cancer"

Stephen didn't disagree with stem cell research that the pages kept referring to. He knew however that stem cells could be harvested as easily from placental afterbirth rather than killing an unborn child to get them.

Thousands of births happened across the country every day. It would be much more efficient and effective to harvest those stem cells for research. Going through a court battle was costly and they had to deal with social acceptance. There was only one reason they did it this way. They wanted to change public opinion. Stephen didn't know the forces of darkness were guiding this fight not logic.

Stephen looked up at the clock. The workday had passed quickly. He'd gotten quite a bit done in the last couple of hours. He was sure that his supervisor would be pleased with the work. He'd developed a strong investment recommendation concerning the last three accounts in the umbrella group of Aurora Finance Unlimited.

It usually it took a while for a securities investor to land an account like Aurora. This account had just landed in his lap. He'd thought it had been more a fluke than anything. He'd given his supervisor advice on a couple of large accounts. The advice had turned out to be dead on the money. He hadn't expected to be so accurate. Stephen hadn't seen the angel that whispered the same advice into his ear before he had repeated it to his boss.

His superiors had been regarding Stephen as one of the shining stars of the company. They'd brought him in on the Aurora account on a "guts" move. Stephen was both excited and a little scared. He intended to make the most of the opportunity. He was confident he could do the job well.

He had set the alarm on his watch to remind him to pick up Candy. He shut down his computer and headed for the door. Stephen didn't see the angel behind him turn a page in the magazine on his desk. Stephen would look at it tomorrow and be drawn to the third line.

It showed a subsidiary company of Aurora Finance Unlimited. The subsidiary claimed a forty-seven percent profit for the quarter. The company name was only abbreviated "HCDC". The client register showed that "HCDC" stood for "Happy Care Daycare".

The angel stood guard over the magazine manifesting the light of Heaven. The forces of darkness would not be allowed to approach. This page of the magazine was something that the Father had ordained that Stephen would see. What Stephen did with the information was completely up to him.

Stephen's office hadn't gone unnoticed by Molech's minions. They reported what they saw instantly to their master. Molech was livid. He had hoped for more time since the warning from before. He knew that Jenoch had put a ring of warriors around the little man. That should have been enough.

How could a single angel have gotten through his ranks? Stephen was unclaimed. He shouldn't have needed guarding. Molech raged up and down the length of the room.

He swatted assorted imps and demons aside as he did so. Every so often he grabbed whomever was within reach and screamed.

"How did this little messenger of God get past you?!"

When the whimpered response failed to mollify Molech, he threw the demon away.

One particularly bold demon answered with "He didn't get past me master. I've been on duty across town for you."

That earned him a good beating. Molech slammed the imp alternately from the floor to the wall and back. He screamed something about respect while he foamed at the mouth.

He was the picture of insanity. His minions cringed away from him. They looked imploringly at each other as if one of them had the answer that Molech wanted. Eventually Molech regained control of himself and glanced about the room. Fully a third of those present were beaten beyond recognition. The rest were fairly roughed up. A few would never recover completely from their wounds.

He'd thrown four of the demons he'd attacked from the room. They passed through the roof and sailed more than a mile. They finally came to rest in various places in a nearby playground. A child got off the merry go round. He walked through one of the wounded demons while going to his mother.

Cold chills and a wave of nausea shot through the little boy. He fell to his knees and started vomiting violently. His mother ran to him with worry on her face. She picked up her son and started for her car. She was completely unaware that she was surrounded by wounded demons.

The demon dragged himself over to his fellows. A broken and torn wing dragged limply behind him. Whimpers broke from several mouths or muzzles as they came together to talk. They discussed what they were going to do now. They were all in pretty bad shape. Black ichor wept from several wounds on all of them.

The discussion took an unexpected turn. One severely beaten demon spoke through torn lips.

"If we go back, Molech may decide to banish us rather than let us back in. Our presence would only be a reminder of his temper. He won't allow that in the ranks."

They agreed with his assessment. They would not be going back to Molech. There were rumors that Marduk had plans brewing in the north. After a brief discussion it was agreed that they would seek out Marduk and offer their services to him.

Chapter 38

Molech's memory flashed back to the time of his ruling the land of Canaan. That was the time of his greatest glory. He had been the god of the Ammonite peoples. He held sway over all of the land that would someday be given back to the people of Israel. His will was law during that time. He was held in high favor in the courts of Lucifer.

Lucifer himself had directed him to turn the Nephilim into a ruling body. He became one of the demon princes in Lucifer's court after his death. Life was sweet while he had lived. He'd had many of the powers of his father Semyaza. He had been killed early in the first rebellion. The humans romanticized it. They told the corrupted portions of the story as "The Iliad" or "The Clash of the Titans".

Semyaza was the leader of the watcher angels. He and his two hundred brethren had broken their allegiance to God. Their duty was to observe the human race. They were not to interfere or give aid unless directed to do so. Semyaza was very curious about the human act of reproduction. There were no female angels, so he had no experience for comparison.

A large number of the watcher angels were obsessed with the beauty of the human women under their charge. More than a few of them had expressed interest in experiencing the human act of sex. As a good commander should, Semyaza listened to the council of his officers.

That council had awakened the curiosity in him. His curiosity led to obsession. He started observing the human females exclusively. He no longer had interest in observing the course of humanity as a whole. He watched the females interact with each other. He watched how they interacted with the men. He observed courtship rituals. He began to suspect his dilemma when he began watching humans in the act of love. His obsession had grown unbearable.

Semyaza called a council of his officers. It was well known that they were all obsessed with the human women. They had all danced around the subject of taking power on this world. Semyaza had

246

decided it was time to bring the matter out into the open. They were immortal. If they seized power here, they could theoretically hold it forever.

His captains looked expectantly at him.

"I call you all here to speak of the unspeakable. We have all spoken in whispers of taking power on this world. None here could stand against us. We could rule as we choose. We could have progeny of our own." He'd added the last as a tantalizing remark. He wanted to get the subject of the females in the very front of this talk.

"Everyone here knows that this is a great disobedience. We all know that the punishment will be equally great IF we are defeated. As the leader I say that we will either do this or put it away. The time for a decision is at hand.

"We will not do this if we are divided. I will not drag another into punishment that he hasn't earned. We will decide this day. If we decide no then the matter is settled, and we will not speak of it again, ever."

Semyaza paused for a moment. He wanted everyone present to know that there was the opportunity to say no.

"If we choose to do this however, we will not do it by half measures. We will claim this world and make the race of man into a race of our descendants." The captains all looked back and forth between each other. Semyaza was talking about altering the human race outside of the will of the creator.

None of his captains were aware of the time spent with Lucifer. Semyaza had sought the council of the light bringer on this matter. Lucifer had shown Semyaza a brilliant plan. If the human race was to be redeemed, there had to be a human race. If they succeeded in altering the human race beyond their humanity, redemption would be impossible. The creator would fail, and they would win their prize.

His captains posed the question of how to go about taking power. Semyaza had laid out how it would be done. He neglected to tell them that almost all the plan had come from Lucifer. He didn't want to give up his position as leader. He had answers to every question they had. Every problem had a solution. When all was considered, they had decided to take power.

They all fathered as many children on the human women as they could. Where natural means were unsuccessful they turned to other means. Speed was of paramount importance. They needed to create a race of non-humans that were angelic and human in nature. Some of the beings were very alien due to the nature of the angel acting as the father.

Semyaza had fathered hundreds, possibly thousands of children. A number had been stillborn. A large number were humanoid in form. Those were more powerful than a human but not comparable to an angel. Two of his children had been born showing a great deal of his nature. The eldest of the two was more powerful but not by much. He had named him Zeus. The lesser he had named Molech.

Molech and Zeus had both appeared to be immortal in nature. Molech had been the dutiful son of the two. He was obedient to his father's commands. He had shown respect to his mother until she had passed as an old woman. Zeus had chafed at his father's rule. He was often rebellious until faced with punishment. Then he submitted grudgingly.

Semyaza had set them both up as the heads of their own kingdoms. They were his two most powerful vassal kings. They ruled their kingdoms in autonomy but paid tribute to their father on a yearly basis. The brothers were fierce rivals, but their father thought this a good thing. If they were competing with each other, they had little time for rebellion.

Molech had heard the rumors of Zeus' desire for lordship of this world. He knew his brother to be rash and sometimes erratic. He considered the rumors to be just that, rumors. Their father after all was far more powerful than they. Even together they would have no hope of overthrowing him. So, he had not been prepared when the day of battle came. Molech had lived so long that he hadn't considered that he could be killed.

He had lost his life when the stylized "Zeus" had decided the time for rebellion was at hand. Molech had been caught in his courtyard with only a light guard. It was a surprise attack. They had overwhelmed his guard. At least twenty had seized and subdued him. "Zeus" who had gone by many names before and since approached.

"I see that you were unprepared to defend yourself brother." Zeus purred with a smile. Molech didn't bother answering his brother. Zeus drew the bright blade at his side.

"I am the elder brother. Rule of this world should pass to me. Alas, our father is immortal. As I understand it, he is to be bound. With him out of the way, I need to remove serious contenders to the throne. You alone could challenge me in might. That is unfortunate for you." Zeus stated mournfully.

His face lost its amiable expression. He raised the shining sword and growled, "Any last words dear brother?" For a moment Molech glared into the face of his brother. Then he leaned forward as far as he could and spit at Zeus. The spittle landed short of its target. Zeus looked at the spittle on the ground, then up at his brother.

"I'd thought as much." He'd almost laughed and swung the sword in a broad arc. Molech's head hit the ground and both his body and his head burst into flames. In a moment there was nothing but a pile of ash.

That memory always troubled him. He had been alive. He could feel. Now he was burdened with this half-life. He still retained a good portion of his powers. It had taken years to master them again in this form. Through the ages he'd found priests of Molech who'd served as his willing avatar. It had been better than this life, but it wasn't the same. Now he'd been eons without a willing avatar. Worship of Molech had dwindled after the flood.

Molech was incapable of feeling remorse for any of his actions. He was however rather regretful. What he had done to his subordinates went completely against the directives he had been given by Lucifer. He didn't understand this philosophy of forgiveness and tolerance. Lucifer brought this forward in mimicry of the Father. He also knew that Lucifer didn't brook disobedience.

The problem was that when anger overtook him he had no control. His essence has been corrupted when he had died. He supposed part of the problem for him was lack of belief. He really didn't believe Lucifer was stronger than the Father. In the core of his being he didn't believe that Lucifer had a chance at all against the Father.

Regret showed more than anything else. In times like this he cursed his birth as Nephilim. He hadn't asked to be born. He'd been born because an act of disobedience by his father. He would pay for that disobedience as much as his father would. In those moments he had one thought. *"Where is the justice in this?"*

Chapter 39

The drive home had been a quiet one. Candy was a little tense because Argass was on edge. He felt that something had gone wrong, but he didn't know what it was. He had refined his control over Candy. Over the last few weeks, she had begun to mirror his moods.

This meant she had become more and more erratic. Her parents were getting seriously worried about her. Stephen pulled onto their street. Argass saw the glow in the distance. He'd hoped it wasn't what he thought it was. When the car reached the driveway, it was evident the worst had happened.

The house was aglow with the light of Heaven. Argass leapt from the car and flew screaming to the imp who was waiting outside the house at a distance. Argass tackled the imp and started pummeling him.

"What have you done fool? How did the light of Heaven surround this home? You were left alone for only a few hours and I come back to see your utter failure. The master will have your hide for this. I will see to it!"

This brought the imp out of his fearful stupor. "I didn't allow this you idiot!! Do you think I would invite any of the host of Heaven into this home?! Do you think I don't know that Molech will be furious?! Why do you think I'm sitting so close to this burning light?!

"I'm trying to get as much information for the master as I can offer him. I didn't allow this but I'm trying to salvage as much as I can. I've only been in this home for a few days. You however, have been here for weeks. You've been given special permissions by Molech. You should think of how to solve this with me instead of trying to lay the blame at my feet."

These last remarks caused Argass some true fear. Candy started having some sort of seizure the moment the argument began. She growled every word that was coming out of Argass' mouth. Her voice became raspy and her fingers clawed at the air. Her nails scratched Stephen's face as he tried to cradle her in his arms.

Stephen started yelling for Rachel as he carried Candy into the home. Candy screamed in pain the moment he crossed over the threshold. Her cries were little more than pitiful wails. Rachel came to the living room. She became terrified at the sight of Stephen carrying Candy. Blood was trickling down his face. He hadn't even noticed that he was bleeding.

Rachel's voice was shrill, "What is wrong with Candy?!! Why are you bleeding??" Stephen did a double take at Rachel, "Bleeding? What are you talking about? Candy started having a fit when we pulled into the driveway. I don't know what's going on with her."

Rachel took a deep steadying breath, "Stephen you are bleeding pretty heavily from your cheek. What happened that Candy started acting out?"

Stephen laid Candy on the couch and turned to Rachel, "Get a cold compress for Candy. She must have scratched me when I was carrying her into the house. I will take care of it when you come back. I don't want to leave her alone."

Rachel was frustrated. He had completely ignored her questions. She turned, half-walked and half-ran to the kitchen. Her hands trembled as she opened the drawer to the washcloths. She got one out and ran cold water over it from the sink. She hurried back into the living room. It struck her that Stephen's face was ashen. He was scared for Candy.

This scared her. She knew that Stephen didn't scare easily but this had shaken him. He took the cloth from her and started blotting gently on Candy's forehead.

Rachel prompted. "Honey, you need to check your face in the mirror. If Candy wakes up and sees you bleeding, I don't think that will help her."

Stephen stiffened for a moment. Then his body sagged a little. "You're right, I'm sorry. I'm so scared for her. Rachel, what is wrong with our baby?"

Rachel's eyes brimmed with tears, "I don't know honey. Let me do that while you clean up."

Stephen reluctantly got up and went into the bathroom. He was shocked when he saw himself in the mirror. Rachel had told him he was bleeding, but he wasn't prepared for what he saw. The left side of his face had a large smear of dried blood. There was a thin line of blood trailing down the side of his face and dripping onto his chest. He couldn't believe that his daughter had done this to him.

Stephen turned on the hot water and reached under the sink and got the first aid kit. He made sure to grab a colored washcloth, so the blood wouldn't show so much. He dropped the cloth in the sink and opened the kit. He turned the water off and wrung the cloth out. As he wiped the blood away he saw the long thin scratch that Candy had inflicted on him. It wasn't deep except for the lowest part. If luck favored him, it wouldn't leave a scar at all.

He dabbed at it with the antiseptic. He quietly sucked in his breath with the sudden shock of pain. He was amazed at how much pain flashed through his lower jaw from this little action. He took the antibacterial ointment and applied it to the wound. He left a bandage off of it for a while. He wanted it to get some air.

He heard the doorbell ring and wondered who it could be. He also heard Candy scream. Thankfully it was brief and hopefully the person ringing the doorbell wouldn't have noticed it. He decided it would be best for him to finish cleaning himself up before going out and greeting company. He didn't want someone to walk into the house and see Candy in her current state. He didn't think it was a good idea to answer the door bleeding either.

Mrs. Simmons had been sitting in her living room watching the Grace channel. She felt a powerful urge to go and check on the Beaumont's. She knew that Liz's daughter lived two blocks down. She had only visited there twice before. She was familiar with the Beaumont's since she'd visited Liz every now and again. She'd run into Stephen and Rachel more than once.

She felt a huge sense of urgency. She stood up and hurriedly retrieved her purse. It was an unconscious action. She didn't think she would need her purse. She wasn't completely conscious that she had it with her. She didn't see the angel whispering in her ear to go and go now.

He whispered to her to grab her purse and take it with her. He even prompted her to say a prayer before she left her home. She did all of this without resistance or conscious thought as to why. She knew that she felt prompted to do these things. She was a mature Christian. If she felt prompted she would act without question.

Urges of this nature always seemed to work out for the best. She had trained herself not to question them. She silently prayed all the way over to the Beaumont home. Her hand unconsciously checked her purse. She felt the small bottle of olive oil she kept in it. When her hand touched it she relaxed.

She stepped up to the door and rang the doorbell. She heard the shriek as her hand came away from the doorbell. A pang of fear gripped her. She realized that she'd been brought into this home to do battle. When the shriek ended she bowed her head in prayer. Silently she asked to be a vessel of the Lord. She prayed for the safety of the family.

Rachel opened the door with a frightened expression on her face. Angela Simmons was not quite ready for what came next. She heard a deep raspy voice behind the door scream.

"Get away from this house praying bitch!"

The ferocity of the scream startled her for a second. Rachel gave her a look that was full of confusion and fear.

Angela gathered her courage and held up a hand.

"Please, don't close the door. You and your family need the help that has come here tonight."

Rachel hesitated. She knew that Mrs. Simmons was a church going lady. She also knew that something was going on here that she didn't understand. She stepped back a little and Mrs. Simmons stepped through the door.

It was like stepping through a heavy curtain. She made it over the threshold and the whole room felt deeply oppressed. Gooseflesh erupted across her back. She couldn't believe the difference that one single step made. It was like walking through ice water. She felt the presence of God here. She also felt the undeniable presence of evil and it hated her.

When she stepped into the living room, Stephen came from the hall. It was easy to see that he had been cleaning a wound. In his haste he had forgotten to change his shirt. There was a bloodstain all over the right side of the chest. Candy twisted on the couch and screamed in pain.

"You are not welcome here, whore of God. Leave here and you may go unharmed!"

Stephen started forward. He was going to put a stop to this. Candy was in pain and he wasn't going to let this churchy lady hurt her any more.

He had barely taken a step when he felt Rachel's hand on his arm. He looked her. There were tears streaming down her cheeks.

"Please honey." She begged.

The fight seemed to go out of him. He thought he would watch. If things seemed to be getting dangerous he would put a stop to it.

Angela dug through her purse unconsciously. She took out the little bottle of olive oil.

Candy saw it and hissed. "Is that for my healing old woman?!!!" She laughed maniacally. Mrs. Simmons stepped forward. She was completely unafraid.

"No, this isn't for your healing. This is for the child. You are beyond healing."

Mrs. Simmons stepped forward and opened the bottle of olive oil. She dipped a finger into it and spoke in an authoritative voice.

"Be still!"

Candy seemed to freeze where she lay. Mrs. Simmons leaned

forward and dabbed olive oil on Candy's forehead. Then she gazed directly into Candy's face.

In a commanding voice, "In the name of the savior Jesus Christ, tell me your name." Candy's face sagged for a moment. In a timid voice she answered.

"You know my name. I'm Candy Beaumont." Righteous anger seemed to well up in Angela.

"You are commanded in the name of Jesus Christ to reveal your name. Reveal it NOW!!!"

Candy's face became a mask of rage for a moment then she leaned forward and hissed.

"My name is Argass, old crone. I roamed this earth when men still thought the world was flat. You have no power over me." Candy's face had a maniacal appearance.

Mrs. Simmons face softened. "You are right. I have no power over you. But I don't come here in my own name. I come here in the name of our Lord Jesus Christ. You will leave this child in peace and you will trouble this family no more. This is the will of him who sent me." Mrs. Simmons was calm as she commanded.

She glanced at Rachel and Stephen then turned back to Candy. "Argass, imp of Satan. You are commanded in the name of the Lord Jesus Christ to leave this child alone and never to return. She belongs to her Lord."

"She is mine!!! She is mine!!! She allowed me in." wailed Candy's voice.

"She is a child, protected by her Father. Her suffering here tonight was to reveal the glory of God. Her suffering is the instrument of her parent's salvation."

Upon hearing this Argass screamed a wail of despair. He knew that his punishment would be great. He was being ordered away in the name of the savior. He couldn't disobey. It was as though he had been flung bodily from the house. He rose from the house and saw the Heavens open up.

No less than a hundred angels came down and circled the house. They were all massively powerful. Their swords were drawn. There is no way any of the dark forces were getting into the home while this guard was on duty. It would seem that the Lord planned on bringing these three into the fold soon.

Chapter 40

Candy slept soundly on the couch. She had simply fainted with the exit of Argass. Her appearance showed no signs of what had just taken place. Stephen and Rachel crossed the room to her. Rachel put her hand on her forehead, tears brimmed in her eyes. Stephen stood close with a stony but concerned look on his face.

What in the world had happened in his normal American home?

He had trouble processing what he had seen and heard. It was like something out of a horror movie. Before this little event he had regarded the spirit world with a great deal of skepticism. Now however, he had witnessed it. He would have thought this had to be fake, but the subject had been his daughter. He was shaken down to the core of his being.

Did that mean that all that stuff those television preachers were saying was true? He always thought they were money barons for false faith. They always asked for money. If they were so concerned with the state of a person's "soul" then why was money always the issue? What about caring about people for the sake of caring?

He watched as Rachel stroked Candy's forehead. A feeling of fierce protectiveness came over him. Something of this stuff was real. He had to do whatever he could to protect his family. He turned to Mrs. Simmons.

"Can you please tell me what just happened?"

Mrs. Simmons thought about it for a moment. She knew that Stephen and Rachel weren't practicing Christians. She also knew they had a worldview that followed the secular desires. She decided to tell him the truth instead of putting him off. What he did with the information was his choice.

"Your daughter was being oppressed by a demon. He had somehow attached himself to her. When he manifested himself, I ordered him to leave your family alone in the name of Jesus Christ. He didn't have any choice but to obey. He won't bother you anymore. That doesn't mean your family is completely safe. It is probable that there are others with their eyes on your family." Mrs. Simmons explained.

That last sentence sent an army of chills down Stephen's back.

"Is there any way to guard against this ever happening again?" Stephen asked. Mrs. Simmons was shocked. She hadn't expected such ready acceptance.

"The only way to guard against this is to accept Jesus Christ as your Lord and Savior. This is something that you should investigate. This is not a magical solution. Salvation is found only by true faith in the Lord. It isn't a formula where you do this, and you are safe. Christianity is a day by day walk with your creator." She replied.

Stephen hadn't expected this. He had been exposed to evangelical preaching a few times in his life. Every time he heard it, was a feel-good gospel message. "Come to Jesus and you will have peace." Or "Come to Jesus and you will find your success." He'd seen too many people try Christianity because they were searching for gold at the end of the rainbow.

Stephen stared down at Candy and made a promise to himself. He was going to research Christianity. After what he just saw, he believed Mrs. Simmons had hit on the truth. If there were truth in it then he would lead his family into the Christian faith to protect them.

His mind jumbled with little Christian sayings he thought were useless. Things kept popping into his head like. '*You have a God shaped hole in your heart. Let Jesus fill it.*' And '*When Jesus holds you up then nobody can knock you down.*' Stephen hated being confused and that is what he was.

He looked down. -- *He wasn't quite up to bowing yet* -- and closed his eyes. In a moment he had offered up the first prayer he had ever formed in his life. It was simple.

All he said was, "If this is real then I ask you to lead me." He didn't see Mrs. Simmons bow her head in thanks. When he glanced back up, she was staring directly into his eyes.

"I know this is difficult for you. If you like I have several Bibles at home. I can give you one and recommend some reading if you are interested. I can also answer questions you have after you've read. I don't know everything, but I can answer the basic questions. I can also point you in the right direction if I don't know the answer.

"You need to understand that Christianity is not a blind faith. God invites people to examine the Bible with an open mind and an open heart. The Bible is a collection of sixty-six books written by forty authors over a period of about eighteen hundred years. When you hear people saying things about the Bible being inaccurate, they are usually only repeating what they've heard others say.

"I'll explain all of this later if you like. Right now you don't need to be thrown into the deep end of the pool. Now is the time for mother's milk, not steak."

Stephen didn't quite understand the analogy but was thankful for the offer.

He hesitated for a moment, "I'd appreciate the loan of a Bible if you are sure you don't mind."

Mrs. Simmons gazed at him for a heartbeat, "Young man I will not lend you the word of God. I will give it to you freely as we are commanded." With that statement Mrs. Simmons turned on her heel. She spoke over her shoulder as she walked toward the door.

"I'm going to get your Bible. When Candy wakes up make sure you give her something nutritious to eat and drink. Don't fill her with junk food snacks. She's been through a trauma and her body needs to recover. I'll be right back."

Stephen turned to Rachel who nodded a yes to everything that Mrs. Simmons was saying. Stephen thought, *Okay, she seems to know what she is talking about.* Again, the feeling of utter helplessness swept over him. What could he do? He hated being in unfamiliar territory.

A sudden feeling of determination swept through him. He would do what needed to be done to protect his family. Mrs. Simmons came back with their Bible and a list of passages to read. She advised mostly at first to stick to the four gospels. That would give them a picture of what had been done for them and how to grasp salvation.

Stephen and Rachel had thanked her profusely, but she refused to accept it. Mrs. Simmons told them it wasn't she who had helped them. It was the Lord. She gave Rachel a hug. Before she walked out the door she gave Stephen a soul-searching look.

"I'll be praying for you and your family." With those words she turned and walked out the door.

Stephen found that comforting even though he couldn't tell you why.

Candy stirred with a whimper, "Mommy?"

"I'm right here, baby." Rachel's answered tearfully.

"Mommy, I'm hungry."

Stephen marveled at the fact that Candy didn't seem to remember the last few hours.

Rachel made Candy a sandwich and a bowl of soup. The rest of the night passed uneventfully. The next morning, Stephen went to work. He walked over to his desk and noticed the magazine. He scanned the page it was opened to but didn't notice anything. Something about the page seemed intriguing. He couldn't put a finger on the curious feeling. Stephen dog-eared the page to find it easily again and dropped it into his briefcase.

He made a mental note to read through the magazine tonight after their little Bible session. The rest of his workday was routine. He went home to a family that he looked at differently now. Candy seemed like her old self again. Stephen and Rachel pored over the Bible from Mrs. Simmons.

They had decided to read the Bible together. They took turns reading out loud to each other, each one taking a chapter. If they came to something they didn't understand they wrote down the passage and their question about it. When they had several questions, they called Mrs. Simmons about them.

They were amazed at her knowledge of the Bible. Not once did she hesitate with an answer. She didn't tell them she was pleased with their determination. She didn't want them to become prideful. She was happy to be of help to them. It made her feel that she was serving the Lord.

On Tuesday night Rachel turned to Stephen after they had read the eighth chapter of Matthew.

"That part about the demon possessed man, made me think of what happened with Candy. Did you notice it?" Rachel shuddered, and Stephen put his arm around her.

"Yes honey, that is the first thing I thought of when we hit that passage. Doesn't it strike you as strange that we've never heard a lot of this stuff? We live in the information age and neither of us knew much at all about what was really in the Bible. We need to mention that to Mrs. Simmons."

Rachel responded "Well we could also ask Amelia, I'm getting a little worried that we are starting to be a bother to Mrs. Simmons. I know Amelia knows a lot about the Bible and we have dinner plans with them tomorrow night."

Stephen glanced up quickly, "Oh My Gosh! I had forgotten all about that. Do you still want to go, or do you want to call and ask for a rain check?"

Rachel stared at Stephen incredulously, "Are you kidding? I've been looking forward to this since Candy's ordeal. It seems like something sane that we can do to take our minds off of what happened. It still creeps me out that she has no memory of it."

Stephen thought about it for a second.

"I know what you mean. I don't see how she doesn't remember. I have to say that I'm thankful that she doesn't though. That last outburst scared the life out of me."

Rachel nodded vigorously, "I know. It scared me so badly that I couldn't speak while it was going on. Her voice was what scared me most. It sounded so evil."

Rachel let out a little shudder. "Stephen let's talk about something else. I don't want to keep reliving that."

They spent the rest of the evening in light conversation. They didn't want anything particularly deep to talk about. They wanted to spend time with each other. They had gone through something together that had fundamentally changed their outlook on the entire universe. Now that the shock had worn off. It was time for them to spend a little time with the familiar. They were safe with each other.

Chapter 41

Argass found himself a little more than ninety miles south of the Beaumont home by the time the force that held him slackened. He was sailing over a large forest. The temperature had risen a few degrees and the climate was more arid. He had only been driven away twice before but never had it been this forceful.

The first time he was forced away, his host had been an old confused man with a bad temper. He had been able to attach himself to the man through his temper. He had stayed with the old man attempting to completely possess him. The old one's family had seen the warning signs. They had prayed and asked the church to intervene. In the end his host had given his life to the Lord and Argass knew defeat.

The last time he was attached to an unfaithful husband. The husband had become addicted to sex and constantly cheated on his wife. She on the other hand was a loving Christian woman. Her prayer had driven Argass out of the husband and out of the home. It had been painful, but nothing compared to this time.

Argass became engrossed in his memories. He and his companions had simply waited outside the house until the husband left for work the next day. He was happy and content, but the fool hadn't prayed or done anything to protect himself from them. They leapt on him as soon as he was over the threshold.

Ah, the sweet nectar of reclaiming what was yours from an enemy who gave away so little. They convinced him to skip work and go to a strip bar. By the afternoon, he wallowed in self-pity, lying beside the woman he picked up in the bar. The two demons of despair in the group kept at him and kept him from going home.

It took only one week for them to convince that idiot to take a handful of sleeping pills. Without his wife, he was no challenge at all. They had hoped that with his death they would have an opportunity to move in on the wife. They hoped to exploit her weakness, but that was not to be.

At the funeral and for at least a month afterward, she was always surrounded by Heavenly warriors. They were taking no chances with her. The demons thought they could call to her from a distance. As soon as she heard the tempting cries, she prayed. No less than ten angels attacked the demons.

They were scattered to the winds. Argass was lucky to escape at all. He'd thought himself lucky to only have lost a hand to a Heavenly blade. The hand had grown back. It had taken a few weeks, and Argass remained in hiding. He didn't like hiding, but he was rather adept at it.

He came out of his reverie. He looked around then drifted down to the forest floor. He couldn't afford to stay in the air. He didn't want to be spotted by any of the Heavenly host. For that matter, he didn't want to be found by Molech, either. It would be best to remain in hiding.

He sailed through the trees skimming over the forest floor. He wondered where he should go. It wasn't long before he heard something. He turned in the direction of the noise and saw a blurred, dark form. It wasn't an angel. It was too small to be Molech or one of his lieutenants.

Argass slowed to a crawl and turned in the direction of the shape. He allowed himself to sink even further until he was sliding down into the earth. Only the top of his head was sticking out. As he approached, he saw what looked like a lesser imp. The imp was talking to someone.

"So, Belchar, what do you think we should do now? We've lost our host, and we've been here for a week. We haven't heard anything from Gremlar. I say we head north. I've heard rumors that Marduk has something brewing a little north of here."

Argass heard a grumpy voice answer. He still didn't see the demon that was speaking.

"Idiot!" scoffed the voice. "If Gremlar returns and we are not here, it will be the abyss for us. Do you want to risk that?" Argass slipped around a tree as the speaker came into view.

There was another lesser imp. He didn't see anyone else. This must be Belchar. He had a horn in the center of his forehead. Argass wondered for a moment what this Belchar had done to earn a horn of authority. He may only have one, but that was one more than Argass had.

Argass debated for a moment whether he would contact these two. He needed to learn what he could from them first. He moved a safer distance away and observed the two. He drifted away from the tree. He could feel the earth and the tree roots slipping through his body. That was always a strange sensation.

He let out an involuntary shudder when his head passed through a rotted log. He stopped just past the log and made sure that he had a good vantage point. Argass closed his eyes and concentrated on hearing. He wanted to make sure there weren't any more imps about. He didn't detect the presence of anyone else.

Argass took a moment to consider the imps. The first one was smaller than Argass. The unnamed imp sat restlessly on a fallen log shifting his broad shoulders. The imp reached up with one hand and rubbed at the side of his wickedly curved beak. Argass noticed that this one had the beak of a predatory bird. He snapped the beak nervously as he listened.

Argass turned his attention to Belchar and realized that he was hard to focus on directly. He wasn't invisible. He was right there. When Argass tried to look directly at him, he wanted to glance away. *What is this?* Argass thought.

He remembered tales he'd heard of Lucifer's appearance. *They say you could only see his outline. You can't see his features because light itself won't touch him.* Argass shivered again. This time it had nothing to do with tree roots or earth. He turned his attention back to the other imp.

This Belchar was the one in charge. He spoke in a deep gravelly voice while waving his spindly arms in a spastic manner. The voice coming from the face of an old crone was disconcerting. Argass noticed when he spoke his movements weren't smooth. They were jerky, in time with his voice.

Belchar peered around as though he'd heard something. Argass wondered if they weren't alone. Belchar couldn't have heard him. He hadn't made a sound since drifting into the clearing. The imp let out a hiss and a clicking sound. Then he stared into the forest for a moment.

Belchar turned to his companion. "I know you are impatient. I can understand that. However, I think we should wait for Gremlar. Another week or two won't harm anything. It will show our dedication to orders. How could he get angry at us for showing such dedication?"

The other imp was silent for a moment, "Very well. You are the one with the horn, after all. Tell me this. After this much time, do you think that Gremlar will return?"

Belchar seemed to consider his words before answering. "No, I don't, Galug." Belchar slouched over and sat on the log opposite Galug. "Consider this. I have seen demon lords punish imps who waited at their post for years. We can only wait what we believe a reasonable amount of time.

"After that, we can try to find ourselves another lord. Three weeks of doing nothing is a great sin in the eyes of most demon lords. That is what we were told to do, though." Belchar paused and then repeated, "'Wait here for me. I will make contact and receive instructions. I will return for you.'

"If we wait, we won't appear to be disloyal. That will be a point in our favor. Waiting is the safest thing we can do. Do you remember what Gremlar did to Shorak for leaving his post? I for one do not want to be thrown unceremoniously into the abyss. We will have our time there soon enough."

Galug looked around sharply. "You know you could get punished for saying that! The lords want us to believe we can win."

Belchar stared at Galug for a minute. "Do you believe we can win, Galug? Have you ever seen even one of the Heavenly warriors harmed by our kind? The best we seem to be able to do against them is hold them at bay. We can only do that when we have a large horde built up. How many of our kind have you seen sent to the abyss by an angelic sword?"

Galug stared at Belchar for a moment and turned away. There were some questions that were best left unanswered.

So, thought Argass, these two are waiting for one called Gremlar that they don't believe is going to return. At least they aren't playing the cruel little dominance games that crowds of demons play on each other.

Argass considered. *There seems to be little to fear in revealing myself to these two. I may even find two traveling companions.* Argass began to drift through the earth back in the direction he came. He didn't want them to know that he had been eavesdropping on them. Some things you didn't reveal if you were cautious. He would appear to stumble across them.

When he was far enough away that he barely heard their voices, he rose up from the earth. He turned in their direction and called out.

"Hello? Is there anybody there?" Silence met his ears. They had obviously heard him. He waited a moment and then called, "Hello? Is there anybody out there? Anybody at all…"

It was a few moments before he got a response. It was Belchar who answered.

"Over here. Come forward and identify yourself. No sudden movements mind you." The last words came out with a bit of venom that Argass knew Belchar would back up, so he decided to move forward slowly.

Argass made sure he had grown to his full height. Wanting to be as close to an equal as he could, he concentrated and drifted in the direction of Belchar's voice. Argass floated about a foot and a half off the ground until he came into the clearing and viewed the area. Belchar was sitting on a log staring at Argass with a ragged sneer on his face. Galug was hiding behind a stump regarding Argass with worried eyes.

Belchar glared at him. Inwardly, Belchar was happy that this imp didn't have any horns. He still had rightful claim to leadership.

"Who are you? Where are you coming from and why are you here?" came the questions from Belchar without preamble.

Argass watched the expression on Belchar's face. He had hoped to gauge his response, but no such luck. Belchar wasn't giving anything away emotionally. Argass considered for a moment and then decided on the truth.

He answered, "My name is Argass. I was formerly in the employ of Molech, the demon prince of lord Satan. I was assigned to corrupt a child and, ultimately, her family. I am here because the Heavenly host intervened and saved the family. I was thrown many miles away. I wasn't released from the force that held me until I fell into your forest. I heard you talking to your companion. I followed the sound of your voices, and here I am."

Belchar's eyes grew wide at the influx of information. He regarded appraisingly at Argass.

"I worked in a small task force lent out to Molech once. That one gets crazy mad. You should probably learn to hold back on all of that blatant honesty when telling stories like that."

Argass threw back his head and laughed. He hadn't heard humor from another demon in years. When he regained his breath, he peered at Belchar.

"When my existence is in danger, I tell nothing but the truth to my superiors. I may be an imp, but I'm not a fool."

This time it was Belchar's turn to throw his head back and chortle. After a hearty chuckle, Belchar straightened up.

"It would seem you know your place."

Argass waited a moment, "I don't have any horns. I must know my place or expect discipline."

"That is true. So, what would you have of us here?"

Argass considered for a moment, "I am seeking for my own kind. I can't go back to the region I came from. The prayers of a saint expelled me. Since I can't go back to my own area, I can only search for others of my kind."

"What have we here?" asked a booming voice. Argass, Belchar, and Galug froze where they were. None of them wanted to look around. The voice had carried so much power. The words hit them like a physical blow.

That must be Gremlar. I see why Belchar is so afraid of him. Then he realized that wasn't the case. Neither Belchar nor Galug showed any recognition of that voice. Argass hoped that Belchar would step forward and say something. Nobody moved. *Fearless leader!* Argass thought fiercely, cursing his own terror.

The owner of the voice came into view. He was monstrously huge. This one dwarfed Molech. Argass realized that what he had mistaken for small trees were actually legs. The demon prince stepped toward them on the legs of a huge spider. Glistening black fur played across rippling muscles of a human torso. His attractive human face bore a roguish smile. This being stood taller than some of the trees around him.

The demon prince moved forward. Argass expected to be destroyed where he stood. Laughter filled his head and the rest of his being. Argass didn't understand where the mirth came from. Finally, Argass gathered his courage and glanced up. He saw the smiling face of the demon prince.

Argass' head swam in confusion. What was the smile about? None of this made any sense. If this wasn't Gremlar, then who was it? Argass peered around at Belchar and Galug. Belchar was standing there with absolute terror on his face. Galug was crying. Again, this didn't make sense.

A voice invaded his head. "What are you afraid of, little ones? I am here to give you a purpose. If you would prefer, I could consign you to the abyss." This last remark brought forth a whole new round of laughter inside his head.

270

The fear in his mind was driving him insane. This couldn't be right.

This was a demon prince. He was the largest demon prince that Argass had ever seen. Why was he toying with Argass like this? Then the voice invaded his mind again.

"I am not toying with you. I am seeking servants. Join me. I can offer you protection, for the time being."

Argass terror was overwhelming. The demon lord had invaded his mind without his knowledge. This lord could view his innermost thoughts as though they were written on a wall. Argass surveyed the area and saw that Belchar didn't seem to be afraid. Galug was another story though. He was even more fearful than before.

Without ceremony the demon prince reached out and scooped up Galug. He held Galug aloft for a moment and then turned to his left and stared at a spot in the air. The spot opened up and Argass could see that this demon lord had opened a place into the abyss simply by thinking about it. He tossed Galug into the hole and it winked out of existence as soon as Galug was through it.

The demon lord turned back to Belchar and Argass. He surveyed them for a moment.

"I have no need of cowards. They make things too unpredictable." A huge smile still lingered on his face. "Oh, but I forget myself. Permit me to introduce myself. I am Marduk."

Now Argass knew the terror that had seized Belchar. All of demon-kind knew the name of Marduk. He had been one of Lucifer's favorites years ago. He had fallen out of favor some centuries back. He'd lost control over his dominion in Babylon. His power base had simply withered away over time. A lack of diligence on his part had seen his fall from favor.

He was known to be immensely powerful and unorthodox. The stories made him sound like a wild cowboy. Argass and Belchar were both afraid to move. Neither had answered Marduk and Argass was getting worried that the demon lord would take offense.

"No little one. I understand that you are afraid. I won't punish you for showing fear of me. I'm sure you mean me no insult. I will however, require an answer to my offer. I am offering you my protection in return for your service and your allegiance. If you give me your allegiance, your former lord will have to contend with me if he believes you should be punished. I know it is unusual, but I do know how to reward good service. I don't place blame for things that you have no control over.

I know what you are thinking. Follow this one or be consigned to the abyss. So, I will make you this offer. I want true service from you. If you say no, I will respect your decision and leave you here in peace. If you follow me then I will expect all of your allegiance to be mine. What is your decision?"

Argass considered the words for a moment, "I can't speak for this one, but I for one accept your offer. It has been long and long since I was spoken to with any respect from a lord of our kind. I give you my word that I will serve you to the best of my ability."

Marduk smiled, "Excellent, you will join a group of recruits that I've gained over the last year. They number roughly a thousand. We are massing for some plans I have north of here." Marduk turned his attention to Belchar. "Well horned one? I have your compatriot's allegiance. Do I have yours as well?"

Belchar was silent for a moment, "May I keep my horn my lord?" With that Marduk threw his head back and laughed long and hard.

"Yes, you may. Prove yourself able to handle the squad I will give you. I will double the size of your forces and continue to double them until we find your limit. How does that strike you?"

Belchar's face split in a wide grin. He broke his smile long enough to say, "You have my promise my lord. I will serve you to the best of my ability."

Marduk straightened, smiling. He looked at his two new recruits, "I have a base of operations close by. Follow me." Argass was stunned by the encounter. The rumors that he'd heard of Marduk seemed to be true. It was unusual for a demon lord of Marduk's stature to go around recruiting his own imps. It was rumored that he preferred to hand pick his minions.

Marduk had a spider's scuttling gait. Argass and Belchar tried to keep up by walking at first. When that proved to be next to impossible, they took to the air. They rose to a position in the air slightly behind flanking Marduk. They covered perhaps half a mile before cresting a hill over a valley.

The valley was a hive of actively. There were perhaps a hundred demons flitting back a forth. There seemed to be three large demons coordinating the smaller groups. Demons left a group and disappeared. Other demons appeared and flew toward one of the groups.

"Come along." ordered Marduk.

Chapter 42

The next morning, the Beaumont home was busy. Stephen made sure he had all his paperwork when his eyes fell on the magazine. He took it out and was reviewing the Financials when he saw the Logo for HCDC. He still didn't know what HCDC was, but it somehow seemed familiar.

The angel reached out and touched Stephen forehead. With his other hand, he pointed at the logo. In a voice like thunder he roared, "Remember." As soon as the word was uttered the angel spread his wings and leapt through the ceiling.

Rachel asked if Stephen wanted a cup of coffee. Stephen's attention was drawn to her, and he indicated that he would. He closed the magazine and put it back in his briefcase. Something about this article was gnawing at him and he couldn't figure out what it was. It was starting to become a little maddening. Something in his mind reminded him of the letters from the daycare. "HCDC? HCDC? What the heck is HCDC?"

This thought bubbled away in his brain. He walked into the kitchen and took the cup of coffee that Rachel offered him.

She looked up at him, "Honey, have you noticed the time?" His eyes snapped to the clock on the wall. He was surprised to see that time had gotten away from him. He would have to leave for work in five minutes or he would be late.

This wasn't like him at all. "Thanks honey. I guess I'm a little preoccupied."

Her forehead wrinkled in a questioning expression, "Why?"

He answered with "One of the accounts I've been working with at work is kind of questionable. Something about one of its subsidiaries is odd. I'm supposed to turn in my recommendation today. But hey, we don't have time for this right now. I need to get to work."

Rachel replied, "Okay honey, I will see you when you get home tonight. Remember we are going over to the Carters for dinner."

He smiled, "How could I forget, you've reminded me every hour on the hour since last night. I already know if I cause us to miss this dinner I will be flayed alive."

She smiled back, "And you better remember it buddy."

Stephen leaned down and gave her a kiss, "I've got to run. I'll see you tonight. What is the dress for this evening anyway? I don't want to wear a tie."

She giggled, "No, no tie. This is supposed to be a friendly dinner, nothing formal or fancy."

"I can live with that." He leaned down, stole one more kiss, snatched up his keys and headed out.

The breeze from the closing door made the papers on the island flutter. She walked over to the Island and pulled out the drawer. She reached in and pulled out a manila envelope. She picked up the stack of papers that were on the island. The papers were the letters from the Happy Care Daycare Center. At the top of each letter was the logo "HCDC". She hummed lightly as she put the letters in the envelope to take to the Carter's tonight.

She didn't see Andarel standing inside the doorway. He had used his angelic wind to disturb the papers at the right time to get Rachel's attention. Andarel smiled and leapt into the air. All was coming together. *"Soon,"* he thought *"and the reckoning will come."*

Amelia had just finished cleaning the breakfast dishes. She went about her morning routine and made sure the house was clean. She had a slight pang of guilt and she walked over and picked up the phone. She dialed the number and a few seconds later Roger answered.

"Hey honey." Roger's voice came on the line. Caller ID was such a wonderful thing in today's society.

"Hey honey" was Amelia's answer. She hesitated for a few seconds, "Honey, I know we agreed that we weren't going to tell the Beaumont's about the letters at first. This is really bothering me though.

"I really think we should tell them as soon as we expose that the letters are the same."

There was a silence on the other end of the line for a moment. Amelia was relieved to hear, "You know honey, I was thinking the same thing. I think we should tell them we compared the letters before we called them. Maybe we should do it as soon as they walk in the door. I don't want them to think that we have been deliberately manipulating them."

Amelia felt such a burden lift from her. She had been feeling so guilty. She thought leading this family into giving them what they needed was dishonest. Now she could think of Rachel as a real friend. That made things a lot more worthwhile.

She asked lightly, "What did you want to serve for dinner tonight?" She stifled a giggle when she heard Roger's voice come back on the line in his best AHNOLD impersonation

"Ah you kiddink me? We have to do our best bahbeque for dis family!"

She laughed, "Ok honey. That works for me. I'm glad we are going to be up front with them. Do you want me to do the side dishes?"

There was a short silence on the other end of the line and then she heard, "I tink you already know that the master of the bahheque can't be bahdered with such trivial details as side dishes. I will be producing the magical and masterful ribs of the bahbeque."

Amelia gave in, "Oh, I'm sorry you are so right. I shouldn't have expected such humility from the master of the 'bahbeque'. I don't know what I was thinking... Uhh I mean tinking."

There was a slight pause and then Roger answered back with, "As long as we understand each other." He articulated all of this in a thick Austrian accent.

They exchanged goodbyes and got off the phone. Amelia thought for a moment and decided on potatoes au gratin and homemade coleslaw. That would be a good match for Roger's ribs. She had to admit that he was good at cooking ribs on the grill. She had thought grilling out was a useless male obsession. She almost made fun of him when he'd come home with his brand-new gas grill. He had grilled some steaks for them that melted in her mouth. She had decided to let him have his little male obsession.

It was going to be a few hours before he got home and start the grill. She gathered the ingredients for her side dishes. She put some tea on to brew. She looked in the flatware drawer for a minute or two before she found the potato peeler. She laid it beside the potatoes then went over to her spice rack.

She spent the next hour cutting and chopping. She had the potatoes on the stove when the phone rang.

She picked it up, "Hello?"

Rachel's voice came on the other end of the line, "Hey Amelia, It's me. I was wondering if you wanted us to bring anything with us tonight."

Amelia thought about it for a moment, "Well to tell you the truth I had completely forgotten about dessert. You could bring that if you like."

Rachel offered, "Okay how about my famous homemade chocolate cake from Kroger?"

Amelia laughed, "That will be perfect but I'm kind of shocked to know we use the same recipe. By the way, we are having barbeque ribs, potatoes au gratin and homemade coleslaw. Does that sound okay to you or do you have any particular requests?"

"That is so strange." Rachel noted, "Ribs are Stephen's favorite. Candy adores slaw. Topping it off, potatoes au gratin is my weakness. I love them, but my thighs don't like me to eat them a lot. I don't think you could have planned a better meal."

This came as a slight shock to Amelia. She wondered if the Holy Spirit was buttering up the Beaumont's. A hearty meal is a good preamble to a serious conversation. She really wanted to address the subject of the daycare tonight. Amelia was lost in thought for a moment.

She snapped back to reality, "Well it is going to be great to have company tonight. We don't have company over a lot. My consulting job keeps me busy in my in-home office. A lot of times I lose track of time.

"Roger respects my work, so he doesn't interrupt me. When I'm engrossed in work I'm unaware of the passage of time. There are times when I don't realize it's after eight o'clock. Roger doesn't complain. He just brings me a plate of food and asks if I'm going to be much longer."

Rachel asked, "You are a computer consultant? I didn't realize that's what you did for a living. I thought you were a data entry clerk or something like that."

Amelia let out a little laugh, "To tell the truth it took a bit of a leap of faith to go into this line of work. I had a friend who kept telling me that I could make it as a consultant. I've never been the brave sort though. I don't like to worry where my next meal is coming from. "

Rachel responded, "You know I never asked you what time we should be there. We already have your address. We got it from your son's letter."

Amelia replied, "Brennan is Roger's son from a previous marriage. His mother doesn't have a lot to do with him, so he spends a lot of time here with us"

Amelia smelled something, "Oh My Gosh, my potatoes boiled over. I'm sorry but I need to get off here. You can be here between 6:00 and 6:30."

Rachel answered, "Ok, we will see you then." The phone went dead as Amelia put it back into the cradle.

She didn't see the scaled imp running through the wall to get away. He caused the potatoes to boil over by turning up the stove. He had planned on wreaking havoc on her homemade coleslaw, but he

278

couldn't stand the light of the Holy Spirit. He would be badly blistered for the next couple of days.

Amelia grabbed the oven mitt and lifted the pan from the burner. She turned down the heat and set the pan back down. She was sure she'd set the heat to medium heat after it had started boiling. How had it gotten back on the high setting? Maybe she only thought she had set it to medium. Oh well no one else was in the room, she must have been mistaken.

She wiped the stove top off, soaking up the liquid while being careful of the hot burner. She checked the clock. Roger would be home in about an hour and a half. She wanted her side dishes to be finished before then. That way she'd have time to clean the house a little and talk to Roger while he was grilling the ribs.

She prepared the slaw, being careful of the dressing. Roger didn't like the dressing to overpower the ingredients. She finished making the potatoes and started her cleanup. When she turned to the sink she saw the faucet was running a thin trickle.

She didn't see the imp turn the tap. She shook her head and walked over to the sink. She washed her hands and reached for a fresh towel. There was a crash behind her. The seasoning was on the floor.

She didn't see the little imp diving through the floor to get away from the light. "What in the world is going on here?" she thought. "I know I'm not that clumsy or forgetful in the kitchen. I know I turned that tap off and I didn't put the spices next to the edge of the counter."

She didn't see the angel descending into the kitchen. The room was filled with the reflected glory of God. Tiny cries could be heard from the floor, wall and window. Then all was silent. Amelia didn't see the angel lean forward and whisper

"You are under oppression and attack from the evil one." That bit of business carried out, he ascended back into the ceiling.

Chapter 43

Amelia's eyes went wide. She thought *Oh My Gosh could that be it?* The thought seemed to pop into her head. The spices lay on the floor at her feet. She pushed all other tasks out of her mind for the moment. She didn't want to be tempted to clean the mess. This was more important.

She bowed her head and closed her eyes. She began her prayer as a soft whisper, which grew in strength the longer she prayed.

"Father in Heaven, I don't know if I'm right about this but it seems like this home is under attack and oppression tonight. The enemy doesn't want our two families to get together. I ask that you protect this home and that you protect the Beaumont's until we can be together tonight and share your knowledge with them. As I said, I don't know if I'm right. It is only a suspicion. But I would rather lay it in your hands and be wrong that to ignore it if I'm right. Thank you for your love and your sacrifice. Thank you for listening to my prayer and all of this I say and ask in the name of Jesus Christ, your son. Amen."

Amelia raised her head and a feeling of peace came over her. She thought it was amazing how prayer could help. She cleaned up the mess of the spices. After the floor was spice free she looked around the kitchen for any last minute little things.

Roger walked through the door with Brennan in tow. He carried the large package of ribs that he'd picked up. "I'm home woman, and I brought home the bacon. I don't want to hear no more of that 'I am woman hear me roar' stuff. Got it?"

Amelia narrowed her eyes playfully at him, "Does the man of the house need to be bonked on the head with a rolling pin?"

Rogers face went serious, "Uh, no honey, I was just saying that I'm going to get right to grilling these ribs."

Brennan socked his dad in the arm, "Way to wimp out dad." Amelia giggled, and Roger smiled.

Roger rounded on his son and challenged in a playful voice, "Hey boy, you want some of this?" With that Brennan ran into the living room. "Yeah, that's right you better run. You are lucky I have some cooking to do. I'm the man around here. Honey, hand me my apron."

Amelia went to the cabinet and got out the heavy-duty black apron with "Harley Davidson" across the chest. Well one thing for sure. This wasn't a wimpy apron.

"Stephen and Rachel are going to be here between 6:00 and 6:30 so we need to get to it. Brennan is now drafted into helping me clean up while you grill the ribs, ok?" Amelia asked as she handed the apron to Roger.

"Works for me. He needs to start earning his keep anyway." Roger winked and headed for the patio door. "Brennan" Amelia called. "I need you to come help me."

Brennan's head popped into the archway between the kitchen and the living room. "What's up?"

She explained, "The Beaumont's will be here soon, and I'm almost done with the kitchen. Will you dust the living room while I finish up in here? I'll be in there in a few to vacuum."

"Sure." he replied. He walked to the utility closet and got the duster and walked dutifully back into the living room.

"Well that was easier than I thought." thought Amelia. For the next few minutes she wiped down the countertops. The refrigerator and stove got some attention for good measure. She walked to the utility closet and got the vacuum cleaner. She saw Brennan busily dusting the knickknacks on the entertainment center. In a few minutes they were both done.

She requested, "Would you mind putting the vacuum away as you go? I want to see how your father is doing."

Again, the reply was "Sure" and he pulled the vacuum in tow as he left the room. Amelia walked out onto the patio. Roger flipped the ribs on the grill. The smell of the sauce and the cooking meat drifted over to her and her mouth watered. She was looking forward to this meal and to the fellowship afterward.

She walked over to Roger, "How goes the grill, great hunter?"

"Everything is going fine honey. Did Brennan give you any trouble? I would have told him to do it, but he needs to learn to start taking instructions from you. I hope I didn't leave you hanging on a limb."

Amelia was surprised. She hadn't considered his actions. He was trying to enforce her place in the family in a subtle way. That was sneakier than she would have thought to do it. He'd been there to back her up if it had been needed. Since it hadn't been needed the pecking order was set up.

She answered, "No. He did everything I asked without protest."

"Wow," Roger marveled, "We better watch out. Somebody is going to think we have a well-behaved kid." He stabbed a fork into one of the racks of ribs and turned it in the flame. Some of the sauce dripped into the flame and they heard the sizzle and smelled the delicious smell.

"You know honey, I consider myself really blessed. I have you at my side while we raise Brennan. I know he isn't with us all the time, but we are raising him, not his mother."

Amelia stared at Roger, "I feel the same way." She hugged him and got barbecue sauce on her hand.

"That isn't an apron. That is a bib for you." She stated.

"Yes" he replied, "But a manly bib. "Hey how long before company gets here?"

Amelia checked the clock. She replied, "They should be here anywhere from fifteen minutes to half an hour from now. How are the ribs coming?"

He stabbed another one with his fork, "They will be ready in about ten minutes. I can keep them hot easily enough. I can't leave them on for very much longer though or they will dry out."

Amelia thought about the way circumstances were coming together, "You know, I think they will get here right around fifteen minutes from now." She gave Roger a little knowing smile and then walked back into the house to check table settings.

The doorbell rang precisely fourteen minutes later. Amelia opened the door. The Beaumont family stood on the front porch. Rachel was holding the chocolate cake that she had promised to bring. She had an uncertain smile and an expectant look on her face. Stephen's face was a mask. Candy on the other hand was animated.

Amelia beamed and opened the door wide. "Well, you are welcome here. We are so glad to see all of you."

Stephen's face visibly relaxed at this. He even smiled a little. Rachel seemed to relax and smiled even wider. Candy was hopping on the spot.

Amelia stepped back to allow room for the Beaumont's to enter. She didn't see the crowd of angels that were ringing the house. The Heavenly warriors stood shoulder to shoulder, ringing the house. The Father was providing protection. These families would come together and share a meal without incident or torment.

Rachel, Stephen and Candy stepped inside. Amelia noticed that Stephen was checking his surroundings the entire time. Amelia wondered at this.

Roger walked into the room. He stepped forward and extended his hand with a smile. "I'm Roger, pleased to meet you."

Stephen accepted his hand, "Pleased to meet you too, I'm Stephen."

"Come on in and make yourself comfortable. The ribs will be ready in a few minutes."

Stephen glanced at the patio door, "Would you like some help with the ribs?"

Roger smiled, "No but thank you. They are almost done. I've turned the heat way down. I like to smoke them for a few minutes before serving."

Stephen blinked. "You do that too? Everybody I know thinks I'm crazy for doing that. I give them a little smoke before I pull them off the grill. It doesn't dry them out and it gives them a little tang."

Roger smiled, "Would you like to see my new grill?"

Stephen answered, "Sure."

They both headed for the patio door. Candy bounced slightly at her mother's side. Brennan walked into the room and she gave a little squawk of recognition. "Mommy, I know him. He goes to my school."

Rachel smiled and turned to Amelia "We call the daycare her school. She was much more accepting of school than babysitter or daycare."

Amelia nodded in appreciation, "Isn't it funny? We soften things to make them more palatable."

Brennan stood there for a second, "I know you. You are in the blue group. Your group is doing the out loud chanting. I'm in the turquoise group. Our group is learning to concentrate without chanting to the universe."

Amelia's face slightly blanched at these words. She had walked over to the island and taken the papers out of the manila envelope. The form letter was lying on top. She'd ruffled the papers when she walked from the island.

She asked, "Brennan, what are you talking about? You've never mentioned anything about this before. Are they are teaching you to chant and meditate at the daycare?" Brennan's face was innocent but wary at Amelia's tone.

He looked at her, "Miss Penny said it was something to help us deal with the world around us. She told us it was pretend and that we shouldn't tell people about it unless they asked us."

Amelia's face grew concerned. She turned to Rachel, "Hold on a minute. We need to have our husbands in here for this discussion."

Rachel was taken aback by Amelia's reaction, "I don't understand what you mean."

Amelia hesitated for a second, "I'll explain in a moment, but we need to get to the bottom of this. This could explain some of the things that have been happening around here."

She turned to the patio door and called out, "Roger could you and Stephen, please come here for a moment?" Roger's curious face appeared in the door. Her tone suggested that something was wrong. "What's up honey?"

Chapter 44

Roger stepped into the room closely followed by Stephen. It was evident that he was wondering if they'd worn out their welcome. Nobody saw the angel standing by the island waving at Stephen. Stephen thought he saw a flash of movement at the island. He turned his head toward the island and his eyes fell on the papers on the island.

His eyes seemed to be drawn to the logo on top of the papers. "HCDC"..... He froze in place. He couldn't believe what he was seeing. He had been going insane wondering about that logo and here it was sitting right here in front of him. He turned and walked to the island. Roger walked straight over to Amelia and Rachel.

Stephen saw Candy's name on the paper bearing the logo. Then it clicked. HCDC... Happy Care Daycare.... This was the daycare that they sent Candy to. This company was run and backed by abortionists? This didn't make sense. Why would an abortion chain own daycare centers?

This company touted itself at loving and caring for the future generation. This same company had no problem killing the future generation? How could the execs at this company reconcile this with their consciences? Stephen was so shocked by this. He dimly heard Amelia and Roger's exchange but was so lost in thought that it was just background noise.

Roger walked in and saw the concerned look on Amelia's face. This wasn't good. Something had really brought out her instinct. Roger knew that face. He knew that his best option was to listen to she had to say. He was concerned with what had put her in danger mode.

Amelia's face was rather stern, "Wait till you hear this." She turned to Brennan, "Brennan, I want you to tell your father everything that you just told me."

Brennan seemed to squirm for a moment, "Well, Miss Penny told us we weren't supposed to tell anybody about it. I didn't mean to get anybody into trouble." He had a terrible fear on his face when he finished the sentence.

Amelia's face became softer, "Brennan you did the right thing by telling us this. You didn't do anything wrong and you have nothing to fear. I want you to tell your father what you and Candy told us. I promise you aren't in any trouble."

Brennan relaxed a little, "When Candy came in I recognized her. I looked at her and said, 'I know you. You are in the Blue group.' Her group does the loud chanting to get in touch with the universe. I'm in the turquoise group. We are older, and we are learning to concentrate to get in touch with the universe." Brennan finished his account.

Candy piped up with, "When we first started learning to chant, Miss Penny taught us we were chanting to the funiverse."

Rachel turned to Candy, "The funiverse? Did she actually tell you that?"

"Yes mama." Came her reply.

Roger took all of this in without saying a word. He'd noticed Stephen walking past the group. He'd heard something about Stephen needing to get something out of the car.

Roger turned to Amelia and Rachel, "This is a daycare. Daycares are federally funded, aren't they? Being federally funded, they can't teach any form of religion. This is because the government can't favor any religion over another? Chanting to the universe is a form of New Age or Hinduism and that is definitely a religion."

Amelia offered, "Yes that is why I called you in here. We have the duplicate form letters that they are handing out too. This is starting to look like some kind of sham. I wonder how far this stuff goes."

"Duplicate form letters?" asked Rachel's confused. "What are you talking about?"

Amelia turned to Rachel, "I noticed that the form letter you were supposed to get for Candy was exactly the same as the first letter that Brennan got from them. I was going to show you that today. Candy's letter and Brennan's first letter are lying on the island."

They started toward the island and Amelia felt a small pang of conscience. She wished she'd told them she knew it when she first called. That would have to wait for later if it was needed.

It was then that Stephen called from the door. "You're not going to believe what I have to show you all." He came striding over to them with the financials magazine in his hand. "I was put in charge of a proposal for one of our larger clients. The company is Aurora Financial Unlimited, they own several smaller companies and one of them is a rising star that carries this logo."

Stephen turned the magazine around and showed the group the logo that had been haunting his brain for the last two weeks. He pointed to the form letters on the island, "The name of the company is HCDC or Happy Care Daycare. I've been going crazy over this logo lately and didn't know why. Aurora Financial Unlimited owns Happy Care Daycare."

The group eyed questioningly at him, "Aurora Financial Unlimited makes the bulk of their profits from a huge string of abortion clinics. They own clinics throughout the United States. They are getting money from families either way it goes. If you don't want your child, you can pay them to kill it for you. If you want to keep it, you can pay them to lovingly care for it while you work."

Rachel's face blanched at this. Roger stood there in stunned silence. Amelia glanced from Stephen to Roger. She was at a loss for anything to say. Stephen's gaze went from face to face. "I told you, you wouldn't believe me." He seemed to say. Rogers face took on a resolved appearance.

He stepped forward, "Do you all realize the amount of deception we've found on so many fronts here today?" He waited a moment and when nobody spoke, "Think about it for a moment. A company that owns a string of abortion clinics starts a subsidiary for the purpose of daycare. In marketing that is called hedging your bets. If you can't get them one way, then get them another.

"They made sure to keep the names separated from each other. They gave a logo to the financial magazine. They gave 'HCDC'. That

288

is fairly innocuous. So, it was a pretty safe bet that the finance world wouldn't connect the dots. The heavy hitters in society today are all about money and image. They control the purse strings. This is a free society though. To keep the little people happy, they have to put on a pretty face.

"They kept things that are morally opposed under the same blanket. That is hard to do in today's information age. This was well thought out. You can bet they have an exit strategy for when they are found out. This was a calculated risk to generate income. We are just the ones who found it first.

"When you get right down to it the best we can hope for is a big political stink on the Happy Care Daycare Inc. Aurora Financial Unlimited will blame their lawyers for the acquisition. The daycare is the one that are doing illegal practices. The CEO of Aurora will claim ignorance. All we can really hope to do is raise public awareness. We can expose the daycare for what they are. Other than that, we really can't hurt them."

Amelia, Stephen and Rachel stared at Roger as realization dawned in their eyes.

Amelia voiced, "You can't be serious. Don't you think the moral outrage will count for something? You really think Aurora Financial will come out smelling like a rose?"

Roger waited for a second and looked into Amelia's eyes, "Who is the ruler of this world honey?"

Rachel glanced from Roger to Amelia, "What? I don't understand."

Amelia turned to Rachel, "The Bible says that Satan is the god of this world in 2nd Corinthians chapter 4. Jesus Christ won't be the ruler of this earth until the second coming. That's when he comes back and conquers the foes of God. It will be then that he sets up his kingdom to rule for a thousand years."

Rachel's face showed stark surprise. "I've never even heard of such a thing". She almost cried out.

"That isn't surprising." Amelia offered, "Most people believe that this world only ends during the war of Armageddon. They think that after that all the people will be in Heaven with God. That isn't how the Bible tells it though. Man was made to live on earth, not in Heaven with God."

Roger spoke up with "Ladies, I know this is interesting, but we need to stay on topic. We need to decide how we are going to handle this."

Amelia appeared a little sheepish but smiled at Roger, "Your right. Sorry honey. Do you have any ideas?"

Roger was keenly aware that all eyes were on him. He thought, *Wait a minute, how did I get to be the leader of this chain gang?* He took a deep breath, "First of all we need to make sure that the kids are taken care of. I know they are really hungry by now. We need to offer our thanks, share our meal and then occupy the kids."

He gave a meaningful once-over in Brennan's direction and then stared hard at Amelia.

She got it. "Oh, ok honey." Amelia leaned over and whispered into Rachel's ear. Roger made a show of going out and getting the ribs from the grill. As he turned toward the patio door he saw Rachel whispering in Stephen's ear. An expression of comprehension dawned on his face and then he turned to Roger.

The conversation turned to lighter things during the meal. Roger asked Brennan how his schoolwork was going. Stephen asked Candy if she had learned anything new at school. Rachel asked Candy if she'd made any new friends. At this question Candy became rather animated. She explained she'd met a new little girl name Shan and that they both liked a lot of the same things.

Rachel hadn't heard of Shan before. It turned out that she was a little African American girl whose parents worked in accounting. Candy stated that Shan was sad when she first started coming to 'school' but that now she seemed happy because she had made so many friends.

Candy went on, "She was so quiet when she first showed up but now she screams at everybody. She even yelled at her mother yesterday."

Roger gave Amelia a level look at this. She understood his meaning. When the meal was finished Roger prompted Brennan to show Candy his game system. This was a no-brainer because Brennan didn't care who he played with as long as he got to play on his system.

When Roger suggested it Brennan's face had lit up like a Christmas tree. Brennan politely asked Candy if she'd like to play Nova Fighter 08 with him. She didn't know what that was but was happy to go and play.

When the kids were out of the room Roger spoke up, "Ok, now we can talk freely. I didn't want the kids to hear any of this. We don't know what they might give away. Feel free to jump in with any suggestions.

"I was thinking how we could handle this. If we show up the daycare is going to put on a show. If we confront them with the duplicate letters we will get stonewalled. We will hear 'I didn't have any idea that was going on.'

"What we have to do from this point forward is gather information without their knowledge. I have three wireless pinhole cameras. We could mount them on something small. We could put one on Brennan's shirt at the second or third button. The same could be done for Candy. The last one could go on Brennan's backpack.

"We don't know how effective the backpack camera will be. It would be better to throw out as big a net as we can though. Afterwards we check and see what we get. We shouldn't have to do this for more than a couple of days. We are trying to get their day to day activities.

"The range on the cameras is only a couple of hundred feet. The receiver is going to have to be somewhere close by. Hanging around in the parking lot would seem suspicious. Parking a rental car close by shouldn't raise any red flags though. I can set the receivers to record for 8 hours at a time.

"We have a bit of luck. The kids on are spring break this week. They will spend the whole day all week at the daycare. That gives us a one-week window of opportunity. That is going to give us the best chance of actually getting something.

"I can rent a car tomorrow morning and then park it close to the daycare. I'll have the receiver in the trunk. It will just be a parked car. I'll need somebody to pick me up after I park the car. I'll need help with the picking the car up too. I think the pickup time should vary every day."

At this Amelia spoke up, "Well I can do the drop off, but I have a meeting tomorrow at 4. I don't know how long it is going to take and this client is the kind who needs a ton of hand holding."

Stephen offered, "I can do the afternoon pickup if you can wait until about 4:30. I can cut out a little early from work and come straight there to pick you up. I think I should drop you off about a quarter of a mile away from the daycare though. I don't think they know we've become acquainted. The less information they have on the subject the better."

"Now that's what I'm talking about." Roger stated. "The biggest part of the plan is to make sure we have everything set up. Honey, can you get one of Brennan's shirts? See if he has one with black buttons so the camera will be inconspicuous? We need to see if we can work the camera into the front part without it sticking out like a sore thumb. I was wondering if Candy would like to wear a necklace tomorrow.

"I have one camera set up to look like a pendant but she would need to wear it outside of her shirt. What do you think?" Roger turned to Rachel. She replied, "Candy will wear any jewelry we give her and think she's big stuff while she's doing it. Can the pendant stand up to scrutiny? I know my little girl. She will show the necklace to anybody who has any interest. If it can't take scrutiny, then it won't work."

Roger thought that Rachel showed some foresight. He replied with, "I could hand this thing to you and there is no way you would think it is a camera." Roger was surprised at how simple things were becoming. He'd done a ton of investigations. There was always something that got in the way. Aside from putting a pinhole camera on Brennan, this plan was coming together. Something was bound to mess it up.

Chapter 45

Outside, Heavenly warriors stood in a ring around the house. Beyond the Heavenly light was a huge blob of darkness. The angels knew it was a nest of evil waiting to come crashing down on the families. Some of them wondered what the Father would do about this but none of them worried about it because they knew who they served.

Wicked moans and shrieks came from the darkness. After a long shriek came maniacal laughter. The demons were trying to shake up the angels. They never succeeded with this technique, but they always tried. A huge shape moved inside the darkness and Molech stepped out.

His face was absolutely wicked with hatred. He started to move his lips and saliva dripped from his jaws. He licked his lips in an obscene gesture. Smiling wickedly he spoke. "These humans are mine. I lay claim to them. I will drag them down with me little angels. Your precious Father won't keep all of you on them forever and when your numbers wane then we will strike. We will kill the children first. That will shake their faith in their precious Lord. Three of the humans aren't Christians. They are mine already. They won't give themselves to the Lord once we kill their child."

Molech started to laugh a long loud cackling laugh. It was shrill and meant to be unnerving. One of the largest angels stepped forward from the ring. It was Dayanel. He had been the one chosen to watch over Candy. He held out his hand. A huge glittering silver sword appeared there. He spoke in a low, calm but carrying voice.

"The Lord rebukes you, evil one."

Molech staggered back as though struck and howled in rage. His howl had a wheeze in it that sounded unclean. Molech held out his own hand. A huge red tinged black battle axe appeared in his fist. Green mist began to waft up from its edge. "Come to me little warrior. I will take your head back to my minions to play with. They would appreciate such a play thing."

Dayanel didn't flinch. His face remained impassive. Molech was trying to tempt him into pride. He merely spoke again. "Again, I say, the Lord rebuke you evil one." With that Molech dropped the axe and doubled over. He howled in agony. He threw up a green slime that smoked on the ground.

Four of his larger minions stepped forward to help their master. He lashed out when they touched him. He cuffed two of them aside. The remaining two retreated back in to the darkness. Molech straightened and stood facing the angel. He was so angry that he was foaming at the mouth.

His face contorted, "We will meet in true battle soon heavenly warrior. On that day I will take your head. Once the battle is joined your Father won't protect you." He waved his hand and the axe on the ground disappeared. Molech turned and walked back into the darkness.

Dayanel stood stock-still. *So it has come to this,* thought Dayanel as he watched Molech's form melt back into the darkness. *Here we stand, but surely you know your fate.* Dayanel took up a song of praise. The sound was stunningly beautiful. He sang only a moment before his brethren joined him in praise. The Heavenly light grew with the Father's approval. The cloud of demons began to scatter and dissipate.

Molech shouted. "I'll be back. I will never stop fighting!" The Heavens answered with a booming voice, "Yes you will but it will profit you not." These words hit the demons like a bomb. They scattered like roaches running for cover. Unearthly screams rent the night as the fled the words of the creator.

Back in the house the two families talked calmly. They had no idea of what had occurred. They didn't know that Heavenly warriors had camped around them. They were unaware that demonic forces waited to strike at them.

Dayanel had turned and taken his place back in the ring. The song of praise continued into the night. The Carter home seemed a secure and peaceful place.

Roger asked, "Having any luck with Brennan's shirt honey?"

He was all-thumbs with a needle and thread, but Amelia was a veritable whiz with them. She had learned how to sew from her grandmother as a child.

She glanced up at Roger, "I'm not sure this is going to work honey. Can you disguise this, maybe like a sheriff's badge? Brennan would wear something like that all day if we let him."

Roger thought about it. "I know a guy who specializes in that sort of thing. He is the one who put the one camera in a pendant. I can do it tomorrow but that means we will have to postpone this little shindig for at least one day assuming that he can help me tomorrow when I see him."

Nobody saw the smoking form of the imp dive into the floor and disappear. Nobody saw his charred form rise from the earth a couple of miles away. Molech was there. He had been waiting.

The imp was a sight. He had endured a great deal of pain. That was better than being consigned to Sheol. His fear of failure gave him a desperate strength to endure. He knew he would heal. Burns this bad would scar terribly though. They would be honored battle scars though.

Molech's face split into a wide grin. He listened to the imp's tale with great interest, clenching and unclenching his fists. He heard the families plan to expose the Daycare. The imp had been told to travel underground to get into the house. He was supposed to get a find out what was going on in the house. Molech had provided a distraction.

Molech thanked his little servant and told him to get some rest. The imp peered at Molech expectantly. He dared hesitate only a moment. Then the imp seemed to deflate as he turned to go. "Wait little one. I do not mean to overlook you. I forgot in the heat of the moment, but service of your magnitude deserves a reward."

He stretched out his clawed hand and placed it on the little imp's head.

In a moment the imps form began to swell. He grew about a foot and tiny horns sprouted on his head. His hide grew thick and his claws began to drip a green slime. Molech pulled away and the demon shuddered in ecstasy.

It had been a small empowering, but it had still been an empowering. The little one took off like a shot. He couldn't believe his luck. Not only had he been empowered he had been granted horns. They were small horns, but horns they were. He had been given a bit of leadership.

Molech called his lieutenants. They spoke of the next day's activities. Laughter came out of the darkness. Molech turned to Jenoch, "Take ten of your fighters. Follow the Carter man tomorrow. Learn what you can of their plans. We may not be able to attack him but maybe we can harass his allies. Take your forces and go."

Jenoch hissed, "Yes my lord."

Jenoch let out a low screech and ten large demons appeared out of the darkness.

The largest of the group spoke up, "You called captain?"

"Yes." Jenoch growled, "We get to have some fun torturing a human monkey. Make yourselves ready."

The assembled demons hooted their approval. Two of the demons brought forth wicked looking blades.

They were being given license to harass a human. If the human was protected they couldn't kill it. They could harass it though. They might be able to kill it if it wasn't protected. They would have their fun first though. A long game of cat and mouse would be in order. Jenoch and his demons rose into the air. They began to soar into the direction of the Carter home.

Molech turned to his remaining lieutenants, "Organize another open-air sermon for my pet human. Do it in the parking lot across from the daycare."

Barak spoke up, "I will go to our forces that influence his elders. We will have it organized within a few hours. The pompous old man is easy to control. He knows the owner of the shop with the parking lot. The only issue will be the timing. We should be able to get everything set up by the day after tomorrow."

Molech smiled at this. "Very good, get it done and report to me. I want to know the instant that all is set. Any more ideas of what we can do?" The assembled demons didn't know how to react to this. Most demon lords offered violence at a suggestion. Molech stood before them asking for one.

One of his lesser lieutenants finally spoke up "My lord, perhaps we should send forces back to the Carter home. This would keep the angelic forces focused on them. They might get suspicious if they think we have left them alone. An enemy directly in front of you tends to distract what is going on behind the scenes."

"Good." hissed Molech, "Take all of the forces you need. See that it gets done. I am going to check on my pet. I will influence him for the wonderful 'message' he is going to deliver when the sermon is set." With that the band of demons separated. Most of them flew in different directions. Molech simply disappeared.

Chapter 46

Eddie lay on his bed and watched television. It had been a bland day. His prayers seemed to be jumbled together. He wasn't receiving any revelations for his next message. He wasn't worried about it though. The next open-air session wasn't until next Saturday. There was plenty of time.

He was confident that the next message would be 'given' to him long before the time came. This particular moment was a rare opportunity to kick back and relax. 'The worker is worth his wages' Eddie thought. Everybody needs to take time to relax. 'And on the seventh day the Lord rested from his labors'

The church that he preached for might find his choice of television programs interesting. He was watching an action adventure movie that showed a lot of skin. He thought of himself as no longer married. In his mind he wasn't being unfaithful to a wife who had passed on.

Eddie didn't see Molech appear right beside the television. The room went rather cool and the television went off. Eddie looked around the room. He felt a presence. He thought that this might be some sort of demonic attack. He slid from the bed and landed on his knees. He started praying.

"Father I come before you as one of your servants. You have blessed me so much with money and a flock to care for. I call upon you for your protection this night. I rebuke any demon near me at this time."

Molech grinned. He knew that this little preacher had succumbed to the sin of pride. He had indeed rebuked Molech, but he had done it by his own name. He hadn't done it in the name of Jesus Christ.

Molech manifested a shrill scream that seemed to trail away. That would fool this idiot into thinking he was winning a spiritual battle.

Eddie's eyes went wide. He thought, "*I did it. I rebuked a demon and it had to leave.* The Bible says we will have the power to cast out demons and I just did. I never dreamed I would be battling the forces of darkness for real."

Molech assumed a beautiful angelic form. He had used this form every time he spoke to Eddie. The room filled with an unearthly light. Eddie saw the light and was filled with a form of ecstasy. He believed that the Lord had smiled upon his prayer.

Molech stepped over to Eddie and placed his hand on Eddie's shoulder. "Hail favored man of god. You are much loved by your lord. The evil one sent his messenger to block my path. Your prayer made him leave." Eddie shuddered when the words entered his mind. He felt so honored and small at the words. He couldn't speak. He felt unworthy to speak so he listened.

Molech spoke in a syrupy tone. "I have need that you deliver a message tomorrow. Your elder will contact you. I have placed in his heart an urge for my children. The way will be made clear for you. You will deliver my word to those that have need of it tomorrow."

Eddie hesitated for a moment. "What shall I say Lord?"

Molech answered "I prosper those who call upon me in my name and leave those alone that have no need of my son's name. Give this word to my children. A sign will follow you for proof. You are my mouthpiece. Your worth will be proven to unbelievers tomorrow."

The phone rang, and Eddie went to pick it up. "Hello?" He expected it to be Mr. Edwards. It was.

"Hello there, young man. I hope this night finds you well. I was talking to a friend of mine a little while ago. He owns that little strip mall in the middle of town. You know the one across from that new daycare center?"

"Well hello Mr. Edwards. Yes, tonight turning into a fine night what can I do for you?" Eddie managed to keep the surprise out of his voice, but only barely. He had been told about the call but was still shocked that it actually happened.

Mr. Edwards boomed. "Right to the point, I like that. My friend said it would be ok for you to do an open-air sermon day after tomorrow in his parking lot. I was trying to get it set up for tomorrow, but he has a few friends in town that he would like to hear the gospel of Jesus Christ without it looking contrived. It is late now so we really can't expect you to come up with a great message on such short notice. But you will have all day tomorrow to put something together."

Eddie didn't care for sneaking up on someone with the gospel. He had already received his instructions though. "That will be fine sir. Are the details of the tent and the chairs set up already or would you like me to make some calls?" Eddie asked.

Mr. Edwards replied, "No young man, you need to work on your message. I'm taking care of everything. We will even be offering a light lunch right after the service, to the crowd that gathers. What better way to get people to listen than to feed them?"

"You know," Eddie remarked, "That is true. One of the most well-known miracles of Jesus was the one where he fed five thousand with five loaves and two fish."

Mr. Edwards gave a chuckle and a hum of agreement. "Right you are young man. You keep that in mind while you are preparing your message. I will see you morning after tomorrow. Your message is set to start at ten-thirty. A local caterer is setting up a meal for eleven-thirty. Everyone will have a choice of pork or chicken. You will have an hour for your message. Make sure to offer an invitation to the meal at the end.

"Don't take up an offering. This whole thing is for the benefit of some friends of mine. They are suspicious of the Christian faith. They think that the church only wants their money. If they see an offering plate they will focus on that and not your message. I want them to get a good dose of the gospel.

"Don't worry about the cost. It has been taken care of. Please point out that we aren't taking up an offering. Stress to them that the Lord has already provided. Try to do your best to make them feel as welcome as you can."

Eddie took all of this in and thanked Mr. Edwards. He hung up the phone and started wandering, lost in thought, to the kitchen table. He decided that his sermon would have to be about the Lord's provision. He sat down and starting jotting down notes.

He was trying to work in his earlier revelation. He wrote down 'Call upon the Lord' and 'God can't violate his own character'. He started to write 'God must answer your prayer' when he hesitated. This bothered him, but he kept writing. There was a small voice in the back of his head saying that this wasn't the true gospel. God is sovereign, and it is his choice to say yes to prayers. Eddie thought of his revelation and shoved the voice away.

That little voice nagged at him. When he allowed himself to pay attention to it, it distracted him. He couldn't focus on the message that he was supposed to get ready. He thought of that still small voice as his enemy. He did his best to ignore it.

He worked in how he had claimed the lottery ticket in the name of Jesus. He wrote down how if you claim something in the name of Jesus then the nature of God has to grant your prayer because God doesn't let his name disappoint those with real faith.

Eddie wondered what the sign would be during the sermon. Would he to be given a clue so he could preach with real confidence? Eddie bowed his and prayed silently to himself. "May I know something of what will happen tomorrow? Will you only reveal it when the time comes?"

Molech was still in the room. He was so excited he was salivating. He reached out and touched Eddie's shoulder. In a soft voice that sounded loving he crooned, "Faith child, have faith, a healing will come tomorrow. Through you one of my children will walk for the first time."

Eddie became ecstatic at these words. He never dreamed he would be used in such a miracle. He felt so humbled. Thoughts of the nagging little voice were completely banished from his mind. He wondered how it would happen. If people who didn't believe the gospel saw this happen then there was no way they wouldn't believe in the power of God.

Eddie sat at his kitchen table with his head bowed. He appeared to be in prayer but he wasn't. He was lost in a fantasy of how he was going to be the one channeling God's power to heal. They would all see him. If he were lucky some of his old associates from his former church would be there.

They would know they had let him go at the wrong time. He was thinking of famous preachers of the day. He couldn't name one that had presided over an honest to goodness healing. He knew there were charlatans out there. He considered himself 'The real deal'.

"Yup," Eddie thought. *"I've got it covered."*

Molech smiled. This puppet was coming along nicely. Molech wondered how long it would be before Eddie considered himself above speaking to the people after his sermons. Sooner or later he would ask for an assistant to help him weed out the sincere. That at least would be his excuse

The next morning dawned crisp and clear. Eddie woke up still at the kitchen table. He had been at the table thinking about the day of the sermon. He had written down notes, but a lot of his time was spent thinking of how fortunate he was to be a preacher. He had also thought the Lord was lucky to have him on the team. He had spent a good while wallowing in his own pride.

It had been his faith that had won him his lottery winnings. It had been his dedication to the Lord that had enabled him to become a preacher. It had been his faith that had caused him to speak out at the lottery office. He didn't consider divine providence.

He moved about groggily and saw that the kitchen clock showed eight-ten AM. He still had the whole day to put his sermon together. He had to work these kinks out of his neck and back. He was still a young man. A sedentary lifestyle had let him get out of shape.

Drinking alcohol hadn't done his health any favors. His complexion was pasty most of the time. His congregation simply thought it was from worry. They believed he suffered long nights of prayer and fasting on their behalf. They were dedicated to him for this.

He shuffled into the bathroom and got his trusty toothbrush. He brushed his teeth vigorously. He didn't see the imp jump from the sink to the floor. There were four imps jumping around the bathroom. They couldn't attach themselves to Eddie, but they could get awfully close. They didn't have Molech's strength, but they could endure a fleeting touch if Eddie was distracted.

Molech had called them deep into the night. He had told them to watch over his human pet. They were to ensure that he got to work on the sermon without any incident from the Heavenly host. They were instructed to call Molech the instant something threatened their mission.

Molech was meeting with one of his lieutenants to set up the 'healing' tomorrow. They capered about Eddie's legs with little to do. Eddie's mind was on himself and his future. He was becoming a self-important individual.

Eddie looked around his tiny apartment and shook his head. The thought popped into his head, *"Don't I deserve a better place than this to live? I'm the Lord's messenger. The Lord surely has something better than this in store for me. When the healing happens today the congregation is going to grow. When that happens, I think I'm going to ask for more of a salary than this 'Take care of my basic needs place'."*

Eddie smiled to himself. Yes, things were certainly coming together for him. He and the Lord were going to do big things together. Eddie picked up his electric razor and started shaving. Today was going to be a good day.

Eddie shaved and stepped into the shower. He took his time and made sure that he was squeaky clean when he got out. He dried with his favorite towel. It had the Ten Commandments embroidered into it. It had been a gift from a member of his congregation.

He always felt like he was cleaner when he used that towel. He finished his cleanup ritual with putting on his favorite jeans and a t-shirt that advertised, "Ask me how to get to Heaven" on the front. He put on his socks and hunted around the room for his tennis shoes.

It took a few minutes for him to remember that they were in the living room beside the couch. He stepped out of his bedroom in his stocking feet and padded into the living room to find his shoes exactly where he remembered. He sat down on the couch and put his shoes on.

He was suddenly struck at how hungry he was. He usually didn't eat in the morning, but a hearty bacon and egg breakfast really sounded good. He had couple of twenties in his wallet that weren't earmarked for bills, so he thought he would indulge himself at the Waffle House down the street while he worked on his notes.

He grabbed his watch off the coffee table and put it on. Then he went through the ritual of filling his pockets with his spare change, his keys and the breath mints that he was always in the habit of carrying since he had started drinking. He hopped up off the couch and picked up his notebook. Eddie headed out the door with his unseen honor guard of imps.

They were starting to get nervous. They had watched Eddie for Molech before and they knew he was stepping out of the norm for his behavior. They were hoping desperately that it wasn't the work of the Holy Spirit, bringing this one back to the cross. Molech would blame them for that.

Roger had driven to his office and search through his address book. He was looking for John Sterns. He and John hadn't spoken in a couple of months, but they had always been on amiable terms. John was an accountant, but he was also into surveillance in a big way.

He was like Einstein when it came to small electronics. He could make anything small appear unobtrusive. Some of the things that he came up with astounded Roger. The guy had creativity that was beyond Roger.

He had shown Roger a baby's pacifier that was completely unremarkable. The thing had been an audio recorder and video camera with a range of a quarter mile. The camera had been incorporated into the base under the nipple. It would have been something that would be easy to leave lying around without arousing suspicion. That is of course if you had a small child.

Roger was wondering what John had come up with lately. He found John's number and picked up the phone. He dialed the number and waited. He let it ring ten times like you were supposed to before hanging up. This was strange. It hadn't gone to an answering machine. John hadn't picked up either. Maybe the phone lines were messed up. He would try again later.

His stomach growled, and he realized he hadn't eaten. The Waffle House that he had passed on the way to the office came to mind. He had frequented there since they had opened. Admittedly he hadn't been there in a while. He was watching his weight.

He also watched how much money he spent on incidentals. Amelia had shown him how much money was being spent on meals out. It had come up when they'd balanced the check book a couple of months ago. He had dutifully stayed away from fast food since then.

He didn't like the thought that he was going to be a drain on their finances because he wanted to indulge his appetite. Today however was different. He hadn't been there in a while. Spending a little money on his breakfast once in a while wasn't a bad thing.

He went back downstairs and got in the car. He made the one-mile drive to the restaurant. He parked the car and started walking to the door. He saw Jan through the window. Jan was an older woman who had been waiting tables all her life. She'd lived through two dead-beat husbands and raised three children on her own on a waitress's pay.

She came to this Waffle house when it opened. She was a soft spoken, helpful lady. She generally made more in tips than any of the other girls. Her customers could tell she was genuinely concerned about whether or not she gave them good service. She was the type of person who would refuse a tip if she thought she didn't deserve it.

Roger saw her waiting on a young man that seemed familiar. Roger thought that he'd seen the young man before, but he didn't know where. He opened the door and held it for an elderly couple coming out.

The gentleman offered, "Why thank you young man."

Roger smiled, "You are entirely welcome sir."

Nobody saw the showdown that was getting ready to start. Roger had three large angels with him. They were walking close to Roger. The imps jumping back and forth from the table to the seat in the booth where Eddie was sitting saw the angels and started screaming.

The largest one with the horns turned to one of his fellows. "We will try to keep them apart. Go tell lord Molech what has happened. Three large angels from the Heavenly host are here and we are only three imps to hold them at bay. We need help as soon as he can send it or get here." The little imps nodded his assent and zipped away at incredible speed.

Chapter 47

The patrons in the restaurant started getting nervous. None of them could have told you why. Roger walked through the door and the angels followed him. The imps screamed bloody murder at the angels. Andarel was the lead angel in the group.

He turned to the imps, "What is the problem little one?" The imps recoiled then started screaming again. The one with the horns held out his hand and a short red sword appeared there.

"You will keep your distance from our charge angel!" He snarled.

"Or what? Will you scratch me to death with your little letter opener?" Andarel sneered with a mirthless smile.

The imp took the insult in stride, "We will not be alone for long heavenly warrior. My lord is on his way and you and your human charge will leave this place."

Andarel glared at the imp. It astonished him that the demons believed they could overcome the Father. Andarel looked back at his two angelic comrades. Their faces were impassive. Andarel turned back to the imp, "The Lord rebuke you."

Those words hit the imps like a sledgehammer. They staggered back, and the leader fell off of the table. This was usually enough drive imps away. These imps however, knew that if they failed in their assigned task they would be consigned to Sheol. They knew their ultimate fate was to be consigned to the lake of fire. They wanted very much to delay that fate.

The leader jumped back onto the table. He let out a hiss and leapt at the angels. His small sword flashed. He aimed for blood. The angelic light blistered him but still he came. Andarel was caught off guard and hadn't drawn his sword. He hadn't even assumed a defensive posture.

The demon landed on Andarel. The imp screamed and jumped away. The tiny demon had scored a hit on Andarel's arm. A sensation of pain shot down his arm. The other two imps had recovered their wits. They ran at the three angels, screaming loudly.

Andarel felt a blade slash across his calf as a tiny imp screamed his war cry. The other two angels were taken off guard as well. Andarel threw up his hand and called his sword into existence. He brought it up in time to stop the imp's small sword from reaching his throat. A quick look back and Andarel saw that his two companions had produced their blades as well.

The lead imp pressed hard at Andarel. He decided it would be best to allow the lead imp to back him through the wall. That would lead them away from the people in the restaurant. A demonic blade passing through a human's chest could cause a fatal heart attack. Andarel didn't want any of the people in the restaurant hurt.

He called out to his companions as he backed through the wall. "Take the fight outside." They all cleared the wall. The fight was going badly for the angels. These imps had used surprise to their advantage. One other of Andarel's companions was wounded.

Andarel's wounds were superficial. His companion's wound wasn't. The angel had a long deep belly wound. Silver liquid stained the front of his tunic. He was pale, and his sword moved more slowly in his defense.

Andarel became angry at the sight. He redoubled his attack. He threw off the leader with a vicious sweep of his blade. The little leader lost the lower two-thirds of his arm to Andarel's sword. He fell away screaming, bleeding black blood.

Andarel did a leaping back flip and landed in front of his injured comrade. He brought his sword up in a sweeping arc.

He caught the demons blade on his and screamed, "THE LORD REBUKE YOU!!!!"

The demon screamed and backed away. He threw up black bile and hissed. "The master comes." The words rang in Andarel's ear. Darkness spread throughout the area. Andarel knew that the demon lord had arrived. He looked back at his injured comrade. His comrade was praying. The wound started healing. The wound had closed, and the front of his tunic was clean again. There wasn't a trace of angelic blood on it.

Andarel uttered a quick prayer of thanks and turned back toward the darkness. Molech stood there with seven demons as large as himself. Molech laughed. Andarel felt his wounds close as the Father answered his prayer. He was wondering how they were going to overcome this.

"Father, we need your help in this." Andarel knew that his prayer had been heard and answered. He felt the surge of Heavenly light first. Then he saw it. He knew something, or someone was on the way.

Thunder rumbled through the air. Then the sound of a trumpet split the air. Andarel thought "NO WAY!!!" The correct response to that would have been WAY!!! Andarel saw Molech and his cronies lose their smiles. The very air itself crackled with energy when suddenly an angelic form stepped out of eternity.

Andarel couldn't believe his eyes. He had never personally seen Michael the archangel away from the throne of Heaven but here he was. Michael, God's warrior angel was here to help them. Michael stepped into a place between the demons and his smaller brethren.

The sight of this archangel was beyond belief. He stood on the order of over thirty feet tall. His proportions were that of the perfect muscular man. His face was bronze. A perpetual corona of lightning buzzed around his head. His garments appeared to be purest silver sewn with gold thread.

Michael's garments seemed delicate. There was nothing soft or weak about him. He was an awesome sight. Any demon that challenged him had to be insane. Michael turned to the assembled demons. His deep booming voice echoed through the air.

"THE LORD REBUKES YOU DEMON LORD!"

The demons screamed in pain. Molech stayed standing by dint of will. He hissed at Michael and held out his hand. His large axe appeared there. "You will not go near my human angel. You will stay back and away from him or we will all attack en masse!"

Michael had a smile on his face as he replied, "Do you think I fear such as you? The Father had me strike Lucifer from the Heavens. What threat can you offer me?" This comment caused Molech's minions to stare at their master. Fear was evident on their faces and in their postures.

Molech seemed to gather his courage. "Be that as it may Archangel, we will not leave our charge here. Neither will we allow you or your company into the restaurant." The demon beside Molech let out a crazed scream and leapt forward. His sword was held high.

Michael reacted so swiftly it was invisible. His sword appeared in his hand while his hand was in motion. The crazed demon got within five feet of the archangel and then suddenly he was cut in half. The sword in Michael's hand crackled with lightning along its length. The two halves of the demon went spiraling away. Trails of black smoke rose from the halves.

Michael brought the sword up again. The point was aimed at the assembled demons. "Are there any more among you that would care to challenge the will of the Father?" Molech was visibly shaken. He seemed to realize that the eyes of his minions were upon him.

Molech knew his leadership was in danger. He thought, *"Nothing risked, nothing gained."* He stepped forward with his axe held at the ready. "My minion acted foolishly. He alone has paid the price. Still, I say to you, you will not enter the restaurant. The preacher is mine and you will not have him."

Michael threw his head back and laughed. "You do not understand lord of demons that all things belong to him who created them. You claim what you did not create."

Molech became furious. He stepped forward another step, "I lay claim to those who have given themselves to me angel! Who are you to contest that? Many are those who have paid heed to their own wills over that of your master. Yet you claim that those who have turned from your path and have given themselves fully to me are not mine? Whose then are they angel?"

Michael stood there quietly for a moment, "They are their own. Go where ye list has always been the will of the Father. It was his hope that love would win out for all. Just because they have followed your path, does not make them yours. You will be beside them suffering in the lake of fire. Your punishment will yet be worse than theirs. They at least didn't actively try to corrupt as many as they could before their fate came upon them." This last part Michael stated a little sadly.

Molech roared, "My name is Molech. I was worshipped by many of these monkeys when time was young. I say that someday you will bow knee to me and my lord. I say we are ascended above you and your ilk. I am Molech and aside from my lord I will not be challenged. Again, I say, I will not allow you or your kind in this restaurant. The human is mine."

Michael answered, "The same applies to you and yours. None of you may enter the restaurant. Our charge is there as well. If nothing else, we leave them to each other. When they part company, then they part company. Anything other than that draws us into battle with you. I will not set aside the task I have been given."

Molech did not like this. He knew that he and his minions had no chance against Michael. This reality left Molech with few options. He decided that he would use the current situation and bluster to his advantage. "Very well angel." Molech growled with a sneer in his voice. "If you and yours do not enter, neither will we. Our charges will exit on their own and from there we will take them." Molech spoke all of this with authority.

He did not want to cross blades with the one who had thrown his lord from the Heavens.

Michael seemed to consider his words for a moment and answered. "If your words are true, my task is to abide by your request. If you are false, then I am to take your head."

Molech nodded at this and turned to his assembled demons. "Encircle the restaurant. Call to me if any of the Heavenly host tries to enter. Do NOTHING without my express orders. You saw what happened to your brother. I don't want to lose any more demons here than I have to."

Some of his demon host gave words of assent. The rest simply nodded and then left to encircle the restaurant. He would watch the ones that only gave him a nod. That was three of seven. He would probably have to find more suitable lieutenants in the near future.

Chapter 48

Roger walked into the restaurant after holding the door for the elderly couple. He felt a chill and thought it was due to the air conditioning. The place was almost full. There was only one small booth open. The waitress was almost finished cleaning.

He wasn't sure he wanted to wait. This was only breakfast after all. He was about to turn around when he caught sight of Jan. She looked up from cleaning the table.

"Well Howdy stranger. We haven't seen you around here in a while. Have you found another breakfast spot that you like better?" All of this was offered in a joking tone. It was enough to lower the tension that he felt.

His attitude softened, "No, Jan. I've been trying to watch my weight. I've been having a time with it since I crossed the 'over-thirty' barrier."

Jan laughed, "Don't I know it? I was there while you were still in high school. So, would you like to sit down and have a meal with us today or are you slumming?"

Now Roger felt welcomed. He replied, "I'm here for a meal. Do you remember my usual?"

Jan smiled at him, "What do you think? 'Two eggs over easy, three slices of bacon (crispy), one piece of toast with grape jelly on the side and a large orange juice.' Did I miss anything?"

Roger laughed, "No, you nailed it. Sometimes Jan, you are amazing."

Jan waived him to the now clean booth. "What do you mean sometimes? I'll never win your heart this way." She playfully lamented. "How is Amelia and when are you going to bring that boy of yours in again?"

Roger felt comfortable, "Amelia is fine. I'll try to bring them both in really soon." He slid into the booth and absently picked up a menu. He realized that his order had already been placed. Sheepishly he put the menu in the stack behind the napkin holder. He was fiddling absently with the condiments when he glanced up and saw a young man staring at him.

This guy seemed familiar. Where had he seen this guy before? Roger faced that moment when you either say something or break eye contact. He decided he would say something completely inoffensive. "Man, it is crowded in here today. Isn't it?" He hadn't meant to make it a question. It came as an afterthought and obligated the man to answer.

The young man seemed to think for a moment and then answered. "Yes, this is a particularly busy day around here. The usual crowd seems to have been joined by quite a few more. Where they've come from I don't know." Eddie finished his sentence with a smile and then noticed one of the patrons at the bar slumping a little on his stool.

No one had seen the demons arm go flying when Andarel had struck with his sword. No one had seen the arm pass silently through the restaurant patron. The patron had gotten sick suddenly. He had come in with a good appetite but now he was sick?

He'd been driving all night and was looking forward to a meal that was prepared in front of him. He didn't want anything special, just something that was made to his order. He'd placed his order and received it promptly. He'd thought that it was going to be a good night. The first few bites were delicious. They were everything that he expected.

Then suddenly the mood in the restaurant changed. He couldn't have told you why. Everything was different. He didn't see the demonic arm spiraling through the air. It had an effect when it passed through his body though. He'd just taken a bite of eggs. A horrible wave of nausea struck him.

He didn't think he would make it to the bathroom. He had jumped off the stool and ran to the men's room. Thankfully, nobody was in there. He had gained the room with no problem. He knelt in front of the public toilet and did his business. He had no idea what had made him sick.

The manager knocked on the door "Hey buddy, are you Okay?" He heard the question but was unable to form a response. "Do you need me to call you an ambulance?"

The completely idiotic thought of "Sure, Call me an ambulance. I'm Mister Ambulance." ran through his head before he answered. "No, I'll be fine. I need a moment."

Silence met his answer for a moment and then he heard. "Okay, if you change your mind, let me know."

The manager went back around to the front and took stock of the restaurant. The mood had definitely changed, and he was at a loss to understand why. Oh well that was a worry for another time. He had to do what he could to put the crowd at ease.

He didn't want to lose business because somebody came in sick. He searched for signs of worry or unease. The best business was repeat business. He walked around the room and checked on the other patrons.

In his search his gaze passed over two men in adjoining booths. They seemed to be talking haltingly to each other. He recognized Roger as a sometimes customer. He didn't want to interrupt the conversation. He decided not to bother them.

Jan brought Rogers order. He dove in with reckless abandon. He didn't know why but the food smelled especially appetizing today. He tried his eggs. They made him glad that he'd come in today. He hadn't had a good full breakfast since he started watching his weight and the budget.

He took a piece of bacon and glanced up to see Jan smiling at him. "It does my heart good to see a man enjoying his food." She smiled and turned away.

Roger was about to go back to his food when he noticed Eddie. He was holding a piece of paper that he absently raised from his stack. Roger saw the scrawl, "John 3:16" at the top of the page.

He didn't know what prompted him to ask. The words were out before he thought it was rude to ask. "Are you working on a Bible study?"

Eddie turned and saw his raised hand. He put his hand down a little sheepishly.

"No, I'm working on a sermon for tomorrow. I'm preaching an open-air sermon at that little strip mall across from that new Daycare center. Do you know the place?"

Realization hit Roger like a sledgehammer. He remembered where he'd seen this young man before. He'd been the one preaching when He and Amelia had stopped to listen. He remembered well that he didn't agree with the content of the sermon. He thought about challenging the young man on this. Then he remembered that Jesus didn't beat anybody over the head with a Bible on his way to Calvary.

Roger stopped himself from saying something challenging, "Yeah, I know the place. My son goes to that Daycare."

Eddie smiled at him, "Well if you have time tomorrow stop by and listen to the sermon. We will be serving a meal right after. You are more than welcome to attend."

Roger was shocked at how genuine this young man seemed. He was noticeably Roger's junior, but he seemed streetwise. He stared at Eddie for a moment. *How could someone of his obvious intelligence have been ensnared by a false gospel?* He was going to blow off the open-air sermon. A nagging feeling prompted him to think about it.

If nothing else this was an opportunity to learn something. He may not be able to do anything for Eddie. He could at least become familiar with the delivery of the message. If it wasn't false, then all the better but if it was then he was curious to see how it would be packaged.

"I appreciate the offer. What time is the sermon?" Roger asked.

Eddie seemed to swell a little at the question. "The sermon will start at ten-thirty. We should be serving the meal shortly after eleven-thirty. You don't want to keep hungry people waiting for the truth or for food." Eddie chuckled at his own joke.

He noticed that Roger hadn't laughed. He wondered about this man who was asking questions about his notes. Roger looked steadily at Eddie, "Ten-thirty, you say? I might be able to make that. Not like I have anything better to do for the day. Business has been slow for the last week."

Eddie perked up at this, "Really? What do you do for a living, if you don't mind me asking?"

Roger answered, "I'm a private investigator. I have an office downtown. This has been a pretty good year but the last week has been kind of slow. I'm not complaining mind you. The Lord has seen fit to steer quite a bit of business my way."

Eddie grew interested at this. "What is it like to be an investigator?"

Roger smiled at the question. Most people had this glamorous idea of what the job was. He'd never had a client who was a beautiful woman wanting the aid of the strong man. Most of time it was an old codger who thought his wife was messing around or a middle-aged woman who thought her husband was on the town with a younger woman.

He'd had a few cases of lost dogs. He'd even had a case of a stolen iguana. That one had been dumb. The ex-girlfriend had sneaked into the apartment and stolen the iguana. She claimed that she had put up half the money to buy the pet in the first place.

"It is a job of feast or famine." Roger answered. "It isn't glamorous at all. A lot of the time it is really boring. Most of the people who hire an investigator have some severe trust issues. I've even had clients doubt the proof that I've given when it isn't what they expect.

"I had an older gentleman who thought his wife was having an affair. I tailed her for three weeks trying to catch her in the act. I pulled eighteen-hour days on this investigation. The closest she came to flirting with a man was saying 'Yes, please', to a waiter at a restaurant.

"I did the whole smear, phone taps, electronic listening devices, following her everywhere she went. This woman absolutely was not having an affair on her husband. When I took him all of the evidence I had amassed he called me incompetent. Then he called me a liar. Then he accused me of sleeping with his wife.

"He tried to say that I caught her in the act and then threatened to tell him the truth if she didn't sleep with me. He became so angry that he threatened not to pay his bill. I had to take him to court. I eventually got paid but it sure wasn't worth all the trouble. I've never dealt with anyone so paranoid in my life. Now, when I receive a call, I monitor my clients. If they act particularly paranoid I won't accept the case."

Roger came back to the present with a little jolt. He hadn't meant to go into such detail. Eddie was staring at him. He didn't know what Eddie was thinking. Like most people though, Roger didn't like to be stared at.

He didn't realize that his expression had hardened. Eddie started a bit when he realized he was staring.

"Sorry about that. I don't generally stare. I was lost in thought. I knew a man like that when I was in seminary. That type of person always seems to generate the same kind of chaos around them. They seem to thrive on the discomfort of others. It is funny how the basic personality types mix to form such a wide variety of people. I've read that there are only four basic types but none of the four are set in stone."

Roger thought about what Eddie said for a moment. He had to agree with the sentiment. Roger realized that his food was getting cold. He took a bite and turned back to Eddie. He chewed and swallowed, "What is your sermon going to be about tomorrow?"

Eddie gave a small smile, "You will have to wait until tomorrow to see. A good preacher never ruins the story before it starts."

Roger took a few more bites while Eddie did some revisions on his page. Eddie took a drink of his coffee as he changed a word that he was staring at.

Roger was enjoying his bacon when Eddie took another sip of coffee glanced at Roger from his notes. Jan walked up and discreetly put their checks on their tables. She smiled at Roger before turning and walking away.

Eddie put his coffee cup down, "I hope you don't mind me asking but you realize I am a preacher. Do you mind if I ask what faith you follow?"

The question was harmless enough.

Roger answered, "My family and I are non-denominational Christians."

Eddie gave a surprised smile at the answer. "Well you might enjoy the sermon tomorrow. If you can't make it there will be another one in a couple of weeks. Tomorrow is a special one for some friends of my elders that are in town. They are rather bitter toward the Word of God so one of our elders thought it would be a good idea to have an open-air sermon for them to 'hear' while they were in town."

Roger thought about this. He didn't agree with sneaking the message in on anybody. There were better ways to share the love of God. Roger finished off his breakfast and picked up his check. He pulled some bills out of his wallet and left enough to cover the bill and give Jan a nice tip.

"It was nice meeting you. I may see you tomorrow". Roger stood to go and Eddie replied, "It was nice to meet you too. You and your family are more than welcome to attend tomorrow. We'd love to see you there." Roger nodded to Eddie and headed for the door.

Jan called to Roger as he reached for the door. "Don't be a stranger and remember you promised to bring your son in soon."

Roger turned back, smiled and waved to Jan. "I'll remember, and I'll bring them both in soon. How's that?"

Jan smiled, "Works for me." Roger walked out.

He didn't see the face-off that was going on. He didn't hear the squealing and hissing from the demons when he passed them. He walked between the archangel's legs on his way to his car.

Molech spoke up, "You have your charge. Take your pup and go." Michael's sword tip pointed at Molech. The demon lord would have gone pale if he could. Roger got into his car and checked the paper he'd left on the seat. He would go back to his office and try to call John Sterns again.

Chapter 49

It hadn't been a good day. John Sterns couldn't see all the things that were going on around him. If he could he would have run to the nearest church. He wrung his thin hands together and ran them through his sparse black hair. He stood and stretched his tall wiry frame in an attempt to relax.

This morning had started horribly. His alarm clock hadn't gone off. He could have sworn that he set it to go off like usual. He had set it, but an imp had turned it off. He ran out of hot water in the shower rather quickly. Another unseen imp had fiddled with his water heater. He believed he was going to have to call a repairman.

When he was dressing for work, the arm of his shirt ripped off as he put it on. He didn't see an imp's claws catch on the seam. Then the laces broke when he tried to tie his shoes. He didn't see the imp bite at the strings.

John was under demonic attack. He didn't know it but that was the cause of these things. The morning just kept sort of happening to him. The toaster was obviously on the fritz. He'd set the bread in it and turned it on. In the bathroom during a quick shave, the smoke alarm went off. He ran into the kitchen to find a cloud of black smoke pouring from the toaster. He'd pulled the plug and carried the smoking toaster to the back step to let it cool off.

It had taken him a few minutes to open the doors and windows to try to clear the house of smoke. The house smelled terrible because of the acrid smoke but he didn't have time to do anything more. He decided to leave the exhaust fan in the kitchen and the bathroom on.

He left the small window in the utility room open so that fresh air could come in. This morning had gotten on his last nerve. He felt uneasy and he was late for work. He was a type "A" personality and being late was enough to cause him some measure of distress. When he finally had gotten shaved and dressed he decided that since he was already late he would at least eat something before going to work.

He changed his mind completely when he opened his refrigerator and found that the milk he'd purchased two days ago had curdled. This didn't make sense. It was eight days before the expiration date on the carton. He decided that he might get a cup of coffee on the way to work but he wasn't going to plan on anything for sure.

His briefcase was where he'd laid it the night before. He was in the habit of putting his briefcase beside the front door. That way he would see it on the way out the door and wouldn't forget it. He attributed his bad luck this morning to staying up so late last night working on a pet project.

He'd found a way to make a pinhole camera fit into a toy badge that looked absolutely innocuous. He didn't know why the idea had occurred to him. He hadn't seen the angel drop through the ceiling of his home a couple of days ago and whisper into his ear. He thought the idea was his alone.

The angel wouldn't have scared him as much as the sight of his home this morning. Imps were running everywhere. An imp had turned off his hot water heater. An imp had forced his toaster to keep cooking and burn his toast. An imp had turned off his alarm clock, curdled his milk, broke his shoelaces and torn his shirt when he tried to put it on. They were enjoying themselves immensely. They had particularly enjoyed his fit of apoplexy when he found his back tire flat.

They knew that this man was of the world and didn't hold any particular religious faith. They knew they wouldn't receive any of the blame for his mishaps. They knew he wouldn't call upon the Lord and they knew that they would be able to enjoy this day without fear of reprisal.

John was good with small electronics, but he didn't have all that much mechanical ability. It took him half an hour to change his tire. His hands were dirty. His face was sweaty. He was on the verge of walking back into the house and calling it a day. Then he thought about all that had happened. He could at least look forward to the calm of his office. He had a few projects to finish for his larger clients.

He was his own boss, but he couldn't shirk his duties. He might lose his business. He got in his car. It wouldn't start. He tried it a couple of times with no results. He started to get seriously angry. He put his head on the steering wheel and started taking deep breaths and counted to ten.

The imps were intent on what they were doing. They didn't see the angel rise up through the ground under the car. The angel placed his hand on the underside of the engine and spoke a silent word. John turned the key in the ignition again and the engine caught on the first try.

John muttered, "Now that's more like it." He put the car in gear and backed out of the driveway. He thought "Finally something happened right today. Maybe things are going my way now." His drive to work was uneventful except for the driver who ran a red light and almost hit him.

He couldn't have told you what made him look around. He had an impulse and saw the sports car bearing down on him. He slammed on his brakes and laid on the horn. The driver glared at him and tires screeched as the other car swerved. John got angry as the other driver made a rude gesture to him. The creep was obviously mouthing curses as he drove on.

He was extra careful during the rest of the drive to work. He knew the near miss hadn't been his fault, but he didn't want to take any chances on this particular day. It had gone badly enough already. He decided that he would get a cup of coffee and a pastry from the vending machines on the floor below his office. He did not want to stop and take the chance of something going wrong.

He pulled into the parking garage found that his parking space was taken. That was it. He wasn't in a mood to tolerate this. He drove around to the guard shack and told the guard he wanted the offending car towed. The guard promised she would call a tow-truck and she wrote down John's license number.

She told him he could take one of the visitor spots and an allowance would be made for him today. He thanked her and drove around to the visitor area. As the day's luck would have it all of the visitor slots were taken. He wasn't in a mood to put up with this. He didn't really want to have another person's car towed but his patience was gone.

He made his decision. He parked behind the car in his spot and walked back to the guard shack. He asked if she could find out who owned the car. If she found out would she, please tell them to move their vehicle. If they refused, then go ahead and call the tow truck.

He told her that he was going to leave his car parked behind the offending car. He would move his car when they were ready to move out of his spot. He at least wanted to see the offending party. After all that had happened today he felt that somebody at least was going to apologize to him. John left his phone number with the guard and went up to his office.

The door didn't want to open. The lock seemed a bit sticky. He had to jiggle the doorknob to get the key to turn in the lock. He set his coffee down on his desk. He went to start his computer and the coffee turned over and spread out across the desk and poured straight onto his pants.

John swore. He was not a man given to cursing but this day was just too much. He cleaned his desk with some paper towels from his cabinet. He blotted at his pants and thought that he looked like he had wet himself. That was when the phone rang.

It was the guard. She told him that the owner of the car was on the way down to move it now. He thought to himself that of course they were now. He blotted at his pants some more. They had inconvenienced him. They could stand to wait for a few minutes.

He thought it was fortunate that he was wearing black pants. The spill wouldn't be noticeable. He made sure that he had his keys in his pocket and went to the door. He went downstairs to the garage and started toward his car. As he approached his car he saw the surly man standing by his car.

The man glared at John as he approached. "I'll thank you to move your car, so I can get out." John was in no mood to put up with anything.

"I pay for this parking place. Consider yourself lucky that I didn't have your car towed without a word." Neither of them had seen the car pull up when the man took a menacing step toward John.

John didn't want a fight but with everything that had gone on today he wasn't going to back down either.

"Oh, you think you could have had my car towed?" the man growled.

John stood his ground and snarled, "There isn't any thinking to it. I know I could have and if you don't believe me you can ask the guard." John had a flinty edge to his voice and he was waiting for the other man to make a move.

They were both glaring at each other when an authoritative male voice cut in. "Is there a problem here John?"

The moment of tension was dispelled as both men turned in the direction of the voice. John recognized Roger, "Not as long as this gentleman moves his car out of my parking place."

Roger was a little shocked at John's tone. Roger knew John to be a gentle and generally friendly kind of guy. Something must really be pushing his buttons for him to act like this.

The other man complained, "I can't very well get out of your parking place if you don't move your car." The words came out with a good bit of sarcasm.

John spun on the man. "Look buddy, I'm in no mood to put up with your crap!! This is my parking place. I paid for it. I get here, and I find your car in it. You can get in it now and move it or I'll say to hell with it and have it towed." The words came out rather loud with a good bit of acid in them.

The other man was caught off guard and deflated quite a bit. He didn't say anything he turned and walked to his car. He opened the door and got in. Roger thought that the situation had amended itself but that he wanted to let John know that he wanted a word with him.

"Hey John, I'm going to park my car and come to your office. There is something that I want to talk to you about. John nodded in the affirmative as he turned to get in his car. Roger drove off to the next level to his parking place. John backed away from the car, so the other man could get out. The other car backed out and then peeled away from the parking space.

I notice you didn't say anything to my face buddy. John thought with a little satisfaction. He parked his car and then went back to his office. The door opened easily this time and his pants were nearly dry now. He had stopped at the vending machines to get another cup of coffee and the detour had given Roger enough time to get parked and show up.

Roger knocked on the door and opened it. It was an office, but Roger felt like he would be intruding if he didn't knock.

John stood up behind his desk and offered, "Oh, hi Roger, sorry for my attitude down there. You wouldn't believe the day I've had." Roger could tell that his friend was having a tough time. John was shaking with frustration, though Roger doubted he realized it.

"That's okay. Everybody has a bad day once in a while." Roger noticed the atmosphere in the office was oppressive. This seemed rather strange. Every other time he'd been in here the atmosphere was always light and pleasant. Roger wondered about this and decided that it would be best to err on the side of caution.

He silently offered up a prayer for this man's well-being and protection. Roger noticed that the atmosphere loosened immediately. Roger realized that this man was under spiritual attack. He knew John held no real religious beliefs. He also knew that as a Christian he had an obligation.

Roger thought that first he would get the business at hand out of the way. Afterward he would offer to buy John lunch, so they could talk. During the talk he would give his friend a view of the gospel of Jesus Christ.

Roger spoke up. "John, I was hoping to talk to you today about your hobby."

John's eyes became excited, "Before you say another word I want to show you something I've been working on. I finished it last night."

John moved the coffee cup carefully to the bookshelf behind him and opened his briefcase on his desk. "Take a peek at this." He crooned as he took out the toy badge and placed it in Roger's hand.

Roger stood there for a few seconds gaping at the badge in his hand. His mind simply wouldn't accept that it was coincidence. There was no way this man had finished making exactly what he needed.

Before Roger could speak John spoke up. "It should have a range of about a quarter mile. It picks up video and audio and transmits in color. It still needs to be tested though."

Roger tore his eyes from the badge and spoke a little numbly, "I have a perfect field test for you. That is, if you think it will work."

John noticed his sudden change, "What?"

Roger answered, "I'm doing some surveillance of the new daycare center in town. My son doesn't know it, but I was going to have him wear a camera in there.

I came to you because I needed something that would appear innocuous but something that he would be willing to wear without knowing what it was. To tell you the truth I was going to specifically ask you if you had an audio video cam that fit inside a badge."

John's eyes widened, "Man, what a coincidence!"

Roger stared at him for a moment, "I also want to make sure that the other two cameras are picking up on the receiver while this one is working. You did say the receiver could handle up to five cameras at a time. Oh! And there is something else I wanted to talk to you about if you don't mind. If it is ok with you I'll buy you lunch today and we can chat."

John almost moaned, "Man, after the day I've had, there is no way I'm turning down a free lunch." He paused for a second, "I see why you are concerned. The five-camera limit seems high, but that unit is top of the line. It will handle the three cameras with room to spare.

"I know you've got the other two calibrated to it so if you bring all three and the unit, I can check them out for you to make sure there isn't any configuration problems. What are you going to do with the other two cameras?"

Roger thought about it for a moment. He decided that if he was going to trust John then he had to tell him the whole story.

"I'm going to have a little girl wear the necklace cam that you sold me last year. I'm putting the other micro cam in Brennan's back pack. I figure between the three we will have the best chance of getting what we need." He replied.

John mused for a moment, "That makes sense as long as you don't have any hardware conflicts." John was thinking about how this is the only normalcy he'd had all day. There was a part of him that didn't want Roger to leave. Then he chided himself for being superstitious.

"That is exactly why I brought the subject up." Roger answered.

John let out a little chuckle, "Yes mighty investigator. As far as lunch where did you want to go and when?"

Roger thought about it for a second, "How about Stoney's? You know? It's that little barbeque place down the street."

John whistled, "I know the place. They are a tad expensive."

Roger smiled, "Yes but they are worth every penny. How about I come by and pick you up at eleven-thirty? Hopefully, we will beat the morning rush."

John offered appreciatively, "Sure, man, it's your nickel."

As an afterthought, Roger held up the badge, "I know I didn't formally ask so, do you mind if I use this tomorrow?"

John smiled, "Do you think I'm going to go against the universe and the man who is buying me lunch? Go ahead and take it, but I hope Brennan is at least a little careful with it. You don't need to say anything to him. It is a shock resistant camera. It should take a little abuse. What would be the point of putting it inside of a child's toy if it couldn't take any stress?"

Roger thought his logic was flawless. "Okay, that works. I'll make sure to get it back to you in a couple of days. If we break it, I'll pay you for it. I'll even bring samples of the video in for you to analyze so you can see the quality of it. I would ask for your discretion about this. The investigation is personal and discreet. I would appreciate it if you didn't say anything to anybody about it."

John replied, "No problem, I don't have any kids. I don't know anybody who uses their service. I don't know anybody who works there either. I think you are pretty safe even if I have a momentary slip, *which I won't*."

Roger got ready to turn to go, "Well then, buddy, I'll be back at eleven-thirty to get lunch. Ok with you?"

John smiled "You da man."

Roger was about to leave, then remembered. "I bought those three cameras from you. You're sure this cam doesn't operate on the same frequency? I'm only using two of them plus this one. You know me though. I worry about the little things first."

John peered at him blankly, "Oh, yeah you had me confused there for a second. Make sure you test it to be sure. If it doesn't work the first time, bring the receiver to me. I'll configure them for you. Don't open the box yourself. It is very delicate."

Roger thought about this for a second. He wanted to start the investigation tomorrow. He was hoped the configuration was already compatible. He decided to run home and get the equipment before lunch. They could do the test in the office today. John could make any adjustments.

They would be able to start tomorrow with no problems.

"Okay." Roger answered, raising his hands in mock surrender. "I won't open the box. I'll bring it to you before lunch. Will that be ok?"

John replied, "That works for me. You have me curious about it now anyway. The test will only take a few minutes. Adjusting it will be simple, if it is needed.

The phone on John's desk rang. His gaze snapped to it. "Sorry" he mouthed and picked the phone up. Roger waved to him and moved to the door. He felt a chill and a momentary rush of intuition. He closed the door laid his hand lightly on it. He offered a prayer for his friend's safety. He asked for help today delivering his message.

Roger felt a peace come over him. He turned and went to his office down the hall. Neither John nor Roger saw the imps that had been in the office. Roger didn't see the demons cringing outside of the office. They were hissing curses at him. The door shined brightly now. He had ruined their fun.

There were ten imps that had been tormenting John today. They were about to attack John when Roger had walked in. One of them had been under the floor. He was going to give John a strong foot cramp. One was standing behind John. He was going to grab John's head in and give him a migraine. A third was standing in John's desk facing him. He was reaching for John's stomach. He thought a good dose of nausea was in order.

When Roger had walked in the light of Heaven came with him. They had scattered like roaches in the light. They were filled with abject terror. All ten had exploded out of the office in all directions. After a few minutes half of them gathered out in the hall. They waited for the horrible light to leave.

They could do nothing but stare at the door after Roger left.

Chapter 50

The tiny demon horde waited for the long minutes to pass. This nuisance had taken up their playtime. They hated it when one of these glowing ones came near. It was unpleasant. The glowing Christians only came around trying to offer the gospel message.

John was so secular that the minions of darkness didn't bother to fight for his soul. He was on his own one-way ticket to hell. They watched as the Christian finally walked out. They prepared to enter the room again then something went wrong. They saw the light building from the door that that Christian had exited. The light of Heaven was flooding into the room and settling around the man.

They screamed and cursed at this. Protection from Heaven had claimed this one. They wouldn't be able to enter the room until the light was gone. They didn't know how long that would be. They wouldn't leave though. They were under strict orders to harass this man. If the opportunity presented itself, they would be on him again. They each settled into down to wait.

John was glad Roger came over. It had seemed like the first normal thing all day. Since he'd left everything seemed normal again. It was almost pleasant. He didn't know why he felt so peaceful. It had been a terrible morning. He didn't stop to question it though.

He'd been on the phone with one of his largest clients when Roger walked out. A proper goodbye hadn't been possible. Roger knew what business was like so there was no offense. He worked steadily on the report with no interruptions. He double checked the figures and hit the send button on his email. He looked up and realized it was almost lunchtime.

He liked being able to get work to his clients fast. He loved computers and was adept at his brand of accounting software. He was checking his email when a knock came at the door. Roger came in. He carried the receiver unit with a small bag on top.

He intoned, "Here are the cameras and the receiver."

Roger laid the equipment on the desk. "Do you mind checking them out for me?"

John answered, "Sure thing Roger." He plugged the receiver in and checked the settings. He took the cameras out of the bag and did something with them. Roger saw him arrange the cameras and change some settings.

John set the display and a split image showed up. All three cameras were showing a view of the office.

Roger almost shouted "Sweet!!!!" as soon as the images came into focus. John set the receiver to record and set it running for a few seconds.

"Here is how you view your recording." He touched a stud under the display.

They got a few seconds into video clip and John clicked pause. "What the heck?" He muttered incredulously. John ran the recording backwards. He clicked pause and turned to Roger. "What in the world do you suppose that is?"

Roger gave him a blank stare "What? I don't see anything."

John instructed, "See right here beside the filing cabinet. That looks like a person's shadow. But, there isn't anything there to cast a shadow. The sun is on the other side of the building.

Roger checked the image, then shifted his gaze to the filing cabinet. "Well, whatever it is it isn't there now." He glanced back down at the image, "The scale is all wrong anyway. If that were a person's shadow they would have to be about three feet tall and have some very large ears."

John laughed at that, "Your right. It must have been dust on the lens or a trick of the light." Neither one of them saw the little imp that had stepped into the filing cabinet when John turned the camera on.

Roger asked, "Did the other two cameras pick up okay?"

John answered, "Let me check." He pulled down a menu on his software and changed a couple of settings. They were treated to an image of the ceiling. "The necklace cam worked fine. Now let's see if the last one worked alright." informed John. He pulled down the menu again and made a change and another picture of the ceiling came up. "Everything seems to be in order now, Kemo Sabe. Everything is ready for your little spy mission tomorrow." John announced.

The reference to the lone ranger wasn't lost on Roger. He chose not to comment on it. Sometimes John had a rather warped sense of humor.

"Hey" Roger noted, "It's time for lunch. You ready to eat?"

John glanced at Roger, "Is the pope catholic?" They walked out heading for the elevator.

The small band of demons descended into the office.

The largest one spoke, "The master must be made aware of this. Go and tell him Gort."

"Why do I have to do it Grimja? You always choose me for the unpleasant tasks." The little demon started to sink in to the floor to go. Gort was the smallest and weakest imp there.

Grimja growled "This task will be more unpleasant if you don't hurry up." He glared around at the rest of the imps and hissed. "We wait here for our charges return. There is nothing we can do while he is in the care of the Christian. We can only hope that he doesn't heed the message that the cross is sending him this day."

The group began milling around the office inspecting the odd contraptions around the room. The imps wondered why humans had to surround themselves with things. It didn't occur to any of them to sabotage the recording unit or the three tiny cameras.

Roger and John got into Roger's car. They made the short drive down the street to the restaurant. Stoney's was famous for good barbeque. They had the best Texas style steaks in this area. Usually there was a line that went out the door. Roger knew this. He also knew Ted, the manager.

They'd met at church. Roger had called Ted the night before and told him the situation. He asked for reservations to give his friend a picture of the gospel. Ted promised he would save a table for Roger. They needed to enter from the back, so the line of people wouldn't get upset. Roger agreed and planned on leaving Ted a nice tip.

They parked and got out of the car. There were people standing in a line outside the door.

Roger announced, "Follow me." John appeared confused but changed course and followed his friend. They went around to the back. Roger knocked on the back door.

Ted came to the door. "There you are. I was just thinking about you. Come on in. I have a table ready for you."

They followed Ted in and he seated them at a table that was against the wall. As Ted walked back to the front a matronly graying woman spoke.

"Excuse me but why didn't they have to wait in line like the rest of us?"

Ted replied with "Ma'am, they had advance reservations."

Roger and John perused their menus.

John gave a little whistle, "Man, are you sure you want to eat here? This is the first menu I've ever seen that offers a finance plan."

Roger laughed, "Don't worry about it. I got it covered." Roger wasn't about to show his shock.

He knew the place was pricey. The prices however had almost doubled since the last time he'd been in here. At first, he thought he'd pay with cash, but it was a good thing that he'd brought his credit card with him. Then he thought *"Well if I'm going down, I'm going down chewing on a steak."*

He turned to John, "I don't know about you but I'm having the porterhouse. Want to join me?"

John gave him a short stare, "It's going to be a funeral for your wallet buddy. Okay, I'm right there with you."

The waitress came over, "Are you ready to order sirs?"

Roger answered, "Yes young lady, I'd like the porterhouse, baked potato and a side salad. My friend here will have…." He turned to John with and expectant air.

John took his cue from Roger and smoothly continued "…the exact same thing."

She was smiling as she wrote it down. It was obvious that she was thinking of the customary fifteen percent tip. The meaning of the smile wasn't lost on Roger. He realized he was going to be saying goodbye to more money than he had originally bargained for.

He thought, "I'm doing the work of the Lord. I should be able to enjoy a good meal for the cause. If it costs me a little bit, it will be worth it." That eased his mind a little. He started to think about how best to begin.

He was brought out of his reverie with "And what can I get you gentlemen to drink?"

There was no hesitation on John's part. "Draft beer please." That didn't sit well with Roger. He kept his tongue though.

When the girl turned to him, "I'll have a cola please."

She wrote them down, "Very good, I will be right back with your drinks."

John was playing with the little puzzle that the restaurant left on each table. Roger didn't really like those brainteasers. He spent his time in investigation. He considered that enough of a brainteaser. He watched John struggle with the puzzle. The waitress brought their drinks shortly.

Roger saw a waitress ask a question of a patron with a mouthful of food. *"Are they trained to do that when your mouth is full?"* He wondered. He chuckled at the thought. John gave him an expectant expression.

"Just a wry little thought." Roger explained. "I've been meaning to ask you. I know you aren't married and you don't have any kids. I was wondering what you believe about your life."

John seemed a little wary at the question. "I believe the same thing that most people believe. I try to be a good person. I'm nice to people. I don't lie, cheat or steal. I'm not saying I've never done any of those things. I just don't make a habit of them."

The waitress appeared with their meals. The steaks were still sizzling from the grill. Roger gazed at his almost lovingly. He had requested it medium and was glad to see it was nicely scorched around the edges. John had ordered his medium rare. Roger thought privately that he really didn't see the appeal behind a steak barely cooked.

He thanked the smiling waitress. He picked up his fork tried an experimental bite of the steak. It was cooked perfectly but it needed a little seasoning. He seasoned the steak with steak sauce and not a small amount of salt.

John was staring at him when he finished. "Like a little steak with your salt?"

Roger laughed, "I only do that when Amelia isn't around. She worries about high blood pressure."

Roger considered, *well now is as good a time as any.* "Tell me something John. What do you think happens when you die?"

John seemed to think about the question for a moment while he chewed his steak. "I've never really given it all that much thought. I suppose when you are gone, you are gone."

Roger peered at John, "You don't believe in a higher power or God?"

John smiled a little at that question. "I believe there might be a God, but I don't think he is all that interested in us."

Roger queried, "What if you found out God is interested in you? Would you want to know more about him?"

John got a patient expression on his face, "Was this meal a chance for you to get me alone and preach at me?"

Roger was taken aback by the directness of the question. "No, the meal is because you are my friend. It's also a way for me to thank you for your help."

John stared steadily at Roger for a moment, "Roger I understand that you want to share your faith. Truthfully, I'm not into the whole God, Heaven and run from the devil thing. Can we agree to enjoy this meal and each other's company?"

Roger was slightly deflated, but he knew that you can't argue someone into Christianity. He gave John a smile, "Sure buddy, but if you ever want to know about the Lord, I hope you'll ask me."

John approved, "Okay, you've got a deal there." With that they both attacked their steaks.

The conversation was pretty light after that. John hoped he hadn't offended Roger. Roger thought much the same thing. They finished their meal and John insisted on covering the tip. As they stood up John quietly laid twenty dollars on the table and they headed for the door.

He waved at Ted as he reached for the door. Ted waved back, and they stepped out into the bright sunlight.

Roger unlocked the car and they got in. "I don't know about you, but I'm stuffed. That was an excellent meal."

John agreed and exulted "At least they can say they have a reason for being so expensive."

"Yes, they can. Amelia is going to kill me when she sees the credit card bill. I have to admit though I really enjoyed that meal. We'll have to do that again sometime."

Roger started the car and pulled smoothly out onto the highway. They were both a little lethargic after the large meal. Roger pulled into the parking garage and made the loop to his parking spot.

"Well at least your parking spot is open." John offered that with the air that it still gnawed on his nerves. He had come closer this morning to a fistfight than he had in years.

Roger had decided he was going to do some steady praying for his friend. He might object to being witnessed to, but he could be prayed for without his knowledge. They got out of the car and went up to John's office.

"I'll bring this back to you in a couple of days." Roger held up the badge.

John responded, "No problem, you realize it was only an experiment?"

Roger replied with, "I don't think you realize how much this fit together. If I told you how things have gone you might want me to preach at you a little."

John stared at Roger for a moment. He knew that Roger was a serious man. Remarks like that didn't pass his lips for no reason. He thought about it for a moment. Then he silently gave in to the little voice saying "Naaaaaa…. that can't be right."

He didn't realize was that little voice was an imp. This particular imp had been with him for years. It was calling to him from the hall. Roger put the three tiny cameras in his jacket pocket. Lifting case that held the receiving unit, he bid his friend a good afternoon.

Roger made sure to check the door after he walked out. He stopped for a moment, holding the case in both hands. He closed his eyes and offered a prayer for his friend. He thought about what was going to happen tomorrow. The beginning of an investigation was always the rather exciting for him.

Chapter 51

Roger had shown Amelia the badge camera when he'd gotten home. She had been impressed with it. She had remarked that Brennan would enjoy playing sheriff for a day. That gave Roger the idea that he would take Brennan to the daycare the next morning. He planned to make a show of promoting his son to sheriff in front of the staff.

They wouldn't want to offend a customer. The badge at least would be safe for the day. Amelia had called the car rental agency and agreed to take the rental to about half a block from the daycare about five minutes after he left with Brennan. She would wait for him to pick her up.

He thought about the open-air sermon the young preacher was going to give tomorrow.

He turned to Amelia. "You remember that young preacher we saw at that open-air sermon?"

Her face took on a questioning air, "Yes, what about him?"

He thought about it for a second, "I ran into him the other day at the waffle house. He seemed a little anxious and invited me to an open-air sermon he's speaking at tomorrow. Do you want to go, or would you prefer not to?"

Amelia's face became troubled, "I really don't like listening to sermons containing false doctrine. I know that I know better. I just don't want to get my theology mixed up."

Roger nodded his understanding, "Something about it seemed important to me. I'll drop you off here at home in the morning and go to the sermon. I want to hear what he says. If nothing else I may be able to talk to him about his doctrinal choices."

Amelia looked a little amused, "Are you planning on eating out again? I may need to build some room into the budget this week." She mused the last part with a light chuckle.

Guilt clouded Roger's face, "I know honey and I'm sorry. Waffle house wasn't bad, but Stoney's really put a dent in our pocket this week."

She stepped forward and put her arms around his neck. Her eyes were luminous, "Oh, I think we can allow your little excursions. You are a good provider and husband. I couldn't ask for better."

Roger felt fortunate to have her. "I love you." He whispered into her ear.

"I love you too", she purred with an impish smile. She swatted his backside, "Now, enough distractions. Get to work."

Roger laughed and sat down at the kitchen table. He went over the details of the plan for tomorrow. Roger rubbed his eyes after going through the stack of papers for the third time. He shuffled the stack back together.

Amelia stepped up behind him and started massaging his neck and shoulders. He sagged into his chair.

"You know I can't concentrate when you do that." He almost complained.

Amelia giggled, "Why do you think I do it. Don't you think you've gone over your plans enough for one night?" The last part she offered with a note of expectance.

Roger loved it when Amelia made the first move. He initiated most of the time but sometimes she saw fit to take the reins as it were. He smiled and pushed the papers back into the folder. This night was going to end better than he expected.

"You know, I think you might be right. Where is Brennan?"

"He went to bed about a half hour ago." She informed him, smiling. With that remark Roger took his wife's hand and they went upstairs.

Eddie was thinking about his sermon tomorrow. He thought of the promise that he'd been given. Tomorrow was going to be the biggest day of his life. He wanted to appear immaculate tomorrow. He started the evening by laying his clothes out.

He didn't want to appear stuffy. Open-air preaching required that you try to relate to a casual public audience. He decided he wouldn't wear a blazer. He picked out his favorite tie. It was dark with a small streak of red in it. A shirt and tie were dressy enough for the older members of the congregation. The lack of a jacket was casual enough for the younger crowd.

There were times the crowd got really involved in his sermons. It was during those times he loosened his tie. He tried to be more personable and relaxed. People listened to someone they felt they could relate to.

He laid out his little cross-shaped tie clip, picked up his Bible and headed for the couch. He wanted to spend the evening in prayer and communion. He didn't realize who or what he was communing with.

He opened his Bible to the book of Job. Over the past year it had become his favorite book. He secretly compared himself to Job. He would never tell anybody that. He knew that it was too prideful, but he couldn't help himself.

He sat down on the couch he felt more than heard that soft whisper. It came to him now when he started to pray. He felt so fortunate. Molech was there behind the couch. He softly crooned to Eddie. He despised these humans, but they were the key to the winning of creation.

Eddie slipped into his ecstatic state easily now. Molech leaned forward and whispered more insistently into Eddie's ear. He selected Eddie's sermon for him. It was going the story of Jesus healing the people.

Molech's face was blank as he concentrated. He sent out his thoughts and Jenoch heard him. He wanted a report on the 'healing' tomorrow. Jenoch arrived roughly five minutes later. He sailed through the ceiling and landed in a crouch.

He bowed his head, "I come as ordered master."

Molech smiled. Eddie started to shiver. It wasn't cold in the room. Molech looked at Eddie and then turned to Jenoch.

"Let us depart some distance. It appears this human can sense when two large demons are near."

They both ascended through the ceiling. Together they flew to the edge of town with Jenoch behind in the submissive position. They landed and Molech was pleased to see Jenoch bowing to him again. It felt as though he was receiving worship.

Molech demanded, "What news do you have of the healing tomorrow?"

Jenoch responded with "All preparations have been made master. The actor will be there tomorrow when the sermon starts. He has been in town since yesterday.

"One of our pets is pushing him around in a wheelchair. Everyone who has seen him believes he is paralyzed. We got him from two states away. There is little chance of him being recognized. His training as an actor should help him make his healing believable."

Molech smiled at this. "Good" he lightly purred. I want tomorrow to go exactly as planned."

He saw a movement out of the corner of his eye. An imp was sailing toward the town. He was about twenty yards away. Why would an imp be entering his territory?

Molech decided that he needed to find out. He covered the twenty yards in two bounds. Molech reached out and seized the imp that was trying to pass by so unobtrusively. The imp had a piece of spirit parchment in his claws.

Molech rasped, "Why do you pass through my territory? What is this that you hold in your slimy little fist?"

The imp gasped and writhed in pain. "I am merely delivering a missive my lord. It is from one of the hierarchs. It is written on spirit parchment. It will disappear once it has been read."

Molech took the parchment from the struggling little imp's claws, "Let me see this." He unfolded the parchment and started to read.

My dear Chernobyl;

In your last letter you were worried because your charge is becoming more confident in his Christianity. You need not worry. In fact, you should be jumping for joy. It is when they are confident in their faith that they try to "Go it alone". The idiots think they can handle it. These are the times that you can best use to your advantage. You've had your charge long enough that you know his weakest points. Use those points in the moments that he seems most confident. He will fall to one of them. I guarantee it. When he does, you simply move in and start feeding him the thoughts of how he has failed as a Christian. If he is the man you describe, then he will despair. In his despair, instead of running to the enemy as he should, he will instead hide himself -- or try to -- from the all present enemy. The first instance we know of this was in the Garden of Eden itself. When the man and woman fell -- Sometimes I can't remember their names, but then again who among us cares? -- The first thing they did was hide from their creator. While he is attempting to hide himself, you will need to appeal to the basest part of his nature. Get in touch with Slumgorm and see if he can arrange for his attractive charge to offer understanding (and a few other things) to your wounded little man. If you handle this right he will be turn away from his faith entirely as being impossible to live up to. It is impossible of course but the humans are constantly forgetting about the abundance of Grace from our enemy.

Your affectionate mentor,

Shacklebolt

Molech screamed, "This is spirit parchment!! If it isn't fully read by its intended recipient, it will never fade. Isn't your master aware that humans can both see and handle spirit parchment? Doesn't your master realize that if letters such as this fell into human hands it would constitute absolute proof of our existence and purpose?

"Take this back to your master and pray that I do not speak to lord Lucifer before your master can get to him." Molech then threw the little imp from him back the way he came. He saw and enjoyed the fear that he had engendered.

Molech turned to Jenoch, "You may go back to the tasks you were working on before I called you. Keep me apprised of the situation if there are any changes."

Jenoch bowed, "Yes, master." He rose into the air and flew back toward the center of town.

Molech thought to himself that he needed to get back to his pet human. He still needed to 'inspire' his pet's sermon for tomorrow. He couldn't allow his anger to offset his plans.

He rose into the air and bellowed, "We will see how much trouble you are in lord Shacklebolt. You may be part of the hierarch of hell but none who endanger our struggle are safe from our lord Lucifer's wrath. I will enjoy causing you pain."

Chapter 52

Molech streaked over the land back to Eddie's apartment. He needed to ensure that the sermon was sufficiently inspiring. When he got back he noticed that Eddie was nervous at the loss of contact. This was a good.

His pet human relied on him for the messages he preached. He took his place behind Eddie and started to whisper. They maintained this pose for a couple of hours. Molech would say prompting words. Eddie scratched words onto his notepad.

Molech murmured his approval or disapproval. Eddie reacted by underlining, leaving alone or scratching out what he'd written. There was such enjoyment in controlling this misled preacher. Molech couldn't contain his grin.

The sermon was finished. Eddie stretched and knelt before his couch to pray. Molech sat on the couch in front of him. He pretended that he was the object of Eddie's worship. In an odd sort of way he was. After a little while in prayer, Eddie stood up and headed toward his bed. It was late and he wanted to be rested for the morning.

It was still dark. Roger's eyes popped open. He looked over at the alarm clock. There was still twenty minutes before the alarm was set to go off. Roger was a little aggravated at that. There wasn't enough time for any meaningful rest. It was also a little early to get out of bed.

He quietly got out of bed and padded to the bathroom. He closed the door slowly, so it wouldn't make any noise. He didn't want to wake Amelia before she had to get up. He'd learned early on that she hated being awakened before she had to get up.

He shaved and cleaned up for the morning. For some reason this morning felt different. It didn't feel like he was starting an investigation. This morning he felt like he was preparing for battle. He hadn't seen the angel that had guarded their sleep all night.

He heard the alarm clock go off. It blared for a moment then it went off. He knew that Amelia was awake now, maybe not up but awake. He came out of the bathroom and noticed that the bedroom was still swathed in darkness. No way was he going to turn the light on.

He padded to the dresser and found the clothes he was looking for. He got dressed in the dark in silence.

"Why does the morning have to come so early?" asked Amelia's voice out of the darkness.

"That's why they call it morning, honey." He answered in a neutral tone.

She let out an explosive sigh and shoved the covers away. She sat up on the side of the bed and chided with a little twist in her voice, "I would have gotten more sleep if somebody hadn't kept me awake."

Roger smiled, "I wasn't the one who started it last night."

Amelia let out a little giggle, "Well sometimes a girl has to take charge of matters."

Roger replied quietly as he pulled his socks on, "Thank you for explaining that to me. I'll try to remember it in the future."

His mind snapped to the day's activities. "Are you sure you don't want to go to the sermon with me?" He asked in a quizzical tone.

She answered, "Yes, I'm sure. I don't feel right about going. Do you have the badge handy for Brennan?"

He replied that he did as he was tying his shoes

It occurred to him to check the battery in the badge itself. He'd changed out the battery pack in the receiving unit. He didn't know how long the battery in the badge would last. This thought worried him a little.

"Mind if I turn on the light?" he asked.

Amelia affirmed, "Sure, go ahead. I'm awake now." He went to the door and found the light switch and flipped it on. They both shared that little moment of discomfort when you go from darkness to bright light.

Roger walked over to the dresser where he'd laid the badge the night before. He wondered what size battery this thing took. He was able to put his finger on the back and give a little twist. The battery cover came off. He examined the small watch battery that would power the unit.

A thought occurred to him and he walked over to the chest of drawers where he routinely put his stuff. There it was. He'd bought a little laser pointer and spare batteries last week on a spur of the moment purchase. He stared at the spare batteries and his knees went weak. They were the same batteries. This had to be divine providence.

He turned to Amelia, "You aren't going to believe this." He prompted.

Her face assumed an interested expression, "What?"

He explained, "I was wondering if the battery in this thing was new enough to last all day like we want. I checked the battery. Then I remembered that little laser pointer I bought last week. It had spare batteries with it. Well the batteries are exactly the type used in this badge. How freaky is that?"

Amelia let out a delighted little laugh. "I love it." She exulted. "Every time we run into something like this it is evidence that God is working with us even when we don't know it." Roger saw where she was coming from but wasn't all that comfortable with stuff like that.

Roger put the badge in his breast pocket. He went down the hall to Brennan's bedroom. Light was showing under the door. That was a clue but not enough. Brennan had gone through a period of getting up, turning on the light and then laying back down.

Roger walked over to the door and knocked lightly.

Brennan answered, "Yes? I'm getting dressed."

Roger thought it was funny that his son was modest. "Okay buddy, I was making sure you were up." Roger heard the almost exasperated sigh from the other side of the door.

Roger went back into the master bedroom. He smelled singed hair. Amelia was in the bathroom using the curling iron.

Roger absently said what he was thinking. "It's a good thing I'm not a woman. I wouldn't do all that. I would make a very unkempt woman."

She laughed, "You know honey, you are right. You wouldn't make a good woman at all. Besides that, you really don't have the legs for it." She giggled.

He shot back, "Hey wait a minute, what's wrong with my legs? I was a body builder for five years, so you can't say I'm not good enough."

She smiled, "Honey! Nothing is wrong with your manly legs. You appeal to me immensely, but they aren't feminine, and neither are you. If you were I wouldn't have looked twice at you. You are my M. A. N. Got it?"

Roger sat there for a moment taken back by her rather bald explanation. Amelia was usually reserved but, in these moments, alone together she was capable of being blunt and kind of …. sexy. This was something they were going to have to talk about soon.

He set about finishing getting ready. He wore his usual tie and sport coat. He didn't like wearing a tie. He'd found out early on that the public expected an investigator to appear professional. One impertinent young lady had asked him where he kept his disguise kit.

He finished tying his tie in a crisp double Windsor knot. He didn't like the single Windsor it was too lopsided for his taste. Then he called out from the bathroom.

"Brennan? Are you ready buddy?"

Brennan answered back, "Almost, I need to get my shoe's on."

Roger took out his cologne and applied a small amount to his face and neck.

Amelia complained, "Oh you would wear that on a day like today and that is my favorite."

Roger smiled, "Well a guy has to look his best honey."

"And who is all of this for?" she asked rather quickly.

He turned to her innocently, "Why you of course."

She laughed at that, "You really don't think I'm that naïve, do you? You are getting ready to leave me for the day. I know. I know.

You need to have a nice professional appearance for the public. I don't expect you are chasing other women honey, because I know you know what would happen to you in your sleep if you did." She finished her last sentence with a smile and a little narrowing of her eyes.

Roger experienced a moment of 'Wait a minute, I don't remember that conversation'. He was about to deliver a rejoinder when a knock sounded at the door.

Roger answered, "Yes?"

Brennan opened the door, "I'm ready, but why are you taking me to the daycare and not Amelia?"

Roger replied, "Because buddy, Amelia has an appointment and I'm trying to help out in the time factor."

Brennan's face dawned with understanding, "Oh, Ok Dad, I'll wait in the living room." Roger gave his Ok and Brennan closed the door.

"That boy is getting too inquisitive." Roger complained.

Amelia smiled, "He is his father's son. By the way, when is Susan going to pick him up, after spring break? I love having him around. I want to be prepared for his absence."

Roger thought about this for a moment and had to take a deep breath and face reality. He replied, "Susan, will be picking Brennan up the Sunday after the end of spring break." Roger had a really hard time when it came to anything to do with his ex-wife. In this one area his pride had destroyed him. He had tried to be a good husband.

He had prayed for her. He had been patient and he had done everything that he could find in scripture that a husband is supposed to do. With all of that, still, she had left. Their family had broken up and there was nothing Roger could do about it. He knew he needed to forgive her.

Amelia didn't make a response. She knew her husband's feelings on the matter. Roger walked over to her and gave her a kiss.

"I'll drop Brennan off and wait for you."

"Ok honey. I'll be a few minutes behind you. You'll need the few minutes to set up the badge thing."

"Yes." He answered.

He unconsciously reached to his breast pocket where he had stowed the badge. "Love you." He told her as he turned toward the door.

"Love you too" came her response behind him. He closed the bedroom door and walked down to the living room.

Chapter 53

Brennan sat on the couch playing his game boy. He looked up when Roger walked in. He started shutting it down and got up.

"Ready?" Roger prompted.

Brennan smiled at him, "Did you forget that I've been waiting on you?"

Roger gave him a playful push, "Watch it kiddo."

Brennan laughed, "I was only telling the truth. We do value truth in our family don't we?"

"Oh, ha ha very funny." Roger replied. He turned toward the door with Brennan right behind him. They got into the car and Roger did one last check to make sure that the badge was still in his pocket.

He started the car and let it idle for about half a minute. As he sat there he went through the plan for the day.

Brennan asked, "Is something wrong Dad?"

Roger came out of his reverie, "No, everything is fine. I'm going through my mental list for the day."

Brennan offered, "Make sure you remember the one about pick up a nice gift for my wonderful son."

"Oh, we are just full of ourselves this morning aren't we?" Roger shot back.

"Amelia always says I'm a morning person." was the chipper reply. Roger was enjoying the banter. He usually didn't spend much time with Brennan in the mornings.

He put the car in gear and pulled out of the driveway. He drove to the daycare and only passed one car on the way. He thought it was strange that there weren't more people on the road and then he remembered that it was spring break. All of the teachers, school kids and moms weren't on the road this morning. He wondered how much traffic this group actually made up.

They got to the daycare and Brennan moved to get out of the car.

Roger announced, "Hold on cowboy, I've never met the daily

staff around here. I'll go in with you."

Brennan made a little face indicating the thought, 'Dad, please don't embarrass me.', before he got out of the car.

They walked in and Roger studied the layout. A young lady in her mid-twenties walked up as soon as Roger came through the door.

"Hello, Brennan. Is this your father?" She was staring at Roger with barely disguised admiration as she asked the question.

Brennan answered, "Yes Miss Judy. This is my dad." She stared at Roger for a moment longer than would be polite before saying,

"Pleased to meet you Mr. Carter. Brennan here tells me you are an investigator."

"Yes, ma'am I am. I'm working on a case for a corporate entity at the moment."

"That sounds vague enough to be a little cloak and dagger", she said.

He replied with "I have a duty to my client to protect their identity."

She stated, "That is understandable. By the way, Brennan is a big help around here. I would say he is something of a natural leader."

Roger thought this was some grease for the wheels to disarm him. He didn't let that thought show on his face,

"Thank you." He turned to Brennan, "I'm going to go now buddy but before I do I'm going to promote you." He reached into his pocket and pulled out the badge. He pinned it on Brennan's shirt, "You are my sheriff for the day. If Miss Judy here gives us a favorable report on you, I will get you that gift you asked for."

Brennan's face brightened, "Really Dad? I'll be good. I promise."

Judy's smile was large, "You will be lighter by the cost of the present because Brennan is good every day."

Roger smiled at that, "If he acts out any, I expect you to let us know."

Judy replied, "We always communicate with the parents if their child misbehaves. You haven't heard from us because Brennan is as good as gold when he's here."

"Thank you, ma'am," Roger answered.

Judy smiled broadly at him with a little flirt in her voice, "Oh, please call me Judy."

She had reached out and taken hold of his arm. Roger looked down and she pulled away quickly. "Sorry." She tittered, "I'm something of a touchy person."

"That's quite alright." Roger turned to Brennan, "I'll see you tonight son."

Brennan had a strange expression on his face as his father turned to go. He had evidently noticed the flirtatious vibe that Judy was giving off and didn't appreciate it. He planned to talk to Brennan tonight and make sure that everything was okay between them.

"It was nice to have met you Mr. Carter." Judy called as he was walking out. She was still smiling at him.

"Same here" He called back as he closed the door. He got in the car, drove a block toward home and waited.

It was only a minute before Amelia pulled up in the rental car. He got out and crossed the street.

He called, "Pop the trunk honey." He heard the faint little click, and the trunk came floating up on its' hinges. He lifted it the rest of the way and inspected at the dark gray box inside.

He unclipped the latches and lifted the top on the receiving unit. He powered it up and checked to see if it was receiving a signal. It was receiving all three signals. Evidently the Beaumont's had dropped off Candy before or was doing it now.

Roger clipped the lid back on and closed the trunk. Amelia had gotten out of the car and he heard the chirp of the auto-lock system as she pointed the key fob at it and pushed the button. She stared at him questioningly. He gave her a thumbs-up and they both walked to his car.

He opened the door for her. She slid into the seat and reached over to unlock the driver's door. He walked around and got into the driver's seat.

As he buckled himself in, she whispered "This seems like we are on a mission."

He turned to her and whispered back, "We are, but why are you whispering?"

She laughed at that and shot back, "I don't know." He started the car and pulled smoothly away from the curb. They drove the rest of the way home in silence. She seemed rather tense at the moment and he didn't want to make her feel self-conscious.

They pulled into the driveway and he killed the engine.

Her face became questioning, so he explained, "I thought we might be able to share a cup of coffee together before I leave for work."

She smiled, "Okay, but it will have to be a quick one. Remember I have a meeting with a client today and I need to get there early to set up."

He announced, "Okay. That works for me. I still need to do a little research. I do have more than one case at the moment." They walked into the house. There was half a pot of freshly brewed coffee as he knew there would be. Amelia never made a full pot because of the waste.

They weren't big coffee drinkers. He went over to the pot and poured two cups. He put two sugars in hers and made sure to pick it up in his left hand. He walked over to the table and sat down. He laid her cup in front of her and took a sip of his coffee.

"You know I wouldn't ask you to do anything dangerous in one of my investigations don't you?"

Her face softened, and she replied, "I know honey, it was so weird the way we planned this all out. It's like being in an episode of Mission Impossible".

He laughed, "I understand Mrs. Phelps."

He took another drink of his coffee. He noted, "You don't want your coffee, do you?" She hadn't touched it.

She replied, "Not really but I didn't want to turn down your company". He leaned over and kissed her.

He pulled away, "I'm going to go ahead and go then. Don't worry. Everything is going to go off without a hitch today."

Silently he thought, *"I hope"*. She voiced an Okay and they both got up. He took the cups to the sink and she started toward her little in-home office. He called out to her, "Good luck today honey. I love you."

She called back, "Thanks, you too. I love you too." With that Roger went back out to his car and drove to his office.

He'd planned to work for a couple of hours before going to hear the sermon that Eddie was preaching. Neither he nor Amelia saw the angels that were accompanying them. They were under Heavenly guard today. None of the forces of darkness would be allowed near them.

He got a call from the restaurant chain. He'd handled a case for them last week. They wanted to know if they could have access to the data that he'd collected. He told them that as long as they paid the bill that he'd sent them earlier in the week he'd give it to them with no hesitation.

Their representative told him they'd have a check ready tomorrow. Roger told them he would prefer a cashier's check and that he would bring the data tomorrow if the check was ready. He didn't want to appear untrusting, but he'd been burned a few too many times to be naïve about American business.

His last phone call was from a gentleman named Rick Thompson. Rick was in a business partnership with an old friend. He explained he didn't want to accuse anyone, but money seemed to be disappearing from the business. He wanted Roger to investigate his partner for embezzlement.

The business wasn't incorporated. Liability could become a major issue. He didn't want to risk his personal assets because of dishonesty. He asked Roger if he could help. Roger considered before he answered.

Roger asked, "How long do you think this has been going on?"

Rick answered, "I noticed the numbers being odd about two months ago. The numbers indicate something odd about 4 months before that. I didn't want to say anything to him about it because we are friends. Numbers don't lie though. Somebody is stealing money. I can't afford that. Can you help?"

Roger explained, "I can help but I'll need access to your company's bank account data and the incoming profits and outgoing expenses. You can black out the account numbers, but I'll need the data in digital form, so I can analyze the data and see what should be going on versus what is really going on. I'll also need salary information on all of your employees including yourself and your friend. I'll need tax data and any charitable donations that you currently have going out. How much do you think is currently missing?"

Rick thought about that for a few seconds and stated, "I hate saying this, but I think it is in excess of $200,000.00."

Roger's mouth fell open. "Mr. Thompson, why didn't you do something earlier? You realize that the most probable thing is that you won't recover any of that money. You'll be able to take the business and control of it away from your friend. That is about all you will be able to do though"

Rick lamented, "I know. I know. I didn't want to believe he would do this to me."

Roger commiserated, "Sir, I admire your loyalty to your friend but sometimes loyalty is misplaced. If he has placed the money into an account and I find that he is guilty, you can charge him with grand larceny. He will plea bargain through his lawyers. You can take the hard line that you will continue to press charges until he releases half of the stolen funds to you. Since it is a partnership he was entitled to half the funds anyway. You will also demand complete control of the company's operations. They will fight against this. You will have to stand firm and say that he's proven himself untrustworthy in running the company. You can't back down on either of these points. If you do, you will lose in the end."

Rick questioned, "Okay, what do we need to move forward?"

Roger instructed, "Get me the data that I told you about. If you need, I can email you a list. Make sure it is a private email, that only you have access to. Nobody else is to know of this investigation. Are you married?"

Rick replied, "Yes".

Roger commented, "I'm formally advising you that I will not perform this investigation if I so much as think that you are informing your wife. I'm serious about this. Not only does this cover the investigation, my threat now covers you against your wife. You tell her what I said, and she can take her anger out on me."

Rick responded in a quiet voice, "You've been doing this for a while haven't you?"

Roger asked, "Yes I have. How did you hear about me?"

Rick answered, "I saw your ad in the phone book. I was afraid to ask anybody about an investigator because there would have been too many questions."

Roger disclosed, "That is the smartest thing I've heard you say since you called me. I have a meeting to go to in a few minutes. Are you aware of my rates?"

Rick answered, "Yes and I think they are perfectly reasonable. I'll gladly pay your rates for results and even offer you a fifteen percent bonus."

Roger informed him, "Sir, that won't be necessary. I'll be doing my job, but I really do have to go now. Email me the data as soon as you get it to Rcarter@reasy.com. Do you need me to email you a list of what I need from you?"

Rick returned, "No sir, since I started worrying about this I've gotten into the habit of recording all of my phone calls. I'll play back the recording and dictate it into a hand recorder. My handwriting is messy. I type much faster."

Roger was a little shocked at the confession. He knew that as long as one person in the conversation knew it was being recorded then it was legal. Mr. Thompson was only covering his back. Roger commended him, "That was actually another smart move on your part. Have you come across anything that can be used in the courts? You know, things like conflicting statements about profits or expenditures?"

There was a momentary pause on the line and Rick came back with, "Yes, several but I would want your opinion on them before I submit them as evidence." Roger was increasingly impressed with this man's shrewdness. He was definitely a savvy businessman.

He had fallen into the friendship trap. You like a friend so much that you don't want to believe that they would cheat you. Roger had seen this situation more than once. It almost never resolved to the satisfaction of the person cheated. They always seemed to lose something.

Roger offered, "Well sir, I really do have to go. You have my email, my phone, and you know my rates. If you want to proceed, please email me the information. After that I'll start my investigation for you. I will contact you every night to give you an update on how the investigation is proceeding.

"If you have any further questions, please write them down and put them in a place that is readily accessible but away from prying eyes. Do we have an understanding?"

Rick affirmed, "Yes we do. I'll call you later tonight to make sure of receipt of the files I'll be sending you. Other than that, there is nothing more to discuss at this time. Until tonight then" Roger stated,

"Until tonight." They both hung up.

Roger reached into his pocket for his key. He turned off the lights and the coffee maker. He locked the door and headed for the elevator. He was wondering what Eddie's sermon was going to be about as he headed for the car.

Chapter 54

Eddie had finished writing his sermon the night before. Since there was supposed to be a healing he'd thought it fitting if the sermon were about God's healing. He skimmed through his notes as he waited for the crowd to gather in and settle down.

He saw the gentleman he'd met at the Waffle House. He admitted that he was surprised to see him there. So many people said yes to get away from you. After that you never saw them again. Witnessing to people about the Lord was becoming increasingly difficult.

He saw Roger take a seat in the third row at an aisle seat. Eddie thought, this man had to be a practicing Christian. Most non-practicing Christians came in and took a seat in the back. Non-Christians sat as close to the door as they can get.

The crowd was quiet and looked around expectantly. Eddie saw Mr. Edwards walking to the podium to say the opening prayer. Eddie realized he had only a couple of minutes before his sermon was supposed to start. Mr. Edwards scribbled something on a piece of paper and laid it on the podium before beginning the prayer.

Eddie didn't listen to the prayer. He trusted Mr. Edwards to be sincere and heartfelt. He ran through his key points in his mind. The prayer finished, and Mr. Edwards introduced Eddie.

Mr. Edwards seemed to be fond of the fact that Eddie's last name was Cain. His last remark would always be, "Ladies and Gentlemen I present to you, a man named Cain who truly believes we are our brother's keeper, Mr. Eddie Cain."

Eddie walked up to the podium when Mr. Edwards started away. He saw the note that Mr. Edwards wrote. "The food is ordered and will be here on time. Don't worry. Just concentrate on your sermon."

Eddie looked at the shelf on the podium. The cold bottle of water was there. He straightened his pages on top, reached underneath and took the cap off the water bottle. Eddie raised the bottle to his lips. He took a sip and swirled the cold water around in his mouth. He took a moment to gather his thoughts.

"Good morning ladies and gentlemen. I hope this morning finds you in the Lord's favor. Today's message is about the Lord's healing power. I've read that there are 39 different types of diseases. Jesus took 39 lashes for our healing. You will hear preachers say that it is not always God's will to heal.

"I say that God is a loving God and if he loves you then he wants to heal you. Can you imagine a loving Father not wanting to heal his child? I lost my daughter not too long ago and for the life of me I can't picture God not wanting to heal his children.

"All through the Bible, God is portrayed as a loving God and a loving Father. Can you picture a loving God allowing his children to suffer with cancer or Down syndrome? Jesus said, 'When you ask for something from the Father, believe that you will receive it'

"Why would God grant a request when you don't even believe he will do it when you ask? Matthew 21:22 says that if you believe you will receive what you ask for and have faith then you will receive it.

"Now we all believe that the Bible is the word of God. The passage that I quoted is in the Bible. So that passage is a promise from God and God can't break his promises. If he did he would be lying, and God can't lie because he would violate his character if he did.

"Another thing God can't do is fail. If he sets his mind to do something, then it is a done deal. It will get done in His time and his manner. We don't always get what we ask for in the way that we ask it. How many of you have had a prayer answered but not in the way that you asked for it?" Eddie asked the crowd.

He looked around. He could tell he had their rapt attention. He scanned the crowd and saw a young man, probably in his mid-twenties. He was handsome. Eddie noticed that he was sitting in a wheel chair. He wondered how long this young man had been confined to the chair.

He continued, "God has answered many prayers for me not in the way I asked. I've also had times when God answered my prayer in a very short time and in exactly the way that I asked.

"When I was a boy, my father was in a truck accident. He was in a coma for three days. I prayed for him constantly for those three days. At the end of the third day he woke up and just stared at me. He had tears in his eyes, 'I heard you talking to God for me. Son, Thank you.'

"That was the day I decided to become a preacher. I'm ashamed to say that I turned my back on the Lord not too long ago. As I said earlier, my wife and I lost our daughter some time back. It wasn't too long after that that I lost my wife in a car accident. She over corrected her car and drove into the river. She drowned before the E.M.S. workers got to her.

"I can honestly tell you that I had never been in more pain in my life. I was so close to turning my back on the Lord. I can't tell you how scary that is. I found out soon that the Lord still had a use for me. He had a healing for me that I didn't expect. I know this is going to sound hokey, but I think the Lord has a healing for somebody here today."

Eddie peered intently at the crowd again. He was trying to gauge their reaction to his statement. He noticed the man that he'd met at Waffle House was staring at him with a grave expression on his face. The young man in the wheel chair seemed enthusiastic and excited.

He wondered for a moment if this young man was the one who would receive the healing that he'd been told of. Molech crouched behind him with his muzzle close to Eddie's ear. He was waiting for the moment to prompt Eddie to call for the healing and that moment had arrived.

Molech's disgusting saliva was dripping from his muzzle. It passed through Eddie as he preached. A drop would pass through Eddie and he would feel a thrill in his stomach. He interpreted as the approval of the Lord.

If he had known who was helping him, he'd probably had a heart attack. At the very least he would have run away in terror. Molech prompted Eddie to notice at the wheel chair. He told Eddie that the chair was the enemy. The chair represented sickness.

He made sure that Eddie was fixated on the chair and what it represented. Molech didn't want him to consider who provided the healing. Eddie was suddenly seized by a hatred of the wheel chair. He was overtaken by emotional stress.

He wanted to serve the Lord, wanted to be one of the chosen. He didn't care about the truth so much anymore. He cared about being right. He steeled himself and gripped both sides of the podium. The forces of evil were going to take a beating tonight. He would be the one to deliver that beating.

He spoke in a voice that mimicked thunder. "God is the ruler of this universe. God is the owner of this universe. God is sovereign here. God says that he wants to face the enemy and vanquish him. God will vanquish the enemy here today."

In his ecstasy, Eddie turned to the young man in the wheel chair. "Young man, how long have you been in that wheel chair?"

The young man seemed taken aback for a moment. Finally, he responded, "Since I was ten sir. I was in a car accident. I lost my mother and my father was gravely injured. I was raised in foster homes all my life."

Eddie fed off that statement. "Young man I say to you that the Lord has a healing for you today. You only need to believe." The young man spoke, "Sir, I was raised to believe in God. I believe in the power of God. I also believe that people should accept what God given them. He knows better than we what is in store for us."

Eddie stepped back from the podium and stomped. He called out, "This is exactly what the Lord was speaking of when he said, 'Such faith I haven't seen in Israel. Come on up here young man."

The young man was crying by the time he maneuvered the chair down front. He wiped at his eyes with his fists. Eddie addressed the crowd now. He spoke fervently.

"Ladies and gentlemen, I plead with you to join me in prayer for this man. God has a healing for this man on this day. We are going to see a miracle here today. What is your name?"

The reply came, "My name is James."

Eddie noted, "James, like the brother of Jesus."

The front row had six middle-aged women that were praying fervently. Four of them were in the middle of a spiritual ecstasy. Roger was surveying around the tent. He was trying to take this all in and keep the incredulous expression off of his face.

He didn't like the way this seemed. The atmosphere in the tent was getting tense. This situation might possibly get out of control. Eddie raised his hands and began his prayer.

As soon as he started a woman in the front row fainted.

"Dear Lord, we come to you today and lift up your child James to you. He can't walk Lord. We ask that you take pity on him. Please give him the use of his legs."

Roger watched as James's leg twitched. One of the women down front screamed and fell to her knees praying. Then the other leg twitched, and his foot hit the floor. Two men came forward and stood on either side of James. They gingerly took his upper arms in their hands and lifted him to his feet.

They let go. He stood for a second and then swayed and fell back into the chair. Eddie stepped forward and they lifted him again. He put his hands on the James's shoulders and started a fervent prayer.

He immediately started speaking in tongues. A young gentleman in the third row collapsed in a storm of tears and tongues. When they let go of him again he stayed standing. He spread his arms like a child learning to walk. He took a shuffling step forward. His knees wobbled but he stood unaided.

Roger watched it and didn't believe any of it. He decided to stick around after the service. He planned to follow James when the excitement was over. The whole tent was a scene of Pandemonium.

Two women lay in a half stupor. An older gentleman waved smelling salts under their noses. The young lady that had swooned was still lying on the ground. One man had stepped into the aisle, dancing and singing.

Someone took the wheel chair away. James was helped to a chair beside the podium. Roger looked around and thought to himself that this was turning into a mess. Eddie practically screamed in glee while trying to pray or preach or something. It was unintelligible.

In a short time, Eddie calmed enough to speak.

He offered, "Well ladies and gentlemen, I think we will stop the service here. We won't see a blessing bigger than that today. I do have one question for this young man."

Eddie turned to James, "Tell me something. What did it feel like when you were able to support yourself?" James was still wiping his eyes when he spoke "When they first lifted me out of the chair I got this really strong tingling sensation in my legs and lower back. Then I could stand."

Mr. Edwards came forward and whispered something in Eddie's ear. Eddie turned to the crowd in the tent.

"I've been informed that the food has arrived, and the meal is ready to serve. At this time, I will ask Mr. Edwards to give the blessing since he's the one who took care of all of the food preparations."

Eddie stepped back deferentially. Mr. Edwards stepped forward, "Let's all bow our heads please." The subdued chatter in the tent ceased. Everyone in the tent obediently bowed their heads.

Mr. Edwards offered in a carrying voice, "Father in Heaven, we come before you this day thankful of your presence and the miracle that you've provided today. We thank you for the healing. We thank you for the food we are about to share in your fellowship. We ask blessings on the people gathered here and on this ministry. All this we pray in your son's name. Amen."

Nobody saw the troop of Demons that capered about Molech in glee. They were in celebration mode. Human souls were on the way to being corrupted. The kingdom of Heaven would lose souls to false doctrine. Word of this miracle would spread like wildfire in this small community. It would soak like a sponge into the surrounding communities.

Molech crouched behind Mr. Edwards. He had his claws on Mr. Edwards and Eddie. These two were working out very well. He had a satisfied expression on his face. His eyes gave away a wary expression though.

The Heavenly host had been present here today. He eyed Roger and the two Heavenly warriors that flanked him. The angels had their swords drawn. They were shining slightly giving off the glory of God.

He hoped these three weren't aware of his plans. He'd worked hard developing this little tent group. Roger regarded James intently. James sat in the chair by the podium. Several people gathered around him talking animatedly. One of them was the gentleman that had danced in the aisle.

James gave off a satisfied air. The more Roger watched this man the more suspicious he became. Roger didn't see the angel that leaned over and whispered in his ear. He ran through his plans to follow this guy.

He wanted to find out how the guy got here. What car was he riding in? Who drove him around? Roger checked his little key chain digital camera. Pictures of James, his companions and the car they drove were in order.

Roger made a decision. *I can't stand here staring like an idiot. Someone will get suspicious.* He stepped over to the serving line. It had thinned out now. He took a piece of chicken and a glass of tea. He took his food and drink to the corner of the tent. He made sure he had a good view of James and his admirers.

Roger planned to follow at a discreet distance. He watched the group as some of the crowd took to their cars and left. Molech leaned over Eddie and whispered in his ear. Roger saw Eddie's head turn. He looked directly at him.

Eddie's face split with a wide grin. Roger thought, *"Oh great, this is just what I need right now. I need to keep an eye on this guy."*

Roger decided he would trust that the 'fans' around James would keep him busy for a while. He stood up as Eddie reached him.

Eddie had his hand out and Roger took it. Eddie asked, "Well, how did you like the sermon?" Roger made his face a mask.

He replied, "That was something I've never seen before. I've never seen a healing in person. It seemed like you knew it was going to happen. How is that?"

Eddie's face took on a somber air. He answered, "Last night while I was praying, I had a vision. The vision showed a man being healed. I was hesitant to believe it." Eddie shifted his weight to his other foot.

He continued. "Then I saw James over there in the wheelchair. When he wheeled that thing in here a voice in the back of my head spoke, 'He's the one.' I didn't have a choice but to believe it then." He stared at Roger expectantly.

Roger offered, "I've heard of that happening before. I've never seen it in person."

Eddie smiled at him, "Well friend, you've seen it now. God gives faith to the faithful in boundless measure."

Roger didn't want Eddie to become suspicious. He offered a conciliatory, "Amen to that."

That seemed to put Eddie at his ease. It appeared the problem of Eddie was going to solve itself. Mr. Edwards walked toward them.

He hoped this gentleman was going to take Eddie away. Mr. Edwards approached and cleared his throat. Eddie turned around,

"Mr. Edwards that was a nice blessing you gave before the meal."

Mr. Edwards smiled his thanks, "Can I please have a word with you Pastor Cain?"

Eddie answered, "Sure." Then he turned to Roger, "If you will excuse me please."

Roger nodded, "No problem."

Roger watched and saw James with his fans. They were

gathered over the remains of their meals. He heard Mr. Edwards say something about church membership. He resolved to sit in his car and watch until James left. His car windows were tinted. That was the next best thing to invisible.

Roger thought about it for a moment and then took out his key chain camera. He walked over to where James stood chatting with his new fans. He turned the camera on and walked up to James.

"Do you mind?" He indicated the camera, "My wife isn't going to believe this."

James gave him a broad smile, "Sure, this will be the first picture I've taken standing up in sixteen years."

Roger thought, *if this guy is acting then he really gets into his part.* He stepped back and aimed the camera at James. He snapped the picture and turned to go.

One of the women stepped forward with a business card in here hand. "Excuse me sir, I don't have my camera with me. I'd really appreciate it if you'd email me a copy of that picture." Roger looked at the business card.

His eyes went a little wide when he read 'Edith Barnes, Regional Director, Happy Care Daycare'.

He replied, "Sure ma'am. No problem."

She offered her thanks and returned to the line. Roger tucked the card into his shirt pocket and headed for the door of the tent.

Chapter 55

He silently prayed, *Okay Lord, I know you set that up. No way was that a coincidence.* Ten minutes later, Roger sat in his car with his binoculars. These were advanced binoculars. They would take a clear picture at any focus setting. They also had an infrared feature.

Every couple of minutes or so he would glance in at the tent gathering. He was watching for James every time. Roger sat there for about an hour. Finally, he saw Mr. Edwards leading James to his car.

Roger thought, *why are they leaving first? This guy was the star of the whole show.* They got in and Roger started his engine. He put the car in gear and waited for Mr. Edwards black Mercedes to drive past.

He fell in behind the car. They drove through town for a couple of miles. Mr. Edwards pulled into the parking lot of the Brand hotel. Roger pulled to the curb. *"Well this guy isn't a local."* Roger thought.

Roger sat there watching for a couple of minutes. James got out of the car. He walked over to a white Honda and got in. Roger thought, *"Now all I have to do is follow him. When he parks, I'm going to see if that car is modified for a paralytic. I bet there is nothing modified about that car."*

Roger raised the binoculars and focused on James. He was waving and smiling at Mr. Edwards. James turned back to the car and opened the door. Roger zoomed in the binoculars. He could see that there was nothing modified about the car. He quickly snapped a picture.

Mr. Edwards pulled out of the parking lot as James got into his car. Roger made sure his car was in gear. He hoped that James would be going in the same direction he was pointed. As fate or God would have it, he was.

Roger pulled out and fell in line about 100 yards behind James. He slowly inched his way up to about 20 yards. He checked traffic to make sure that he was about to do was relatively safe.

There were no cars coming so he raised the binoculars. He zoomed in on the back of the car and snapped a picture. He pulled closer, focused on the license plates and snapped another picture. Roger made sure to take the next turn. He didn't want to chase this guy down.

He planned to use his contacts on the police force. They would track this guy down for him. He thought the way things were going was interesting. One of the higher members of the church was in on this scheme. He wondered how far this little plot went.

Roger drove to his office immediately. He connected the binoculars to his computer. He turned the system on and waited for it to boot up. When it was done he checked the pictures contained on the binoculars. Roger copied the files to his hard drive. He printed all three images to check their clarity. When he was satisfied, he called his contact in the police department.

The phone rang twice, and a voice answered.

"City Police, Sergeant Tanner may I help you?" intoned the voice on the end of the line. Jeff Tanner was a muscular black man with piercing eyes. Officer Tanner spoke into the phone like it was an enemy.

"Hey Jeff, this is Roger. How's it going?" asked Roger.

"Well, everything was going swimmingly until I found out you had a couple of hours of overtime work for me to do for free," replied Jeff, relaxing in recognition.

"Oh, come on. I never do that to you and I always compensate you for the little favors I ask of you." said Roger, feigning a wounded tone."

"Yeah, yeah right. Free pizza for looking up the bad guys. Well, you know me, will work for food. How are Amelia and Brennan?" asked Jeff. His voice changed to warmth at the last question.

"They are doing fine. Brennan is staying with us for the school break this week." informed Roger.

"Good deal" offered Jeff "I always thought it was a raw deal that you got out of that custody battle. She was never around, and you were the picture-perfect dad. You should have gotten custody."

Roger came back with "Thanks man, I appreciate that a lot. How are Bonita and the kids?" "They are doing fine. Between the video games and the designer tennis shoes they will absolutely die without, they are about to put me in the poor house."

Roger laughed at that, "I know what you mean. Brennan drives me crazy for the latest games and game systems that are out there. I don't get to see him as much as I'd like so I hate to say no to him. He has to hear 'No' every now and then so I make it a 50/50 ratio of denial."

Jeff replied with, "That won't work in my house. If I say no more than half the time Bonita will break down and say yes. That whole growing up poor thing and wanting to give them everything you didn't have, you know?"

"Yeah I got you." Roger noted.

Jeff replied with, "Well enough of the sappy stuff, what do you need man?"

Roger replied, "I've got somebody in the city that I think is running a religious scam. You know that tent ministry that formed a while back?"

"Yeah" Jeff answered.

"Well they had a healing today and I was there. This guy got out of his wheelchair and walked. I was suspicious, so I followed him after the service. One of the leaders of the church drove this guy to the Brand hotel. This guy gets out of the car. Then he gets into the driver's seat of another car. This car hasn't been modified at all for a paralytic. I followed and took pictures," Roger explained.

Jeff commiserated, "Yup, sounds like the classic religious scam. Next thing you know they will be hitting the people up for tons of money to do the 'Lord's work'."

"I don't know what their plans are at the moment. I want to expose it before it goes any farther. People's faith and souls are at stake when something like that happens," Roger stated.

There was silence on the line for a minute and then Jeff's voice came back on the line with "So what do you have for me? Some license numbers to run?"

"Good guess. Am I that predictable?" Roger asked.

Jeff laughed, "It's the same thing you asked for the last four times you needed help. Give me the numbers and I'll call you back later with some information. It will only take about a half an hour for the numbers, but I have a couple of things on my desk I need to clear off before I do anything else today."

Roger picked up the pages lying in front of him, "Okay, the first is a black Mercedes, Kentucky license plate R1S-914. The second one is a white Honda, Illinois license plate J1A-370."

Jeff offered, "Okay man, I'll be getting back with you soon, got to go now."

The line went dead. Roger thought of that. Jeff never waited for a goodbye from the other person. He figured that he had notified of the end of the call and hung up. "Oh well, everybody has a quirk or two."

Roger thought about what he was going to do with the information when Jeff called back. He didn't want this to make a huge scene. He hoped there were only a few people involved. He decided to wait to see what would present itself. This was God's rodeo, he was just along for the ride.

He checked the clock and realized that he hadn't eaten all day. He thought that today was shot. He hadn't done any work on his business. He decided he could afford one day. He chided himself. He was doing the Lord's work wasn't he? Where was his faith?

On an impulse, Roger looked up the number for the Waffle House he'd gone to. The number showed on the screen, and he wrote it down. He picked up his phone and dialed the number.

A male voice answered, "Waffle House, May I help you?"

Roger recognized the voice of the cook. "Hey Ed, this is Roger Carter. I don't know if you remember me. I was wondering if Jan is working today."

There was silence for a moment then Ed's questioning voice came back on the line, "Yes she is. What do you need?"

Ed was a man of few words. Roger knew they were trying to run a business. He asked, "Could I speak to her for a moment please?" Ed didn't like his business being interrupted, but he also knew that Roger was a customer.

After a brief pause, he replied, "Yes but keep it short."

Roger heard that he had turned away from the phone. Ed's voice came through as background noise. "Jan, phone for you."

There was a moment of silence then Jan said, "Who is it?"

Ed informed, "Roger Carter."

Jan was curious, "Well what does he want?"

"I don't know." Ed shot back irritably and added, "Keep it short."

Roger heard Jan's voice come on the line with a questioning note in it. "Yes, Roger. Is there anything wrong?"

Roger offered, "No Jan, nothing is wrong. I need to know. You know that young man that I was talking to the last time I came in?"

She replied, "The young preacher? Yes, I know who you are talking about?"

He thought that was one hurdle jumped. Then he asked, "Do you know how often he comes in if at all?" He held his breath as he listened.

She answered, "He comes in almost every other day at twelve o'clock for lunch. Why do you ask?"

He said, "I was wondering how I could get in touch with him again. Thanks, Jan. I won't keep you. I'll be seeing you soon."

"Okay." Her confusion was evident. He heard the click.

Okay, now I know how to contact this guy if I need to confront him about his teachings and the healing. The thought was rather cynical.

Amelia came to mind. She would be dying to hear about something like this. Roger decided to tell her tonight. She would have some questions. He didn't want to spend a lot of time trying to give explanations over the phone.

Chapter 56

Candy had played with the other kids for an hour or so. She showed off the necklace to everybody that would indulge her. She started swinging it around like she'd seen on one of the gangster shows. She wasn't paying attention to where she was. The pendant struck the counter with a loud crack.

She examined it. There wasn't any obvious damage. She didn't know that she had destroyed the camera inside it.

The imp stopped screaming at her and giggled. "That's one down and one to go." Then he flew over to where the kid's backpacks were stacked.

He levered a little girls pink backpack until it fell. It landed directly in front of Brennan's backpack. He knew the camera was completely blocked. "Well," He sighed. "My work here is done. I will go report to the master. Right after I have a little fun about town that is."

He leapt into the air and passed through the ceiling. He didn't see Brennan come out of the bathroom. Brennan polished his badge with a paper towel. The reception on this particular camera was excellent. Since there was a tiny angel standing on Brennan's shoulder, it was going to stay that way.

The lead Child Development Specialist, Judy was having a conversation with her assistant, Diana.

Judy informed, "I know it's early, but I have an appointment this afternoon. Let's take care of the special training now instead of this afternoon."

"Okay." Diana replied.

Judy walked to the front of the floor. She called out. "Turquoise group form a line in front of me."

Diana walked to a spot at the rear of the building and called out "Blue group, form a line over here in front of me."

The children obediently broke up into the separate groups. They formed straight lines in front of the two women. As soon as the lines were formed the ladies called for quiet. The two lines of children grew still and quiet.

Judy's voice became coaxing. "Okay kids form a circle around me." They did so with a practiced ease. It was fortunate that she was facing Brennan directly. Her reflection was clear in the badge.

"Okay, close your eyes and take deep slow breaths." The kids were quiet as they complied. After a minute of this, "Now I want you to picture yourself lying in a meadow of green grass. It is a sunny day. The wind is blowing softly. You feel the breeze against your skin. You are calm. Now reach out with your mind and talk to the universe. You are part of it. It is part of you. You can feel the consciousness of the universe. Now talk to it in your mind. Tell it how you feel and what you want. Then listen to see if it says anything to you."

Several of the kids appeared to be in a stupor. Brennan wasn't affected at all by this effect. None of the children of practicing Christians had been affected. No one took note of this.

Roger had been working when Jeff called.

"Hey buddy, how's it going? Man have I got some news for you." Jeff offered. Roger's mouth went dry before he could say anything. There was a silence on the line and Jeff prodded, "Roger? You there man?"

Roger finally found his voice, "Yeah Jeff I'm here you caught me off guard. I got a little too excited there."

Jeff answered, "Well I'll try to be a little more sedate for the elderly." He laughed a small laugh.

Roger returned, "Okay then young man what do you have for me?"

There was another slight pause as Roger heard papers rustle in the background. Jeff's voice came back on the line

"Okay, let's hit the mundane stuff first. The black car belongs to a James Edwards. He's a real estate guy. He's also one of the richest men in the state. He is rather reclusive, so nobody knows all that much about him. His record is squeaky clean. He lost his wife to brain cancer and his only daughter to a car accident. He never remarried. Everything I see here says he's a pillar of the community. Aside from what you have on him, this guy is squeaky clean. Do you want his phone number?"

Roger thought about this for a moment. He decided that this guy was doing the wolf in sheep's clothing. Either that or he was a recent turncoat. He was going to have to mull this one over for a while. He didn't like not understanding his adversary.

Roger picked up a pen, grabbed a pad and instructed, "Yeah, go ahead and give it me. It will at least save me looking it up later."

Jeff offered, "His home number is 606-351-3692" The system doesn't show a cell number for him. It's probably because he doesn't like cell phones."

"Okay then what else do you have for me?" Roger asked hopefully.

Jeff replied with "Well this is where you struck gold. The white Honda belongs to James Wagner. He is a marketing rep for a company called Starfire Marketing out of Chicago, Illinois. That in itself is unremarkable.

"His hobby however is what sets him apart in this case. He is an amateur actor. He's taken all kinds of acting workshops and he's appeared in several plays in the Chicago area. Your boy wants to be a famous thespian Roger.

"His current employers probably wouldn't approve of his recent religious activities. Marketing is about presenting an image. The image must be one of perceived honesty. Otherwise the Marketing Firm has no chance of doing business.

"This guy's activities could cost his employer a lot of business. I bet he would fold if you pressured him with a job threat. I know you want to contact this guy. Are you ready for his cell phone number?" Jeff finished with that.

There was a pause and Roger answered, "Yeah, I get you, Jeff. Not only have you handed me the information. You also gave me the means to use it to my advantage. Thank you so much. Go ahead and give me the number."

Jeff informed genially, "Well you know how it is with us geniuses. We can't keep from sharing our vast knowledge. The number is 312-817-4909. Hmmm… instead of pizza I think I want a nice lasagna lunch. What do you think?"

Jeff's last statement had such an air of self-confidence that Roger let out a big belly laugh.

"I'll get you a twenty-five-dollar gift card for Mancini's that way you can choose the day you want to go Italian," Roger allowed.

Jeff answered in a mollified tone, "Well, sir, it has been a pleasure doing business with you, but I have about three more of those 'get done now' things. Call me sometime at home when you have time to talk. We need to catch up. I miss the days when we were workout partners. Ever think about getting back into body-building?"

Roger ruefully stated, "Yeah, I think about it. That seems to be as far as it goes. Who knows maybe we'll both get motivated. Sometimes I'd love to pick it up again. I'll try to remember to call you. Sorry man, I haven't been spacing you off, I've been busy."

"I know man, life happens. Talk to you later." Jeff replied. With that Jeff hung up.

Roger thought wryly, *"Now that would bug some people."* Roger looked at the clock. It was two o'clock. He had time to call this guy if he thought he should do it today.

He considered it and decided there was enough going on today. No sooner was the decision made, he felt an overwhelming urge to call. He didn't see the angel whispering in his ear. He silently prayed. *"Okay Lord, I'll take that as your desire for me to go ahead and make the call."*

Roger picked up his phone and dialed the second number he'd written down. After 3 rings a cheerful male voice answered, "Hello". Roger asked, "Is this Mr. James Wagner, actor?"

James answered with "It sure is. What can I do for you?"

"Mr. Wagner, You work for Starfire Marketing. Is that true?"

There was silence on the line for a minute. James' voice came back across the line sounding uncertain. "Yes, it is. Who is this? Is there something that I can do for you?"

Roger stated, "Mr. Wagner, my name is Roger Carter. I'm a private investigator with Rest Easy Investigations. As I understand it, you recently attended a service in Littleton, Kentucky. During the service, you deceived the congregation into believing you were healed of paralysis. Is that accurate?"

James was sweating bullets right now. This guy knew where he worked. He seemed to know all about him. From the tone of his voice he seemed unhappy with the information he just shared. James decided he would cooperate for now.

He answered guardedly, "Well yes, but it really wasn't like that."

"Wasn't like that? You mean you didn't show up in a wheel chair and lead these people to believe that you were paralyzed? You didn't pretend to be healed and then walk around talking to the congregation saying you hadn't walked in sixteen years? Which part of that was inaccurate?" Roger replied stiffly.

There was a long silence. "Well, all of that was accurate." His voice shook slightly. Roger was irritated now, "Mr. Wagner, I really don't think you realize the severity of your actions. You obviously profited from your actions. You aren't going to tell me you drove from Chicago and did this for fun. If you don't cooperate, I promise that you will be prosecuted for your actions. I also believe there is a good chance you will lose your job. So, tell me, Mr. Wagner, what's it going to be? Do I need to contact your lawyer and your employer? Or would you care to cooperate instead?"

James was literally sweating now. He didn't dream this little lark of a job was going to land him in this kind of trouble. He knew it was dishonest and had considered saying no. The three thousand dollars that James Edwards had offered had assuaged his conscience.

"Mr. Carter, I will cooperate with you, but I honestly didn't mean any harm."

Roger got angry at this point. He replied rather hotly, "You didn't mean any harm?! You didn't mean any harm?! Mr. Wagner, do you have a faith that you follow?"

James was shocked by the anger in Roger's voice. "Well, no, not really."

"And that is precisely why you don't understand what you've done. The people that believe you were healed believe that they've witnessed a miracle from God. You may not understand that, but it's true," retorted Roger.

His voice was dripping with sarcasm at this point. "People of faith base their lives on their beliefs. They live their lives in the service of the God that they believe in. Then you walk in and mock their faith. I'm sure you had a good laugh on your drive home." Roger finished.

James lamented, "Sir, I'm sorry. I didn't know. What do I need to do to make it right?" Roger was so glad to hear those words.

Roger informed him, "Mr. Wagner it is a good thing you don't live around here. The truth is going to hurt a lot of people. You won't be a popular person when the truth comes out.

"What you've done can be repaired but you are going to have to admit to the truth. It would be best coming from you. First I need to know how many people in the congregation knew about this?"

James replied, "The only person who approached me was Mr. Edwards. I don't think anybody else in the church knows." Roger felt better at this remark. At least Eddie is a sincere preacher. He may be misled but he is still sincere. That at least would make him more approachable with the truth.

Roger offered, "Okay Mr. Wagner, I will get you Eddie Cain's phone number. I want you to call him and tell him the truth." James balked at this, "Mr. Carter, I've never been what you would call a brave man. Can I provide you with a recorded statement, family pictures and a video clip of me in my last play?"

Roger's heart sank. What James had suggested would be sufficient, but Roger added, "I'll go along with that if you allow me to provide your cell phone to Mr. Cain. If he wants to contact you, you will be open and honest with him.

"That's the best I can do. Oh and no changing your cell number. You do that, and I'll call your boss with all my evidence. Mr. Wagner, will you agree to this?"

James thought for a second, "Well let's be honest with each other. I don't really have much choice in this do I? I wish I'd never met James Edwards." Roger thought about that for a moment. While he felt a certain amount of compassion, the truth had to come out. This was the only way the church would heal.

He related, "Mr. Wagner, you would have been better off if you hadn't met him. In a spiritual sense you now have much to answer for. The Lord doesn't take it well when his people are led astray for money. I realize I'm speaking from a faith you may not share."

James' blood ran cold at that thought. Maybe there was something to this religion thing. This might be something he needed to look into. Roger heard the long silence on the line.

He knew that James was taking stock of his life. Fear was evident in his voice when he spoke of the statement.

Roger asked, "Mr. Wagner, you say you don't have a faith that you follow. Doesn't that seem a waste of an existence? Do you honestly believe we are here for nothing?"

James thought about that for a moment. "I never really thought about it like that." He replied thoughtfully. Roger expressed, "Okay, I'm not going to preach at you. I know at this moment you really aren't ready for it. Right now, you are just trying to stay out of trouble.

"You need to consider is that 'staying out of trouble' is one of the main aims of Christianity. One of the first reasons Christians become

Christians is because they are trying to stay out of trouble."

James was confused at that statement. "What do you mean?" He asked.

Roger answered, "In the Bible, hell is a bad place, full of pain. A lot of people become Christians because they want to avoid hell. Isn't that the same thing as trying to stay out of trouble?"

James hadn't heard most of this before. He hadn't really considered the rest. He'd been living his life on his own terms.

Roger voiced, "Mr. Wagner, after this has settled down, feel free to contact me. I would be happy to help you with your questions or concerns about Christianity."

James nodded, a useless gesture on the phone, "Oh okay, I'll do that."

Roger returned, "Back to the subject at hand. Let me give you my email address so you can send me the material you were talking about."

James hedged, "Mr. Carter, I don't have a pen and I'm not anywhere that I can get one."

Roger offered, "Fine then, when we hang up I'll call right back. Don't answer the phone. I'll leave a message with my email in it. I expect to receive an email from you by the end of the night. Is that too soon?"

James answered, "No. That will be fine. I'll make sure to send it to you before 9:00PM tonight." Roger said, "Okay, I'll expect your email. Bye for now." James gave his farewell and they both hung up.

Roger called back, and when the message tone sounded, "Send the materials to r-c-a-r-t-e-r @ r-e-a-s-y.com." Roger hung up and wondered, *when will I have time to handle that?"*

Chapter 57

Roger's mind returned to the problem of the day. He was keyed up because of worry for Brennan and Candy. He wondered what kind of evidence the cameras would produce. He hoped he wouldn't have to run the setup again tomorrow.

He reminded himself to pray for the kids and the video evidence often. He sat at his desk and wondered what Amelia was doing. It was almost 4:00 o'clock. He decided to call her.

The phone rang as he reached for it. He picked it up and intoned "Rest Easy Investigations, Roger speaking. May I help you?"

Amelia's voice replied, "Hey honey, it's me. I just wanted to call and ask you to pray for the kids. I've been worried about them all day."

Roger shot back, "I'm way ahead of you. I've been praying for them all day. Could you please call Stephen and Rachel? If they are still coming, I'll pick up two large pizzas on the way home. I don't want you to miss any of our little meeting because you are cooking."

Amelia breathed a sigh of relief. "Thank you honey. I was going to suggest takeout tonight. I've been keyed up so badly today." Roger offered, "Well if you'll call the Beaumont's, I'll call in the pizzas. I'll leave at four-thirty today, so we can see what we have today.

"I can pick up Brennan on the way home. You can drive me to pick up the rental car after we get there. He'll be ok alone for all of fifteen minutes. If you aren't comfortable with that he can ride with us."

"I think he can ride with us. I'll drop you off a block before we get to the car. That way he won't know where you are going." Amelia stated.

"Ok, I'll see you in a bit honey. I'll pick up the pizzas on the way home in the rental." Roger informed in anticipation of the night's adventures. He ended the call and hit star-zero-three on his speed dial. That was the number to "The Pizza Joint". They made the best pizza in town.

He wondered idly if he had his priorities mixed up. He had a pizza place on his speed dial before the police. The phone picked up and a youthful female voice came on the line saying, "Pizza Joint, may I help you?"

Roger answered, "Yes, this is Roger Carter, I'd like to place an order for two large pepperonis for pickup please." A moment passed, and the voice intoned "Roger Carter, 555-4735?" He answered with "That's me."

She voiced, "Yes sir, I've placed your order. Your total will be $18.95. Your order will be ready in approximately thirty-five minutes. Will there be anything else?" Roger returned, "That will be all. Thank you much. I'll be there in a bit."

Roger hung up and checked the clock. He went through what he called his 'work shut down' ritual. He ensured his office door was locked, then headed for his car.

He was a bit nervous on the drive home. He really wanted to see what the cameras had picked up. He didn't see the angelic guard sitting in the car with him. He didn't see the two huge angels flying over his car. He also didn't see the one in front and the one behind his car.

A band of demons followed the car. They were agitated. They searched for an opening that wasn't there. Their orders were to attack the little human investigator. The angelic blades held them at bay.

Roger stopped at the daycare and picked up Brennan. Brennan was full of energy and happy to see his dad. Judy was still there, and she was openly smiling at Roger. Roger asked if Brennan had behaved himself and she affirmed that he had. Roger thanked Judy and told Brennan to get his backpack.

Brennan ran to the stack of backpacks and dug through it until he found his. He put it on and walked over to his dad. Roger noticed the shoulder strap on his backpack was directly over the badge. He thought, *"Well it doesn't matter, we are headed home now."* Roger gave his goodbyes and thanked the staff. They turned and headed for the door.

Once in the car and Brennan asked why Amelia hadn't picked him up. Roger explained that Amelia had a meeting and wasn't able to. Brennan accepted the answer without protest. Roger pulled out of the parking lot and headed for home.

They made it home a little later than usual. Roger told Brennan to stay in the car because they need to go pick up something. He got out, unlocked and opened the door. He called out to Amelia, "Honey, we're home. Are you ready?"

She called back from the living room, "Yes, I'm getting my jacket. I called Stephen and Rachel. They will be here at around six o'clock." Roger heard the living room closet door close and Amelia appeared in the hallway sliding into her jacket. "Did you order bread sticks with dipping sauce?"

Roger winced, "No honey. I didn't even think about it. I'll see if I can get an order of them when I get there."

She had a smirk on her face, "You never think of my favorites." Then she assumed a small pouting expression.

Roger looked a little stung, "I promise I'll pick up some for you. I won't leave 'The Pizza Joint' without them."

She smiled, "Honey, I was teasing you. I really do like the breadsticks and sauce though."

He answered, "I know honey. Sometimes I feel like I'm selfish because I don't think of things like that."

Her face was a little shocked, "Roger Carter, you are one of the most selfless people I know. I don't ever want to hear you say that again. You work hard to provide for this family. You spend lots of time with me. You make time for Brennan and you spend time with him on his homework. You volunteer your time once a week at the church as security and you talk to your parents at least once a week. Don't let some stupid breadsticks make you feel selfish."

Roger was shocked by her reaction and had nothing to say

in reply. He simply replied, "Time's a wastin' honey. We better get going."

Amelia gave him a little glare, "Okay, let's go but this conversation isn't over. We will talk about this more after the Beaumont's leave tonight."

Roger secretly hoped she would forget about it by then. They went out the front door. Amelia went to the passenger door while Roger locked the house up. He hadn't unlocked the passenger door. He liked to open doors for her, so he had gotten into the habit of leaving her door locked so he could unlock it and open it for her.

She had balked at this at first. She was a grown woman, perfectly capable of opening a door. She could tell it mattered to him though. Amelia had decided to allow him his chivalry.

He dutifully walked to the driver's side door and opened it. Then he smiled at her, "Honey, don't you remember that you are dropping me off?" Her face took on what Roger called 'one of those looks'. She walked around the car and got into the driver's seat.

She sat there for a moment and reached up to close the door.

He asked, "Honey, don't you think you will need the keys?"

She peered up at him with consternation on her face and replied, "Look smart guy. Are we doing this or not? I didn't think we had time for a comedy routine."

Roger held up both hands. With an impish smile, "Hey, I'm just saying." He held out the keys and she snatched them with a smile. He closed her door for her. He noticed Brennan giggling in the back seat.

He didn't hear Brennan say, "That's a point for dad's side."

Roger wondered what was going on when he got in the car and Brennan was giggling.

Amelia softly ordered, "Oh hush young man."

He figured he'd picked on her enough, so he let it go. She started the car and backed out of the driveway. They drove most of the way there in companionable silence.

Roger fiddled with the radio and Brennan made gagging sounds at the older songs. A block before they got to the rental car she pulled over to the curb.

Amelia turned to Roger, "I believe this is your stop kind sir."

He replied, "Well yes, it is dear lady. I will meet you back at the house as soon as I finish picking up the pizza *and* breadsticks with sauce." He leaned over and kissed her.

To Brennan, "See you at home, champ."

Roger got out of the car and started walking up the block. He heard the car turn around and head for home. None of them saw the swarm of angels that surrounded them. Half of the swarm split off to stay with Roger. The rest stayed with Amelia and Brennan.

There was another swarm hovering behind the angelic warriors. These weren't angels. The demons were searching for any break in the angelic ranks. They wanted to get to the Carters. From the determined looks on the angelic faces, that wasn't going to happen.

The demonic ranks shrank back from Molech's anger. The demon lord's anger was terrifying.

"What do you mean you didn't know that there were three cameras?! You were the one that I trusted! You were the one that I sent! When Canaan fell you were the only one I did not punish! You were my most trusted servant!

"I gave this to you to prove to the others that it would be done without difficulty. I give you my trust and you failed me!! The humans have evidence now because you failed to realize there was another camera!!" Molech screamed in absolute fury.

Braylor cowered on his stomach before his lord. He knew that his failure would cost him dearly. He didn't know how much.

In a sniveling voice, "My lord, our intelligence was that they only had two working cameras. I only followed the directives that I was given."

Molech leapt to his hooves. Saliva flew from his mouth as he screamed, "Since when do we trust in our intelligence completely?

You think to lay the blame of your failure at the feet of someone else. This is your failure Braylor and I will pay the price for it. However, you will pay your price before I do!"

Braylor cowered at the words and wished he could disappear. He sincerely wished he hadn't been created. What could he do in the face of his lord? He knew he was about to be banished but running was not an option.

An imp such as Braylor didn't have a prayer against a demon lord. He couldn't match him in a fight. He had no chance of outrunning him. On top of all of that Braylor would be a hunted down if he tried to hide.

Braylor rubbed clawed hand nervously across his grey warty forehead. The slime he sweated coated his palm. Small rivulets of the slime ran down his veined neck. His tongue snaked out across gapped and broken teeth. He nervously awaited his fate.

Molech lunged forward and grabbed Braylor by the nape of the neck. Molech called one of his underlings over. The large imp came crawling over. Molech growled, "Take this out to the country." With that, he pulled Braylor's head off and handed the imp the body.

Braylor begged for mercy. Molech held Braylor's head by one of his ears. He reached up and drew his claws through the air. Braylor saw the portal open. Loud wails came from the portal. Molech unceremoniously tossed Braylor's head into the portal. The assembled demons heard Braylor's screams as Molech closed the portal to Sheol with a wipe of his hand.

Chapter 58

Roger picked up the pizza and got the order of breadsticks and dipping sauce. *"I'll be back in her good books when I bring this home."* He thought. He picked up a couple of bottles of soda and headed for home. He made sure to get caffeine free soda.

Brennan would be hyper if he had caffeine at dinner. Roger wondered what had been recorded during the day. He considered making the meal informal in the living room. Remembering that Brennan and Candy would be present, the video would have to wait.

Roger planned to suggest Brennan show Candy how to play his video games. He was prepared to offer a small bribe to his son if needed. He made it home in fifteen minutes. He pulled in the drive and saw the Beaumont's car coming down the street.

He hadn't realized how long it had taken to pick up the dinner. He got out of the car with his arms loaded. He called a hello to Stephen and Rachel. He noticed that Candy was swinging the necklace she was wearing. He hoped it was Candy-proof.

Roger didn't have a free hand, so resorted to pushing the doorbell with a knuckle. Amelia came to the door in a minute.

She gave Roger a speculative glance. "Did you lock your keys in the car?" she asked.

He gave her a look, "Sorry honey but I didn't have a free hand to use my keys."

"Oh" she replied, "Sorry about that." Roger invited the Beaumont's in as he stepped over the threshold. They followed him in the house, leading Candy by the hand. Nobody saw the angels that came with the Beaumont's.

The angels took their places inside the formation of the other angels that were ringing the house. Roger walked over to the kitchen table and put his burdens down there. He moved the pizzas and soda to the kitchen island.

Amelia had gotten out the paper plates and they were already on the island.

"So how have you guys been doing today?" Roger asked.

Stephen replied, "It hasn't been a bad day. We are a little anxious, well you know."

Roger gave him a meaningful glance, "I know exactly what you are talking about."

While they were talking, Rachel rummaged in her purse. She pulled out a silver locket necklace. She spoke to Candy saying, "Hey sweetie, want to trade?" Candy's eyes went wide. The locket had a dove intricately etched into the top. She took the locket and handed the other necklace to her mother.

Rachel held out the necklace to Roger. Roger took the necklace, pocketed it, "What if we need to do this again tomorrow?" Rachel's face became questioning. It was obvious that she hadn't thought of that before acting.

Roger raised his voice for the benefit of the kids. "Who is ready for some pizza?" Brennan and Candy both reacted enthusiastically. Roger instructed, "Ok, let's wash our hands, say the blessing and then we can eat."

Everybody took a turn at either the kitchen sink or the downstairs bathroom washing their hands. When they were finished they all formed a circle and joined hands for the blessing of the meal. Roger prayed in his deep steady voice.

"Father in Heaven, we thank you for this food and for this time of fellowship and family. We acknowledge you as God and we ask your blessing on this meal and these families. We also ask for your blessing on the endeavor we are engaged in together. All this we pray in Jesus name. AMEN"

All those gathered in the circle echoed his amen and they all released hands. They filled their plates and sat at the kitchen table. Amelia and Rachel chatted about scrapbooks.

Stephen asked in a low voice, "Have you had a chance to check anything yet?"

Roger eyed the kids pointedly. Understanding swept across

Stephen's face. Roger shook his head almost imperceptibly. The kids had attacked their food like they were starving. Pizza was Brennan's all-time favorite food. He was enjoying this night if only for the meal.

Roger prompted, "Brennan, when we finish with dinner, why don't you show Candy how to play 'Mutant Ninja's Revenge'?" Brennan looked skeptical. Roger added, "Any time you use teaching her to play won't count against your time limit for the night."

Brennan's face brightened, "Okay, Dad."

Nobody saw the four large angels walk through the wall. They stationed themselves in the kitchen, living room and Brennan's room. The fourth one was Andarel. He spoke up to the other three. "Make sure you keep an eye on the floors. They are using that trick a lot lately. Any imp or demon that you see, sound the alarm and banish it with your sword."

Roger and Stephen made small talk as they ate their dinner. Roger glanced over at Amelia. She was dipping a breadstick and getting ready to bring it to her lips when she noticed his gaze. He must have had a satisfied expression on his face because she took on an impish smile. She raised her breadstick as if to toast him, "Thank you honey."

Rachel seemed a little lost at this exchange. Amelia explained, "Roger knows how much I adore breadsticks and dipping sauce." Roger smiled and turned back to Stephen. He hadn't realized that Stephen had been speaking.

Stephen seemed a little put out. Roger apologized, "Oh man, I'm sorry. I didn't mean to ignore you. We had a little moment."

Stephen's face lost its' edge, "No problem. I do that sometimes too. So, is there a plan or are we winging this?"

Roger answered, "Oh there is a plan. I'll let you in on it in a little while." He cast a meaningful glance at the kids. Candy was basically finished. She picked at her food and sipping on her soda. Brennan on the other hand showed no signs of slowing down.

Roger asked, "Candy, aren't you going to eat more than that?"

Stephen answered for her, "She probably doesn't have much of an appetite at the moment. I gave her a little snack before we came over."

"Yes, I know you did. You are always sneaking her little treats when I'm not paying attention. You ruin her appetite at least 3 times a week." Rachel grumped.

Stephen's face became sheepish, "Well she's daddy's little girl and I like sharing a special little moment with here every now and then."

Roger glanced between them and commented, "Do we need to break out the gloves and get a referee or will this not devolve into violence?"

Rachel replied with a red face, "Oh we aren't arguing. There are a few little things that we don't see eye to eye on. Sorry. We didn't mean to bring this into your home." A few minutes later they all finished up.

Brennan had finally found his limit. He put half a slice of pizza in the refrigerator with the rest of the leftovers. Candy had managed to eat a full slice of pizza. She was slowly nibbling on a breadstick.

Roger prompted, "Buddy, are you going to take Candy upstairs and show her your games?"

Brennan answered, "Okay Dad. Come on Candy." Brennan led Candy up the stairs to his room.

Rachel announced she was going to go upstairs with the kids. She wanted to make sure they didn't come downstairs unannounced. She said, "The last thing we want is for them to go back to the daycare and say that their parents were looking at pretty pictures of the daycare on the television."

Roger responded, "That is a good idea. If we have anything good, do you want me to burn a copy for you to peruse later when you get home?"

Rachel perked up, "I was going to ask if you could do something like that."

Roger explained, "I'm going out to the car and get the receiving unit. I'll have it hooked to the television in about 10 minutes."

Amelia spoke up, "I'll clean up from dinner and put on some coffee."

Stephen chimed in, "Okay, now that we all have a plan, I'm going to sit on the couch and pretend to be lazy."

Roger and Amelia laughed at this. There wasn't anything for Stephen to do at the moment. Roger headed out to the car. Video game noises punctuated the evening. Candy's delighted squeal drifted downstairs now and then. One time they heard Brennan saying, 'I'm going to get you.'

Roger came in carrying a leather case and the receiving unit. He took them to the living room and put it on the floor beside the entertainment center. He maneuvered an end table in front of the entertainment center. He placed the receiving unit on the end table and connected it to the TV.

Amelia finished up in the kitchen and asked if anyone would like a cup of coffee.

Roger answered, "I'd love an after-pizza coffee."

Stephen gave a hearty, "Yes, please."

Amelia replied, "How do you like your coffee?"

Stephen told her, "Cream and three sugars please."

Roger joked, "Like a little coffee with your sugar?"

Amelia went to the bottom of the stairs and called up to Rachel. Rachel answered no, and Amelia went back to the kitchen. She came out of the kitchen a minute later carrying a tray with three coffees on it. She set the tray down, "Are we all set yet?"

Roger offered, "Yes. We were waiting on you. I didn't want you to miss any of this. This first setup is the camera that we put on Brennan's backpack." He raised the remote and pushed the play button. For a few minutes they were treated to an image of the main childcare area.

Roger hit the fast forward button and scanned through. A few kids moved around then the image shifts around. A shape is seen to roll in front of the backpack. Roger noted, "Another backpack rolled down in front of Brennan's. The camera is probably going to be blocked for the rest of the day. Let's scan through the whole thing to make sure."

He clicked fast-forward until the T.V. was showed the maximum view speed. Fifteen minutes later they had gone through all 8 hours of the video feed. No image appeared until Brennan dug the backpack out to go home.

Roger commented, "Well, that's one down. That didn't do us any good. Let's see what the necklace that Candy wore did for us." He stepped up to the receiving unit and set it for playback on camera two.

Roger sat back down and took a sip of his coffee. "Good coffee honey." He complimented as he hit the fast-forward button on the remote. The screen showed an image of the outside of the daycare from the perspective of a short person.

"Hey, what have we here? That is showing good quality video and at least the necklace is turned the right way." Roger rattled off.

That proved to be an unfortunate statement. There was nothing holding the necklace in place. It showed a view of what was in front of Candy. Then motion would cause the necklace to flip. During those times it showed a black screen because it was facing her chest.

Before long the image started whirling around in a crazy manner. Roger was looking at the screen, "What the heck is that?" Then the whirling would stop.

Stephen commented, "I think I know what's going on. I saw Candy swinging the necklace around in a circle when we picked her up. I bet that's what is doing that."

Roger commiserated, "Well that explanation makes sense."

They watched the playback when the image started doing the whirling motion again. Then suddenly everything went black.

Roger stated, "I think she may have broken the camera by hitting something with it. Let me run it back and then do a replay with the audio on."

Roger ran back the video to the last point that the video feed was working. He adjusted the audio to make sure they would hear it then he hit play. The noises of kids playing in the background were heard. The whirling motion started then a loud crack sounded. The video and audio went out.

Roger noted, "Yup, that's what happened. That is one camera down for the count."

Stephen apologized, "Roger I'm so sorry. We will pay for the camera."

Roger rebuffed him, "No, you won't. This is also a field test of this equipment. We didn't ask you to join us on this, so we could weasel money out of you."

Roger's face took on a thoughtful expression. He turned to Amelia, "Well, so far we are two-up, two-down. It isn't looking too good for the home team." Amelia knew that tone. She didn't like it when her husband spoke like that. She knew he was feeling a little inconsequential at the moment.

She prompted, "Well, honey, we still have one camera to go. Remember, one soul with God is a majority. God doesn't always give us what we want but he does give us what we need."

Andarel was standing in the corner by the entertainment center. He glanced at one of his fellow angels and stated, "I like that woman. She knows where her faith belongs."

Roger stepped over to the sending unit. He set it to show the third camera. He turned to Amelia with a hopeful expression before he sat down. The look he gave wasn't lost on Amelia. She spent a moment in silent prayer for him. She knew he thought he had failed his family if this plan didn't work.

Roger hit the play button. The scene showed a little boy's face. The child had been speaking to Brennan. Roger fast-forwarded for a few seconds. Then hit the play button again. The scene came back with Brennan speaking to one of the Daycare workers. He asked her when snack time would be.

She laughed, "It will be soon, you little walking stomach."

Roger fast-forwarded again for a minute. The scene flashed up, and Brennan was playing with a truck. Roger fast-forwarded again and finally hit pay dirt.

When he hit play, the image was of one of the daycare workers talking about the universe.

Roger spoke up, "Hold on now. I think we have something." He hit rewind and watched the video play backwards until he could tell the kids were forming a circle around someone.

He recognized the woman as Judy that he had spoken to when he dropped Brennan off. Roger, Amelia and Stephen sat electrified watching the video. They listened to the meditation that Judy led them through. They watched as Brennan shifted around. They saw several children swaying to the sound of Judy's voice. It was rather hypnotic.

Roger found himself getting angry. The daycare was taking money from trusting parents. They had flaunted that trust. They intentionally disregarded the parent's belief systems and attempted to instill their own.

Roger glanced over and saw the expression on Amelia's face. She was as outraged as he was. She also looked panicked. Roger wondered what was going on in her mind. They watched through the entire meditation.

Roger started doing the fast-forward hops again. He wanted to see if they spouted any more new age jargon during the day. The cursory scan only took about half an hour. Roger didn't want to miss anything.

When they reached the end of the video he prompted, "We've got exactly what we need."

Stephen responded, "I don't understand how this is such a bad thing. How can this help us?"

Roger explained, "Any child care facility has federal funds available to it, if that facility meets certain guidelines. One of those guidelines is that they can't promote any religion or faith system above another while receiving federal funds. They can lose their business license for doing this, not to mention facing some hefty fines from the Feds.

"I can set up an appointment with the district attorney and take this in as evidence. Religious cases are a firestorm of controversy, so I know the district attorney will pursue this. It is a good way for him to make a name for himself in legal channels."

Amelia spoke up and her voice was a little strained. She asked, "How long is this going to take? I don't want to send Brennan back into that place. They are feeding him spiritual poison."

Roger felt as though he was being a little callous when he answered, "Honey, if we are going to make this case stick we have to be outraged parents with their son in this Daycare at least until the case gets started. If we pull Brennan out now we will appear unreasonable to the general populace.

"Remember if they go to the press they can turn this around on us because this country was formed based on religious freedom. We have to keep the focus on them and not give them ammunition to focus on us. Keep in mind that we have federal law on our side."

Amelia stared at her husband for a long minute. Then she replied testily, "Okay, you are the expert in this. I'm not comfortable with Brennan going to this daycare. If he has to until the case gets started, then he has to. We are going to pray for the kids every night and we are going spend time with Brennan every night in the Bible. This is spiritual warfare." Amelia's voice got higher the more she talked, and a tear trickled down her cheek.

Stephen thought that she was over reacting but didn't say anything.

Roger offered, "That is fine honey. I agree with you and we can do that. It is actually something that we should adopt every night. We could spend 15 minutes in the Bible every night as a family. That would arm Brennan and us against worldly ways."

Stephen started to wonder about this conversation. He liked the idea of being a Christian. He'd seen what prayer had done for Candy. He also thought all things in moderation.

Chapter 59

Molech hovered outside the house. His hearing was such that he heard everything that was said. He was absolutely livid with rage. Molech hissed "Jenoch, come to me." A moment later Jenoch was at his side, bowing to his master.

Jenoch murmured, "Yes master, what is your will?"

Molech snarled, "Take twenty imps and assault the house. I don't care about the risk. I want you to get an imp hidden inside. The one that you choose to hide is to gather as much information as he can.

"In two days he is to leave the house and report directly to me. You stay back from the fighting. You are too valuable to me to risk."

Jenoch smiled at this, "Yes master. It shall be done."

Jenoch called his seventeen imps and one of Molech's other lieutenants to gain the other three that were needed. The lieutenant's name was Chamdar and he gave up three of his imps as soon as Jenoch asked for them.

It was common knowledge that Jenoch was one of Molech's favorites. It did not do to go against one of the favorites. Actions like that would get you banished to Sheol. Chamdar spoke in a slovenly manner, "Are you sure you only need three? I would be happy to provide more for the master's cause."

Jenoch smiled. He adored the position of power that he occupied. "No. The master's orders were explicit. His instructions were to take twenty. We are to get one hidden in the house. I will not deviate from his wishes."

Chamdar understood that. To deviate from your master's plan was to invite punishment. Sometimes even the smallest deviation was enough to cause an already irritable master to demonstrate banishment to the rest of his underlings.

"That is well understood." barked Chamdar. He took his leave, melting into the darkness. Jenoch whirled to face the assembled imps.

He snarled, "Each of you produce your weapon of choice."

Obediently the imps screwed up their faces in concentration and held out their hands.

Some of them produced red axes. Some produced black swords. One produced a slimy bow with a quiver full of dripping black arrows. The last one produced a black spear with a huge spear tip that glowed red with a green hue around it.

When they finished, Jenoch selected an imp. He was the one that had produced the bow.

Jenoch rasped, "You, I want you to wait outside of the assault. As soon as an opening breaks, I want you to dive into the house and hide. Don't give away your position. Listen to all that they say. Watch when you can.

"Two days from now, leave the house and report to Master Molech. You are to tell him everything you see and hear. Watch for a weakness in the family. Search for information regarding the daycare. Try to bring back as much information as you can."

The little imp holding the bow bowed and offered an oily "yes" then waited expectantly.

Jenoch took charge of the other nineteen imps. He selected four of them at random, "You four come with me." He led them to the side and spoke. "When the assault is well under way, I want you four to dive into the ground and try to surface inside the house. If you see any angelic warriors come up behind them and assassinate them. You are to prepare the way for the bowman. Is that understood?"

The assembled imps answered in the affirmative. Jenoch appeared to be lost in thought for a moment, "In the event that you find yourself alone in the house with your brothers slain, hide and listen to the family for the next two days. Gather as much information as you can and then leave the house underground for at least a mile, then come and report to me. I will take you to Molech. Remember, your main objective is to attack any angelic warriors that you find inside the house."

The imps nodded. They knew the part about gathering information was a contingency plan in case the bowman was dispatched. They wouldn't say anything about it. If it turned out badly they wanted nothing to do with it. If it turned out well then let Jenoch gather his own reward at his own risk.

Jenoch said, "Remember, wait until the assault is well under way." With this he turned back to his remaining imps. "Follow me." He leapt into the air and stood in the air about one hundred feet from the house and twenty feet above ground.

The fifteen remaining imps leapt into the air and formed a crude line behind him. They were all brandishing their weapons. The angels ringing the house started moving. Half of them leapt into the air. Silver swords appeared in the hands of the angels.

They formed a staggered formation like a pyramid ringing the house. In about ten seconds they had formed what looked like a honeycomb over the house. Then the whole formation started rotating in a clockwise motion.

The speed of the spinning increased until the angels couldn't be seen any more. It appeared that a barrier of light shaped like a cone formed over the house. The barrier was made of the bodies of living angels. Lightning bolts flashed from the barrier to the sky and back again. The demons could see the barrier, but they couldn't see the house anymore.

Roger, Amelia and Stephen sat on the couch. Roger had his laptop on the coffee table with some cables leading to the receiving unit. He had a pile of five DVD's on the coffee table in front of him.

Amelia asked, "Honey, do you really need so many copies?"

Roger replied with "Well we need one original, one copy for Rachel, one copy for the DA, one copy as a backup, and one copy for the daycare's attorney because they have the right to confront the evidence of their accusers. That's five."

Amelia followed his logic and replied with a simple, "Oh, Okay." What they didn't see was the pinpoint of light that started out in the middle of the living room floor about five feet off the floor. The point of light grew and swelled filling the room with light.

An opening formed in the center of the light until it was the size of a set of double doors. Brilliant white light poured from the opening. Then suddenly angels started stepping through the opening. There were four angels already in the house.

Angel after angel stepped through the opening. Ten more angels had entered the house. Their leader was a large brawny blonde angel. He stood nearly seven feet tall. He had a huge two-handed sword in his hands.

He commanded, "Fan out into every room. If an imp comes into a room banish it with your sword. We will conduct active searches. This house will stay clean of their influence. Such is the will of our Father."

The other nine new angels fanned out through the house with their swords drawn. They greeted their comrades as they went. Outside the house Jenoch drew up his battle line in a 'V' formation. He floated to a point twenty feet behind them and shrieked, "Kill them!"

His imps charged forward with their weapons flailing. They slowed as they got close to the barrier. They became tentative as they swung and jabbed their weapons at the barrier. It took a few moments to find the edge of it.

One of the imps inched forward and swung his axe. His axe clanged against something. For an instant the outline of an angel appeared. The angel parried the axe stroke with his sword. Impossible as it was to believe this wasn't only a barrier.

It was the group of angels spinning so fast that it gave the appearance of a solid barrier. The lead imp let out a shriek of triumph and understanding. He began to methodically swing his axe at the same point over and over. His brethren converged on the point where he struck.

Suddenly there was a knot of demons at the same spot. They all swung or thrust their weapons into the same spot. The clang of angelic steel on demonic metal rang out through the night. Demons hissed and cursed while they battled. A dog howled an eerie howl somewhere close by.

Jenoch floated over to the bowman, "Start casting your arrows into the barrier while I look for an opening little one." Obediently the little imp notched an arrow to his bowstring and drew the arrow back. He fired the arrow right above the knot of demons that were hacking at the angelic barrier.

After the first arrow was away he fired another at the same spot. His aim was true, and the second arrow found the same mark as the first. He continued that way over and over. His speed increased with each arrow until he was only a blur of motion.

Strangely enough, the number of arrows in his quiver never lessened. When he drew an arrow, another dripping black arrow appeared in its place. The skill of the angels couldn't be denied. Every axe stroke, every sword swipe, every spear thrust, and every arrow was turned aside.

The demons were concentrating all of their efforts at one small area of the angelic barrier. This began to take the toll that Jenoch hoped. The bottom part of the barrier was noticeably thinner than the band containing the assaulted portion.

Jenoch saw at this and smiled. *"Just a little bit more"* He thought. He looked back and signaled the four imps that he had instructed to go underground. They saw the signal and immediately sunk into the ground and started moving toward the house. Jenoch scanned the battle.

Angelic swords were clearly visible in the barrier. The barriers spin had slowed down noticeably. The outlines of angels could be seen.

Jenoch screamed at his imps, "You have an advantage now. Use it my warriors."

His voice was a ragged high-pitched wail. It was like the imps had been injected with adrenaline. They doubled their efforts. Their speed was blinding. The angelic barrier was thickening at the attack area. Then it happened.

Jenoch saw exactly what he was searching for. The barrier developed a small opening at its base. Jenoch surged to the bowman in a flash. He grabbed the bowman by the nape of the neck and hissed lowly, "Here is your opening imp. Now go."

Jenoch hurled the imp like a spear. The imp shot through the air straight and true. He was through the opening in a blink. He changed direction when he cleared the hole. He headed straight for the house.

The four underground imps were proceeding slowly through the ground to the side of the house. It is hard to move when you are essentially blind. Every now and then one would raise his head enough to make sure of their direction and distance.

They were inside the barrier now. They wouldn't make entrance to the house before the bowman though. The demons assaulting the barrier seemed to sense an easy victory. They started getting sloppy.

Two of them came too far forward to engage the barrier and were cut in half by a single stroke of an angelic sword. The imp with the spear made too deep of a thrust and his spear was parried away in a circle. He lost his grip on the spinning weapon and had nothing to parry with of his own. An angelic sword thrust out and impaled him on the chest. He dissolved in a puff of smoke and brimstone.

One angelic warrior broke ranks momentarily. He swung a two-handed sword. He cut the heads off three imps in two lazy appearing strokes. Then simply sank back into the barrier.

The bowman passed through the wall of the house. As soon as his head passed through the wall it was cut off by the downward swing of an angelic blade. He dissolved before his body made it completely through the wall.

Two imps with axes hacked at the angelic barrier with ill-timed strokes. They got the ornate heads of their axes stuck together. An angelic sword swept out of the barrier and swept off their heads.

The four imps rose up through the floor into the dining room of the Carter home. They had the good fortune of rising behind an angelic warrior. The lead imp leapt up and struck the angel square in the back.

Two angelic warriors were floated into the room as this was happening.

In unison they screamed, "NO!!!!" They surged forward as their comrade dissolved into pure silver light. An instant later the angel appeared before the throne of Heaven.

He felt a moment of chagrin before the love of the Father washed over him.

A voice entered his mind, "Your part in this is done my child. Take peace in the knowledge that your part was accomplished perfectly."

The angel turned and addressed the throne, his head bowed. "But Father, I fell in battle. I didn't even know the attack was coming." A light laugh came from the throne. "You did not fall in battle you were transferred here when you were struck. There is no punishment for my elect angels."

In the house the fight was raging. The two angels rushed into the dining room with their blades drawn. They methodically hacked the imps to pieces. It took about ten seconds for the battle inside the house to be over.

Andarel peered at two of his companions, "You two, attack the demon horde in a short sortie. I want them driven back from the barrier."

Chapter 60

A pinprick of Heavenly light formed in the middle of the living room. It expanded and became a gateway to Heaven. Fully thirty angels stepped through the gateway. In a few seconds, thirty-two angels leapt into the air and dove through the house to aid their brethren.

They passed through the roof. In a second, they passed through the angelic barrier. Jenoch's face took on an expression of stunned horror. When he saw the knot of Heavenly warriors turn toward him, he screamed.

"Attack them!" He turned to flee.

He knew his imps were lost. Neither Molech nor he had anticipated this. He wasn't going to wait around to be banished by the Heavenly host. Jenoch started flying toward Molech's lair.

Fear gripped him when he realized he was being followed. There were at least ten angels behind him. Jenoch weighed his options for a moment. He believed Molech would banish him, if he led the angels to his lair.

He knew he wasn't a match for ten angels so 'stand and fight' was not an option. He only had one option left. He would run away. Jenoch did a ninety-degree turn at top speed. He was going as fast as he could.

He chanced a quick glance behind himself. They weren't gaining but they weren't falling behind either.

"This isn't going to work. It appears I can't outrun them." He thought. *"Maybe I can lose them."*

With that thought in mind he dove straight down. He passed effortlessly into the Earth. He couldn't see at first. It took a minute for him to alter his perceptions. Finally, he could see. He changed direction in the hope of throwing off his pursuers.

He was still going flat out through solid rock and dirt like it was nothing. He chanced another glance behind to see if the angels were still on his tail. He did not like what he saw. They were there, and they were getting a lot closer. This was not looking good.

If he started a zigzag pattern it would cost him valuable speed. *"There is nothing for it."* He thought, *"I can't outrun them."* He changed direction to dive straight down for a few seconds then banked hard left.

Jenoch was approximately thirty miles below the surface of the Earth. He checked behind again, and they were less than twenty feet behind. Rage boiled up in him and he thought. *"If I am to be banished by these angels then by the Heavens I will take a few with me when I go."*

Jenoch whirled to face his pursuers and came to a stop. He produced a huge two-handed sword and started swinging it at the lead angel. The fight didn't last long. Jenoch swung his sword three times at the Heavenly warrior.

He realized he'd been surrounded. Four angelic swords came at him. He was skilled enough to block two. The other two however cut through him like he was smoke. Then suddenly he was smoke, inside of solid rock. His scream as he was banished was hideous.

The angels gathered together and started back toward the Carter house.

"Well, that is one demon that will never corrupt another soul." The lead angel noted in a satisfied tone. His fellows heartily agreed with his assessment.

They burst through the ground into the open air loudly singing praises to the Father. The throne of Heaven smiled upon them. They arrived at the Carter home in a few minutes. The scene there was serene.

Andarel saw his fellows approaching and flew to meet them. "How did it go?" he asked.

"He won't be bothering anyone anymore", Was the reply. Andarel was happy to hear this. He joined the rest of his fellows in song.

Together they flew back to the house. The line of angels that surrounded the house had returned to normal.

Andarel instructed, "We are to guard the families for the rest of the night. They will not be molested by the forces of darkness by the will of the Father."

Inside the house, Roger gave Stephen the DVD he had finished putting into a case. "Here you go. Would you give this to Rachel please?"

Stephen accepted the DVD, "I'll put it in her purse."

He got up and walked over to the end table where Rachel had put her purse when she came in. He dropped the DVD into it. "She is going to be so interested in seeing this." He noted.

Amelia was getting a little jittery. She was unaware that she was somewhat sensitive. She was sensing the battle raging around them. She glanced at Roger, "So what is the plan now?"

Roger considered for a moment, "I think it would be best if the four of us pay a visit to the District Attorney tomorrow. I could take it alone but if all four of us go it will make more of an impression on him.

"We should probably take the kids to the daycare tomorrow before we drop the bomb on him. He will want to speak to us. The presence of the children would hamper the conversation. He will want to talk to the children but not at first. The first meeting he will want the facts and our evidence."

Amelia was a little miffed, "If we disapprove of the daycare's methods, I still don't see why we need to leave the kids in there. What if we ask the District Attorney's opinion about it?"

Roger replied, "Okay honey. If he says it won't hurt the case, we'll find a sitter and take them out of the daycare.

"We need to get Rachel down here, so we can plan how we are going to do this tomorrow."

Amelia answered, "Okay" in a more mollified tone. She got up and went to the stairs. "We aren't watching the video any more so there is no need for her to be upstairs. I'll go up and get her."

She went up the stairs.

While she was gone Stephen offered, "Rachel is going to react the same way that Amelia did."

Roger was quiet for a moment, "I know. I don't blame them. I feel the same way about it. I guess men have the ability to be more emotionally detached than women."

Stephen observed, "Well if you really want to start a good fight say that in front of Rachel. She doesn't believe in the men one thing, women the other thing stuff. That really gets her dander up."

Roger smiled, "I'll try to remember that." Amelia and Rachel came walking down the stairs then. They were talking amiably, and Rachel laughed at something that neither Roger nor Stephen heard. Neither of them thought it worth the effort to ask what was funny.

Amelia and Rachel took a seat on the couch. They looked at Roger and Stephen expectantly. Stephen stood the gaze for a moment and understanding dawned in his eyes. He turned to stare at Roger as well.

Roger finally broke down, "What?"

Amelia stared at him with an innocent expression on her face, "We are simply waiting for your words of wisdom, Oh wise leader." Somehow, she held on to a perfectly straight face while saying this.

Roger's eyes narrowed. "And just what is that supposed to mean?" he asked.

Still maintaining her innocent appearance, "Oh nothing wise one. We simply stand in awe of your august presence."

He glared at her. "This isn't August this is March." Amelia lost her innocent face at that. She and Rachel started laughing and it took a few minutes for them to regain control. Amelia finally spoke, "Rachel wanted to see how you guys would react if we acted like that."

She affected an unhappy little girl appearance. "You could have done better than that." She cooed in a small voice. She sounded like she was hurt.

Roger retorted, "Oh come on honey, we are here for something serious."

Amelia replied, "Oh honey, what good is this life if we can't laugh every now and then? We've been facing a lot of tension lately. We just wanted to break the tension. The devil is our enemy, but he doesn't own us. We have the protection of someone greater."

Roger replied, "Alright, point taken. Let's get down to business though."

Amelia raised her hands in surrender, "Okay, Okay. So, what is the plan Snookums?" Roger gave her a reproving look.

He spoke with a tight voice, "Okay, here is what I think we should do. We take the kids to daycare one more time. We all meet here tomorrow at 8:00 in the morning. Is there a problem with any of this so far? Will you all be able to take the time tomorrow to do this?"

He glanced around at their faces. He could see that Amelia still absolutely hated the idea of taking the kids to the daycare but at least she didn't say anything about it. Stephen had something of a troubled expression on his face. Roger searched his face, "If there is a problem you need to let me know now."

Stephen replied, "No there isn't a problem. I'll have to take a personal day tomorrow. It won't be a problem, but I think there is a meeting that I'll miss. I was wondering how important it is."

Roger gave Stephen an "Okay." He turned to Rachel, "Is everything okay with you so far?"

Rachel replied, "Well, truthfully, I'm not too keen on taking the kids back to the daycare. I'll go along with it for now, though. I think the D.A. is going to say yes, that we can take them out. I don't have a problem with taking off tomorrow. I never miss work so one day in three years isn't a big deal. I'll call in."

Roger nodded at this. "The district attorney's name is Jack Collins. He's a driven man. He is also honest. I've known him for about six years now. He is a long time divorced with an estranged daughter. His wife took their daughter and left because he was so much of a workaholic.

"I'll call him tomorrow morning and tell him we have a blockbuster for him. He knows I wouldn't call him like that over something trivial, so I know he will see us. We'll take the DVD that I copied and the portable DVD player. That way we will be prepared to show him the video.

"Stephen make sure you bring the information that you found about the daycare and the abortion clinic."

Stephen nodded at this, "Will do."

Roger continued, "Amelia and Rachel, I want you to appear appropriately outraged at the information that we give the D.A."

Amelia answered, "Oh don't worry about that. I won't be appearing anything. I AM outraged, and I know Rachel feels the same way."

"Darn right", Rachel offered in support.

Roger smiled, "Okay I think we have the basics covered. Stephen knows his part. Amelia and Rachel make sure you bring up the changes in the kid's behavior after going to this daycare. I also want Amelia to be the one to bring up the duplicate letters.

"She is the one who found it and I want her to explain how. Make sure you bring the scrapbook you were making. Rachel please bring your copies for comparison.

"Okay we have tons of information to deliver. If we deliver it correctly, I think we are going to blow this thing out of the water." He looked around and saw Amelia, Rachel and Stephen grinning at his words.

He instructed, "Okay, it's getting late. We have a lot to do tomorrow. I think we need to get to our beds soon, so we will be fresh for tomorrow. Remember to gather your materials tonight. If you have to, put them in your cars so you won't forget them tomorrow."

Rachel and Stephen stood up. Roger and Amelia followed their action. Rachel walked to the bottom of the stairs. She called out,

"Candy, come on down. It's time to go sweetie." There was silence for a moment.

Brennan's voice came down the stairs, "She fell asleep. She's lying on the floor. Do you want me to wake her up?"

Rachel answered, "No, I'll come get her."

Stephen offered, "Honey, you've had a long day. I'll go get her."

Rachel's expression turned grateful. She smiled, "Thanks honey."

Amelia watched with a grin. Roger saw this and thought, *Oh boy, I'm going to hear it now. I'd better order flowers soon to stem the tide.* Roger and Amelia saw the Beaumont's to the door and exchanged their goodbyes.

They were heading up the stairs to the bedroom when Roger thought of his conversation with James Wagner. He touched Amelia's shoulder. She stopped and searched his face. He told her, "Honey, I just remembered something. I'll be up in a few minutes." She nodded and continued up the stairs.

Roger went back down into the small in-home office and turned on the computer. When it booted up, he signed on to his email account and checked his email. He was glad to see an email from Jwagner101.

He read the email and downloaded the files to his system. He listened to the recorded statement. He was glad to hear Mr. Wagner admit to the truth in the statement. He referred to the family pictures and the video clip from his last play that plainly showed he wasn't paralyzed.

Roger reviewed the pictures and the video clip. When he was satisfied, he burned all of the files to a CD, labeled it, and put it in the top desk drawer where he knew it would be safe.

Chapter 61

Nobody saw the imp. He'd taken a position in the farthest corner of the kitchen floor. Only one ear was in the room. He couldn't see the families. He could only listen. He constantly feared discovery and dispatch by an angelic blade. The time limit wasn't over, but he had to warn his master.

The ear disappeared, and the imp shot through the side of the foundation. He headed for Molech's headquarters. He was scared to give this information to him. He knew if he didn't, it would be worse. Ten minutes later, he arrived at Molech's lair. Five minutes after that he'd been kicked across the room out of anger.

Molech frothed at the mouth. The froth was a mixture of red and black. When it dropped to the floor it actually sizzled and smoked. The imp begged for mercy and whined. That didn't work. It only seemed to enrage Molech more.

Molech screamed incoherently then lunged and kicked the imp across the room again. He heard one of the higher demons shudder. That drew his rage from the imp. He leapt across the room at the demon that shuddered.

He landed amongst his followers. In a blind fury he flailed about with his fists and his wings. He even started spitting venom at those that were too far away to reach. The scene became one of positive bedlam.

Molech didn't speak. He wasn't punishing the guilty. He wasn't trying to find out anything. He had let his fury drive him into a berserk rage. He had just dismembered four of his followers.

A huge voice crackled in the air. It only commanded one word. "HOLD!" The assembled demons became quiet except for Molech. He was still in a rage. A huge dark hand came up through the floor and grabbed Molech. It picked him up as though he were a doll. It lifted Molech off the floor and shook him.

The voice roared, "Who will you command little one when you have disabled or banished all who serve you?" The voice and the grip seemed to snap Molech back to his senses. His voice was groveling and thick when he replied.

"My master, My Ba'al, Lord Lucifer, I am sorry. I lost control of my temper. The work that we have done here is unraveling. It is all because of the work of some puny Christians. They are protected by the Heavenly host. They are given an unfair advantage by the Creator."

Lucifer snarled, and the hand shook Molech violently again. "What do you expect Him to do?! Help you?" Lucifer's voice was dripping with rage and sarcasm, "Listen to me my little lieutenant. You serve me at my pleasure. We do what we can in the confines of the rules that have been set down. Sometimes we win. Sometimes we lose. All we can do is our best."

Lucifer's Head came up out of the floor beside his hand. The screams of the tortured damned came from behind him. Deepest darkness swirled about his head. Maniacal laughter and lunatic conversation echoed in the air around him.

The entire room went icy. Even the assembled demons were terrified of the palpable evil in the room. His features became visible as if through thick smoke. To say the least they were terrifying. The demons that stared at his face had to look away.

His eyes started out being beautiful then they started to smoke before boiling and melting out of their sockets. Every time the cycle ended a tortured scream clawed at the edge of awareness.

His mouth appeared as a positively beautiful smiling mouth with even white teeth. Then it would cycle slowly to rotted crooked fangs with a tongue covered in pus. Wriggling maggots crawled across the tongue.

The nose appeared straight and lovely. Then it cycled to a broken, flattened bloody set of nostrils. The cheekbones were smooth and high. Then they cycled to gaunt undernourished jutting cheekbones with open sores.

The chin started as a set strong-jawed chin. Then it distended to the point of being unusually large warty. Maniacal laughter was heard inside the head of the observer. Then the voice of a small child begged for help.

"Pay heed to my words imps and demons. I will give you the plan of what shall be done since this lieutenant of mine is too enraged to consider." Molech affected the appearance of chagrin and shame.

Lucifer turned his head and gazed around at the assembled demons. He hissed, "Tomorrow my children, we will attack the little Christians on their way to the law offices. We will attack without mercy. We will kill anything that gets in our path."

The image of his face licked its cracked dead lips. The skin of the lips seemed to age, crack and fall off. Pain was obvious on that face. He was in real and severe pain, not the impression of it.

None of the assembled demons were brave enough to ask him the cause of his pain. The assembled imps and demons became excited at the thought of attacking the Christians. A few actually started foaming at the mouth.

They capered about screeching and laughing. The scene was one of insane evil. Laughter and insane gibbering came from them. They didn't see the angels that were observing them.

Andarel was glaring at the scene with obvious disgust. He watched his companion, "So now we know their plans for tomorrow, but the Father knew their plans before time began." His companion grunted his agreement.

Andarel stated, "We need to plan what we are going to do tomorrow."

His companion turned to him, "No we don't. The Father will give us our instructions. You know this. What is the cause of your pain brother?"

Andarel felt a moment of shame and replied, "I hate seeing these fallen ones plotting the destruction of our Lord's chosen. I don't understand why the Father is waiting." Andarel's companion was Leldorel, a captain in the angelic forces.

Leldorel answered. "We are limited Andarel. Our Father however is not. You know that we need to wait on the Lord. Your anger is righteous, but you need to keep it in check. Now, let's go tell the rest what we have found."

Wings appeared on Leldorel's back. He spread them and leapt into the air. It wasn't long before Andarel was at his side. Andarel asked, "My captain, what shall we do?"

Leldorel laughed, "You already know. We wait upon the Lord. I was there when Daniel prayed and waited. Three weeks, he waited for an answer that he believed should have already come. I wasn't a captain then. We were facing Molech and a horde of demons. They were fierce. Some of them seemed to throw themselves on our swords.

"Fully half our number was cut down to appear before the throne of Heaven. Then the Father sent Michael to our aid. Michael was like a lightning bolt across water. He cut through their ranks like a hot knife through butter.

"He cleared a path and told me to take the message to Daniel while he held the horde at bay. He had destroyed a fourth of them on his first pass. He had them fearful. I don't think I've moved that fast before or since."

Leldorel smiled at the memory. "I had to deliver the message and leave soon. The prince of Greece was already on his way. The battle was shaping up to be a long and drawn out. That was when we went through the changes of the early empires. There is our enclave up ahead. It appears something might be going on. Let's go see what all the excitement is about."

They both flew down into the small church. It was a beehive of activity. Leldorel and Andarel passed through the ceiling and headed for the altar. A commander of the host stood before the altar singing praises and offering prayers. Leldorel was respectfully quiet while he waited for the commander to finish his duties to the Lord.

The commander's song ended, he put down the silver bowl. Leldorel stepped forward. "Is there any news sir?" he asked in a subdued voice.

The commander glanced up. His eyes were shining after his time of worship. "The horde plans to attack tomorrow. Lucifer himself will be part of the attack."

Leldorel's eyes went wide. He breathed, "Sir this is unheard of. Will our forces be augmented?"

The commander smiled a small smile, "No, we are to hold on our own."

Leldorel noted, "Sir we can't match their numbers."

The commander got a stern expression on his face, "Do not forget the one we serve."

Leldorel's face became chagrined at this.

The commander oredered. "Captain prepare our forces for deployment. We will guard our human charges as soon as we can deploy to their homes.

"Cut the forces in half. We have two families to guard. I wish we could have them together for the night. I am afraid though that they don't know each other well enough for this thought to have occurred to them."

Andarel had been silent up to this point but spoke up at this time. "Sir, we could make a suggestion to the males in the family."

The commander seemed to think it over, "No. Our instructions don't include this. We will not get ahead of our Lord. Captain, you have your instructions. Carry them out please."

Leldorel and Andarel turned on their heels and walked away to carry out their orders. Leldorel started barking orders. His orders were immediately followed.

He turned to Andarel, "You will be in charge of the second force that will be going to the Beaumont's home."

418

Andarel countered, "But sir, I've never been in command." The commander had silently walked up behind them. He startled Andarel when he replied with a gentle smile. "Well I guess you better get used to the idea lieutenant."

Andarel's jaw dropped. Then he heard the whisper from the throne of Heaven. He was being promoted because of his dedication to his work over these last years. He turned to the assembled angels and began to issue orders for the plan that appeared in his mind.

Chapter 62

The alarm clock went off loudly. Roger reached over and switched it off. He rolled over, nudged Amelia, "Time to get up honey."

She moaned a little and opened her eyes, "Five more minutes?"

This was how their day started every morning. He reached over and reset the alarm. A small smile played over his lips. This was a morning ritual they had developed.

Five minutes later the alarm clock went off again. This time Amelia didn't offer any protest. She knew it wouldn't do her any good. Roger got out of bed and put on his pajama bottoms. He walked down the hall to his son's room.

He woke Brennan and made sure he got up before he left the room. He walked back into the bedroom to find Amelia had fallen back to sleep. He used his patented 'Yank the covers off the bed' move. That irritated her a little, but she understood why he did it.

She got up and felt the cool of the carpet on the bottoms of her feet. She started toward the bathroom and heard Roger in the bathroom brushing his teeth.

She walked in, "Good morning honey."

He spit out toothpaste, "Good morning. Are you nervous about today?"

She winced a little, "I've been trying not to think about it. I didn't get to sleep until about 2:30 this morning."

He offered, "I know. You tossed and turned all night. I'm going to run to the office and change my answering machine, so my clients know that I won't be in today.

"I'll call Jack then. I know he'll work us in. If he complains I might have to bribe him with lunch."

She raised an eyebrow at that, "Well that's fine but don't spend a week's pay on it." Roger got a guilty look on his face.

"I won't. I won't." He returned in mock surrender.

Amelia assumed a pout, "I don't remember the last time you took me to Stoney's."

Roger wilted, "I will amend that as soon as I can honey. I promise." His face was so guilty that Amelia felt sorry for him.

She cajoled, "I was only playing with you honey."

He replied, "You know it isn't nice of you to say things to me in jest that you know make me feel guilty. If you want to go to Stoney's just say so. I didn't know you wanted to go. You are the one who keeps saying it is too expensive."

She was shocked at his reaction. She thought, *I think I've pushed him too far with the playful guilt tactic.*

Then she crooned, "Honey, I'm sorry. I was only playing. I didn't mean to hurt your feelings. I don't care if we go to Stoney's or Burger King. I just like spending time alone with you."

Roger softened at this, "I know honey. We've both been so busy lately. How about this? Next week Brennan will be back with his mother. How about we plan a night at Che Royale, a room, dinner in their 4-star restaurant, the works?"

Her eyes went wide at this. She had wanted to go there for a long time but was worried that Roger wouldn't like it. She took two quick steps and threw her arms around him. "Oh honey, I've wanted to go there for such a long time. You don't think it will be a waste of money?"

He replied, "Absolutely not. If it makes you happy then we will do it every few months." She thought, *"I'm so lucky."* They couldn't see the pair of imps in the room that had been trying to start an argument.

They'd been standing on the counter screaming at the humans. It looked like they were going to succeed. Then Andarel entered the bedroom and started singing praises to God. Roger and Amelia shared an embrace. The imps cursed and hissed at Andarel.

Roger broke the embrace after a short time, "Honey we've got to get moving. We've got a lot to do today. Since I'm going out anyway, why don't you let me drop Brennan off at the daycare?" She answered this in the affirmative and he gave her a little squeeze.

He turned around, disrobed and stepped into the shower. Ten minutes later he was stepping out and toweling himself off. Amelia was used to him being first in the shower. He never took long for a shower and she usually took twenty-five minutes or more.

She was scrubbing her face when he was toweling off. She took a minute to towel her face dry. He was walking into the bedroom to get dressed. It always worked out well by doing it this way.

Roger was dressed in under ten minutes. He went downstairs started preparing breakfast. He had breakfast ready in about another ten minutes. The table was ladened with scrambled eggs, sausage, toast and jelly. He poured juice for Brennan and a cup of coffee for himself and Amelia.

Five minutes later they were all sitting at the table eating breakfast. Admittedly Amelia was in her bathrobe. She didn't want to wait to get dressed and let her food get cold. They generally ate breakfast in silence for the most part.

Roger wasn't chatty in the morning and Brennan was proving to be his father's son in that respect. When they finished breakfast, Roger and Brennan stood up to leave. It was an understanding between them. Since Roger had prepared and laid out the breakfast that Amelia did the final cleanup.

Roger poured some coffee in his travel mug while Brennan gave Amelia a goodbye hug.

Roger walked over and gave her a kiss, "I'll see you later honey. I love you." He didn't want to tip Brennan off as to what they were doing. They didn't want him to know for fear that he might let something slip.

They trooped out the door. A minute or so later Amelia heard the car start and pull out of the driveway. She was nervous about today. She offered a prayer to the Lord about the day and their safety. She thanked the Lord for his answer, no matter what it was. When she gave her amen peace flowed into her. She didn't even notice it.

She stood up and started gathering the dishes. She hummed a praise song under her breath as worked. She didn't see the angels that were in the kitchen with her, watching over her. She felt safe and at peace.

Roger drove in silence. Brennan sat quietly in his seat. He was looking at his hand-held video game. Neither of them saw the two angels in the back seat. They didn't see the ones that were flying alongside and above the car.

The larger angel in the back seat turned to his companion, "Wow! Real chatterboxes these two are. I wish they would shut up, so I could think." His companion grinned at him and, "Oh be quiet, Bonorel. You know a lot of the humans aren't 'morning people'."

Bonorel became serious, "I wonder how things will go today."

His companion's face took on a serious expression, "It will be what the Father will's it to be." Roger pulled up to the daycare. He and Brennan got out. He walked Brennan to the front door. Roger opened the door and followed his son inside.

Judy was her usual smiling self when she saw Roger. Brennan didn't seem very happy while Judy was obviously flirting with his dad. Roger made a mental note to tell Amelia about it. He didn't want any misunderstanding on his part. He especially didn't want Amelia to think he was hiding something.

He thanked Judy and headed out the door. He drove straight to his office and looked around first. It was a habit since he was an investigator. He always sampled his surroundings.

He went to his answering machine and listened to the messages. There were three. They were all from different clients. They were asking for information that wasn't particularly urgent. He made notes on all three.

He changed the outgoing message to let his clients know that he wouldn't be in for the day. They shouldn't be too disgruntled. He didn't do this often at all. They would have to understand when he gave an explanation.

He headed back down to the parking garage and headed for home. He checked his watch. He was going to make it home in time to meet the Beaumont's. He got in the car and started out of the garage. He cleared the garage, took out his cell phone and dialed Jack Collins number.

Jack Collins was a driven man in his mid-forties. He was slightly muscular because of his workout routine. His workout served to keep him trim and toned. He was the district attorney. He hoped for an appointment to district judge. His aspirations weren't without a cost.

He was divorced after fourteen years of marriage. His wife and daughter had left him without a word of explanation. His daughter was thirteen. The divorce had cost him his emotions. He'd thrown himself into his work.

The cell phone chirped, and Jack hit the talk button. "Hello?" He was driving to work and wearing a headset. He could use his phone while driving. There was no way he was going to do anything to get a reckless driving charge on his record. He still hoped for the District Judge's position.

A voice came on the line, "Hey, Jack. This is Roger Carter. How are you doing?" Jack recognized the voice and gave one of his only friends a hearty greeting.

"Roger, how are you doing old man? It's been a while, fella. Why such a long time between contact? Is something up that I need to know about?"

Roger was glad to hear the cheerful hello. That meant this would be much easier than he had anticipated. Roger answered, "Jack, I've got something to tell you, something big. I don't want to talk on the phone. Can we meet today? I will bring some witnesses with me."

Jack thought *"Witnesses? What's this about witnesses? Man, this must be big. Roger wouldn't call me and talk like this if it wasn't."* He said out loud, "When do you want to come in?"

424

Roger thought *"Swish, slam dunk."* Then he offered, "How about 8:45? Is that okay for you?"

Jack answered with "Don't worry about it. Come in. I'll have to rearrange my schedule, but I'll have my secretary make it happen. Can you give me a hint what is has to do with?" Roger thought it over for a minute, "I'll have to be vague, but it has to do with federal funds and you'll get a lot of press."

Jack thought. *This is the sort of thing to boost me into the limelight. I may not make district judge out of it but I could possibly get circuit court judge from it and that is another step closer.*

He instructed, "Roger, I'm going to have to get off of here. I'm almost at work. I'll need to talk to Sharon as soon as I get in. She hates the rearrange game. She gets cursed out by clients when she has to do it."

Roger countered, "Okay, I'll see you in your office at 8:45. I'll have three people with me. Amelia will be one of them."

Jack answered, "That will be fine. Talk to you later." With that he hung up. Now he was really curious. He thought, *Roger never involves Amelia in any of the cases that he works on.*

He pulled into his parking place. He grabbed his briefcase from the passenger seat beside him. He bounced into the office like he was on a spring. He was really wired from that phone call.

Roger closed his cell phone. He had a broad grin on his face. He said, "Now Lord, do you think you could have made that any easier for me?" He sat there for a moment. He didn't expect an audible reply. He reflected on the circumstances. Jack hadn't done any of his usual complaining about having to rearrange his schedule. He hadn't hinted that lunch might be a good way to pacify him after such an affront to his orderly life.

Roger saw he was getting close to home. He didn't know why but his attention was suddenly drawn to the billboard about a half of a mile ahead. There was about a gap of about three feet between the ground and the bottom of the billboard. Roger saw the bottom part of a police car parked behind it.

He automatically looked down at the speedometer. He was doing ten over. He immediately hit his brake. By the time he passed the billboard, he was doing the limit.

After about a quarter mile, Roger mused, "Now you are just showing off. Oh, and by the way, thank you." The angels guarding him laughed uproariously. They loved it when the Father did things like that.

Roger cruised along at the proper speed limit now. He was about ten minutes from home and would be making it with a couple of minutes to spare. He was in prayer while he was driving. He paid attention to the road, but he was relating the things of the past few weeks.

He was astounded at how neatly everything had fallen into place. He had a feeling in the very heart of his being that this was going to be one big slam-dunk. He knew that the enemy was already defeated, and it was just a matter of time to prove it.

The rest of the way home passed quickly. He pulled into the drive, making sure to pull to one side leaving room for the Beaumont's to park beside him. He got out of the car and walked up to the front door. He was fumbling for his key when Amelia opened the door for him.

She wore a beige skirt and jacket with a white dress shirt. She had on a hint of makeup and perfume. She knew this was Roger's favorite outfit. She artfully dodged him when he reached out for her.

She giggled, "Honey, you will mess up my makeup. Now behave."

He grinned at her then reached over and closed the front door.

He mused, "Now I can't help but think that you wore that on purpose. You know it's my favorite outfit and you are wearing my favorite perfume."

She grinned, "Well I have to keep you interested with a tease every now and then don't I?"

He offered dryly, "Oh yeah, only on the most important day we've had in a long time."

She was smiling when she countered, "Honey, that's what makes it such a good tease. So there."

The doorbell rang. Roger went to the door and opened it. Stephen and Rachel were standing there expectantly.

Roger told them, "Come in. Come in.", in his most welcoming tone.

Stephen asked, "Aren't we leaving?"

Roger answered, "Yes we are in a few minutes. Would either of you like a cup of coffee?" Stephen accepted while Rachel declined.

Roger turned to Rachel, "Would you like some tea or juice?" Rachel returned, "No thank you. I'm fine."

Her eyes lit up when she saw Amelia. She walked past Roger and Stephen with a little squeal, "Let me see your outfit."

Roger gave Stephen a look that said, "Women?" Stephen returned the exact same expression.

Stephen accepted his coffee. He took a sip while watching Amelia and Rachel coo over clothes.

"This is good coffee." He complimented.

"Thank you." Roger accepted. Stephen finished his coffee around the same time the ladies stopped talking about clothing stores. They all headed out to the car.

Roger held the door for Amelia then got behind the wheel of the car. Roger drove to the D.A.'s office. Nobody saw the swarm of angels around the car. There were even some under the car. They were to guard the family from an underground attack.

Andarel was nervous. He knew there was going to be an attack, but everything was quiet. Where were the demons? He wasn't scare of the attack or the demons. He was worried about his own performance.

He pushed the anxiety out of his mind and concentrated on his mission. It wasn't up to him to question the Father's planning. His job was to do as he was told. They pulled into the parking lot. The angels saw Molech and his horde were there.

The angels pulled into a tight formation around the families as they got out of the car. The Carter's and Beaumont's had taken three steps from the car when the silence was broken.

Molech roared, "Attack!"

The angels tightened their formation around their charges.

The heel of Amelia's broke. She staggered with an exclamation. Everybody stopped to see what had happened. None of them saw the angelic sword cut her heel off to get them to stop for a minute. The demons surged forward with their weapons raised. The angels tensed and braced themselves.

A huge black axe appeared in Molech's hand. He screamed in rage as he ran forward with his axe raised over his head. Half of the angels left the little formation and surged forward. Angelic swords flashed like lightning in the dark.

The angels and the demons collided not twenty feet from the families. The sound was horrendous. The angels were outnumbered three-to-one. The fight was vicious. The demons had the advantage and they knew it. They coordinated their attacks so that each angel was being attacked at least three-to-one at first.

Andarel looked around and saw three of his fellows cut down. As their advantage increased, the demons increased their attack ratio. It went from three-to-one to five-to-one in just a few seconds. Half of the angels had been cut down while only two demons had been dispatched.

Andarel called for his group to tighten up and stand back to back to increase their guard. He parried a black axe that came screaming toward his head. He swung his sword and separated the demons head that had attacked him.

He tried to recover his sword to the guard position. He had too many demons around him. He couldn't move fast enough. He felt the flash of pain as the demonic spear bit into his side. The pain was blinding. He searched around again and saw his comrades falling beneath demonic weapons.

He saw his last comrade fall as he felt his body dissolving. He began to lose consciousness. He appeared before the throne of Heaven. He stared around and saw all of his fellows bowing and singing praise to the Father.

The assembled demons turned toward the families. Roger was peering at Amelia's shoe.

Molech roared, "Stop!!! They are mine."

Angelic blood dripped from his axe. He floated to the front of the horde. He was no more than twelve feet from the families. He raised his axe over head.

He screamed maniacally, "Kill them now." They started toward the families when, suddenly, a light brighter than the sun appeared between them and the families.

The light was so concentrated and bright that the form of the man standing in the light could barely be made out. No detail could be seen. The demons surged forward. They couldn't stop before the light burned them.

A voice like thunder boomed, "NO!"

Lightning burst from the figure in multiple tongues after the word was spoken. Molech screamed in pain and realized that this was a manifestation of the savior. He started to retreat as fast as he could. His only hope was to get away.

The voice spoke again. "These are mine. I will not allow you to touch them!"

The lightning burst forth again. The assembled demon horde fell into shambles. Many of the demons had been struck by the lightning and had utterly dissolved upon contact.

Molech had retreated fastest. He was badly burned, and his left arm hung limply at his side. More than three fourths of his horde had been destroyed. He ran and hoped that the last few of his minions would keep the Heavenly host off his back.

Amelia glanced around nervously. She had gotten extreme cold chills. Fear had settled over her in a horrible pall. In an instant the fear was replaced with a feeling of peace. She was calmer than she had been in more than a month.

The Carter's and the Beaumont's all heard a soft voice in their heads.

"Be at peace my children. You are under my protection."

They all stared at each other in surprise.

Roger asked in a shaking voice, "Did you hear what I heard?" Amelia had tears streaming down her cheeks.

She answered, "Yes honey, I know I did."

They didn't see the light gradually fade and finally disappear. The feelings faded and they all became aware of their surroundings again.

Roger announced, "We still have a job to do."

It was amazing how they all snapped back into business mode.

Roger still had Amelia's repaired shoe in his hand. He had put the heel back on the studs. It should last until they got home, and he could glue the heel back on. He gave her the shoe and she put it back on. They turned toward the D.A.'s office and started walking toward the door.

Chapter 63

Jack Collins sat at his desk. He was making a list of the things he wanted to ask Roger when he got there. He had instructed his secretary to send the Carters and his party right in. Jack knew Roger and he knew that Roger wouldn't play around. If Roger said the case was big it was big.

His secretary Sharon called him on the intercom. He answered, and she let him know that Roger Carter and party were here. Jack got a little nervous and told her to send them in and to please send in a tray with coffee. He had learned that people open up easier when you showed them hospitality.

Two ladies walked in. Then a man he hadn't met came in followed by Roger. Roger made the introductions. It struck him that in all of the time he'd known Roger he'd never met his wife. He looked at Amelia for a moment and then shook hands all around.

By the time he finished the obligatory few minutes of small talk with Roger, Sharon came in carrying a tray with a carafe of coffee, various condiments and cups. She was quiet as she came in. She demurely placed the tray on the small serving table.

Before she left she glanced at Jack, "Just call me if you require anything else Mr. Collins."

Jack liked her professional manner in front of clients. When they were alone she was friendly, even a little affectionate. She called him Jack and wasn't above a hug when she was leaving for the night.

Jack stated. "That will be all, thank you Sharon."

She smiled, turned on her heel and walked out. She closed the door quietly behind her.

Jack turned to Roger, "Well Roger you have me curious. What is this all about?" Roger looked like the cat that had swallowed the canary.

He asked, "Do you know the new daycare here in town? They are called the Happy Care Daycare."

He opened a briefcase. He took out a small portable DVD player and a case with a DVD in it.

He informed, "I checked with the federal childcare agency. They are accepting federal funds to help defray their costs. As you know, if you accept federal funds you can't favor any one religion over another. You especially can't teach a religion."

Jack offered, "Okay, I take it you have evidence that they are teaching religious practices to the children without the parent's knowledge or consent?"

Roger replied, "Yes, but that isn't all we have. We have a lot of evidence of bad business practices."

Jack tried to make his swallow imperceptive. "What else do you have?"

Roger smoothly returned, "I'll let my witnesses present their evidence."

Jack thought about this for a second. He opened his notepad, got out a pen, "Okay, go ahead."

Roger asked, "Do you want to see the video evidence first or would you like for everyone to present before you watch the video?"

Jack mused, "Let's get everything in perspective before we get to the video." Roger was exultant when he heard this.

He knew Jack would answer this way. If he heard all of the evidence first and then saw the video, he would be filing charges tomorrow. He would probably be setting up a press conference the next day.

He replied, "Okay, how about we start with Amelia and Rachel Beaumont. What was done wasn't necessarily illegal, but it was dishonest and reflects terrible business practices."

Jack gave Roger a steady gaze and finally instructed, "Well Roger, this is your show. Let's do it your way, as long as I get all of the information."

Roger turned to Amelia, "You have the floor honey." Amelia pulled a folder out of her purse. She gave Jack a steady gaze, "We've been using Happy Care Daycare for a while. Every month they send

432

you a letter telling you how your child is doing in the daycare." She pulled some papers out of the folder and laid them on the desk in front of Jack.

She offered, "These are the letters we've gotten over the last several months for Brennan."

Jack picked up the letters and read through the first couple of them. He couldn't see where this was going yet. "Okay, how is this, a big deal?"

At this point the other woman named Rachel spoke up. "Well we didn't think anything of it at first. Then when we got to know the Carters we compared the letters for both our children." She laid her letters on his desk.

He picked up the first one and read through it. He noticed right away that it was identical to the one for the Carter's. The names and personal pronouns had been changed but that was all. Nothing illegal but it is a dishonest business practice. He thought, *this is the kind of thing that tabloids love and juries hate.*

He turned to Roger, "What else do you have?"

Roger replied, "Well Stephen here has some interesting information."

Jack turned his attention to Stephen, "Yes?"

Stephen cleared his throat as he pulled out a magazine from his briefcase. "This is a financial periodical that my company receives."

"You will notice that Aurora Financial Unlimited actually owns the Happy Care Daycare chain. If you do a little more research, you will find that Aurora Financial Unlimited also owns the largest chain of abortion clinics in the United States.

"I don't know about you but that seems to be a little bit of a business conflict. Does that mean in their business if you can't kill them then you can help raise them?"

Jack sat there for a minute. He was stunned. This was so much more tabloid ammo. He realized that it wasn't against the law to have diverse business interests, but this was a polar opposite. A jury would eat this up alive.

"How in the world did you come across this information?" He asked. He surveyed the room. Roger appeared satisfied. "I know this isn't all you have for me is it?" He asked.

Roger answered, "No it isn't. I told you this was big, and I wasn't exaggerating. This is going to be a huge case for the public eye if you play it right."

Jack sat there for a second, "Well so far you haven't given me anything I can use to press charges." Roger smiled, "You know that Daycare's are federally subsidized. And you know that being federally subsidized they aren't allowed to teach any kind of religion. If they accept federal funds and teach religion regardless it is considered a felony."

Jack countered, "I know all that. I don't need a lesson in law."

Roger replied, "No you don't. I'm setting the stage." Roger put the DVD in the player, spun the player around so Jack could see the screen. He leaned forward and hit the play button.

Jack sat there riveted to the screen. He couldn't believe his luck. They were accepting federal funds while teaching religion. That coupled with all the other dishonesty, this was going to be a big case.

When the video was over he looked up at Roger. "Who else knows about this?" he asked.

Roger replied, "Only the people in this room know about this investigation and evidence. We used audio video equipment disguised on our kids to gather the video. The kids were unaware of it. We went to great pains to keep the kids ignorant, so they wouldn't give it away."

Jack nodded approvingly.

Amelia spoke up, "While we are talking about the kids, I would like to ask if you think it would be alright for us to pull our kids from the daycare? They are teaching our kids religious practices that we consider occult practices. I for one don't appreciate it."

Jack leaned back for a second, "Ma'am, I don't blame you and a jury wouldn't either. Go ahead and take your kids out today." After a moment's hesitation he added "but don't give a reason why. If they press the issue, tell them that you found an in-home sitter that is more convenient."

Amelia gave him a grateful smile and nodded. Rachel put her hand on Amelia's and they both shared a smile with each other. Jack saw the expressions and could tell that these were two determined mothers. Jack glanced down and wrote a few notes.

When he turned back he saw Amelia giving Roger a challenging stare. *I wonder what that is about?* He wondered.

He instructed, "This is how it's going to work. You all are going to go home or back to work or whatever you would normally do. I'm going to go to the courthouse and file charges. I'm going to dispatch a deputy to serve the charges to the district manager of the Happy Care Daycare chain.

"I'm going to make about thirty copies of this DVD for the press conference tomorrow. I'm not going to submit your names as witnesses until I absolutely have to. As soon as the charges are filed, I'm going to contact the newspapers, radio station, and the television news crew.

"I'm going to schedule a press conference for early tomorrow morning. I'm going to present all of the main evidence to the news. That way it won't be possible for their slick lawyers to keep the evidence out of a courtroom.

"Nowadays that is the only way you can make sure the evidence isn't kept from the people. Now I'm not going to lie to you. This move will probably ensure that this case will never go to trial. Aurora Finance is huge. They have tons of high priced lawyers. If we went strictly by the book, none of the evidence would be heard in court and we would lose within a week.

"This way we embarrass the big boys to the point that they have to take action to save their public image." Amelia's face took on an outraged expression.

She almost screeched, "You mean because they have several tons of money they can manipulate the system to the point that we have to play angles to get any justice at all?"

Jack answered, "Yes ma'am. The system isn't perfect, but it is the only one we have. We can rest easy in the fact that it works better than the communist justice system." Amelia seemed slightly mollified but only slightly.

Jack offered, "I'm sorry to be abrupt but this has given me a ton of legwork to do. I need to get on this before the well runs dry, as they say." He posed the last remark as a joke but nobody in the room laughed.

Roger was aware of Jack's drive and ambition. He wondered if he hadn't prepared the group for this quick change of mood and focus. He stood, and the others stood following his lead.

He thrust out his hand to Jack, "I know we've brought this to the right person. I know that as an officer of the court you will follow this to the end of the rope." Jack smiled and took Roger's hand.

He promised, "Roger, I'm not going to let go of this until I've made sure that Happy Care Daycare has been sufficiently drug through the mud."

Roger thought for a moment, "Jack, what is this going to cost you?" Jack looked at him and smiled. "This isn't going to cost me a third of what it is going help me. I'm in the catbird seat and you put me there. There is no way that I can be harmed more than this situation helps me."

Roger thanked Jack and led the others out of the office. When they got outside of the office, Amelia and Rachel were absolutely charged up. They started talking about possibilities. Roger stopped in the middle of the parking lot and reminded them that more than likely it wouldn't even go to trial.

Amelia didn't like that, but she and Rachel stopped talking about what they thought was going to happen. They all went to the Carter's house. Roger and Rachel got out of the car and started to say their goodbyes.

Roger asked, "Aren't you guys coming in?"

We aren't going to pick up Brennan until the regular time. That way it won't seem unusual and won't set off any alarm bells." That made sense to Stephen but Rachel and Amelia seemed a little grumpy about it.

Stephen and Rachel joined Roger and Amelia at their table. They ate sandwiches buffet style after saying the blessing for the food. They prayed for Jack Collins safety and his salvation. They prayed for the children under the care of the Happy Care Daycare chain. They thanked the Lord for his provision and his protection.

They sat around the table, ate, drank and enjoyed each other's company. The throne of Heaven smiled upon them. When the afternoon was nearly over Roger and Stephen spoke of who usually picked up the kids.

Usually Amelia picked up Brennan and Stephen usually picked up Candy. After a brief discussion it was decided that they would stay as close to normal as possible. If needed, Amelia would give their planned excuse.

She didn't have to tell them it was she herself that would be watching Brennan. Since she worked at home it would be simple given Brennan's age. They would easily have time to find another sitter.

Stephen would say that since Rachel's mother had been taking care of Candy that they had been talking to her about it. This was true, but they had never asked her if she would be willing to resume. They knew she wanted the opportunity that had been offered to her.

After this little plan was set Amelia spoke up, "Hey guys, do you want to stay for dinner? I'm sure that Roger would like to use his atomic space grill to cook ribs. I'll cook up some sides and we can all share a hot meal as two families."

Roger looked delighted at this suggestion, as did Rachel. Stephen however seemed a little shocked.

He turned to Rachel, "Honey, what do you want to do?"

She replied with, "Are you kidding? I'd love to stay and spend time here." Stephen seemed to think about it for a moment. He turned to Roger, "Okay, we will come back and have dinner with you on one condition."

Roger had a note of caution in his voice when he asked, "What is the condition?"

Stephen answered, "Well we shouldn't be the ones eating at your house all the time. Don't get me wrong you guys are great cooks. I'm starting to feel a little guilty. Next time you guys get to come over to our house and let us cook for you."

Roger and Amelia both laughed a little and offered assurances that there was no need for guilt.

Then Roger challenged, "Okay big guy, what are you going to cook to match my ribs?"

Stephen smiled, "Well ribs are good, but I've got a recipe for T-Bone steaks that will make you jealous of my gas grilling powers."

Roger stared at Amelia with an incredulous expression, "Oh it is so on now. Just wait until this pretender to the throne samples my seasoned grilled flounder. He will beg for my forgiveness for this insult."

Amelia turned to Rachel, "You know, I think in the future we might not have to do so much cooking when we get together."

Rachel laughed, "That's fine with me. That will give us more time to chat. What is it with men and grilling anyway?"

Amelia mused, "I think because it is outdoors and involves fire. It brings out the caveman in most men. I do have to say you are in for a treat. Roger's grilled flounder is to die for. He won't even give me the recipe."

Stephen cut in smiling, "Amelia we better go get our kids before we wind up late. I'll go ahead and leave now. Give me 5 minutes and

438

then you can come after Brennan. I'm usually there and gone before you get there."

Amelia answered in the affirmative and Stephen was out the door.

Roger stood up, "Well I'm going to get started on the ribs. They will take longer than your sides. What are you going to do? Bake potatoes and salad are always a good fit with ribs."

Amelia offered, "Okay that works for me." Roger walked over to the fridge and got out a large packet of ribs. He went over to the sink and filled one side with hot water. He put the ribs in to soak. He wanted to thaw them as much as possible before putting them on the grill.

He got lost in what he was doing, getting the food ready. He glanced up and saw Stephen and Candy coming through the door. He hadn't realized how much he had busied himself. Stephen told them that he had passed Amelia about a minute after he left the daycare.

Roger stated "Okay, I better get a move on." He turned back to the grill and put the ribs on. He sprinkled the dry rub on the ribs and turned them over quickly. He seasoned the barely singed side. The ribs were done on one side by the time Amelia got back.

She peered at Roger, "That went easily. They didn't even ask why." Roger felt a slight surge of relief.

He offered, "Well that's one less thing to worry about. These will be done in about 10 minutes. You might want to start on the sides."

Amelia gestured in the affirmative and walked over to the fridge and started preparing the side dishes.

Stephen walked over, "You know, it was the same with me. They didn't even ask why. That one lady Judy said Okay."

Roger thought about it for a moment, "That is rather strange. If a business starts losing customers, you would at least expect them to question why."

They didn't know that one of the Lord's angels was in the daycare influencing the young lady not to ask questions. The families sat down to a nice meal. Stephen had to admit, these were some good ribs. After the meal they had some good fellowship.

They didn't see Molech lurking around outside. He didn't dare come inside. He was sure there was a compliment of Heavenly angels in the house guarding the family. He was right of course. God was watching over these families.

Chapter 64

The next morning started out normally for the Carters and the Beaumonts. It was not a normal morning for Jack Collins. He was absolutely in his element. He had called all of his news contacts and set up a press conference in the conference room of the community center.

He got there early and went in to set up the video equipment. He checked the setup of the chairs and the table. He had a table in the back that held the drinks, doughnuts and some small snacks. Provide them with food and drink try to appear like you cared about their comfort. The press would react more positively to your point of view.

He checked his printed material. He had printed out all of the accusations against Happy Care, so the press would have something to go on if they didn't take good notes. He made sure to put the stack of pages and the DVD copies under the top of the podium.

He didn't want any one of them getting the material before the others. The press tended to be touchy about that. He checked his watch. He still had thirty minutes before the press got here. He went to the back and poured himself a cup of coffee. One of the things Sharon could do is brew an excellent cup of coffee. She was a good legal assistant. She was also a domestic breeze.

He started perusing his notes. A few minutes later he heard the door open. He glanced up and his heart sank. Sandy Greene was walking toward him with a lupine expression on her face. She was the top reporter for the Clarion Call. It was one of the larger papers in town.

She was generally held as one of the most ruthless journalists in the city. He knew she was going to try to pump him for information before anybody else got here. He made up his mind that he was going to be firm and not give her anything.

She affected a grin as she approached, "Hey Jack, how's it going? Do you have some good dirty laundry for us today?"

Jack gave her a brittle smile, "Yes, you will have to wait until everybody gets here."

She pretended to be downcast, "Oh come on. Give me a little hint as to what is going on." It was then that Ray Davis walked in.

He groused, "I might have known that you would have gotten here first and would be trying to wheedle information out of Jack before the rest of us got here."

Sandy crooned, "Now Ray you know that a good journalist is always on the story."

Jack didn't want this to turn into a back-biting argument, "Hey guys, why don't you get some coffee and a pastry before they are all gone. It's close to time for everybody to get here."

They grumbled a little, but they went to the back table to help themselves. People were coming in at a steady rate now. He recognized the local news anchor from Channel 5. His name was Greg Jensen. He checked his watch and saw that there were only a couple of minutes to go.

He gave his hellos to a couple more of the crowd coming in. He went to the back and topped off his coffee and then started for the podium. When he got there, he put his coffee on the shelf in the podium. He took out his printed material and laid it on the podium.

He saw one of the young photographers that he knew. He stepped up to the young lady and asked her if she would mind distributing the material. She was glad to do it and he went back up to the podium.

He cleared his throat and the room went quiet. "I made sure to print a list of the news items that I wanted to impart to you today. Young Miss Trimble is passing them out now. I'd like to go over them with you and then I have a video to show you."

Ray was perusing the pages that he'd been given. "Is this for real Jack?" He asked. Jack answered, "Yes, and I have proof of every item on those pages." There was a buzz around the room as people started reading the items on the pages. Every now and then a shocked gasp could be heard.

"Okay, listen up." Jack called, in his assertive voice. He knew he had to take charge and keep control or this would turn into a shouting contest by the reporters who wanted their questions answered first.

"If you will check the first page about halfway down, you will see the initials HCDC. The first page is a page out of a financial journal. If you look a little bit past the initials HCDC then you will see that HCDC is a subsidiary of Aurora Finances Unlimited.

"Aurora Finances Unlimited made a good percentage of their money from their family planning clinics. They own the largest chain of abortion clinics in the U.S. They own the company HCDC. HCDC stands for Happy Care Daycare."

People in the audience furiously scribbled notes. "So, it would seem ladies and gentlemen, if they can't kill children before they are born, then they'd like to help raise them."

Greg Jensen spoke up, "That may seem like an unethical business practice, but it isn't illegal."

Jack smiled at him, "I know that Greg, I'm just getting warmed up. Now, see if you see anything strange about pages two through seven. They are letters addressed to separate families, but they say the same thing about the children. These letters are word for word the same. They only changed the gender and the name of the child where it was needed."

Greg Jensen spoke up again, "Again, rather unethical but not illegal."

Sometimes Jack thought that Greg leaned toward the dramatic. "I know that Greg. I'm not done yet. Bear with me. If you look on page eight, you will see that it is a listing of daycares in the U.S. that accept federal funds. Check bullet number thirty-three. You will see that Happy Care Daycare does indeed accept federal funds."

Sandy spoke up this time. "Jack, ninety-nine percent of the daycares in the U.S. apply for federal funds to subsidize their budgets."

Jack clenched his teeth for a moment. He hated being challenged before he could get the facts out. "Yes, Sandy, that's true, but when you receive federal funds, it is a felony to teach a religion. It is a violation of the Constitution."

When he finished saying those words, pencils and pens scratched paper like mad.

Greg Jensen spoke up again. He was shuffling through the pages in his hand. "Now wait a minute. I don't see any proof of this in these pages."

"That is where this comes in, Greg," Jack grated somewhat stiffly.

He turned around and hit the play button on the DVD player. The screen lit up, and a pin drop could be heard, aside from the noise from the T.V. A few minutes later, the video was over, and Jack was besieged with requests for copies of the video. He held up a DVD, and the room went quiet. He instructed, "I have one for each of your offices. Please take only one."

He asked Miss Trimble if she would do the honors again, and she was happy to do it. Besides, she thought Jack was kind of cute. When she took the stack from Jack, the first thing she did was pocket a DVD. "So, what we have here are several unethical practices and a federal offense from a company that is built on trust."

He'd tossed that out because he wanted to plant that thought in their heads. It would give the company a bigger headache if he their public trust were undermined. The crowd started breaking up and a couple of people left as soon as they got their copy of the DVD. Sandy walked up front and gave Jack a smile.

She noted, "You worked this one well Jack. I wouldn't be surprised if you get a promotion out of this." Jack gave her a blank stare, "I'm just doing my job."

She grinned back at him, "Okay, let's stick with that story. Check page one or two of our paper tomorrow." She turned on her heel and walked out. It was then that the young janitor Tommy walked in.

He looked at Jack, "Is this place ready for cleanup, sir? I saw the room clearing out."

Jack returned, "Yes, that will be fine. There are a couple dozen fresh doughnuts there. Would you like them?"

Tommy bleated, "Sure, leave them. I'll take them to the front office. They won't have a chance to go stale around those guys."

Edith Barnes unlocked her office the next morning. She saw the deputies' car pull up. She didn't know what to think when the officer walked in with a manila envelope.

He was solemn when he asked, "Edith Barnes?"

She replied, "Yes."

The deputy informed her, "I understand you are the regional director of the Happy Care Daycare chain. Is that correct?"

She replied with "Yes, officer. That is correct."

He opened the manila envelope and pulled out a sheaf of papers. "Ma'am, charges have been filed against the Happy Care Daycare chain. As the regional director, you will be required to notify your superiors and to answer the charges in a court of law." He handed her the papers.

She took them. She was rather flustered. She wasn't used to dealing with the police and like most people found them intimidating. The deputy turned around and walked out. Edith picked up the phone with a shaking hand and called her superior. Needless to say, the news wasn't well received.

To say that judge Farrell was angry would have been laughable. To say the judge was furious would have been more accurate. Judge Farrell was a tall thin man in his twilight year. He was fit but being seventy-one showed on him now like age hadn't before.

He saw the story in the paper. He heard the story on the radio and he knew that the local T.V. station was running the story today. He was waiting on the phone for Jack Collins.

The evidence for the court case had been distributed to the news media. It had been done without the knowledge of whether or not it would be admissible in court. He had endured a half hour of unpleasant conversation with the law team of HCDC.

They didn't have any real authority over him. They were however big enough that they could make life unpleasant. When Collins finally picked up the phone the judge was ready to disembowel him.

"Jack, why did you hold a press conference releasing evidence to the public? Some of that would have been rendered inadmissible. You realize you risked a mistrial on this?" There was considerable heat in his voice, and that wasn't lost on Jack.

Jack replied with an equal amount of heat. "Oh please! Tell me you aren't stupid enough to think this would ever have made it into a courtroom. You know as well as I do that my office couldn't put enough pressure on a company that rich to get them into court. Hell, they probably own a third of the judges in the state."

The judge was silent for a minute. Then he concluded, "That might well be true, but we are going to proceed under the assumption that this is going to trial. They are guilty of a federal offense. We don't let that slide.

"Now I better hear how you are building a case for the courtroom. You've turned this into a media blitz. Keep the pressure on so that they will be doing more damage control than attacking us."

Jack and Judge Farrell had both calmed down considerably.

Jack countered, "Your Honor that is a tall order. They have a virtual army of lawyers. My office has Sharon and I. Are you going to let me get at least two temps in the office to handle the overage until this is over?"

Judge Farrell responded, "I'll speak to the Mayor about it. No promises, though."

Over the next week and a half, the customer base of the Happy Care Daycare dwindled to practically nothing. It was made public that the Happy Care Daycare chain was being dismantled. The Happy Care Daycare name was becoming worthless.

The facilities were sold as a single owner operation. Jack Collins wasn't surprised when the case had been taken from him. The lawyers for Aurora had started their own media campaign.

They talked about how Christians were so intolerant of other's beliefs. They had psychologists on talk shows. They explained how no real thinking person would be a Christian. They concluded in their expert opinion you had to be an idiot to take the Bible literally.

Aurora's army of lawyers had filed a change of venue and gotten it. They cited the fact that the evidence had been released in the city where the offense was to be tried. Impartiality and the inadmissibility of the evidence were also cited. The governor had granted the change of venue himself.

The paper reported the change of venue. When Amelia read it her outrage came back.

Roger reminded her, "Honey, I told you this would probably happen. They're shutting the daycares down. That was about the best we could hope for."

She replied, "I know." She was cranky after dealing with the crowd at the grocery. Honey, I'm still not feeling well would you mind fixing dinner?"

"I'll fix dinner honey." He offered. He was worried that she might have an ulcer. She had been nauseous every day over the last two weeks.

Roger was headed to the kitchen to start dinner. Amelia announced that she was going to the bathroom. Roger was alone in the kitchen when Rachel called. Brennan was watching T.V. Roger was in the middle of fixing burgers and fries for dinner. He asked if they wanted to come over and play cards tonight or have dinner.

She answered Stephen was up for some cards, but they were already in the middle of dinner. He returned an okay, but that Amelia was a little under the weather. Rachel told him they would be over in about an hour and a half.

Roger gave his agreeing "Okay" and they got off the phone.

Roger was finishing the burgers when Amelia came into the kitchen with a stunned expression on her face.

Roger informed her, "Oh, good honey. Your timing is perfect." He saw her face and immediately became concerned.

"Honey, are you alright?" he asked. She didn't say anything. She stood there with her hand in front of her. His eyes trailed down to her hand and saw the white plastic implement. There was a blue stripe running across a window that was made into it. Roger's mouth dropped open.

"Is that what I think it is?" he asked.

She still couldn't speak. She nodded. He stood there with his mouth hanging open for a minute.

Then Amelia glanced up at him and breathed, "Honey, I'm pregnant."

Roger grabbed Amelia and hugged her fiercely. He whispered how much he loved her.

Brennan walked into the kitchen, "Is dinner ready yet?" Then he saw his parents in their embrace. "Yuck, get a room."

Roger and Amelia both laughed.

They sat down to their meal. They would talk about this tonight. They both wondered how Brennan was going to handle it. They wondered if it was going to be a girl or a boy. Roger wondered what Amelia would say to the name Geran if it turned out to be a little boy.

An hour or so later the Beaumonts showed up. They played cards and had a good night of fellowship together. Nobody saw the ten angels milling about the house. Then again, they weren't supposed to. Andarell smiled. He liked the way this had turned out.

Epilogue

It was dark and dank. He sat there in the cold cursing the day and the night. He knew that if Lucifer caught up to him he would be consigned to Sheol. All of his minions were either in Sheol or on the run.

He would have to go into hiding for some time. Molech was as miserable as he had ever been. He heard a rustling sound. His head snapped up and he saw one of his fellow demon lords. It was Marduk.

Marduk shambled into the clearing on his eight legs. He had a malicious grin in his face.

Marduk growled, "I see your failure, brother. How long will you stay in hiding?"

Molech snarled, "I would guess at least two hundred years. Our master has a long memory."

"This is true," agreed Marduk. "I have plans brewing in Chicago, if I can be of assistance, you will find me there."

Roger got up on Saturday morning with a rather sad duty to perform.

He rummaged through the pictures that he had printed off a few days ago. He put the pictures in an envelope. He found the CD he had burned from his email from Mr. Wagner and put that in the envelope.

He gave Amelia a kiss and told her where he was doing.

She replied, "Alright" and wished him luck. He drove to the Faith and Hope Baptist church. He found out from Pastor Johnson that Eddie wasn't there.

Roger asked if he knew where Eddie might be. Pastor Johnson gave Roger Eddie's phone number. Roger got in the car and dialed Eddie's number as he drove away. Eddie answered on the second ring. Roger explained who he was and was a little surprised when Eddie remembered him.

Roger asked, "Mr. Cain, Can we meet somewhere? I have something that I have to show you. You are going to be very interested in it."

Eddie answered, "We can meet at that little Waffle House if you like. I can be there in ten minutes."

Roger agreed and headed for the Waffle House. He walked into the restaurant and noticed that Eddie wasn't there yet. He was a little relieved. He walked over to an empty booth. He sat down, and the young waitress walked over and asked if he would like to order.

He instructed, "Yes, I'll have two coffees. I'm meeting a friend. I take my coffee black but bring cream and sugar for him. I don't know how he takes it."

She replied okay and walked away. She came back in a couple of minutes and poured two cups. She sat one down in front of him and one on the table across from him. She laid the condiments on the table.

He gave her a thank you, and she walked away. It was about then that Eddie walked in. He glanced around and saw Roger. He strode over and sat down across from Roger.

"So how are you?" Eddie asked with a slight smile.

Roger looked him in the eye, "I'd be doing a lot better if I didn't have to do this."

That really got Eddie's attention. He was mixing his coffee. He took a sip of it, "What's going on?"

Roger prodded his memory, "Do you remember the tent service where the young man was in a wheelchair and walked by the end of the service?"

Eddie gave him a wary glance, "Yes. What about it?"

Roger offered, "I hate to say this to you, but you've been lied to. You've also been led into preaching a false message."

Eddie's eyes narrowed, "You are going to have to prove that to me."

Roger asked, "You do remember the young gentleman in the wheelchair?"

Eddie replied, "I've already told you that I do."

Roger silently slid the manila envelope across the table.

450

Eddie took the envelope and pulled the sheaf of pictures and the CD out. He started flipping through them, and at first, his face became defiant. He skeptically stated, "All this shows is him walking around after being healed."

Roger offered, "Does that car look like it is set up for a paralytic to drive? On top of that, if you check the back of three of those photos I made sure to put his name, address, and phone number. He promised that if you don't believe me then you can call him and even set up a meeting.

"That CD contains a personal statement from him. It also contains some family pictures of him growing up and a video clip of him in his last play. The play was performed only a few months ago. He is a part time actor. That is why Mr. Edwards hired him in the first place."

Eddie felt a sharp pang in his stomach. He took a nervous gulp of his coffee, "Mr. Edwards hired him?"

Roger said, "Yes he did, and he paid him very well. He was paid three thousand dollars. He was convincing. That was why you wound up preaching that it is always God's will to heal.

"Don't forget that God is sovereign. His will is supreme. Look at how long he allowed Job to suffer. He healed him in the end because Job was the most righteous man in the world.

Remember God's reply to Job from the whirlwind? 'Where were you when I laid the foundations of the Earth.' In other words, he was saying, 'Who are you to question me? I'm God.'"

Eddie felt like the room was spinning. "I'm not calling you a liar, but I'm going to have to call this guy to get his story." Eddie's mind was full of doubt. The evidence in front of him at the moment was compelling.

It terrified him to think that he had been led astray to the point of preaching a false message. He thought of Mr. Edwards. *How could he hire someone to fake a healing? How could he lead his congregation on in the belief that they were so blessed?*

These thoughts brought fear to him, but they also made him extremely angry. He got angry with Mr. Edwards and himself. How could he so easily allow himself to be led astray? Then, as if from a distance, he heard Rogers' voice.

"I wouldn't expect you to simply take my word for all of this. That is why I've provided you with his contact information."

Eddie's face was bleak as he stood up. "I thank you for bringing this information to me. It would have been easier for you to walk away."

Roger looked at him, "I would have to answer to the Lord for that. I don't want any more to answer for than I have to." Eddie stepped out of the booth and walked away without a word or a backwards glance.

Roger felt bad for him, but at least he was being told the truth. Roger thought that Eddie was facing the rod of correction. Then he thought that it was better to face the rod of correction than to face damnation.

With that he called the waitress over and handed her a ten-dollar bill. "Keep the change, Miss." She gave him her thanks and he got up and headed for the door.

When he got home, Amelia asked how it went. He told her as well as could be expected. She could tell he didn't want to talk about it so she changed the subject and they discussed the baby. She agreed that if it turned out to be a boy they would name him Geran.

Eddie headed for his apartment. He was heartsick emotionally. He secretly hoped that this turned out to be a lie. He knew that if it wasn't he was guilty of terrible pride. He got into his apartment and went straight to the phone.

He looked at the back of several of the photos until he found one with the contact information on it. His hands were shaking as he dialed the number.

A male voice answered "Hello?"

Eddie said, "Yes Hello. Is this James Wagner?"

452

The voice answered in a mournful tone, "Yes sir it is. May I ask who is calling?"

Eddie replied, "This is Eddie Cain. I was preaching recently at a tent revival. I was told that you were the man who was healed. I was also told that the healing was nothing but a sham. I was told that you are a paid actor. I was told that Mr. Edwards paid you three thousand dollars to pretend that you were healed. How much of that is true?"

There was silence for a few moments. Then an agonized voice came on the line, "Mr. Cain, I'm sorry to say that all of it is true. I work for a marketing firm. I'm a part time actor. I've never been paralyzed. Mr. Edwards supplied the wheel chair.

"I practiced in the chair for two weeks before the tent service. That way I could be more convincing in it. Mr. Cain, I'm so sorry. I didn't realize the magnitude of what I was doing. I don't practice a faith of my own. Mr. Carter explained it to me.

"I feel terrible for what I've done. Please use the materials that I've sent to set your congregation straight. Please forgive me."

He was so sincere that Eddie couldn't stay mad at him. Eddie was hurt, but he still had his Christian roots. He had been corrected, and like King David, he wasn't going to hide from his punishment.

Tomorrow was the Sunday service. He knew what he had to do. He thanked Mr. Wagner for his honesty and told him that he was forgiven. He made a mental note to pray for James Wagner. He dialed another number.

The familiar voice came on the line, "Hello."

Eddie explained that he needed the laptop projector set up for tomorrow. The custodian promised he would see to it. Eddie thanked him and hung up. He picked up the phone and dialed another number.

Pastor Johnson's voice came on the line, "Hello?"

Eddie explained that he had something that needed to be said tomorrow. He asked if Pastor Johnson would mind giving him about ten minutes at the end of the service tomorrow. Pastor Johnson replied that he would but would like to know what it was about.

Eddie said that he didn't want to let the cat out of the bag too early. Pastor Johnson accepted that answer. They exchanged pleasantries for a few minutes and hung up.

The next morning Eddie got up and dressed in his best suit. He spent a while in prayer. He earnestly expressed his sorrow and begged for the Lord's forgiveness. He got up from his knees and mentally prepared himself.

He drove to the church and checked to make sure the video equipment was set up. It was. He sat through the service, dreading the moment that he would be given the floor. The moment came, and he found that his emotions were somehow turned off.

He didn't see the angel that whispered encouragement to him. He didn't hear the calming words, but they worked all the same. He walked up to the Podium, cleared his throat and started to speak.

"Ladies and gentlemen, I come before you today to inform you of something that I just found out. It is something that is disturbing but you deserve to know the truth." He scanned the congregation. The faces he saw before him were expectant. He saw Mr. Edwards. A pang of anger flared up inside him.

He started to speak again. "Do you remember when we had the tent revival and the young man in the wheelchair was healed?" The congregation appeared interested and supportive. Some of them seemed inspired as they nodded.

He spoke up. "It has come to my attention that the healing was false." Mr. Edwards blanched at these words, and the congregation was buzzing with comments.

Eddie continued, "It turns out that the man's name is James Wagner. He is an amateur actor from Chicago, Illinois. He works for a marketing firm and was found out by an investigator that was in the congregation that night.

"This individual was so skeptical he decided to do some digging of his own. I would like to play a personal statement recorded by this man. I would also like to show some family pictures showing his life growing up.

"In the pictures, he is obviously not paralyzed. Lastly, I would like to show you a video clip of him in a play done a couple of months before the tent service. He is also obviously not paralyzed on stage."

The congregation was aghast. Some of them whispered furiously between each other. One man stood up and yelled, "What are you talking about?! We were there. We saw the man healed. The Lord touched this congregation that night."

Eddie's face became sorrowful. "No, sir, that man wasn't healed. He was never paralyzed. The Lord didn't touch this congregation that night. Mr. Edwards did at the cost of three thousand dollars to hire that young actor to deceive all of us."

Mr. Edwards stood up and screamed, "That is a lie."

Eddie calmly walked over to the laptop that was connected to the projector. He took the CD from his pocket. He inserted it into the laptop and hit the play on the software that automatically came up.

The audio came up first. Everyone heard the confession of Mr. Wagner. Then the presentation went through the family photos in a slideshow style. Finally, the video clip came up. It showed Mr. Wagner running around energetically and screaming his lines.

When the presentation ended, the church was silent. Everyone was looking from Mr. Edwards to Eddie.

Eddie spoke up, "I want the congregation to know that I was deceived into believing the Lord was working through me. I was preaching a false message. It is not always God's will to heal. God is sovereign. He is not a cosmic genie. Outside the word of God, we can't say we know the will of God.

"I preached a false message to this congregation. I didn't do it on purpose, but I did do it. I led people in this congregation astray through my own pride and ignorance. I am not fit to preach the word of God any more. I repent of my actions. I ask for forgiveness, and I resign my post here as tent minister." Eddie hit the eject button on the laptop, and it spit out the CD. He took it and put it back in his pocket.

He turned to Mr. Edwards who was still standing there mutely. The congregation stared coldly at him. Eddie noticed a few in the congregation watching him the same way.

Eddie began. "Mr. Edwards, my part in this was out of ignorance. Your part was with full knowledge. You owe this congregation an explanation and a sincere apology."

Mr. Edwards affected a look of astonishment. "Apologize? Apologize?! I built this church, boy! They should be thanking me. If that fool Wagner hadn't come forward, the people of this church would still believe in the miracle and still be saved!"

Eddie stared at him with pity. "That's where you don't get it. You can't be saved believing a lie. That is what got Adam and Eve thrown out of the garden." With that statement, he turned to the congregation. "Once again, I'm sorry and I hope the Lord heals this church. Goodbye." He walked down the aisle and out the door. He got into his car and thought about what he was going to do. He thought about Mr. Wagner from Chicago.

That thought stuck with him. He couldn't see the angel whispering in his ear, but the word Chicago stayed insistent in his mind. He finally took the clue and thought, *trying to tell me something, Lord?* He didn't hear the angel's delighted laughter. He did, however, feel a small measure of the pleasure of the Lord.

As soon as he got home, he started packing. When he thought about it, he didn't trust the beater of a car to be reliable all the way to Chicago. His neighbor had expressed interest in the car. He decided he would let the car go for a few hundred dollars.

He still had ninety thousand dollars and change from his lottery winnings. That would last him for a good while. He packed his clothes and a few meager belongings into two suitcases.

He had a gym bag he could use as a carry-on. He packed his toiletries in that. The apartment came furnished so there wasn't much else left. He decided to leave the rest behind.

The next day, he called the apartment manager and explained that he would be leaving. He agreed that he would be forfeiting his last month's rent and his damage deposit. Since the rent included the utilities, he didn't have to worry about that.

He called the phone company and asked if the phone could be turned off and how much his balance was. They replied that he was paid up and there would be no charge. He intoned a thank you and hung up.

He went over to the neighbors and asked if they were still interested in the car. The neighbor gave an eager yes. They hammered out a deal for four hundred dollars. Eddie signed the title and gave it to them. He trusted them to get it changed over, not the smartest move.

Eddie called a cab and instructed the driver that he needed to go to the Littleton Airport. It was a small airport, but it did service three of the major airlines. When they got there he paid the fare and got a cart for his luggage.

He stepped up to the counter and informed the attendant that he would like a one-way ticket to Chicago.

"That will be $347" was the crisp reply.

Eddie counted out the money and put it on the counter. The attendant checked his baggage and handed him his ticket.

Eddie turned from the counter. He noticed a striking woman sitting in one of those plastic chairs you find at the airport. Eddie noticed the complimentary coffee on the table next to her chair. He felt drawn to talk to her, but he had that nervousness that most people feel around a stranger.

He cleared his throat and spoke up. "Going to Chicago?" She looked up startled. "What? Oh, yes." He asked, "Going for work or family?" She replied, "Work, and you?"

Eddie smiled a rueful little smile. "I'm going to find work. I was the tent minister at a local church. I found some illegal practice going on in the church. So, I resigned my position. I don't know why, but I feel drawn to Chicago. By the way my name is Eddie Cain."

"Oh, I'm Liz Douglas. Luckily, I have job waiting on me." Eddie said, "Maybe we will run into each other in Chicago."

Neither of them saw Andarel smiling. "Oh, don't worry. You will." With that, Andarel leapt into the sky, and with a song of praise on his lips, he passed into eternity.